D1639441

CRASH COURSE

By the same author

FICTION

Blockbuster

NONFICTION

The Search for Air Safety
Fire
The Secrets Business
Bondage
That Thin Red Line

1817

HARPER & ROW, PUBLISHERS

New York Hagerstown

San Francisco

London

CRASH COURSE

A novel by Stephen Barlay

 For information address Harper & Row, Publishers, Inc., 10 East 53rd Street, New York, N.Y. 10022.

FIRST U.S. EDITION

Designed by C. Linda Dingler

Library of Congress Cataloging in Publication Data

Barlay, Stephen.
Crash course.
I. Title.
PZ4.B2567Cr 1979 [PR6052.A654] 823'.9'14 79-1696
ISBN 0-06-010326-4

79 80 81 82 83 84 10 9 8 7 6 5 4 3 2 1

For Christopher Sinclair-Stevenson

PART ONE

Window seat H1, starboard, was empty. It had been allocated to Mr. Li Wong at the check-in counter fifty minutes earlier. Some passengers were rather irritated when the stewardesses began to count and recount, identify and reidentify everybody on board; and people near the lavatories laughed when the agitated girls in their smart uniforms searched, checked and rechecked each cubicle in a hurried rotation, as if the entire crew were victims of a dysentery epidemic. But there was no doubt about it. Passenger Li was not on the aircraft.

Loudspeakers bellowed out his name incessantly and so classified him as the most wanted VIP of the moment at Singapore's Paya Lebar airport. He still failed to answer the urgent calls, and, after a final recount of 182 people aboard flight SN03 to Sydney, security had to be alerted.

Captain Cornelius Penn was not pleased. A mix-up with catering supplies had already caused fifteen minutes' delay. Now he could not take off with unaccompanied luggage on board. If Mr. Li had disappeared, his suitcase would have to be found and removed. It might be bulging with the innocuous travel chattels of a man who had suffered a heart attack or left the airport for some perfectly honest personal reason without canceling his flight. Or it might contain a bomb. The Captain could not take chances, though he was anxious to leave Singapore as soon as possible. The monsoon was playing havoc with the runway. According to the forecast, more rain was imminent. The time was 1835. And the air traffic controllers had scheduled a token one-hour stoppage in support of their demand for better working conditions. If Penn was forced to start the arduous luggage identification process and perhaps evacuate the aircraft, the flight would be caught in the vise of rain and strike, maybe all night. Hardly the best advertisement for a young and ambitious airline, irrespective of valid explanations.

Penn unstrapped himself and swore quietly, without anger or malice, as he had to writhe his wiry six feet two with vermicular contortions through the gap between seat back, central pedestal and sloping overhead panel, so that he could climb out of his driving seat and stretch. "You must think thin on this bloody crate." He loved his Sarissa, still fresh from the production line of this magnificent new generation of aircraft; but he always claimed that in addition to her Mach warning horn and fire horn a shoehorn, too, ought to be standard equipment to facilitate movement on the flight deck.

The door opened and Colonel Mihir Gupta, chief of airport security, appeared. He stopped, measuring his bulk against the width of the opening, then decided to stay outside. "We don't like it. We're searching all the buildings." He noted Penn's frown, and added, "If that nincompoop is still here, it shouldn't take long."

"Thanks. We can spare perhaps ten minutes. After that we might as well start the hunt for his luggage, because we'll be running into the ATC strike anyway."

The Colonel left, and Penn turned toward the right-hand seat. One man at least would be pleased by the unexpected delay. First Officer Mitchell, the co-pilot, was waiting for news from London. His wife had gone into labor prematurely, and her mother telephoned Mitchell only to reassure him that it was perfectly all right, no complications, nothing to worry about, which of course made him just as worried as she wanted him to be.

"Go ahead, Mike, ask the tower to make another call for you," said Penn and turned to the PA microphone.

The general buzz in the cabin subsided quickly when the speakers above the seats came to life.

"Good evening, ladies and gentlemen. This is Cornelius Penn, your captain, speaking. I was hoping to introduce myself later on, in the air, with some more cheerful information, but unfortunately an administrative hitch beyond anybody's control is causing some delay in our departure. Although torrential rain is also trying to keep us in this delightful city, we'll do our best to get you on time to Sydney, where, according to our latest reports, the sky is impeccably cloudless, and where we might cause a riot if not an armed insurrection if we're late in with half the Imperial Ballet whom we're proud to have on board. So please be patient a little longer, we'll get you away as soon as possible; and in accordance with company policy, we'll pay the self-imposed penalty—the full Sarissa range of refreshments, that is, with the compliments of SupraNational Airline. Thank you."

Penn had hardly finished the announcement when a first-class passenger spat out the cold stub of a spent cigar and rose from his seat as if trying for a moon shot. His nicotine-stained middle finger hit the service call button.

"We'll want to know more about that administrative hitch, and I want a coffee, now! Where the hell is that stewardess?" He beat out a one-note toccata on the call button while he looked down at the dark hair of the young woman in the next seat. "We'll want to know a lot more about that hitch, right?"

"I'm sure there's nothing to worry about," she said.

"How the hell would you know?"

Tiny Malloy, probably the loftiest stewardess who could be accommodated in a standard passenger aircraft, came up running and caught the last sentence. "Because Miss Boone is a journalist, sir, and rather knowledgeable about aviation matters."

"Then—"

"Do sit down, sir," Tiny asked him with the self-assurance of a four-star general, "and I promise you'll be the first to be served once we're airborne. Until then, perhaps Miss Boone can answer your questions. Will you, Miss Boone?"

She looked up, and her blue eyes darkened as she scanned Tiny's face. "Sorry, should I know you? Have we met before?"

"No, Miss Boone."

"Then how do you know me?"

"Captain Penn asked me to take special care of you."

"That's very kind of him."

"He's a kind man, Miss Boone."

"I'm Mara. I used to be a stew, myself."

"And I still am, Miss Boone. But I'll tell the Captain how helpful you were."

"As you wish."

"You must have made a great impression on him last night."

"You're most observant. I'll take it as a compliment."

Tiny left and that was the cue the man was waiting for. Though obviously quite blind to beauty, he stared at Mara and the yellow fingers produced a slightly steamed card from the breast pocket of the tweed he always wore, disregarding the climate, whenever away from Mobile, Alabama.

"Chuck Benning is the name and I'm in turpentine, ma'am. I find it intolerable the way they treat us these days. I mean all I wanted was an explanation and a cup of coffee." He paused to cough and his hand, driven by habit as much as a will of its own, stretched toward the service panel. Mara's finely drawn chin line moved imperceptibly from side to side, and the hand withdrew. "A plain cup of coffee. I mean I'm a simple man of simple tastes, and that's a fact."

"No kidding?"

For a second he searched her face for any sign of irony, but her face remained as earnest as her voice.

"Right." He nodded for emphasis. "I'm a plain coffee and donut man, and that's d-o-n-u-t, if you please. None of your fancy moussaka, lusaka, vinaigrette, cerisette, no. They can throw it all straight into the trash can for all I care." Again he paused to cough chestily, and Mara used the opportunity to insert a solemn "Is that a fact?" He nodded. "And I need a smoke." His hand was up, and, before Mara could interfere, he pressed the call button.

The time was 1841, and the entire airport resounded with the name of Li Wong, who was urged, requested and begged to contact any desk clerk of SupraNational or any other airline, any official, just anyone, if he could, please, but without any further delay.

That Thursday in August was much younger in New York, only a little over seven hours old, but already as hot and humid as many of its past elders. The jeans-and-T-shirt girl hurrying toward Manny's on 48th Street stopped and looked at the sky. She guessed the time, followed the sun rays back down and into the shopwindow as they lit up more and more of the guitars and other instruments inside, but all she wanted to see was the guitars, and not even all those, only the one on the right, the Gibson Heritage Custom for just under four hundred dollars. She had set her heart on that one several weeks earlier and visited it every day while saving up for it, hoping that it would still be there. On Wednesday, when she had the money together, she reached Manny's ten minutes after closing time. But the Gibson Heritage Custom was there all right and now there would be no chance for anyone else to beat her to it. It was silly, really. She meant to be there only a few minutes before the shop opened, but she had woken up several times during the night, and each time when she fell asleep again, the nightmare of people running away with her Gibson Heritage

Custom continued. At six-thirty she gave up fighting it and decided to wait at Manny's.

She was not sure how long she had been pacing up and down there. Might have been half an hour. Or more. She was clutching a roll of sweaty bills, and suddenly she panicked. The bundle felt too small. Perhaps she had lost some of it. Or left some at home. She wanted to count the money, but she was afraid to stand there and start spreading out such a fortune in the open. What if somebody attacked her? She needed a hiding place. The sunken plaza in front of the McGraw-Hill Building, between 48th and 49th. It had a bench, too; it would do nicely.

As she crossed the street, she had a strange feeling that something somewhere did not look right, but at first what it was did not register. Then she noticed it. Of course. The water in the fountain was pink. Even red. Could be some peculiar morning reflection of the sun. Or a new feature to brighten the sight. That's right. She decided she preferred the fountain as it used to be. Plain, watery water.

She entered the plaza and saw something hanging from the pool of the fountain. A hand. And that was red, too.

She turned and ran out screaming. A policeman caught her arm. She was on the verge of becoming hysterical and that made her a little incoherent. The policeman noted the dollar bundle and, to be on the safe side, took it from her. It might be important evidence. It's not often that one can catch them on the spot, red-handed, so to speak.

Forty-five minutes later, at 0459 Pacific Time, nine telephones began to ring in Charles Drayton's California beach house. All three of his direct private numbers were unlisted and changed from time to time, and when he bestowed the secret of such a line upon any of his executives or close associates in the aircraft industry—government and the rest of the world should find the time to contact him through his secretaries or other proper channels—the recipient always regarded the gesture as the equivalent of a knighthood.

"If anybody calls me at night he'd better have a goddamn good reason. And if he did have a good reason, I'd want to hear the goddamn bells wherever I am in the house, on the beach, in the boat or my lady's chamber" was his frequently quoted principle, although, in fact, his lady's chamber was the only place in the house where the telephone could not be heard. On the other hand, since it was she who had demanded a bedroom of her own, away from his goddamn telephones, his lady's chamber became the only place he never visited. Which not only solved the problem of the telephones, but also rang the death knell of their physically dull and emotionally dated relationship.

He glanced at the pulsating red digits of the electronic clock, clapped twice to activate the motor that drew the curtains, squinted as the early light hit him in the eyes, and picked up the phone on the second ring. "Drayton."

He listened, gasped and swallowed hard. Singer gibbered with excitement at the other end of the line and not without good reason. The president of AeroCorp was also shaken by the news, but his crisis manager was not to know it.

"Now stop, slow down and start again."

After a pause, Singer's voice grew flat and tired. "Joe Hannan is dead."

"First you said he was murdered."

"The two statements are not incompatible."

"Don't try to score, Henry, just give me the facts."

"Right. He was found less than an hour ago with five, possibly seven, separate stab wounds."

"Where?"

"Neck, chest, face—"

'I mean where was he found?'

"In New York, by McGraw-Hill's on Forty-eighth. Dumped in a decorative fountain."

"Sounds like a job by one of his jealous boyfriends."

"Yeah. That's just what the police thought, too."

Drayton nodded with some satisfaction. The quick exchange showed that Singer had recovered his composure—he was always aware of the risk of being overheard on an open line—and Drayton was anxious to support the most obvious police theory about the murder in every way he could. For although the loss of Hannan was a serious blow, Drayton wanted no more investigation than, presumably, the murderer did. Only the instigators of the murder would have different ideas, he knew. That they must be competitors seemed to be beyond doubt. The spectacular dumping of the body would ensure extra publicity leading, they must hope, to the discovery of the AeroCorp connection. For Hannan was a superb fixer, aircraft salesman on paper, who was about to obtain political backing for the first major sale of Sarissas in Germany. That must remain a secret. But there were some worrying questions. Had he concluded the arrangements before he was killed? Had he paid in cash? The recipient might deny it, of course, if he knew about Hannan's fate. Singer would have to move fast.

"There's something else," said Singer. "I wouldn't have called you at once only because of that, but now that you're up anyway—"

"Come on, Henry, come on."

"There were two stoppages during the night shift. For very, very trivial reasons."

The emphasis was not lost on Drayton. Singer must have tried to imply that such unreasonable industrial disputes were likely to have some hidden causes. Somebody might be stirring things up. Nothing serious yet, just the odd hitch in the production, but viewed together with Hannan's death, the message could be read loud and clear. About to make the first big breakthrough for Drayton's brave and unconventional grand design, the Sarissa project was under attack. Competitors must be worried—and not without good reason either. Drayton smiled with shameless vanity. Hannan's death could be regarded as a compliment. Except that Drayton never really thought that any of his competitors would react as quickly and fight as dirty as that.

"I read you. Meet me at the plant in thirty minutes."

He rang off and pressed a button at his bedside three times. Breakfast and his pilot with the chopper would be ready for him in fifteen minutes. If the Sarissa and all the prospects of jobs, contracts, dreams that went with her needed protection, it must not make any difference that this Thursday had only just begun in California.

"And I bet you don't know what a terebinth is."

"No," said Mara without the slightest doubt that she would not be kept in the dark for long. Ever since disembarkation, Chuck Benning had stuck to her all the way to the transit lounge and proved himself to be an inexhaustible source of information about turpentine, a grossly underrated and unappreciated substance and topic.

"It's a tree."

"No kidding?"

"It yields Chian turpentine. And that's a fact."

She could have left him many times without even touching her reserve armory for routine defense against party bores, but somehow she did not have the heart to dump him. For all his aggression and tall tales about his business exploits in Alabama and the rest of the world, Chuck Benning seemed rather unsure of himself and lost. Perhaps it was his first flight ever, perhaps no other time had he left the coniferous forest where, to spare his trees, he himself might secrete some of his beloved oleoresin in the dead of night. Penn came to rescue her at last. He reassured Benning that, although the strike had lasted almost two hours longer than planned, everything would soon be back to normal and the flight would be leaving well before midnight.

He led her to the VIP lounge, where she chose to have a brandy instead of yet another cup of stale coffee, and he joined her with a toothless Bloody Mary—his name for plain tomato juice. They sat, sipping their drinks, finding it difficult to say anything, yet enjoying the long silence they actively shared.

"You look tired," she said.

"Harassed, rather."

"The ballerina?"

He nodded. "And the rest of the company. And the other passengers. And the strike committee. And the engine fire warnings."

"You mean we had a fire?"

"No, just a warning-light malfunction."

"Poor you."

He shrugged his shoulders. "One of those nights."

"I still don't know where that missing passenger was found." Without ever taking her eyes away from his tension-furrowed face, she noticed his incessant mute drumming just above the edge of the table. She reached for his hand and the fingers came to rest.

"Li? He was caught with his pants down. In the loo, that is."

"Was he stoned? Or hiding?"

"Just flaked out. Exhaustion. He'd been traveling for something like thirty hours." He withdrew his hand slowly, reluctantly. "It's a long stretch by any standard."

"Like yours now? Lucky you had a good long rest last night." Her voice was indifferent, conversational. Penn could not detect any trace of double meaning. Yet once again, like the night before, there was a blunted edge, a touch of animosity, which he could not understand or verify. It might be his imagination only.

"I'm sorry about last night," he said quietly and looked away.

"Why should you be?"

"No reason. Just a statement of fact."

Her smile was convincing; she hoped it was light acceptance

of a cold statement. Only her big toes curled upward, digging the nails into the soft leather, trying to vent frustration like an attic fire searching for a chimney.

Their previous evening was one of those that could have, perhaps should have, stretched into the night, the dawn, the day, another evening, another night. It did not. She was not hurt. Not even angry. Not with him, at any rate. Only with herself. The last thing she would want was to like him.

The evening began peacefully enough. Mara met Penn and his team, who were waiting for the plane they would take over from the London–Singapore crew and fly to Sydney. She told him she was assigned to produce an "in-depth portrait" of a pilot and explore the new airline concept that was to be embodied in SupraNational, the operation of Sarissas and the marketing onslaught with everything from Saricola and Sarinade to Sarishirts, Saribags and Saricigars. He took her to dinner and they talked airplanes and schedules and fatigue limits and landing aids, and it was odd that even the coldest references to sink rates and all-up weights sounded somehow personal. She was determined to ignore the mood of warmth and intimacy that grew on them, and both of them tried to overlook the more blatant, though accidental, sexual undertones.

"Why me?" he asked several times throughout the evening. "Why is it me you want to write up?"

"Random choice."

"At least you're not trying to flatter me."

"Are you used to flattery from women?"

"Nothing personal about it, just one of the perks. It's the uniform they can't resist."

"Is that why you returned to regular airline service?"

He studied her face carefully. "How did you know I had been away from it?"

"It's a small world." He was clearly dissatisfied with the answer. She shrugged her shoulders: "All right. I lied to you. You were not a random choice."

"Your editor's choice?"

"No. Mine. All right?"

"Why?"

"I wanted to know you."

"Why?"

"Why not? Aren't there enough intriguing stories about your alleged adventures and fights in circulation? Some even show you as a hero."

"So now you do flatter me, after all."

"It's a tool of the trade."

"Thank you for being so frank."

"You're welcome. It's free."

That odd edge. She could not have any personal reason to be hostile toward him. He smiled to make the question sound lighter than it was: "Isn't it dangerous to give away the tricks of the trade so readily? How can you expect me then to fall for them?"

"I said *tools* of the trade. I don't use tricks. What I do, the way I do it, the tools I choose are all open and self-explanatory."

"But not your motives."

"What do you mean?" She hoped she did not sound alarmed. He could not suspect her motives. Surely.

"Do you ever go to bed with your interviewees?"

"Might. Does it shock you?"

"For fun or good reason?"

"Fun is a good reason."

"You're quick."

"Particularly when I dislike the tone of a question."

"I'm sorry."

"I'm not hurt."

"You're a hard and tough one, aren't you?"

"Do you prefer the soft ones, the women who're gullible, naïve and defenseless to your charm and the masculinity you wear like a badge?"

"More flattery, this time with double edge? Your technique should be taught in schools."

She hated every bit of it. That she was attracted to him—to the catlike precision of his movements, to the dark, searching eyes with the sheaves of wrinkles in the corners when he smiled, to the tightly stretched skin on strong cheekbones. She hated it that he so readily submitted to probing, that he made her feel secure and serene, like bathing in the nude in trusted company and comforting darkness.

He wanted her, that was obvious, and wanted her badly, and she made it no secret that it pleased her. He cut the dinner short, and as they were staying in the same hotel, he walked her to the elevator, where she waited for him to pick up the keys of their rooms. His gait was light, always in perfect balance, as if ready to kick out any time.

When the elevator stopped at her floor, she stepped out, and before she had time to turn back, she heard him say good night. The door closed and he was gone. She kept telling herself half the night that she was not hurt, but she was delighted when he called early in the morning and suggested breakfast, which was followed by a long, leisurely day of more airplane talk at the airport, at the feet of the giant Buddha in the Sakya Muni Gaya temple, at the poolside, over Malay satay at a street stall in Beach Road, and aboard the Sarissa when he checked out preparations for the evening flight. She kept wondering why he had rejected her the previous night. Was he suspicious of something or just impotent? Perhaps he was too much in love with someone else, simply did not want her or preferred boys. It did not matter anyway, not at all, but it still bugged her as they finished their drinks, their much-delayed plane almost ready for the flight. Neither of them wanted to get up and go, though the renewed silence was becoming too meaningful and must be broken.

"Thanks for telling Tiny to take special care of me."

"You're a special guest," he said with the uniform smile that must be taught to pilots, together with landing techniques in the simulator.

"She's in love with you."

"Tiny? Don't be silly."

"Didn't you know?"

"Absolute nonsense."

"Just a statement of fact."

"You're wrong. I've known her, what, as long as I've known my wife."

It was his first reference to the fact that he was married, and she tried to pay no attention to it. "That's no argument. Do you expect only strangers to fall in love with you? Women who know nothing about you and trust you blindly?" She knew this was uncalled for and regretted it. So she added, hurriedly, "I'll have to meet your wife, too. To complete the portrait of an airline pilot. What's her name?"

"She calls herself Candy."

"What do you call her?"

"Candy."

"There must be a story in this somewhere. I'll make a note. . . . Any children?"

"A son. But don't ask me about him, for I'm biased. And what's even worse, I'm proud of it."

The impromptu interview was interrupted by Mitchell, who had at last got through to his wife in the hospital. "It's a boy!" he shouted to make sure that everybody heard it. "They say the all-up weight is below the economy factor, but who cares as long as the load distribution is okay!" People smiled, some of them cheered.

"I envy you," said Penn. "Women have conned the world into the glorification of motherhood alone. The joy of becoming a father is grossly underrated."

Mitchell needed no encouragement to try to remedy the situation. The constant overflow of a juicy big smile remained on his face throughout the flight preparations, and it made even the monotonous pilot–co-pilot dialogue of the engine prestart check (Rudder boost switch? Guard closed. Compasses? Checked and synchronized. Cabin signs? On. Emergency exit lights? Guard closed . . .) sound like an extended hurrah of victorious light infantry. Penn wondered if the smile would last all the way to Sydney and then the long haul back home. The checklist had just been completed when the control tower called to tell him that the predicted downpour was fast reducing the runway visual range. Visibility was now down to a hundred and fifty yards.

Singer talked to several people on the night shift of the sprawling AeroCorp plant, and he knew now for sure that the petty dispute and the disruption of the Sarissa production must have been some troublemakers' doing. They would have to be watched closely, he decided, and he had his informers all over the shop floor ready for just that kind of a job

He drove across to the tall executive building, where only Drayton's windows were lit up, rode the elevator to the top in the silence of the dead building, and waved to Ms. Etch, Drayton's secretary, even before he had a chance to see her. Everybody knew that she was never separated from her boss by more than a single door, day or night. He entered the inner sanctum, where every piece of Drayton's fine Venetian mirror collection was carefully positioned and angled to make even those visitors who were used to it uncomfortably self-conscious. Singer's answer was to stare directly at Drayton and so avoid watching his own small and large, distorted and fragmented fleeting images.

Drayton seemed unhurried and relaxed, but Singer was one of the few people who could detect and gauge the true level of tension.

"Coffee, Henry?"

"Please." His ears stretched to detect the swish that revealed that Ms. Etch was already present. She never knocked, entered or approached; she materialized. This time with a Saripot of coffee and two exquisite Sarimugs.

"What's the last we know about Hannan?" Drayton asked her.

"We were orally advised," she said slowly while pouring the coffee remained her main concern, "that Mr. Hannan wished to effect certain material approaches which in the light of post-Watergate and post-Lockheed morality might be interpreted by the malicious as unethical."

Drayton nodded patiently. "In other words, he was about to bribe the fucking bastards."

"You may put it that way, sir."

"But did he pay out or not?"

"Arrangements to provide him with funds had been made, but that's all we know. Anything else, sir?"

"Yes, sweetie. If any goddamn reporter calls, Hannan's position within AeroCorp must be de-emphasized. Is that clear?"

"Yes sir." De-emphasize was one of Drayton's favorite words, and she would need no further explanations.

Singer waited for the second swish to tell him that Ms. Etch had dematerialized. He never ceased to marvel at the perfect team she and her boss made. She demanded as much attention as any roll of embossed wallpaper, while he stood out in any crowd. A Canadian Gargantua, driven by a man-size chip on his shoulder ever since he had broken out into the big open business plains of the United States, Drayton was a big man with an enormous white patriarchal mane, huge appetite and lust for life, and big jokes about his bigness in every department. He was a kindly man, a good listener with a disarming ever-ready smile, who had plenty of time for all callers from cleaners to cabinetmakers. He would offer them refreshments, ask them about their families and flatter them by telling Ms. Etch, "Please cancel everything. I'm out even for my mistress, my bankers or the President of the United States, in that descending order." But Ms. Etch would keep reminding him of vitally important matters that required his immediate attention until, at last, the caller would feel embarrassed by taking up so much of Drayton's time and leave without a proper answer or decision, which Drayton would promise to give him soon. In this way, without ever making snap decisions, Drayton enjoyed the reputation of the man who would answer any problem on the spot—if only he had the time his visitor had wasted with all the initial niceties, family news and waiting for refreshments.

"So where do we go from here?" Singer asked.

"You tell me, Henry. I trust your judgment implicitly."

"Okay. I'll pick up the pieces, and try to conclude Hannan's unfinished business."

"No—no. That's the one thing I can't let you do. I can't expose you to any physical danger. You know too little about these things. Ever heard about a Brigadier Mott?"

"N-no, I don't think so. Who is he?"

"Believed to be a dangerous man."

"Is he involved in this?"

"Perhaps."

"I'll find out."

"Not you, Henry, not you."

"It's vital for us, and as AeroCorp crisis manager, I'm responsible."

"You're goddamn right about that. But your job is to manage and not to go bananas and risk everything. You're too valuable to all of us, to tens of thousands of us whose future depends on the Sarissa. No, we'll have to use somebody much more expendable."

Singer turned away. He knew what was coming. But he wanted Drayton to spell it out for him. "Such as?"

"Well, let's see . . . how about Salah Termine?"

"He's a crook."

"I dislike that word, Henry; it's handed out too readily for everyone ever since those things have been filling the papers about Mr. Nixon. All right, he hasn't got your neat haircut, decadent eyes and Harvard Club tie; and perhaps the Termines are not as old an American family as the Singers"—he pronounced it with a mock German accent—"but he isn't weighed down by all the Ivy League nonsense, he's goddamn keen and he has good family connections all over Europe."

"What family? The Mafia? Or rather the Algerians in the Marseilles Casbah?" For the first time, he was losing his flat, controlled Bostonian accent.

"Give him a chance, Henry, give him a chance!"

Give him a chance, indeed. Singer knew only too well that Drayton had built his entire spectacular career on the one great discovery that no American could resist the temptation to give a man a chance. Singer knew that Drayton used, with incredible insolence, to apply for jobs for which he was clearly unsuited by training or background, and land them with equally incredible regularity because it seemed only fair to give him a chance. It was, of course, a mark of his brilliance that he made good use of every opportunity he had thus gained. And Singer knew that now, despite everything, he himself found it hard to argue against Drayton's plea. But he tried to resist it. "The man is a creep you found under a stone."

"But you employed him. And he's changed, Henry. Three goddamn months in Washington worked wonders. It was you who told me."

"I didn't say it made a gentleman out of a crook."

"Words, words, words, Henry. You're a master of turning a gentleman into a crook by the use of the correct amount of baksheesh, yet you object furiously to a reformation the other way around. All right, make sure that Termine does everything the way you want him to. Manage him."

Running out of arguments, Singer meekly mentioned the press. "They might get wind of it."

"Good point, Henry. We'll have to leak a bit of information

to the public in advance." Drayton pressed the intercom button.

"Yes, sir?"

"I have to talk to Mara." Drayton turned to Singer: "Mara Boone, that is."

Singer looked away, only to confront his own drawn face in seven mirrors.

"She's away, sir," Ms. Etch said over the intercom.

"Don't I know that, sweetie. But where's she now?"

"Should reach Sydney quite soon. Shall I ascertain?"

The Sarissa that was supposed to be approaching Sydney still sat ankle-deep in a newborn river. Paya Lebar meant "wide swamp." The rain tried to force the airport to live up to its name-giving past. At midnight, local time, Penn had to apologize to his passengers yet again, and explain the delay, and be at his reassuring best to forestall the avalanche of complaints that would hit the airline, if not the headlines of the international press. He restarted the Muzak tape to restore the cozy parlor atmosphere in the cabin without knowing that he only caused further problems for Mara.

"Not that again!" growled Turpentine Benning as soon as he heard the first chords, and he went in a beeline for the service call button.

"Don't you like music?"

Mara's innocent question stopped him just in time. "Of course I like music. Everybody likes music."

Mara smiled. She had saved Tiny Malloy and the other girls yet another unnecessary journey up the aisle. "What sort of music do you like, Mr. Benning?"

"Oh, well. I'm a plain waltz-and-schmaltz man, you could say."

"No kidding?"

"Nope. Waltz-and-schmaltz, that's me all right. None of your fancy pop, rock, Nashville revival, papa Bach, Beetho-whatnot and the rest. You can keep them all. And that's a fact. But this is an airplane, not a dimestore or a cheap dive. I expect the crew to look after us, not entertain us."

Unknown to him, he was in full agreement with Penn, who, already annoyed to near the limit of his endurance, had to put up with the irritation caused by Mitchell's ceaseless "Ohwhata beauuuutiful baaaby, ohwhata beautiful day" and then "ohwhata beauuuutiful morning, ohwhata beautiful day," only to revert to the baby version, which he sang with even more feeling. Penn exchanged a few meaningful glances with White, the flight engineer, but neither of them had the heart to ask Mitchell to shut up for Chrissake.

Mitchell hummed through his checklists and stopped only when Ground Control reported a further deterioration of RVR: strong gusts had compressed the loose knit of the rain curtain into rain blankets in front of the aircraft, reducing visibility below an acceptable minimum. To make it even worse, an electric storm was interfering with all radio transmissions, and every communication became as strained as talking to the hard of hearing; even the best jokes and most heartfelt swearing tend to lose their impact through repetition.

Mitchell hummed about the beautiful baby as he consulted his wind vector diagram, and hummed as he redid his sums, at Penn's request, for the take-off data chart allowing for the water on the runway. Their V1 velocity, which Mitchell would call out during take-off, and at which Penn could still abort take-off if necessary, would be 133 knots. At 150 knots would come VR, the second call to Penn to rotate: pull back the yoke and take off. Mitchell had calculated the point at which V1 would be reached, and penciled it on his map of the airport and runway. That would be their point of no return, beyond which the aircraft could not be stopped safely on the remaining length of the runway. There the Sarissa, aptly named after the long and slender lance of the ancient Macedonians, would have to raise her nose and leave the ground so effortlessly that most passengers would not realize for quite a while afterward that their actual flight had begun. Penn decided to start the take-off run as far back as possible in order to make maximum use of the waterlogged runway length.

Through heavy static, the tower called, "SupraNat zero-three, do you wish to taxi into holding position or return to ramp?"

"SupraNat zero-three. We're next in line, we'll taxi into position and hold." Penn still hoped to slip away as soon as the wind dropped and gave him the slightest gap in the weather.

"Krrm, krrhhm" was the controller's answer, and Mitchell mumbled, "We have better transmissions from the moon!"

"Moon, SN zero-three? No moon tonight."

"Roger." The pilots laughed. At least it gave them a brief respite from Mitchell's humming. "We'll hold if it's OK with you, sir."

"Roger, zero-three."

Penn looked out and saw only the first few of the runway center lights. "Center lights go all the way, don't they?"

More amplified noise of cats scratching doors and windows alternately, and ". . . the way down . . ."

"All the way, I understand. Thank you."

Then with sudden absolute clarity: "Oh good, SN zero-three. Thank you. We'll recheck RVR at once now that you see the lights all the way."

"No—no! I'm *asking.* Please verify if the lights go all the way."

"Oh, that. Yes. Affirmative."

"Thank you. I'll want them on full brilliancy."

"Roger, zero-three."

Mitchell was humming again, and Penn decided he preferred the static.

In London it was midafternoon, and Barraclough was angry with himself. He had no one else to blame. He had told himself repeatedly that tea at Fortnum and Mason's would be a waste of precious cash and not so precious time because Brigadier Mott would not turn up. But Barraclough was not a man to break long-standing routines and promises on the spur of the moment. As always, at 1559 precisely, he stood with his back to the Royal Academy in Piccadilly and looked up. He noted that the sky was overcast, the wind westerly and the forecast of 18 degrees Centigrade (to him, deep down, 64 Fahrenheit) just about correct. Details mattered to him.

A massive man of military bearing who was never thought to be more than forty-five years old, he crossed the street without once dodging the heavy traffic—man and motorized beast instinctively recognizing his individual right of way—and stopped on the thin strip of a traffic island which, being parallel with the curb, formed a narrow lane exclusive to buses. He now stood opposite Fortnum and Mason's, his eyes on the clock held by huge leaves at second-floor level above the entrance to the majestic old store. The hands moved and, right on the hour, two sizable doors opened on the left and right of the clock. Two erect stony-faced gentlemen appeared—Mr. Fortnum in turquoise suit with red waistcoat, Mr. Mason in red suit with turquoise waistcoat. They glided out to meet in front of the clock, bowed stiffly to nobody but each other a few times, the privilege of dead shopkeepers, and returned to their respective cells for another hour of privacy.

Barraclough raised his wrist; yes, both his watch and the clock were right. Disregard for timing precision had killed many good men he liked. He crossed to the curb and entered the main food department, where he passed pâtés, smoked salmon, glacé fruits and morning-coated assistants at an even speed, paying no attention to anything or anyone, but noticing everything from new faces to the latest increase in Beluga caviar prices.

At the far end, he took the few stairs up to the tearoom, which belonged to another age, reviewed the scene in a single sweep—seven small six-arm chandeliers, pink and turquoise waitresses, red carpet, garden-type furniture, green marble tabletops, patisserie counter—and took a seat in the corner on the right, a vantage position which was, yet again, quite miraculously, empty, waiting for him. The elderly waitress, to whom he never talked, was on hand at once, and attentively she took his order—tea for one—as if it had not been the same every Monday and Thursday.

Normally, by now he would have classified all the customers—regulars, tourists, pharmaceutical supersalesmen, Arab time passers, impoverished past-timers, the cake gobblers and the girl who always sat sideways since somebody had once remarked on her classic profile. But today he was not quite his usual self. The sight of savory delicacies, the drifting sweet scent of fresh pastry and the homely fragrance of vanilla worked furiously on his taste buds. For the second day running, Barraclough was hungry.

"Here we are, sir."

"Thank you."

"Anything else, sir?"

Meat, you bitch, good meat and chunks of freshly baked bread, and make it snappy, because, believe it or not, I could dislocate your neck with my fingertips, hangman-style. "That will be all, thank you."

He glanced toward the patisserie counter. No sign of the Brigadier who called him his friend these days but would always remain his superior in total command of his loyalty. For it was Mott who had spotted his physique, wide-ranging technical skills and meticulous methodology during the war; who had trained him to cause death singly and liquidate small or large groups hostile to king and country (in that order); and who had recognized his ability to take professional pride in the planning and finely chiseled details of tailor-made operations on the ground, at sea or in flight. Oddly enough, he was never actually blooded in action. Too valuable to risk in the field, he became a back-room boy, an "extermination technician," as Mott nicknamed him in a rare lighter mood.

After the war, Barraclough knew that killing was probably doomed to be a dying business, but he trained to become a karate instructor and studied ceaselessly to keep up with wide-ranging technical innovations and scientific discoveries. He had "one-off" missions and lengthy "on-loan" assignments in Malaya, Cyprus, Kenya, Vietnam and the Middle East. It was a good life, but then, out of the blue, premature retirement. With a decent pension, of course, except that it could not allow for the unforseeable factor: his voluntarily assumed responsibilities for crippled veterans, old comrades' widows and the odd bystander or two who had been his victims through accident, all of whom had come to rely on the lilac envelopes which contained his modest monthly anonymous donations and a punctilious note of "best wishes." Heavy inflation nibbled away at his savings, and soon he had to economize severely. Only one seemingly superfluous item remained on his list of expenses: "Tea at F and M, Mondays and Thursdays at 1600." Because Mott wanted it for clandestine contacts, "just in case . . ."

Waiting for Mott was a fixation, Barraclough knew, but there were precedents to keep it alive: the Brigadier did turn up with work for him on three occasions, and the money thus earned helped to tide him and his beneficiaries over for a while. Besides, he argued, I'm not a sadistic slaughterman for occasional hire. I'm a professional, and one's profession cannot be changed jus'-like-that! When I cease to be a soldier and a pro, I'll be reduced, even retrospectively, to the level of a paid butcher.

His tea was cooling fast. As he raised the dainty cup to his lips, he looked up. At the patisserie counter, the lights shone on a silver sheet of hair. Mott. Barraclough did not try to catch his eye. The Brigadier would buy some cakes, then leave. Twenty minutes from now, he would expect Barraclough to be in the third cubicle on the left in the half-circle of telephone booths at the Piccadilly Circus underground station.

"Somebody must have turned the tap off up there," said White, the flight engineer, when the rain stopped as abruptly as it had begun.

Penn's eyes ran a fast scan check across his instrument panel. The radio was still as pleasant to listen to as a first-batch Laurel and Hardy sound track, but now the contents were sweet: a brief repeat of some basic data, altimeter settings QNH 1007.1 millibars, QFE 1005.2 MBS, headings after take off, assigned cruising height of 28,000 feet (something that Penn planned to get revised when airborne, for he would have preferred 34,000 for his near-sonic aircraft), and the instruction to tune to 118.3 megacycles, his departure frequency. He asked for the latest wind condition report on runway 2.

"Surface wind zero-sixty—zero-six-zero, that is—at twenty knots gusting thirty."

"Roger." Penn looked at Mitchell, who nodded. We'll have to watch that crosswind, their glances agreed. They were a good team. "Good night, sir."

"Good night, SupraNat zero-three."

Mitchell turned the dial to the new frequency and requested clearance for immediate take-off. There was only a slight pause, and the departure controller granted him clearance.

White was ready with his pink card, the final before-take-off checklist. He read it out fast but clearly, waiting each time for the pilot or co-pilot or both or he himself to answer the items from "flaps" to "transponder." Meanwhile the passengers listened with utter boredom to the stewardesses, who, at Penn's request, had to put on a repeat performance of instructions concerning seat belts, no smoking, exit signs and life jackets.

Tiny Malloy apologized to the entire ballet company. Yes, she knew that they were experienced travelers but the Captain was a real stickler for regulations, and some passengers might have forgotten what she had told them a few hours ago, before the delays.

Turpentine Benning became rather agitated once again because he tried but could not locate and feel his life jacket under the seat. Mara told him it must be there.

"I want to *know* that it is there."

She promised to help him find it as soon as they were airborne.

"Might be too late. We'll be flying over water."

"Not for the first few minutes," she reassured him.

White was nearing the end of the checklist. "Cabin crew call" —he paused to give the signal to the cabin crew to take their seats and fasten their seat belts, then answered the item— "three presses." He asked himself about the cabin air compressors and told himself that they were checked with No. 3 being On/A-11 Off. "Transponder . . ."

Penn was staring out, examining the long wet stretch of bituminous concrete ahead of him, the straight line of white center lights that turned into yellow for the last 1500 feet.

"Transponder . . ."

"Sorry," Penn answered. "It's On."

"Before-take-off check . . . completed."

As was his habit, Penn then looked up to recheck that the cabin signs were On and the autopilot Off (he liked to hand-fly her up to 6000), moved his control column slightly forward and back, and the half-wheel aileron control left and right. With this, his private checklist was also completed. He turned around: "All set?"

Mitchell and White gave him the thumbs up. While releasing the brakes, he called the tower: "SN zero-three is rolling to take off."

"Roger."

The company flight manual permitted "the commencement of take-off from a static or rolling condition," and this time Penn chose the latter for extra length of runway. He moved the throttles gently forward, and the aircraft mewed and shivered a little as she began to gain momentum. As soon as the Sarissa moved, Mitchell started his stopwatch and, apart from the occasional quick glance outside, fixed his eyes on the speed indicator. As the throttles were opened, the wheels gathered speed fast and, crossing the threshold bar of sixteen green lights, the plane swept down the runway.

Forty . . . fifty . . . sixty knots . . . Penn had his left hand on the small wheel that steered the nose, and his right hand on the thrust levers, which were now fully forward. Mitchell maintained a light forward pressure on his control column to help keep the nose firmly on the ground until Penn was ready to rotate, and held the ailerons into the wind, as instructed by his captain, to compensate for the pressures exercised by the strong gusts across their path. White monitored the performance of the engines and all was fine, strictly routine.

Seventy . . . eighty . . . ninety knots . . . Penn depressed gently the pedals to coordinate the rudder with the nose-wheel steering and keep the aircraft on the center line. He made such a fine job of it that the wheel began to bump and hammer annoyingly with growing frequency on the lights as the Sarissa accelerated, and Penn moved the wheel just a shade to the right of the center line.

"One hundred knots," Mitchell called and saw that Penn was releasing his grip on the steering wheel to take over the control column.

"I have it," said Penn, and Mitchell let go of the stick. The speed indicator moved to 110, 120 . . . Gusts brought some puffs of rain, blanking out the farthest runway lights for half a second at a time, but that was no problem. "Shit." The nose wheel started hammering once more. Not that it mattered. Only a couple of seconds or some 500 feet to go on the ground. . . . 130 knots . . . 133 . . . "V one," called Mitchell. . . . 140 . . . 145 . . . 150. "VR. Rotate."

Penn nodded. He held the half-wheel firmly and applied the small backward pressure that would be enough to make the nose lift off. The stick resisted him. He pulled a little more, but it still worked against him. Acceleration was normal. Engines running perfectly. His eyes took a snap of the flaps selector: correct, green light On.

"Rotate!" Mitchell urged him. They were beyond the point of no return. They had to take off. They could not stop on the runway any more. "Rotate!" His hands were itching to get on the control column, but he held off. Training was stronger than instinct.

Penn knew exactly how far down the runway they were. But the elevator did not work! The triplicate system was foolproof. It could not break down, he knew that for sure. Except that it did not work. How much harder could he pull that stick? He quickly trimmed back a little.

In any other situation there would be time to experiment. To diagnose what was wrong and find a way. To remedy. To circumvent. Improvise. Something! But not now, hurtling past the yellow lights at 250 feet a second. Some pilots loathe to apply extra force, in case they break something. Penn knew he could not break anything. There was nothing to break—except strict regulations. At this speed, he must take off, absolutely must, no matter what, unless he reckoned that a disaster on the ground would be more survivable than a crash after take-off with a faulty aircraft. He pulled harder on the yoke. No good. The gustlock? No—it was off. *If* the indicator was right.

He saw the end of the runway. He heard Mitchell's yelling. He knew he had no elevator response. Something gripped and squeezed his throat. Oh no, not again! He swallowed hard. He saw no chance of forcing a single sound through the cylinders that mangled his larynx.

"Abandon take-off." He heard his own voice. It was weak and guttural, which made it sound cold and calm. Somewhere in the back of his mind he felt a tickle of pride at not screaming the word "abort," but that thought embryo never lived to be born. There was no time. The airspeed indicator approached the 170 mark.

Three pairs of hands went into well-rehearsed action. From the corners of his eyes Penn registered that the dots of runway lights were fused into a continuous strip because of the speed. Now the strip turned yellow. They were well into the last 1500 feet of runway.

Penn pulled back the throttles and guided them through the gate that prevents accidental application of reverse thrust. The throttles kicked back. He tried again. Better. The brakes he touched only lightly, just tapping, intermittently. The thunder of the engines began to die away. Four seconds since his decision to abort.

Mitchell had the spoilers fully extended. He could do no more to assist in stopping this hurtling mass of metal, kerosene and flesh. He pressed the stick forward to hold the nose wheel to the ground. It felt light, too willing to comply. The wheels might be aquaplaning. He did not envy Penn, who must be fighting for directional control, too. "One-fifty . . . one-forty . . . one thirty." He called out the speeds of deceleration in an unemotionally tinny tone.

A final grumbling murmur of the engines. A gasp of silence. Then the high-pitched whine, at last. Reverse thrust beginning to help. The whine turned into wailing.

Penn touched the brakes again and balanced his half-wheel as finely as if weighing a bean against a pea: the ailerons must keep the wings level for maximum brake effect. If only the grip on his throat would ease. Panic spread down his chest.

A strong gust caught the flank of the Sarissa, trying to make her veer off the remaining short stretch of runway. Nose-wheel steering was completely ineffectual. Penn's feet played the rudder pedal, but even that was no match for the wind. He had to use asymmetrical thrust. He willed his hand to move. The outer starboard engine roared into life. The aircraft fought the wind and straightened up on the runway.

In the seven seconds that had passed since Mitchell's first call of "VR. Rotate," the Sarissa must have traveled some 1400 feet. Mitchell saw the end of the yellow lights. "One-twenty . . . one-ten . . ."

"SN zero-three, SN zero-three, do you read me?" Questions and more questions nobody had the time to answer. Then, embedded in static, a thin Chinese voice: "My God, she's running off the runway!"

Penn was aware of the pandemonium that had broken out on all the airport frequencies, but his ear was waiting for a slight thump . . . now! The nose wheel had left the threshold. He hit the brakes hard just when the main wheels would plow into the waterlogged ground.

Full reverse thrust again. Blown by the engines, a whirling cloud of water and bits of turf began to soar, blocking his view.

A bump and a jolt. The nose wheel was shorn off clean as it crashed into the edge of the perimeter road. The flight deck pitched forward and the cone cut a deep furrow path for the plane. It helped her slow down. But still too fast.

A bang and some knocks fused into a rattle. The wing tip sliced through a fence, an orchard of landing lights and then an ILS localizer installation. That impact spun the aircraft around thirty degrees to make her head straight for a cabbage field and some parked bulldozers. But the three men were still fighting fit. More rudder. More asymmetric thrust. Only the far end of the damaged wing hit a tractor. The Sarissa, spewing fuel as she went, veered toward a ditch.

Fire warnings came on. Penn was shutting off everything in sight to stop more fuel reaching the torn pipes at the gap left behind by a lost engine. Mitchell and White discharged all the built-in fire extinguishers. White prayed aloud.

Another bang and jolt, this time louder still. The main gear could not stand any more of the battering. The struts snapped off and the plane sploshed on her belly, forcing up a spray of soggy ground, cabbages and debris. The nose pitched forward again as it tipped over the edge of a ditch and shot toward the boulders in the wall of the far side.

Something huge, dark and angular reared up, filled Penn's horizon and lunged toward him. Penn ducked. All the lights went out, and in the brief eerie silence only the Chinese voice kept repeating, "SN zero-three, do you read me? SN zero-three . . ."

Singer heard the swish and did not need to stop reading and look up to know that once more Ms. Etch had materialized.

"An ATC strike and storm had delayed her flight, but two minutes ago, when I got through to Singapore, the aircraft was already lined up to take off," she said.

"Thank you, sweetie, you're worth your weight in gold," Drayton drawled, and Singer would have sworn that tears made her eyes go opaque.

"Anything else, sir?"

"No, sweetie, that's all."

"You want me to contact her in the air?"

"No, let her sleep. Sydney will do. But catch her right on arrival at the airport for me, will you?"

Like an apparition which realized that it was past her bedtime, Ms. Etch disappeared. Drayton turned to Singer. "Have you finished?"

"Almost." He would have to be careful not to reveal how very impressed he was with Salah Termine's confidential report. It had come to Drayton directly because Singer was away. Termine must have seized the opportunity. Singer read on, and every line convinced him more and more that Termine was after his own job and that Drayton might not be entirely alien to the idea.

"Quite something, isn't it?"

"Quite. But not much more than what could reasonably be expected in the present climate." Which was a blatant lie.

Singer was stunned by the implications. Although Termine had not yet produced material evidence, his findings gave a clear indication that, in Europe, the international competition among aircraft peddlers was ready to go a long way beyond the relatively innocent games of Lockheed-type who-bribes-whom and "If you buy two generals then I'll buy a king and see who's crying now, so there." Hannan's death in New York might be just the proof Termine's report lacked.

"It's going to be tough, very tough," whispered Drayton, and Singer knew that his eyes would detect every nuance of his reaction.

"I'm ready," said Singer a little too loudly in an effort to make it more convincing.

"Naturally. What else? But of course I'll want your own public role to be de-emphasized."

"Right." Singer studied the report. "Who's this man Mott Termine refers to?"

"That's the Brigadier I mentioned to you—ex-British intelligence."

"Ex?"

"That's what he claims, but Termine will check him out."

"What's he now?"

"Calls himself a consultant and spends a lot of time in Paris and Teheran. A high-class mercenary, I guess."

"You want to buy him?"

"If we can. Termine thinks he may already be on the payroll of one of our more alert competitors."

Singer had an ear for the cutting edge of such softly delivered remarks. He knew that some European outfits would use professional trouble stirrers like this Brigadier seemed to be, but how the hell should he have prevented it? It was not his job, and anyway . . . He was too tired to follow the thought right through. All he knew for sure was that Termine might not be easy to manage. So he would have to find a way. So Drayton must be played a little. So Termine must be allowed to make mistakes. So he would have to be on his toes. But not now. No. Now he just wanted to go back to bed, curl up to the S shape of sleeping Anna and forget about bribes, Drayton, the Sarissa project and Termine's motto that "Only the dead are your allies forever."

The doors of the fire station flew open as the first tender zoomed past them.

"This is tender one. Did you say square eight or eighteen?"

"Eight! Zero eight!" shouted a near-hysterical controller trying to overcome all the static.

"And you said emergency. Is it full emergency or declared emergency?"

"Full! Full emergency! It's an accident! One hundred and eighty-three on board. One eighty-three."

"Tender one calling all fire appliances. Tender one calling . . ." The voice was swallowed by another burst of static

The race toward square 8, located on the grid map at the far end of runway 2, had begun, in fact, even before the Sarissa came to a halt in the ditch. The alert departure controller raised the alarm when SN03 was still on the runway. 121.9 MCS was the frequency cleared for the sole use of the emergency units, but the poor reception seemed to cost valuable seconds of the progress of a full turnout. The first rescue vehicles reaching the scene of the crash could not be driven right up to the aircraft; they were stranded on the far side of the ditch, had to reverse on the mud track and make a long detour. Tender one sped down the runway itself and was within sight of the Sarissa when a small playful flame appeared near the crash site. It was the engine that had flown off by its own. Tender one gave it top priority.

In the cabin aboard the aircraft, silence was absolute. During the deceleration, tremendous G forces pinned heads and knees and hands to the seats in front of each row, eyes were forced to bulge, throats whipped tongues through teeth, abdomens were squeezed and bruised as the forward force tried to prise them free from the clutch of the seat belts. It took passengers long seconds to decide whether they were dead or alive.

Mara knew her face was bathed in blood. But she felt no pain. Her brain could not diagnose whether she was hurt or not. Her hands wiped her face, and she was ready to find some huge gaping hole. But there was no obvious wound. Then she remembered that Turpentine Benning had first been catapulted against the seat back in front, and he had sailed up and hit the roof when the aircraft stopped and the lights went out. Oh, yes. His life jacket. His grumbling. She tried to prevent him from getting up.

Her head began to hurt. The pain came from her neck. But no, no wound there either. She heard all the activity around her. Doors opening, evacuation chutes stretching out, the crew urging people to get up and go. Go! Move! Move, for God's sake! The memories of her own training came to life in her muscles rather than her brain and made her move. A fire or explosion might come any moment now. Yet everything was happening in silence and slow motion. Survivors would always remember that there was no panic.

A woman blocked the nearest exit. Tiny Malloy tried to push her outward or pull her in or just shift her, but she never had a chance. The woman was too big and too determined not to leave the aircraft without her umbrella.

"Go!" Mara shouted at her.

Her voice shattered the silence and everyone began to scream and fight and push toward the doors. The plane was sitting on its belly and it would have been easy to climb or jump out, but people insisted on using the chutes, which were soon torn by sharp shoe heels, and once again evacuation was delayed.

A man jumped at last. He landed in a pool of kerosene but sighed with great relief. Safe, at last. He then produced a cigarette and prepared to light it to soothe his nerves. Mara acted instinctively. She dived through the door and her pulled-up knees hit him in the chest. They both fell to the ground as Tender Two, sirens howling, came to a halt only inches from them.

Mitchell moaned. Otherwise the flight deck was silent.

Penn's nostrils were the first to regain consciousness. The smell of kerosene. His throat ached, but he could breathe now.

"Everybody out!" he shouted even before he opened his eyes and grabbed a handle. The evacuation horn began to wail the grief of a thousand mourners. A huge bump, blowing up fast, began to block his left eye. He turned around. White was there, his hands stretched toward the hole left by his instrument panel, which was, instead, seated in a twisted mass where his head used to be.

The flight-deck door was crushed and blocked. Penn extricated himself and reached for the axe stowed behind him for emergencies. "Give me a hand!" he yelled at Mitchell, who seemed unhurt.

"I'll follow you," Mitchell groaned as Penn tried the emergency hatch. It would not open. The axe soon cleared a passage for him. He wanted Mitchell to go first, but he realized that he himself would be in his way. Besides, as a former pole-vaulter, he could jump and help Mitchell down.

Penn glanced around. Yes, everything that could still be identified had been shut down properly. "Come on." His head hurt, but he forced himself to move and climb up through the hatch. He fought to retain consciousness. Like a sleepwalker he stepped off and fell into the ditch, still shouting, "Come on! Move!"

Two firemen caught him as he was about to collapse and ran with him away from the aircraft. They left him with Mara and Tiny. Seconds later, his undamaged eye began to clear. "Everybody out?"

"Yes."

"Where's he?"

"Who?"

"Mitchell!"

"Haven't seen him."

Before the two women could stop him, he was running toward the wrecked nose of the Sarissa, shouting back at Tiny, who tried to follow him, "Do your own bloody job!" His hand signaled toward the passengers, some of whom were still dawdling about in a daze. Mara went after him. Tiny tried to stop her, but she shook herself free. "You have other things to do!"

All the emergency units were arriving at last. Lucky there's no fire yet, Penn thought. He was convinced he was shouting to them to help him climb the nose of the aircraft to the emergency hatch on top, but he was not sure that they heard him. What the hell took them twenty or maybe thirty minutes, anyway?

It had, in fact, been only four minutes and nineteen seconds since the crash.

A tall well-built girl with a lot of youthful flesh left booth 3 at Piccadilly Circus, and Barraclough took her place. The phone rang almost at once, and he picked up the receiver. It was still warm from the girl's touch, and he derived some sensual pleasure from this almost physical contact.

"I've got some work for you. . . . I mean if you're free."

Barraclough appreciated the gesture. The Brigadier made him feel that he was important, a man whose time was precious.

"Of course, sir."

"Good. How up to date are you on aviation?"

"Near enough, sir. I mean I could—"

"That's all right. Plenty of time. Only contingency planning at this stage. You think you could sink a new type of crate without trace?"

"No reason why not."

Barraclough did not need explanations or justifications. It

was a matter of trusting one's boss. And he trusted Mott despite the rumors that the Brigadier had also quit the Service. True or false, it made no difference. Barraclough was convinced that people such as the Brigadier and himself would always work for the government, in active service or retirement, no matter what. And if the government wanted something . . . He only wondered which country's latest fighter or bomber aircraft would be his target. The Russian Foxbat Mark II? That new Swedish fighter? Apart from these, only new civil airliners came to his mind, and those, of course, would not concern the Brigadier.

"Start thinking about some contingency plans right away. You'll have an immediate advance. Usual arrangements. Use it freely until I give you the details and you work out cost estimates."

"Do we meet, sir?"

"Yes. We'll use scheme two. Any other questions?"

"No, sir . . . except perhaps . . . I mean, could I use any assistance?"

"You mean Fraser. Yes. Give her my regards. Your expense account will be generous enough, so it's up to you."

They hung up at the same time, then both picked up the receivers once more. Mott dialed a long-distance number, and the man who answered without delay had a heavy foreign accent. Mott spoke slowly and loudly. He never trusted a foreigner fully to understand his language, and anybody who was stupid enough not to speak good English must be deaf, too. "It's under way. Please make funds—I mean money—available." He rang off and walked out, passing booth 3, where Barraclough was still on the phone, unable to get through to Fraser—Fraser, Betty M., as he would call her in more emotional moments.

The delay was caused by Mr. Connor, who was making Betty Fraser listen to one of his daily lectures. She had been three full minutes late with the coffee and had spilled some of the paid-for liquid, thus committing one of the "worst of cardinal sins in an ordinary commercial organization which had to earn its keep, unlike the scroungers army in government and other sources of sinecure."

"Sorry, sir," she muttered, and hated herself. But what was the choice for a woman of fifty-three who could not type and had never had any demonstrable commercially useful experience? She answered the phone. "Mr. Connor's office."

"Fraser?"

She recognized the voice. Barraclough never called without an exceptionally good reason. She could hardly contain herself. "Yes!"

"I'll need you. As of today. You may resign."

It happened! It did. Just as Barraclough had predicted. They were back in service. Needed once again. So he was right. Had they married on retirement, they could never be reactivated and assigned together. The risk would be too great. Barraclough rang off without waiting for an answer.

She put down the phone, then turned and slowly and deliberately knocked over Connor's mug. "That's in lieu of my week's notice, sir," she said softly and popped a broken biscuit in the puddle on his desk. "We mustn't waste things, must we, sir."

Penn tried to fight them off, but he was subdued and they gave him the injection that reduced the pain and made him drowsy. But he went on battling against sleep. He heard the sirens, he felt the motion, he tried desperately to focus on the face above him in the ambulance. The girl. What's her name. Mara.

"What happened?"

"Ssh."

"What happened?"

"You got him out."

"Where's he?"

"Another ambulance took him."

"Bad?"

"Probably two broken legs. He was trapped. But you got him out. Now relax."

"Any other casualties?"

She hesitated.

"I know about White," he said with great effort. "Anybody else?"

She shook her head. It was no good telling Penn about Benning. It had been his own fault.

"Listen." Penn's voice was now reduced to a whisper. "If I go under . . . you must talk to the man in charge—"

"In charge of what?"

"Investigation. Tell him to check out the elevator system. It was locked or something. That's where he'll find the cause why I had to abort. . . . Must be an open and shut case . . . open and shut . . ."

Drayton thrived on crises. He listened without a word to the brief Singapore telex translated into Ms. Etch's cool report-writing vernacular. "No female casualty on board."

"Thank you, sweetie." Mara was safe. The rest of the news was just a challenge.

She closed the door quietly as she left, and he knew that nobody, but absolutely nobody, would get through to him in person or on the telephone until he gave her the green light. He walked slowly from mirror to mirror and studied his tanned trust-inducing Southern-senator face in each. He finally confronted his image in the reddish glow of his old favorite though somewhat vulgar collector's item. As usual, he took stock before each battle. His fingers combed through an abundance of good white hair, and when wave after soft wave returned to its normal position, he smiled. There was no empty narcissistic delight in the review of his face. His looks were a tool to be used to win women and allies, and he was pleased with what he saw. At fifty-six, he was obviously at the peak of his powers, and whoever wanted to harm his Sarissa project, be it a competitor or fate itself, would have a hell of a fight on hand.

He derived even more joy from his decision to stay in the office after Singer had left, work through the dawn, greet the morning shift at the gate and say good night to those going home—one of his favorite stratagems—and wait for his senior executives with some fresh information which, however trivial, would still be news to them. This time he would have plenty to tell. And the sweetest act would be to summon Singer back into the office.

He pressed the intercom. "Sweetie, get me Singer." He hoped that the crisis manager would be in bed, fast asleep.

"Singer . . ."

Yes, the voice was sleepy enough. "Sorry to wake you up, Henry, I know you were up all night, but we have trouble in Singapore. An aborted take-off and crash."

"How many?"

"Two dead, confirmed, one or two injured. That's all. But it could spell trouble with the sales."

"Yes, of course. I'm on my way."

"Thank you, Henry. I've already alerted Termine and the go team, but I'd be happier if you yourself took charge." Drayton was sure he heard Anna, the new Mrs. Singer, grumble bitterly about yet another unexpected trip. But that would teach that mediocre actress, Washington PR girl and superb aviation lobbyist not to marry a vice-president when she could remain the president's mistress.

Drayton had lied about Termine and did not look forward to calling the man, even though he would be the best to latch onto this accident, to find out if there was sabotage or any other anti-Sarissa move by competitors, check out all personnel involved, and ascertain if the pilot was an enemy or a fool. And Drayton had to make the call himself, because, given half a chance, Singer might bring in somebody else purely because he did not *enjoy* working with "that crook." True, joy was a nonexistent term in connection with Termine. Too smooth, too sly, too smart and too ugly, Drayton agreed. If he wore a fez and were the only waiter to serve refreshments with a smile from one of those large copper trays in an Istanbul joint, Drayton would have chosen to die of thirst. A less unpleasant way to go. So Termine was a good man to have on one's team. But no joy.

"We don't like it, we don't like it," Colonel Mihir Gupta kept repeating. Delays, a missing passenger, and then the accident —nothing to like, nothing at all. An earnest second-generation Singaporean of Indian descent, he was greatly impressed by his own importance as chief of airport security. He had taken charge of the accident site, the witnesses, the hospital and even the morgue; coordinated the reports from the controllers and rescue services; and assigned armed guards to the wreckage, Captain Penn and First Officer Mitchell. "If the world's spotlights were to be on us, gentlemen," he declared at every opportunity in his somewhat Victorian though localized English, "let us make it a showboat for our drudgery, and no nincompoop please!" And he did make a good job of it. Everything was done according to the book, no souvenir hunter would get away with bits of wreckage, vital pieces of evidence "to adorn his humble homestead."

At four o'clock in the morning Mara knew that Penn had been in and out of X rays and various checkups, but nobody would tell her about his condition, and the Colonel would "most dynamically refuse to talk to the gentlemen of the press or whoever." So she slipped into the kitchen, helped herself to a white coat, hung a glittering corkscrew and a pair of scissors on a chain around her neck, hoping that in the dark hospital corridor they would look medical enough, and walked right up to the guard.

"Anybody in?"

"Only the Captain."

"Good. I hope you know your duties."

"Oh yes, miss—I mean Doctor."

"Right."

She walked past him and into the room on tiptoes. Penn switched the light on. "Hey. You're not supposed to be in here."

"And you're not supposed to be awake."

"So we're cheating. Any news?"

"No, I only came to take your pulse." She touched his hand, then withdrew quickly. "I wanted to know how you were."

"All right, thanks. And it's good to see you."

"Can I do anything for you?" She hoped that he would not ask about the casualties. She felt strangely reluctant to lie to him, and she was not sure if he knew about Turpentine Benning.

"Just one thing. Forget that you're a journalist and be a . . . a passenger? Friend?"

"Why not?"

"The Singapore authorities asked the British Accident Investigation Branch to do the job under the nominal leadership and overall responsibility of some local talent," he said.

"That's good."

"Routine. But, luckily, the Branch has a chap just finishing a military case in Borneo and he'll soon be over here. If you catch him before he comes to see me, tell him about the elevator. Remember what I said?"

She nodded. "A lot of people are on their way from the States, too. From AeroCorp it's Singer."

"How do you know?"

"AeroCorp told me."

"When?"

"Soon after the crash."

"You called them?"

"No."

"You reported to them!"

"I don't work for them."

"Did you tell them about the elevator?"

"No."

"Why not?"

She hesitated. "I thought it was for the investigator in charge. Sort of confidential."

"Thank you."

She shrugged her shoulders and tried to turn away, but Penn's gaze held her eyes.

"Why did you call AeroCorp?"

"They called me."

"Why?"

"To ask how I was."

"Who's *they?*"

"Drayton."

"Was it he or your editor who chose me to be the subject of your article?"

"You were *my* choice. I told you."

"I'm glad."

She busied herself with smoothing the wrinkles in his light blanket and pouring fresh water into his glass. "Have you talked to your wife?"

"Yes."

"Can I do something for her?"

"In what way?"

"I mean when she arrives."

"She's not coming."

"Oh."

"It's . . . it's only that we have a son and she must look after him . . . That's the most important . . . And I'm well enough."

"Of course."

"Don't look so gloomy."

"I never do."

She did this time.

At 0409, Friday morning, local time, heavy jacks were moved urgently to the Sarissa when one of the guards noticed that a child's leg was sticking out from under the wrecked flight deck.

Even before the crushed body could be recovered, it was established that all passengers had been accounted for, and so it was assumed that it must be a local child. At 0457, a shack nearby was visited by policemen. The couple who lived there were known to the police as confirmed drug addicts. Neither parent was found to be sufficiently coherent to make a statement. They had several children, but, according to the eldest, it was "quite likely" that a missing brother would seek shelter and sleep in the ditch or under some bulldozer if caught by the rain.

In London, it was still Thursday evening. Fraser and Barraclough ate their kebabs in a ceremonious silence, drank up their bottle of Demestica—both of them disliked the other Greek wines because of the resinous taste—and went for a stroll along a never-changing route, through the film-set village of Hampstead. Down Well Walk, a whisky in The Flask, out to the edge of and skirting the Heath. Their traditional way of starting and finishing each of their assignments.

There was not a soul in sight when he broke the silence. "I've been thinking."

She nodded. It was his job to think for both of them. Think and come to decisions which were not to be questioned, both during their active service together or since.

"The chief sounded very serious, and I have a feeling that it's going to be a big one." He spoke slowly, with long pauses. "If so, afterwards we'll call it a day, I think. We're not getting any younger. Let others do their stint."

By the time they reached Keats Grove, he had outlined his plan. If it was a major job, there would be a fair amount of money; if they saved enough, they could buy a small sweet shop or something like that on the coast. Funny postcards, ice cream, souvenirs.

"We'll get married, Betty M.," he said.

"If you say so."

He always held that, while they were operational, an enemy

agent could take advantage of their emotional attachment. It would be an unacceptable risk. It was partly this, partly old service habit that made him still call her Fraser.

"How is your daughter?"

"Fine. She's found a better job in a typing pool," she said.

"Good." It was unnecessary to tell her that it was he who had arranged that new job for Sally, their twenty-year-old daughter, who knew Barraclough only as uncle. "If we had the shop with a flat above it, we might have enough room to put her up sometimes. She could even live with us if she wanted to."

"You'd tell her? I mean . . . about us?"

"Perhaps."

She asked no questions about the assignment. She did not need to. If it was for Mott, it would be for the British government. If it was for the government, and if Barraclough decided to do it, it was fine with her. Life definitely looked rosier than only a few hours ago.

A few miles up Hampstead Hill, in a fine Georgian house at the dead end of an elegant cul-de-sac, the telephone rang.

"Hullo?"

"Candy? Is that you Candy?"

"Yes, Mother, indeed. What did you expect at this hour?" Her speech was a living testimony to the efforts of a mediocre elocutionist. "You forgot to tell me something?"

"How did you know?"

"We spoke only fifteen minutes ago. What is it, Mother?"

"Just that, you know, it's not for me to say . . ."

"But you will say it, nevertheless. You always do."

"All right, I won't say nothing then. Except that I'd have thought that you'd be on your way by now to be with your hubby. I mean Cornelius."

"Yes, Mother, I know exactly who my 'hubby' is."

"You're not going then."

"I don't like Singapore."

"I didn't mean a holiday, you know."

"Don't worry. Corrie is all right."

"Because what I mean is . . . you can leave Timmy with me if you decide to go, after all."

"Thank you. *Timothy* would appreciate it."

"Have you told him what happened?"

"Of course."

"It must be quite a shock to him. I mean he's only ten, but he thinks a lot, you know. . . . Candy . . . are you there?"

"Yes, Mother."

"You know what I mean? Timmy thinks his father is God or something, doesn't he?"

"And we all do, don't we? A wonderful husband, a magnificent father. Sounds like an obituary. But after all, he's the man in the left-hand seat, we trust him with our lives, he must be God! Yes, it was quite a shock to Timothy that his beloved father might have made a mistake."

"What makes you say that?"

"Well, you never know, do you?"

The Malaysian Airways flight from Kuching was only two minutes late on touch-down at Singapore. The aircraft rolled to a halt at 0815, and Kevin Stacey was not pleased. The call from the London duty clerk of the Accident Investigation Branch had alerted him at three o'clock, Borneo Time, in the morning. It was a sleepy rush to wind up his almost finished case and hand it over to a local ignorant for processing, more rush to reach the airport with only two minutes to spare, and a flight too short to let him catch up on his sleep. But that was not all the cause of his displeasure. The Sarissa job spelled a further long absence from home, more neglect of his garden, and once again the prospect of missing the North London Butterfly Collectors' annual picnic. And then the inevitable confrontation with international bureaucracy. Intrigue and power struggle, grappling with lies, half-truths and face-saving formulas would be the order of every day in a case that involved a supranational airline, American manufacturers, a worldwide network of subcontractors, insurers in every corner of the globe, Singapore authorities, American authorities, international aviation authorities, as well as British authorities—his superiors who had loaned him to Singapore and who would want him to complete the investigation as smoothly as possible, advise the local government representative in record time—and get out even faster.

One day I'll learn to use shortcuts, he kept promising himself, but because he knew he would never learn, he smiled. Smiled inwardly, that is, as his face, long frozen into a semipermanent frown, with eyes screwed up as if the light was too much to bear, and with one eyebrow slightly raised, left hardly any room for reflecting changes of mood. Perhaps it was this frown that had prevented him for fifty-five years from ever achieving popularity at school, in the neighborhood or at work. Perhaps it was because of this frown that some colleagues regarded him as a sour stickler for unnecessary details. And perhaps it was a subconscious frown at his own abilities as an aviation sleuth whose findings could never quite measure up to the demands of his own insatiable curiosity and his thirst for absolute truth. Whatever it was, the suspicious frown gave no comfort to the anxious Colonel Mihir Gupta, who had parked his car at the foot of the gangway and volunteered to drive Stacey to the crash site.

"We don't like it, not at all. And the sooner we clear this up the better. I hope you agree, sir."

Stacey nodded—half in agreement, half in his sleep.

"I mean I'm not for idle chitchat. I like to get on with it and on to the next job, right? I lead from the front, so to speak, and my chaps know it. By Jove, don't they know it?" And when Stacey said nothing, he sighed with relief. "I'm glad it's you who'll be in charge, sir. We'll get on famously. Neither of us likes to waste words, I can see that."

The Colonel again offered to drive Stacey around the crash

site, but the investigator wanted to walk. On his own and in silence. The Colonel walked some twenty feet in front of him, clearing workmen and firemen out of the way, telling off the guards, exercising authority and no nincompoop.

He joined Stacey as they completed their brisk round. "Well, sir? What do you think?"

"What do you mean?"

"What could have caused it?"

"I don't know. It's too early to tell."

"I mean as a first impression. Just what does it look like to you?"

Stacey glanced around. "An accident, I suppose."

So the irony went unnoticed. "Just what I thought, sir. My very own impressions. An accident. Act of God. Nobody to blame, only to be thankful that there were no more casualties."

"I wouldn't say that. I only meant that we'll now have to get down to finding out what the cause was."

"Right. No idle chitchat." The Colonel began to unbutton his tunic, ready to really get down to it as the man said.

But Stacey had other plans. "Can I talk to Captain Penn first?"

"Of course."

At the hospital, a small fiercely chanting group prevented them from driving up to the main entrance. The Colonel apologized and told Stacey about the dead child who had been found under the crashed Sarissa. "The parents probably think they'll get more compensation if they blame Captain Penn for what happened."

Now that he knew what it was all about, Stacey suddenly deciphered the Chinese accents. "Captain Penn, murderer! Captain Penn, murderer!"

Stacey looked at the Colonel. "Am I wrong to believe that the Captain is still under medical care, in need of peace and quiet?"

"I see what you mean, sir. I shall endeavor to disperse the

crowd without delay and then join you at the Captain's bedside. We must give him the doubt of benefit, right?"

Penn sat on the edge of the bed and stared at the open window. The chanting sounded faint up here, but his eager guard had already informed him about the cause of the demonstration.

"I expected you to be much older," said Stacey, and slowly closed the window, seemingly quite unaware of the shouting outside. "I would have liked to find a more pleasant occasion, but I'm very pleased to meet you at last."

"At last?"

"I just missed you at least twice in Africa. During the Biafran war, to be precise. I not only heard about the mercy missions you flew, but also saw the Dakota you managed to land in the bush. Quite a sight it was. I'm delighted to have the opportunity to congratulate you."

Penn said nothing. He watched Stacey with an uncomfortable mixture of suspicion and apprehension. He disliked accident investigators. They had the reputation of jumping to conclusions too readily, particularly in cases of so-called pilot error findings. So what was the man getting at?

"Must have been the oldest DC3 in Africa. Or anywhere else, for that matter. When I had a chance to examine it, the port engine was missing, the other you must have dragged along the ground. It was held by a single fractured pipe. More than forty per cent of your wing surface was gone when I saw it, and the remains looked like a nice slice of Gruyère. Then there was the tail section." He smacked his lips appreciatively.

"We came through some unfriendly airspace."

For once, Stacey smiled.

"What's so funny?"

"You had an excessive load, you had children all over the floor, even in the cockpit, you made a virtual Stuka dive with a passenger aircraft, you dodged the machine guns of two fighters, and you speak about unfriendly airspace. And I thought I knew something about British understatement."

"I found four dead kids on board."

"And you saved the rest." He took out a tape recorder and a notepad. "You saved them simply by going against the book."

Penn stiffened.

Stacey paid no attention to him. "Yes, those fighter pilots must have gone dizzy just watching your antics. Nobody could have warned them what an ice-cold, desperate and capable pilot might do with a DC3 *if* he's willing to break all rules." He paused. "Well now, about this Sarissa . . ."

As he stopped, there was complete silence. There was no more chanting outside. Penn cleared his throat. "What do you want to know?"

"Everything," said Stacey. "I'll run the tape, but I'll take notes as well if you don't mind. I still don't trust the machine."

Penn told him briefly what had happened. What the stick felt like, what his thoughts were at the time, what he tried, what he did, and what course the disaster would have followed had he taken off by forcing the faulty system. He had no doubt whatsoever about the elevator malfunction. He said it was imperative to find out if this was a unique snag in his plane or some defect inherent in the design of all Sarissas. Stacey was a good listener. He asked only a few questions and every one of them was relevant. Penn began to warm to him. The man was competent. Things began to move in the right direction.

"I had a quick look at the site. The damage to the aircraft is not too extensive. I think we'll be able to test the systems soon." Stacey switched off the tape recorder, and as Colonel Mihir Gupta joined them he added, "If there was a fault, it must still be there."

"What do you mean *if?*"

Stacey touched his arm lightly, almost accidentally. "I'll find it for you. Don't worry."

"Thanks." Penn was on the verge of collapse. The mounting tension, capable of resisting even the sedatives, now peaked out and defeated itself. His eyes closed to slits. He and Stacey did not need to say anything about the urgency of the investigation, about the potential implications, the warnings that might have to be flashed to every operator of the type.

But the Colonel was keen to spell out whose responsibility any delay would be. "Shouldn't we advise the manufacturers and all authorities to ground the Sarissa fleet?"

"Not yet," said Stacey. "Not just yet."

When they left, Penn found sudden relaxation and false security like a high-altitude pilot affected by anoxia. The take-off and the crash, the memory of that panicky throat, the worries and the certainties, life and death appeared unreal, unimportant and inconsequential, and the soft yet omnipresent hubbub of the Singapore morning lulled him into a comalike sleep.

Barraclough spent the night awake. The immediate advance (by special messenger, in used twenties, as usual) reinforced his trust in Mott. He thought about Fraser's reactions and concluded that she had been more enthusiastic about the prospect of running a sweet shop than about the ways of setting up the operation. He also thought about his own reactions and concluded that he was getting too old to cope with the strain of a new assignment. Only recently, he would have thought about the job with white-hot intensity for a few hours, then would have made himself forget about it, relax, and sleep without a worry. He resisted the urge to get up and start work with finely sharpened pencil in hand, but he could not help drawing huge charts mentally, devising headings, selecting priorities and positioning his usual tiny red question marks.

His main question was what sort of plane it was to be. Instinct had told him the answer, but that was not yet a fact. His best line of attack would have to be researched in order to achieve weak-point definition. Question: Was the "crate" to be sunk and destroyed totally or partially—or forced to land in circumstances that would present an opportunity for close examination? If the latter was the case, it might be better to induce a pilot defection, but that was something Mott would have to decide. Presumably, this was impossible, because Mott clearly required a downing. Right. The attack would have to be

External
with
weapons
other aircraft
misrouting
or
Internal
with
bomb on board
techno-sabotage
affecting: aircraft/personnel
arranged by: agent/corrupted staff

Method would be dependent upon level of required secrecy and Appearances (should it seem like an accident or sabotage by a third party clear pointers to whose guilt should be left?) as well as Crash Location (over water, in mountains, near airfield or inhabited areas) chosen for search delay, shock value.

Half asleep at last, he thought about a wide range of military aircraft and tried to guess, once again, the most likely target. By association, he remembered a picture of Prince Charles flying a fighter. A fighter that might be attacked by the enemy, a superior new enemy type, unless a crate was sunk in time—by Barraclough. He smiled. The future king and all his subjects could sleep peacefully. Barraclough was awake. Even Fraser was not supposed to know about such thoughts of his, but heart-warming thoughts they were nevertheless. It was good to be on duty.

Drayton had a good day. He had chaired a meeting of his hastily summoned inner circle of specialist advisers and obtained their unanimous assurance that the Singapore mishap was most likely to be an unusual one, caused by some technical teething trouble, pilot error or sabotage, but certainly nothing that could not be put right easily or would require costly measures affecting the entire fleet. A computer scan of all the reported Sarissa faults and minor incidents had produced nothing that would indicate elevator malfunction. Operators of the Sarissas already in service praised the uniquely uninterrupted serviceability of the aircraft. There had been irritating little flaws in the design, but these were now ironed out and, in fact, several of them had led to quite valuable improvements. False engine fire warnings were the next in line to be cured. Pilots liked the flying characteristics of the Sarissa and a couple of insignificant "handling difficulties" in fairly severe turbulence could safely be attributed to the pilots' inexperience or reporting zeal.

After the meeting, Drayton telephoned and reassured his highest political and aviation contacts in Washington. In return, they promised him off the record backing whenever prospective Sarissa customers showed undue concern because of the Singapore case. A full investigation was, of course, well in hand, and the issue of a detailed report as well as any modifications in design, maintenance or training would be given top priority on all levels.

By late afternoon, Salah Termine reported from New York that the police regarded Joe Hannan's death as a not-so-gay upshot of love among homosexuals, and that the name of AeroCorp was being kept out of it. Further good news was that Termine had found Hannan's German contact a "real gent" who acknowledged the receipt of cash and would continue to honor the deal. One or two loose ends in the case remained but did not require immediate attention.

Safeguarding the good name of the young SupraNational Airline was Drayton's other main concern in the wake of the Singapore accident. For, secretly, SupraNat was very much his own baby, which could grow up one day not only to make the Sarissa a world-beater but also to dent—even destroy—the monopoly held by a handful of household names of international airlines. He called his grand design a "redistribution of wealth in the air," which—though at the moment his own role was strictly de-emphasized—would give him, personally, infinite off-stage political influence well beyond the aviation scene in some fifty countries.

The plan depended on two major *leaps* and a final *step*.

Leap One "into the unknown but not into darkness" was the creation of the near-sonic Sarissa. He knew it was a huge gamble. With a billion-dollar initial development cost, there was no room for mistakes. Frightening examples were plentiful. The inadequate success of the Convair 880 and 990 series had driven General Dynamics out of the aircraft production business. Lockheed, with all its might, experience and reputation, had been broken by TriStar long before the bribing scandals. But General Dynamics had survived the disaster because aircraft production was only about a quarter of the mammoth company's diversified interests, and Lockheed was bailed out because the American government could not let it go to the wall, not while it was the biggest U.S. arms supplier, with sales worth some $4 billion a year, almost two thirds of which came from Defense Department contracts. AeroCorp had no meaningful "other business" to fall back on. So Drayton had to stake the entire corporation on his conviction that the Sarissa was going to be a winner.

Yet, when Drayton gambled, he preferred using loaded dice. In the course of a brief association with some Howard Hughes maneuvers, he had gained access to certain feasibility studies and, above all, Hughes's own comments on them. How this all happened was shrouded in mystery, but, as a result, Drayton had become one of the first men to foresee the gravity of the world's approaching fuel problems. In the late 1960s, when fuel was only about a tenth of an aircraft's operating costs, Drayton had made low fuel consumption the chief guiding principle of the Sarissa design. Also, when most of the world found it indisputable that "big is beautiful" (and cheap) and dreamed about entire villages floating over the Atlantic, Drayton had turned away from the prophets of unstoppable growth and the speed freaks, and spotted the evolution of a potential $50 billion gap in the aviation market. He scorned international partnerships ("They change sides at every corner") and had tried to go it alone. Several hundred thousand engineering drawings later, he now had the 200-seater basic Sarissa, designed to replace the aging 707s and DC8s on a multitude of international routes as the best workhorse of the sky in the 1980s.

If the Sarissa had brought the wrath of fellow manufacturers upon Drayton, his Leap Number Two, the creation of SupraNat and CLIC (Cost-Limiting International Consortium) would make him chief villain in the eyes of airlines and governments. Except that, by then, more than 100,000 jobs as well as several new boom cities and scores of subcontractors would depend on him. It was now a matter of precise timing, confidence in the Sarissa and the good name of SupraNat—all threatened by Singapore even more than the counterplots his enemies must be hatching.

SupraNat was a Dublin-based non-national airline which would operate only Sarissas and would become, Drayton envisaged, the Liberian flag of aviation. The company would own nothing. Sarissas would be "dry-leased" from AeroCorp by small and medium third-world countries, which would then buy a share in CLIC, owner of SupraNat, employer of pilots and maintenance staff, and "wet-lease" the package (planes with air and ground crew) to their own airline.

So far, apart from its built-in tax-fiddle and regulation-dodging facility, SupraNat appeared to be no more than yet another competitor for international airspace, a prestige booster to obscure rulers of banana republics, and a status symbol to those of its shareholders who had been duly impressed by the thought of being one of the earliest operators of a glamorous aircraft which achieved some spectacular sales in countries with advanced aviation—sales such as Drayton hoped to conclude through dead Joe Hannan's "real gent" contact. But then the CLIC would attack its elders where it hurt most: the reduction or outright withdrawal of "fifth-freedom traffic" rights—Big Brothers' right to pick up passengers and freight in foreign countries en route. If the third-world countries were busy flexing nonexistent muscles, Drayton's CLIC would supply them with just the bulging biceps they lacked.

As a result, the conservative estimate was that the Sarissa production run would exceed the sales of 1300 Boeing 727s, the most successfully marketed plane ever, and eventually some 2,000 Sarissas might be in service with widely spread maintenance bases and global interchangeability.

When the Sarissa began to fly, research and improvements continued. In a coup of such magnitude, penny-pinching attitudes were out of order. Innovations to thin any nonvital part of the Sarissa and so reduce weight were encouraged and generously rewarded. Drayton authorized a $30 million program within two hours of the receipt of a proposal for a slight drag reduction that promised a 3 per cent increase in fuel efficiency. All this was widely publicized—but Drayton's final trump, the development of Sarissa Mark 2, was to be the best-guarded secret in aviation history. For after the *two leaps,* the introduction of the new version was to be the *final step* to victory.

Various parts of the plane were designed and manufactured in all corners of the world. Early tests were flown with military secrecy by courtesy of the South Korean government, and four of the new "Whispering Sarissas" were already in the air when still no more than a handful of outsiders knew about the project. The aircraft was to satisfy the three big E's of aviation—

Economy, Energy-efficiency and the interest of Ecology—and it was capable of relatively short take-off and landing, which would bring it into airports in densely populated areas—hence the need for further noise reduction. If Europe was already late to compete, everybody would soon be made a nonstarter when, out of the blue, Mark 2 would have its debut at the Paris or Farnborough international air show.

But now Singapore. Drayton prayed that it would turn out to be sabotage.

"Find something for me," he said to Singer. "If nothing else, just a goddamn suspicion strong enough to justify some leak to the press. They'd love it, wouldn't they? 'European Gangsters Sabotage Winner Sarissa! Competitors Out to Buy Time at All Costs!' What a headline! Just find the bastards, Henry. Find them for me, and you'll sure inherit my empire soon enough."

Soon enough? Singer had some doubts about that. The way things were going for him . . . No, he did not want to think about it. He only mentioned that Anna was not pleased with his unexpected trip, the fourth in three weeks since their wedding. Drayton volunteered to look after her and cheer her up.

On this Thursday, the first convenient flight Singer could catch was the PAN841. After crossing the international date line and losing the next Friday of his life altogether, he would arrive at Manila Saturday morning, meet Captain Brown, Chief Pilot of SupraNat, coming from a conference in Vancouver, and they would take PR501 of Philippine Airlines for the Manila–Singapore leg, arriving at eleven-fifteen local time. With the Manila stopover, it would take Singer fifteen minutes less than twenty-four hours, but he would keep in touch with Drayton in case there was some important development.

At 1335 on Friday, a sensation broke in Singapore.

Local newsmen and international correspondents had besieged the crash site since dawn, but Stacey was not prepared to say more than that the investigation was in progress, it would be much too early to expect any findings. Then the "Captain Penn, murderer!" demonstrators arrived. At the head of the column, a hysterical woman was paraded. Allegedly, she was the mother, but there was some doubt about that, and an alert television crew left to investigate. Colonel Mihir Gupta was determined to have none of this upheaval. He ordered his men to drive the demonstrators away from the site, but the reporters lured him into a dialogue. He begged them for patience. "Mr. Stacey needs time!"

"How much time?"

"A little."

"How little?"

"Very little."

There was an uproar. He was accused of knowing nothing about the investigation of accidents. "It'll take months or years! It usually does!"

"Not in this case. Not when the pilot is alive and can tell us what exactly was wrong with the airplane."

There was sudden silence and he realized what a mistake he had made. Microphones were pushed under his nose. Would he say what was supposed to be wrong with the plane or would he let them publish half-truths and start an international panic among all Sarissa users?

"Look, look, I'll make a deal with you. I tell you as much as I know, but you wait and sit on it, right? In any case, there's nothing to report yet. It's only the Captain's word that there was a small elevator malfunction."

"Small enough for him but big enough to kill two people and an innocent child on the ground?"

"I don't know."

"Shouldn't all Sarissas be grounded?"

"Not yet. It's only the pilot's view."

"He may be lying to save his own skin."

"Yes, that's possible, and I promise you'll be the first to know. But will you promise not to rush to your telephones?"

They promised nothing. It was their duty to press for an answer and report what they discovered. An hour later it was worldwide news that the grounding of the Sarissa fleet might be imminent. Scores of passengers immediately canceled their flights. Everybody in aviation telephoned everybody else.

The first Drayton heard about it was a news flash on television. Ms. Etch was on hand to call Washington and Singapore and all members of the AeroCorp cabinet, except Singer, who was in the air and so could not be of any use.

In London, the BBC seven A.M. news bulletin carried a "Sarissa crash" item, but it meant nothing to Barraclough. He had been up early to surprise Fraser with a cooked breakfast before she caught the first train to Angmering-on-Sea, where her sister lived and where she hoped to find a tobacconist's or sweet shop for sale. She could look around at her leisure during the initial stage of Barraclough's own research when he would need her assistance least.

She left the house at half past seven. An hour later, a messenger arrived with an envelope which turned out to contain only a clean sheet of yellow paper. It meant that Mott wanted to talk. Barraclough rushed down to a public telephone around the corner. He did not see the Brigadier, who must have been watching him from somewhere, for the phone rang as soon as he entered the kiosk.

"I hope you haven't started anything yet, as it's off." And when Barraclough did not say anything: "I mean at least temporarily. Something unexpected happened probably just about the time we spoke. Quite uncanny, the timing, I mean, but it solved the problem for us and made it unnecessary to take action. You know how it is."

"Oh yes." His voice was flat. A beaten man.

"Of course, it may happen after all. You never know."

"No, sir."

"We'll just have to keep an eye on the news."

"Yes, sir." He tried to think what might have been in the news about fighter aircraft, something that canceled the assignment. Nothing. Except that Sarissa sensation in Singapore. That wouldn't affect Mott's plans. It couldn't. Surely. "About the money, sir . . ."

"Oh yes. I'll tell you what. You hang on to it. As a sort of advance on this or some other job. You just use it until then."

"Yes, sir." But he knew there would never be another job. "Until then" meant eternity. A farewell gesture.

"Keep up the old routine so that I can find you as usual."

Fortnum and Mason's, Mondays and Thursdays at 1600 hours. Yesterday's money would help for only a short while. It would never buy the shop. Fraser would feel utterly dejected but try to hide it from him. For she would never get her job back. Not after the tea-and-biscuit walkout. He must think of something before she returned.

His hand hurt. Oh yes, he was trying to crush the receiver. It might be easier to accomplish this nerve-soothing vandalism with one of his old karate chops.

"Yes, sir. The old routine. And good luck, sir."

Penn was still asleep and Mara decided it would be pointless to wake him. Instead she went to the crash site and used the name of AeroCorp to help her cross the police cordon.

In the immediate vicinity of the Sarissa only a generator whirred in the silence. Nobody moved; all eyes were on the makeshift test bed Stacey had rigged up. Several people, standing on the top of some shaky scaffolding, stared through fractures and broken windows into the remains of the flight deck. Mara avoided them and took the steps leading up to the overwing exits. The cabin was deserted. There was a musty smell of dried blood. "Turpentine" Benning. Mara half expected to see him jumping up and down with excitement. She quietly walked down the aisle and stopped behind Stacey, the Colonel and a couple of technicians crowding the flight-deck door, which had been forced open. She knew she would be thrown out as soon as she was noticed, but nobody paid any attention to her.

Her neck craned, she looked over their shoulders. Behind the Captain's wrecked seat stood the pilot who had flown the Sarissa on the previous leg to Singapore. He leaned forward, balancing precariously in his cramped position, placed his hands on the broken control column, and turned toward Stacey.

The investigator raised a large walkie-talkie to his mouth. "Okay?"

"Ready when you are, sir," came the metallic answer.

Stacey nodded toward the Captain, who then began to move the column slowly and gently, forward and back—and again.

"Moves normally, sir," rattled the handset.

"Are you sure?"

"Yes, sir."

Stacey stepped forward, pushing the pilot as far out of his way as he could. "Let me." His hands were on the column now.

"Feels normal," said the pilot.

Stacey turned to go. "Do it again. I want to see it myself."

Mara backed away fast. She ducked behind a seat and let the investigator pass, then followed him to the door and looked with him toward the tail. There could be no doubt: the elevator seemed to respond in the normal way. Stacey jumped out, ran to the tail and climbed the scaffolding there.

Twenty minutes later, Mara was back at the hospital. She was too stunned and desperate to think clearly and sort out why it seemed to her the most important thing in the world to be first with the news at Penn's bedside. She tried to wake him gently but he was totally disinclined to respond.

She held his face between her hands. "You must wake up," she whispered. "They've just made a test. It works."

"What works?" His eyes were heavy, his voice still asleep.

"The elevator."

"What elevator?"

"You must think of an answer fast."

"What answer?"

"Stacey will want another answer."

He suddenly sat up. His head hurt. "What *other* answer? What are you talking about?"

"They're still testing it, but I saw that elevator. It works. Nothing is wrong with it. They'll want an answer from you."

"It's impossible. It didn't work. I had to abort. I had to!"

"I know, I know, you told me."

"Don't you believe me?"

"It doesn't matter what I believe. It's only what Stacey and the others will accept."

"But you, don't you believe me?"

She hesitated. "I do. But I don't know why."

The High Street was drowsy, past the morning rush, the market sleepy, not yet fit for shoppers, the gym behind the railroad lifeless, a mausoleum of long-dead muscle, sweat and aspirations—all-in wrestling had become a regular job, wrestlers fought to the advertised death five nights a week and would have been seen forming a union sooner than be in training. But Barraclough knew what to expect. One of the Leopard Twins, celebrated tag team of the previous decade, would be sitting at his desk in the back room, fully dressed, asleep. He lived at that desk. Not that he could not afford anything else. It was a matter of choice. He liked it there. If gossip was to be believed, his chair was a plumber's masterpiece.

Barraclough knocked, waited for a burst of coughing inside, counted five to give him a chance to relight the stub of a foul Spanish cigar, and entered just as the Leopard shouted an authoritative "In!"

"You still can't sleep?"

"Nope."

"Never?"

"Right."
"Must be bad."
"You get used to it in seventeen years."
End of that subject. Pity. Barraclough did not quite know how to come to the reason for his visit. He sat on the edge of the desk. It would have been no good waiting for any encouragement from the Leopard, who did not regard it as his business to interfere with his visitors' discomfort.
"How's business?"
"Bad."
"Oh."
End of the other possible conversation. The Twins had stashed away a fortune made not so much on their own wrestling as on running a stable of stars who, though now aging fast, still raked in plenty to pay the bills and the everlasting Spanish smokes. Barraclough decided to shoot his last bolt, the only one that would surely elicit a little more than a laconic answer.
"The gym seems empty this morning."
"And so it should. People who worked late last night need sleep. The lucky bastards. And others I'm not interested in. I don't want no male models, bodybuilders and other sissies round the place. Would make my brother throw up."
Which was an intriguing thought. His brother had been dead for several years. Barraclough always hoped to discover which of the Twins was alive but did not know how to ask.
"Listen." He took a deep breath. "I want to do some work."
"You're a fool."
"Not for the money, you understand."
"Makes you a bigger fool than I thought." From constant lighting and relighting, the cigar stub must have been choked solid with nicotine and required all the Leopard's sucking power and concentration.
"I tell you what I had in mind. I could fight a couple of evenings a week . . . You know . . . when you have injuries and you need someone to step in . . . Sort of understudy . . . I mean

. . . you know what I mean." It was becoming harder and harder to keep up the monologue. "You know I used to be good."

"I know."

"Well then."

"Well what?"

"I'm still fit. I could train. Then think up some gimmick. Old Karate Chop back from the grave or something."

"Oh yeah."

"You know what I mean?"

"I do."

"Well then?"

The cigar got going at last. The Leopard puffed at it relentlessly. "You want to die?"

Barraclough tried to laugh. "Not yet."

"It would kill you."

"Exertion? Never."

"Shame. It's the shame that would kill you."

There was a long pause. The Leopard would never say another word. There was nothing to say. Except if Barraclough forced the conversation to go further. He had no choice. "Okay. I need the money."

"I'll think of something."

"I'll be back later."

"Make it the morning. I think better at night."

Penn stormed on board the Sarissa. Stacey greeted him with undisguised indignation but had the courtesy to rerun the test for him.

"I don't understand," Penn kept repeating.

"Neither do I."

"It feels normal now, that's true, but it resisted me during take-off, I swear. Something must have jammed."

"No sign of it."

"Sabotage?"

"Not impossible."

Penn latched onto the new hope. "Somebody might have inserted a wedge or something to lock the elevator."

"Why isn't it there now?"

"It might have been dislodged by the impact."

"It might. Except that it would be on the runway."

"Souvenir hunters! There're always a few around."

"Except in this case. The Colonel sealed the entire area right away."

"Are you suggesting . . ." Penn began.

"I'm not suggesting anything."

"Oh yes you are. You're suggesting that the lack of material evidence and the perfect working condition of the elevator indicate that I killed those people."

Stacey was very cool and deliberate. He took out his notepad and prepared the tape recorder. "Do you wish to make a new statement? You're perfectly welcome to include your accusation against me."

"No. And I'm not accusing you."

"Good. Because I can only repeat that I'm not suggesting anything, least of all making any dramatic statements at this stage. All I'm saying is that I must keep in mind all the possibilities, and it is possible, just possible, that something misled you, and you made a mistake, a perfectly understandable error of judgment in the heat of the moment."

"I did not."

"My job is to prove that. And to make sure that whatever might have misled you, if that was the case, would not be permitted to mislead others."

"I wasn't misled."

"Stubborn repetitions won't take us anywhere."

"What else can I say?"

"Look, I know the feel of the stick as well as you do. Sometimes it worries you a little. Or let me put it this way. In my flying days, it used to worry me how hard I could work it safely in turbulent conditions."

"This was different. In the air I would have forced it a lot more, bit by bit. But at and beyond VR there was no time to experiment."

"Thank you. That's just what the problem may be. If so, the question is What caused the false sensation you had?"

"You're still looking for an explanation of an error. My error. But there was no error. You must believe me."

"I'm inclined to. I know you're an excellent pilot, dedicated to flying. But look at it from an outsider's point of view. If you didn't believe firmly and honestly that there was something wrong with the elevator, if you didn't fight me and didn't claim everything you do claim, that would make you a bad, irresponsible pilot, and not only that, a dishonest man, too. In order to make a genuine error, you must have a genuine conviction of having done the right things."

"Thank you."

"But that doesn't prove that you did do the right things."

"I'm increasingly indebted to you."

Stacey was gradually backing away and Penn followed him. By now they were out of earshot of everybody else on board. Stacey lowered his voice. "You had a lot of problems with that flight."

"You can say that again."

"The missing passenger, the strike, the false engine-fire warning, the weather . . . Were you in a hurry to get away from Singapore?"

"No. Why do you ask?"

"There are rumors that you were embarrassed about the delay, particularly because you had this ballet company on board."

"That wouldn't make me leave before I felt the conditions were right."

"No, I'm sure it wouldn't. But you were under pressure. And perhaps a little tired."

"Not unduly."

"No, it's only those stupid rumors."

"What rumors?"

"That you were out very late the previous night here."

"I had plenty of sleep, if that's what you want to know."

"Personally, I don't want to know anything. But eventually I'll have to write a report and may have to stand up in court, and if the judge asks me, I can't say, 'Sorry, your honor, I just discounted the rumors because Captain Penn is such a nice man.' That won't do. And if they ask me, 'Was the Captain drinking? . . .' "

"You're not suggesting . . ."

"No! I'm not suggesting anything. But there are rumors going round. So I had to get your blood test checked and double-checked before I accepted a sworn statement from the head of the hospital lab that there was no trace of alcohol in your blood twenty two minutes after the crash!"

Penn could not find the strength to apologize.

Stacey followed him out of the aircraft. "The investigation has just begun. Nobody's going to jump to conclusions and condemn you for your decision to abort. But, unfortunately, blaming the elevator and grounding all Sarissas are equally out of the question. The best you can do is to wait and rest."

And that was only the first blow to Penn. The second came unexpectedly as Mara drove him fast through the minefield of microphones and TV cameras, away from the crash site. She told him about the death of Chuck Benning. It did not help him much that she blamed the champion of turpentine for his own fate.

The third blow came on his return to the hospital, where he insisted on seeing Mitchell. The co-pilot was dopey and in pain—and apologetic for being unable to support or contradict Penn: "My hands were off the stick. They were supposed to be off the stick. I never had a chance to feel it. Can't help it, Corrie, I honestly can't. I'm sorry."

"Your job was to maintain forward pressure on the stick to

keep the nose on the ground." The edge in his voice all too obvious.

"Thank you for telling me."

"Well, did you or didn't you do it?"

"You were Captain. You should know what I did."

"Your hands were on the wheel."

"Only up to one hundred knots."

"All right. So what did it feel like up to one hundred knots?"

"Normal, I suppose."

"What do you mean 'suppose'?"

"For Pete's sake, Corrie, it was a few seconds. Do you remember what the first breath of air felt like yesterday morning?"

Penn turned away. "I'm sorry."

"Besides, if it had felt odd or unusual, I'd have warned you there and then."

"Yes. Of course. I'm sorry." Penn smoothed out Mitchell's pillow apologetically. "Any fresh news about the baby?"

At the crash site, Colonel Mihir Gupta "held the front" against the press bravely. He tried to be noncommittal, but he was forced to admit that, so far, nothing had been found against the Sarissa, nothing that would confirm the pilot's suspicion.

"Which means that it was his fault, wasn't it?"

"No comment."

"Does he know it?"

"No comment."

"Will he be banned from flying?"

"He's under medical care."

"So he's not permitted to fly."

"Nobody *is* when under medical care."

"Will the Sarissa be grounded?"

"Definitely not. I mean to this moment in time no such decision has been effected by the authorities in question."

Mara tried to persuade Penn to return to his bed from Mitchell's room. But he was too restless and needed some fresh air as well as time to think.

"Do you want to be alone?"

"Would you like to walk with me?"

She nodded. "I promise not to talk if you don't want me to."

Just outside the hospital they ran into a sea of reporters and onlookers-turned-demonstrators.

"Captain Penn! . . . Captain . . . Just a minute, Captain . . ."

The waves closed in around them and cut them off from the door.

"Do you know the result of the test?"

"Do you realize there's nothing wrong with the plane?"

"Do you feel guilty?"

"Any comment on your guilt?"

He kept shaking his head and repeating "No comment" and "You *know* I'm not supposed to say anything."

"Can't you see he isn't well?" appealed Mara to them. "Leave him alone! Please!"

She was shouted down with accusations of "You want an exclusive, don't you?" And the questions continued. They tried to provoke an answer. Passers-by stopped and made the obstreperous crowd swell. At the far end, a lone policeman began to hew his way through to Penn. The thud of a blow and somebody groaned. A woman screamed.

"No comment, Captain? Never mind how many more are hurt?"

"Doesn't death bother you?" an old woman yelled.

"Any message for the dead child's parents?"

"I'm sorry, you don't seem to understand," Penn mumbled in confusion as he watched the policeman's panic-driven brutality.

"You're sorry?"

"He's sorry!"

"He's sorry!"

"You admit you made a mistake?"

"No!"

"What then?"

"There was something wrong with the elevator."

"Are you sure?"

"I am. I am . . ."

"You say they must ground the Sarissa?"

"I don't know. I think so. I mean until the fault is found."

He knew he should not have said it. But he firmly believed that lives were at risk. Unless he was proved to be wrong, a fool, a murderer by error of judgment.

A few more policemen rushed out of the hospital. But they were not needed any more. The people began to disperse. The news was on its way—killer Captain maintains claim of innocence, blames aircraft.

Drayton spent Friday morning on the telephone and reassured authorities in Washington, London, Ottawa, Bonn, Dublin, Canberra, Vienna and numerous other capitals that, despite the latest rumor initiated by a stress-victim pilot, there was no serious ground for any suspicion about the airworthiness of the Sarissa. He gave a press conference and plied reporters and television crews with Sarissa specials. He revealed that despite his specialists' absolute certainty—"I'm just a goddamn businessman who must rely on the best and best-paid experts in the world"—further tests would be continued to the *n*th degree and every assistance would be given to the investigating authority. He begged them to have compassion on the poor pilot and de-emphasize his plight, because all this "killer Captain" publicity must already have hurt his family badly.

At 1345, Ms. Etch put a call through to Manila airport and, although PAN841 had not yet landed, held the line open. She arranged that an airport policeman should wait for Singer out on the tarmac and rush him to the nearest telephone.

"I understand your concern," Singer drawled sluggishly after the long, boozy flight, and closed his eyes to protect them from the sharp light of the Philippine dawn. "But, frankly, I don't quite see . . ."

"You don't?"

"I mean we shouldn't overreact . . ."

"Overreact? What's the goddamn overreaction in making the fool shut up? And that's exactly what your job is. I don't know how you go about these things. I can't deal with every detail. Make him shut up whatever it takes."

"And what exactly do you mean by that?"

"Just what I said. Convince him or something, but make him shut up once and for all. And if that's too demanding a task for my crisis manager, then perhaps Termine will do it for us. He'll be there soon after you, and I'm sure he'll find a way."

"Look, Charles, I'm worried about the cumulative effect. We try to put the lid on a fly speck, and soon we'll have to cover the lid with a coffin and then a tombstone. It just grows like those Russian wooden dolls."

"And you'd rather leave the fly speck where it is and let it start the rot."

"No, I wouldn't. But Termine is the wrong man for the job. He's the type who'd be banned from the Swiss ski slopes because he's prone to start avalanches."

"You're wrong, Henry. He's the man who wouldn't know that there were ski slopes in Switzerland until he needed to start an avalanche there. But that's beside the point. What do you propose to do?"

Singer shouted a few hullos, pretended the line was very bad, then put the phone down. He would blame the Manila operator for cutting him off.

Penn lay on the edge of the huge double bed, his head in the cradle of his palms, his closed eyelids cooled by a gentle breeze, his ears tuned to the purr of the old-fashioned lazy fan hung from the ceiling. The conventional-modern hotel retained these fans for a touch of the genuine Maugham story atmosphere (a sensible intention backed to death by keen advertising), and Penn preferred them to the air conditioning. Mara had claimed that they had a hypnotic effect on her and so she could not be held responsible for any of her actions. He smiled.

"Why are you smiling?"

"Am I?"

"Mm."

"I thought you were asleep."

"You don't want to tell me? It's all right."

He opened his eyes and looked down. With her ear to his navel, Mara lay naked, almost at right angles to him. When he closed his eyes again, it still seemed he was only dreaming her presence. A miracle. With blurred edges. Like miracles tend to be until they are defined, spelled out and stamped "official." It might have been the alcohol that blurred the edges of the memory. He was not used to drinking. And he had had a lot in the past eighteen hours. Events drifted back to him in individual pictures rather than filmlike sequences. Aboard the Sarissa with Stacey. The demo at the hospital. Mara holding his hand tight, trying to look brave. Roaming the streets of Singapore with Mara. Change Alley and the swimming-pool quality of its incessant drone of bargaining and trading. Entering Raffles for a drink. The waterfront. Entering a bar. Leaving another bar. The bridge. Mara waving to a passing ship. Mara staring down on some lazy junks. Then the warmth of the long friendly silence, sitting with Mara once again at the flat feet of the giant Buddha in the Sakya Muni Gaya.

Faded snapshots of that interminable meal. The bottles of wine. Alcoholic lightness—a novelty to his brain that made his thoughts woolly and convinced him for a while that somewhere, perhaps at a children's party, he must have swapped his head for this floating blue balloon on his neck.

Between the more sharply focused memories of entering her room and holding her, for the first time, in his naked arms, he had only one clear recollection. He was trying to pull down the long zipper that ran—or rather would not run—from the nape of her neck. He fumbled with that wretched hook or whatever that would not give, and he thought, That's middle age for you, when you cease to keep up with the fashion changes in zippers and hooks and ingenious bra fasteners. Lucky she's not wearing a bra. And then the sobering realization that he now suffered the penalty for being out of practice. Candy would laugh and refuse to believe him if he confessed that in their more than ten years he had never been unfaithful. But somehow, being with Mara did not seem to fit into that category. . . .

"All right, smile. Laugh if you like. No explanation is required."

"I thought about you."

"And you found me funny?"

"No."

"Then what made you smile?"

"You said I don't have to tell."

"That's right. But it would be appreciated. I tell you what. I'll swap one secret for another."

"It's a deal. I smiled because I found it odd that I had almost forgotten how good sex could be."

"You're joking."

"It's not funny. Even though it made me smile. Perhaps because it was a surprise."

"Not to me."

"Why?"

"Because I always knew how good you'd be for me."

He put his fingers through her hair. "*Always* meaning seventy hours or so."

"No, I meant twelve, almost thirteen years."

"You were a child."

"Almost thirteen."

"And you dreamt about men?"

"Not men—you."

"You didn't know me."

"I did."

"We met the day before yesterday."

"That's not important. Because I knew what you looked like and that you always wore a cracked bomber jacket with four old bullet holes in it, one of them with scorched edges, and that the zipper was torn but you wouldn't want it replaced. I knew that once you volunteered to fly out kids who were trapped between the Indian and Pakistani armies somewhere in the Punjab and you landed in some forest on fire so that you had to lead the kids to safety on foot."

Penn half sat up and rested on his elbows. There was no chance of interrupting her.

"I knew a little about your childhood, the divorce of your parents and your dream about becoming an airline pilot. And about your fights. What made you such an awful bully? What were you trying to prove? And why did you run guns in Colombia? Whose side were you on? Your current girl friend? I know she was Colombian and very beautiful. And guessed she must have been a fantastic lover. Except that I didn't quite know what being a lover really meant. Which made it even more exciting. And then . . ."

"All right, so you read those stupid articles about me."

"Those and all the bits and pieces of notes and clippings in the archives of the magazine. As a cub reporter I was quite besotted with you. There were reports about your African mercy flights with that Dakota. I knew most of them by heart. I thought I'd recite them for you when we met at that party in Paris."

"What party?"

"You were with a real-life pin-up girl."

"Candy?"

"Perhaps. I began to talk to you, and she took your arm and led you away as if I wasn't there."

"Then it must have been Candy. But why don't I remember you?"

"I looked very plain those days. I blushed easily and it emphasized all my pimples. It was awful. It's better that you don't remember. But it was a memorable party for me. I watched your glamour puss, and when I heard that she was a stew I joined the first airline that would take me."

"And then you forgot me."

"No. I just grew up. At least I thought I did. My infatuation with that printed idol became just a memory. But a friend of mine thought that I must get you completely out of my system."

"A male friend?"

"Yes."

"Close friend?"

She shrugged her shoulders. "If you like."

"What cure did he suggest?"

"To meet you."

"In the flesh? You did. And I thought that I was the seducer, while you were acting under instructions, if I may put it that way."

"Just about the last thing he or even I had in mind. He thought I'd be incapable of what he called 'total love' as long as my old dreams and your image haunted me. He thought a cold, long, searching interview would do the trick. That's why I chose you for this story."

"And luck was on your friend's side."

"He wouldn't say that if he saw us now."

"But he would if he knew that I had crashed my plane and killed three people, and you had found a fallen idol."

"Who's about to get up and start again."

"Start what?"

"Rebuilding the image, of course." She kissed him.

"Well, if you mean . . ."

"No, I don't. It's your work I'm talking about."

"There's nothing I can do about that at the moment."

"Nothing? Can't you fight, make a fuss, shout and scream? You can—"

"That's not on."

"Did you cause that accident or not?"

"I didn't."

"Then you'll fight and clear your name. You'll make a nuisance of yourself. Until they pay attention."

"That's not done."

"Not done! Don't be so damn English! Your country has lost an empire—and more, its self-respect—under that idiotic banner. This is not a game of cricket, Cornelius Penn. This is your goddamn life, your only one, and don't you try to de-emphasize it. Fight." She never even noticed her use of those infectious Draytonisms.

Ms. Etch stood at Gavin Wheeler's elbow and listened patiently as the AeroCorp vice-president in charge of public relations put through a series of phone calls to heads of the advertising departments of major American and European newspapers, magazines and aviation journals. His theme was exactly the same each time: AeroCorp had reached a stage where the Sarissa advertising budget would have to be upped; to work out the details and choose the chief beneficiaries of this spending spree, a confidential lunch/drink/meeting/conference would be perhaps mutually advantageous. The timing of this approach was quite blatant—the message would soon filter through to the editors, who would be free to interpret Wheeler's words as sticks or carrots. The chances were that several headlines dealing with the Singapore mishap would be reduced in size and aggression.

Wheeler had the talent to speak his lines with all the freshness of a first night, but his delivery was slightly spoiled by the presence of Ms. Etch, for she would give almost verbatim reports to Drayton about each call and comment freely on his performance. What he could not guess was that, this time, Drayton had a different priority. He waited for her in her office.

"Have you tried to reach Mara?"

"Once an hour."

"Make it twice an hour."

"Yes, sir. As for Mr. Wheeler's calls—"

"Never mind that. Try Singapore."

"It's only about six in the morning there."

"I know. She was out all night."

"Perhaps she only told the operator not to put any calls through to her room."

"Then make them connect you. Say it's a matter of life or death."

"Corrie!"

Mara was still showering when he joined her in the bathroom. "At your service, miss."

She picked up the soap and tried to sound very casual. "Why did you leave Switzerland?"

"You did your homework, didn't you?"

"Is that your answer?"

"No."

"So?"

"When I finished flying school, a miscalculation of Britain's requirements came to light. There was an overproduction in pilots; we weren't wanted. I was lucky because I had a contract, but that meant only a salary while sitting on the scrap heap. So I was ready to go anywhere, work for anyone, as long as I could fly, accumulate the hours and keep my license. Then I was loaned to that pisspot of a charter operation which tried to fly its pilots twenty-five hours a day. We sometimes fell asleep in the air. It was dangerous, not only illegal."

"So you had a fight with them."

"No."

"Why not?"

"I didn't care enough, I suppose. And there were rich pickings for the less squeamish."

She stepped out and began to dry herself. "But finally you walked out on them."

"No. The Swiss authorities caught up with the company. The operation was closed down, some heads rolled, pilots were dismissed with a nasty taste in their mouths, and I took the first offer that gave me a chance to fly again." He just stood and let the water pour on him. "I'll want a huge breakfast."

"Shall I order something for you?" Mara was the kind of woman who did not try to muscle in on the conversation between her male companion and the wine waiter in order to prove something, allowed men to light her occasional cheroots, and did not feel enslaved, humiliated or disenfranchised if a man opened the door of a car for her. She had just put the phone down as he returned to the bedroom wearing a towel sarong-style. "Was that first offer from Colombia?"

"Yes, through a contact."

"Sounds a dirty job."

"Guns, tourists, racketeers . . . I didn't see the difference. It was a risk, but the money was good and it was flying."

"How did you get out of it?"

"Hey, wait a minute. Is this a part of that devastating interview?"

"It's private. For me alone. Because I must know. Everything."

Over a leisurely breakfast, he told her about his childhood. And mostly about the father he hardly knew. "He was a rear gunner in Lancasters during the war. He had no pilot training, but once he flew home a bomber with both his pilots dead. Apparently he had a real talent for flying. After the war, he traveled all over the world as a service mechanic for a light aircraft rental firm. But I was not to know it. To me he pretended he was an airline pilot. I was only seven or eight. I envied him for his long travels and hated him at the same time for being always away. I remember how hard I tried to be unlike him in every way—and yet how I aped him all the time. I held my fork the way he did, I winked like he did and I spat on my pee every time like he did.

"I was aware of the tension between him and my mother but never understood much of it until that horrid night when they quarreled, yelling at each other. I couldn't help overhearing it. She told him he was a cheat, living in a dream world, lying even to his own son. He then questioned her own lies to me about her motherly love, and she admitted that she had never wanted me or any other children. She said I was an accident. And they were both shouting a lot about abortions, a word which meant nothing to me but conjured up all sorts of horrors in my mind, and it poisoned my childhood. It made me an accident.

"Soon after that night she ran away with another man. A real airline pilot. That was the final irony of it all. And I learned to hate my childhood. My father cried on my shoulder and blamed his own parents' broken marriage for his unhappiness. They gave him no model to copy and build on, he complained, and saw it as an endless vicious circle that would now affect me, too. My mother blamed him for everything. And they used me as a shuttle to carry their poisoned darts. I despised both of them and grew determined to break the vicious circle and become not only a flier but also the sort of father that a child could be proud of."

"I hope you've succeeded." And when he said nothing: "Have you?"

"I hope so."

The telephone rang. Mara was furious. She had left strict instructions . . .

"Mara Boone . . . Yes . . . yes . . . No, I can't . . ." As she looked toward Penn, he stood up and moved toward the bathroom, indicating that she might want to talk in private. She shook her head and pointed at his chair. He shrugged his shoulders and returned to his breakfast. "No, I'm sorry. . . . As you wish. . . . All right, I'll call you back later."

The air conditioning had broken down in the Manila VIP lounge. Captain Brown, Chief Pilot of SupraNat, did not exactly look the part even at the best of times, but after the long flight from Vancouver and in the heat he was an outright mess. Singer felt sorry for the podgy man but he had no choice, he had to tell him. "I know that Penn is your friend, but he'll have to go if he made a mistake. Drayton would insist."

"Naturally."

"Even if he just broke the rules."

"In vain, that is."

"Agreed."

Brown used napkin after napkin to soak up his pouring sweat. But his small sharp eyes never moved from Singer. "I'll first look for discrepancies between Penn's action and the book. And probably we'll have to correct the book."

"Is he that good?"

"I think so."

"He'll have to convince me, too."

"And if he can't," said Brown very softly, "I guarantee that never again will he be allowed to go near a cockpit."

Barraclough walked the streets of South London all night. He trusted, wanted to trust the Leopard. There must be a way for him to earn the money that would buy the shop. He knew Fraser well enough to be sure that she was on the brink of collapse. If he had to tell her that the plans, the marriage, the prospect of telling her daughter the truth were not on, she would . . . He refused to contemplate her reaction any further. But words did not matter. He knew what it would be. There had to be a way. The Leopard owed him a lot; he would have to come up with something. At two o'clock in the morning, he could not wait any longer and returned to the gym. If it was true that the Leopard never slept, it would not matter.

Barraclough knocked and there was only a slight delay in the usual answer: "In!"

"I hope I didn't wake you up or something."

The Leopard ignored the implication. He was too busy lighting a fresh cigar. "You're too old to be credible in the ring. But you could be in a show."

"What show?"

"You'd have to work out some sort of an act. You know, smashing bricks with your fists or toes, things like that. Preferably with a young and pretty assistant reflecting all the horror of it in the background. She could even scream or something."

"I don't know . . ."

"That's all I can suggest. Try someone else if you like. Or work out an act. Make it funny and horrifying. Then come back and I'll get you at least an audition in a nightclub. It might work, you know."

Penn woke up. The room was dark. He did not remember closing the shutters. Mara must have done it before they fell asleep in total exhaustion. He turned; she was not in the bed. He looked at his watch: twenty minutes to noon. The door opened and Mara tiptoed in. She noticed that he was awake, smiled and sat next to him on the bed.

"Where have you been?"

"I told Stacey and the others not to worry if they couldn't find you in the hospital."

"Thanks. Did you tell them where I was?"

"No."

"I thought you fell asleep with me."

"I couldn't."

"Why?"

"I was thinking." He waited patiently. She either wanted to say more, and then why quiz her, or . . . "About you," she said.

"That's nice."

"You ought to do or say what they want, then go home. Fast."

"You think I can do more in London?"

"I don't think you should do anything. Just wait."

"What do you mean?"

"What I said. Wait. And lie low."

"Without a fight?"

"That's right. And dodge the press."

"Why?"

"I can't say more. But trust me. Please."

"That's not good enough."

"I know."

"Then what?"

"I don't want you to get hurt."

"Only a few hours ago you were desperate to convince me that I had to fight. And clear my name. And prove to my son that he has every right and reason to be proud of me. What's the sudden change?"

"The knives are out to get you."

"How do you know?"

"I know. Just one wrong step and you're in trouble. Believe me."

"You talked to someone. Who was it? . . . Somebody rang you here. You couldn't talk in front of me. You rang back as soon as you could slip away. Who was it?"

"Please don't ask questions. Just trust me." Her voice trailed off and she turned away. Penn jumped out of bed to face her. She was weeping.

"What happened?"

She blinked a few times to make the tears dissolve, and managed quite a good smile. "Sorry. I'm not the crying sort."

"I never thought you were."

"Come on." She picked up his clothes from a chair and gestured toward the bathroom. "You wanted to be at the airport when Brown arrived."

As they came out of the hotel, they had to cut through a deserted building site to reach the parking lot where Mara had left her hired car. When they passed a waiting taxi, the driver looked up from his *Straits Times,* rolled his newspaper into a baton, and waved in the direction of three women chattering at the foot of a tower crane. The women suddenly turned, blocked the narrow path, and broke into a rhythmic "Captain Penn, murderer" chant. Mara and Penn tried to hurry past them, but swirling and jostling and tearing at his clothes they kept up the chant until men began to appear from all directions. One of the women screamed for no good reason, and the first man on the scene hit Penn in the face. The pilot staggered back, ducked one raised fist but swayed with his mouth into another. He looked around, dazed and confused, unable to decide what to do, just wincing as more blows poured down on him.

"Run! Come on!" Mara shouted and reached for his hand, but he stood still. His throat was shrinking. His chest felt tight. Circulation in his arms began to slow down.

Then one of the men, perhaps inadvertently, hit Mara. It was a mistake. For it brought Penn back to life. He kicked him in the groin and, with his balance still perfect, head-butted another attacker on his right. There could be no doubt about it: he was a dirty fighter.

"Get the car!" he shouted at Mara. She hesitated. "Run!" He squeezed out the word just before the final turn on the vise closed his larynx.

As the men closed in on him, he climbed the metal ladder of the crane. Two men pursued him some fifteen feet up, where he stopped, keeping them away with his heel. Another three men stood at the foot of the crane, shouting, encouraging the two.

Penn never took his eyes away from the men. When he heard the engine of a fast-approaching car, he only hoped that Mara would be reversing to the site. Then he jumped over the two and landed, hitting and kicking, on the three heads below. The surprise counterattack gave him a chance to run for it. Behind him, one of the men glanced toward the taxi driver at the far end of the site. The driver slowly shook his head. Penn never realized that he was not being chased. He jumped into the car and Mara made a perfect racing start. For a couple of minutes neither of them said a word. Penn wiped some blood off his face.

Mara concentrated on the road. "You were quite impressive," she said at last.

"Was I?"

"You want to go back and ask them?" Penn looked back; nobody was trying to follow them. She glanced at him. "Will you tell me something?"

Penn tested a couple of his front teeth. They still seemed firm enough. "What?"

"Why did you hesitate?"

"Hesitate?"

"At first you didn't fight back. Why?"

"I don't know. I had lots of fights in my childhood and teens. But I haven't thrown a punch in anger for more than ten years. Perhaps it's hard to revert to form."

"Why do you think they attacked you?"

"They think I'm a murderer. And there must be millions of others who agree with them."

At the building site, only a few drying blood patches were left behind as mementos of the scuffle. The taxi driver, already a good mile away, stopped in front of a one-story office building and raised his newspaper toward a woman at the window. She was on the phone, holding an open line to London: "Brigadier? . . . It's done . . . It'll give him the incentive to keep stirring things up, I'm sure. Let me know if you want us to do anything else." The Brigadier sounded so pleased with the demo that she felt justified to charge him for a bigger crowd than what she had actually hired.

Mara had a drink with Penn, Brown and Singer, but soon felt as welcome as a puppet show at a funeral, and left them when they went to lunch.

They found a pleasant restaurant in Telok Ayer Street where they could disappear in a box and talk. Brown asked only a few questions as Penn told them about the accident.

"How hard did you really pull?"

"Impossible to quantify it."

"Did you have a chance to trim back in the meantime to help your effort?"

"Yes."

"Then the elevator trim setting should still show that."

"It does."

"Did you have a quarrel with Mitchell just before take-off?" asked Singer.

"No. Why?"

"It's only that apparently there's something on the voice recorder."

"You didn't tell me. What is it?" Brown looked rather angry.

"Penn says, 'I'll never fly with you again,' or something like that. You remember?"

"Mitchell was humming and singing too much," said Penn. "It was a joke. I even threatened to throw him out of the aircraft at thirty thousand feet." The two men were not laughing. "It was a joke! Or you think that people will take it seriously and brand me as a homicidal maniac?"

Singer had put a call through to Drayton's home and now he spoke from the restaurant manager's private office.

"I can hear music in the background, Henry. Are you already in the old massage parlor in Orchard Road?" And, although Singer told him where he was, Drayton went on regardless: "Sounds good. I hope you have fun. Is the blind little Indian lady still working there? Marvelous hands, really marvelous.

Okay, you may de-emphasize it; it's none of my goddamn business. So how is the rest of *your* business?"

"We're still at lunch."

"Making progress in the right direction?"

"We've achieved a fair level of understanding. That's all I can say so far."

"Good, good, as long as you can make him keep his goddamn trap shut. What shall I tell Anna? I mean, shall I call her and give her your love and say how hard you're working?"

Singer could have sworn that he heard giggling on the line. He felt he had to hand it to the man. Drayton worked hard and played hard and hardly ever slept alone.

At the end of lunch, Brown and Singer talked about the preliminary judicial hearing to be held on Monday morning. They agreed that it was likely to be a brief formality where the less said would be the best in everybody's interest. "And of course"—Singer turned to Penn—"your interest in the first place."

"I'm not so sure, Mr. Singer."

"Henry, please, Henry is my name. And I'm quite positive. You don't want your name in the mud, do you?"

"My name? Why not AeroCorp? Or the Sarissa?"

"Why not, indeed? Good point. But, you see, the pilot is always a chief suspect when there's an accident without an apparent cause. No, don't interrupt me, please. I know it's wrong, I know we may discover some mechanical breakdown and, I can assure you, everybody will search for it. We're already running fresh elevator tests, we'll bench-test all the components and we'll flight-test if necessary. But at the moment we're groping about in the dark, because there are no precedents to go on. No similar case, nothing."

"There's always a first time," remarked Brown a little too meekly for Penn's taste.

"And how do *I* know there's no precedent?" Penn asked.

"Because we've already checked out all our records, all the

incident reports, operators' questions and comments, and there's nothing. And we're an honest and responsible company."

"Every aircraft manufacturer is, if you don't mind my saying, because they can't afford not to be. Whispers about slush funds and the rest are wild and groundless accusations, at least until documented. No, it's your turn not to interrupt, Henry. And I'm sure that questions about concealment of information affecting safety are anything but rumor-mongering—at least until proven otherwise. And even then big corporations and their top men must remain above suspicion. After all, they can't be everywhere; they can only rely on the information and assurances received from some little men down the line, so the blame—"

"I think you've said enough," said Brown.

"Let him go on. Everybody must have a chance to speak his mind," said Singer with all the paternal benevolence he could muster.

"Thank you, Henry."

"Giving everybody a fair chance is Drayton's principle. And that includes you, too, Cornelius, even if you've made a mistake."

"I haven't. And you want me to lie low and let a faulty plane kill a few hundred people before I'm proven right."

"I don't give a damn about anybody being right or wrong. But I want the truth discovered. The facts. And your silence would help to protect thousands of jobs."

"And AeroCorp."

"And you! I can see you as a hopeless modern Don Quixote, charging at airplanes, without noticing that the propeller blades are covered with shit. And I know how you feel. I knew how all the others felt."

"What others?"

"Pilots who cried 'injustice' with nothing to go on. The ones who felt persecuted when only the harsh facts were after them.

The ones who felt cheated, the ones who started drinking, the ones who ended up on the rubbish heap of aviation."

"You forget those, Henry, who won their cases against the easy 'pilot error' verdicts."

"But how many were there? One? Two?"

"I don't know."

"But you do know every one who wrote a book saying, 'This book is not to whitewash a pilot who crashed'—and went on and on doing just that."

There was a pause and Brown cleared his throat to indicate his presence. Singer and Penn turned toward him. "I think Corrie has no reason to say anything but the truth at the hearing."

"Thank you."

"Except that you've already said it. You think it wasn't your fault. You said so; now shut up and wait for the results of the investigation."

"That's what I said," Singer mumbled and tried not to look too gleeful. "All I want is to protect the Sarissa and Drayton's grand design, and to avoid the outbreak of press hysteria. Favorable publicity can't make a winner out of a bad airplane, but gossip, suspicion and lack of confidence can turn even the Sarissa into a loser."

"Fine. How about me?" asked Penn.

"You'll be suspended, but on full pay, of course," said Brown and looked away, anticipating the next question.

"I'm not talking about my status but my name."

"You aborted that take-off beyond VR. With that you put your own name on the threshold. Now help us to prove you right."

Penn spent the rest of the weekend with Mara. They scrupulously avoided any mention of the accident or the course Penn should follow. On Monday, Penn went with Brown to the airport and then to the court where the hearing would be held. They walked down Raffles and Collyer quays, where a young

Chinese with a ready smile joined them, adjusting his steps carefully to theirs.

"Good morning, gentlemen. I'm Mr. John."

"No thank you," said Brown. The extremely unfriendly tone startled Penn a little, but Brown knew better what was to come.

"Very nice private bar with very nice private girls for you, gentlemen."

"No thank you."

"Very nice suit in one day."

"No."

"In eight hours."

"No."

"Six hours? Five?"

"No."

"Radio, camera, Japanese Parker . . ."

"Get lost."

"Oh, you really know Singapore, mister. You in business? We have telex service, accommodation address, can arrange money transfers to and from Hong Kong, Zurich and Bahamas, help with tax reduction, bookkeeping and office cleaning. This is my card, gentlemen. Take the card, please. Very nice tweeds, telex service—"

"Next time. The Captain has no time right now."

"Captain? What captain?" He stared at Penn and almost ran to keep up with the two men. "You Captain Cornelius? Yes!" He spat out. "I don't want your business. You go away. Go away. You in a hurry, you kill people. Go away!"

At the court, Mara met them. She noticed Penn's gloom and pulled him aside. "What's wrong?"

"Nothing."

"You were happier when I left you."

"I know."

"What have you decided?"

"Nothing."

"Please don't start to fight. Not now. I'll do it for you. I have plans. I'll find out the answers to all your questions and prepare everything for you to make the final move, but don't move now. You have nothing to go on. Just wait and trust me as I trust you that it wasn't your fault."

He knew his duty was to wait and do nothing. Mara's outburst made it easier for him. As he turned to go in, she touched his face with her fingertips and smiled. "Pity we wasted the first night when we met."

The hearing lasted only fifty-five minutes. Penn answered a few questions, made a brief statement about his actions and the decision to abort, and turned down the opportunity offered by the judge to make any comments relevant to finding the cause of the accident.

PART TWO

"Ain't goin' to be no white Christmas, guv," predicted the spindly gaffer at the newsstand and nodded a few times in full agreement with himself.

"Nope," confirmed the tall man with the smooth silver skull. He looked up at the blue sky and took a deep breath of the breeze sweeping down from Hampstead Heath. "I'd say it's mild even for London." He bought both the evening papers as usual, and glanced through the headlines as usual. During this brief interval, the gates of the nearby red-brick building would open and schoolboys would begin to pour out into the street. He would then walk slowly toward the underground station. When he was duly overtaken by and submerged in a wave of children, he would smile and he would listen.

It was amazing, really, how much one could learn in this way. Whose parents were fusspots, which master was a poofter, why the Olympic runner's son was a jerk and the TV star's son a lad, why everybody else was a lad, a poofter or a jerk, how far the German mistress was preceded by those floppy boobs, where a blown-up Durex would probably burst first, and where Timmy Penn would spend a few days of the holiday at a friend's cottage in the Welsh Black Mountain district.

Yes, Brigadier Mott found his little newly acquired afternoon routine quite profitable. And pleasant, too, considering the mildness of December.

Drayton was pleased with himself. The major Sarissa deals were shaping up well, and even the Singapore mishap had turned out to be a blessing in disguise. The investigation seemed to have got nowhere (which was only to be expected), and in aviation circles the consensus of opinion was that the Sarissa must be built to exceptional toughness if it had withstood that battering at Paya Lebar without breaking up completely, without bursting into flames and without turning into a mass grave for all those on board.

Salah Termine returned from his travels with stacks of background information on Captain Penn (to be used if need be, but now safely stored in Drayton's private records office) and with the surprise present of an exquisite seventeenth-century Venetian mirror which he had found "in the possession of an impoverished and amorous Italian aristocrat who could be persuaded to swap it" for something Termine had. What it was exactly Termine did not say, and for mental comfort, Drayton chose not to ask. The same blind faith in the man was deemed to be prudent when Termine proposed to research and tie up some loose ends in the Hannan stabbing with the help of some extra funds for expenses. The mirror was put to good use: a TV crew, interviewing Drayton, featured it reflecting a desktop model of the Sarissa in a warm red glow.

Secret progress reports coming in about the development of Mark 2, the Whispering Sarissa, were also most encouraging. The test flights had gone without a hitch, and under certain pressures, backed by a friendly Senator and cooperative Congressmen, the Washington authorities had agreed to conduct the preliminary certification procedure fast and in complete secrecy. Even luck seemed to be on Drayton's side. The next Farnborough international air show had been brought forward, just this once, from autumn to spring. Everybody who mattered in aviation would be there. Cohorts of the world press and television would watch the extensive static and flying display. If Mark 2 was ready, Drayton might book a slot in the show so that the aircraft could make its debut in style, fly in rather than stand in the exhibition, make a low pass or two, whisper to the cheering crowds below, and let all AeroCorp's competitors stew. Just a dream as yet but certainly worth the pulling of not a few strings to make it come true.

Drayton locked away the reports and took out an electric razor. He was not really in need of a shave, but it was fun to use the new mirror on the wall and he wanted to feel in top form with a baby-bum chin, as he called it, for his next appointment.

Mara's unexpected call was, in fact, the crowning triumph of his day. For, apparently, his tactical patience had paid off.

After Singapore, he had seen her once. It was only to say goodbye, she told him. He was stunned and did not try to hide the fact. "It's rather sudden," he said.

She waffled something about life and diverging paths and all good things coming to an end one day.

"So my little scheme has failed."

"It was just a joke, Charles."

"Perhaps. Yet to me, at the time, it seemed so logical. And cleverly psychological. I thought one meeting would cure you."

"So did I."

He stared at his face in the nearest mirror. "But unexpectedly, two-dimensional infatuation grew into three-dimensional love," he mumbled.

"You may put it that way."

"Yet you didn't sleep together the first night."

"How would you know?" She was more surprised than angry.

"Sorry, it's none of my business, of course, but one hears about things. I mean, you know I always hear about people who are important to me."

"I'm flattered."

"He may turn out to be a paper tiger. Paper lover, to be precise. We must remain friends until then, shall we?"

"Why not?"

"And you must give me a fair chance. After all, you know that he's married."

"Don't I know that you are, too?"

"Ah, but that's different. I'd divorce to marry you."

"Really? I thought that you were opposed to goddamn divorce. It's not cost-effective, you always said, didn't you?"

"I still do. But you're an exception."

It was pointless arguing any further. Drayton decided that time must be on his side and patience would pay substantial dividends. He knew he had a lot going for him. He knew he was the sort of man that impressed Mara, he knew she found a sexually acceptable father figure in him, he knew she realized the full effect their relationship had on her status and career. It should only be a matter of time.

In the months since then, the omens had been good. Drayton was informed that Mara had not been to London or Penn to the United States, and that they had had no more than perhaps three telephone conversations, each of them initiated by Penn. And now at last her call announcing that she was in town asking to see him. What more could he wish for?

When Mara entered his office, Drayton resisted the temptation to kiss her. She looked even more beautiful than he remembered her. He almost told her just that but decided against it.

After a few overpolite remarks and embarrassingly long pauses, Mara said, "You've probably guessed that I'm here to ask for a favor."

"I thought—no, I hoped it was something more personal."

"I need some information about the original design of the Sarissa elevator system and also the various last-minute improvements introduced just before the prototype was built."

"All right. You know you only have to ask."

"Thanks, Charles."

"Besides, it may also help us."

"I knew you'd look at it this way."

Drayton buzzed Ms. Etch and told her to arrange research facilities for Mara. "She may see anything she wants to." He turned back to Mara. "By the way, how did you hear about those improvements? At that stage, they weren't publicized."

"Oh, somebody mentioned it at the NTSB." Then she added in a hurry, "Or was it some other place? Can't remember who it was or where. Does it matter?"

"No, not at all." Drayton smiled, but it was bad news. It meant that Mara might have some well-placed source Drayton had heard nothing about. For he knew perfectly well what Mara was up to, what she had done in the past few months, how she was going about gathering information, whom she talked to and about what. Not that he knew of anything that required extra secrecy, but he did not like her undue interest in the case, her presumed intention to help Penn, and the possibility that she might stumble on, misinterpret and publish some minor items of fact that would be at the very least a red herring for the investigators and so delay the final exoneration of the elevator system. Besides, a resourceful, much-respected and successful Mara would be less likely to return to him than a frustrated, disconnected journalist.

When Mara left, Drayton told Ms. Etch exactly what degree of cooperation was to be extended to her: she should be given access only to items already on public record. He then agreed to a long-requested lunch with Mara's editor, who would be encouraged to approach Drayton personally rather than through Mara in the future. Finally, a hint or two in the right places in Washington would surely reduce Mara's popularity and image of reliability with off-the-record information.

He then called Singer. "I have a problem, Henry, and you can help me, but only if you want to, because it's goddamn personal. It concerns Mara."

The phone rang. Penn picked it up at once. Yet another reporter on the line. Would Captain Penn care to comment on the news that three more countries have joined CLIC and SupraNat has taken another batch of eight Sarissas? No, Penn would not wish to make any comment. But . . . No buts. He slammed the phone down. In some mysterious way, the pressure on him was growing all the time, and it was harder and harder to keep his mouth shut. And he hated the telephone. Gradually, the damned instrument had grown into a fixation. He became afraid of leaving the house in case he missed an important call. He had an additional extension installed in the bathroom, and every now and then he checked each set to make sure that nothing was out of order. If Candy spoke to someone, on the phone, he urged her to keep it short and clear the line. And every time the bell rang, infrequently though it was, adrenaline flushed his entire circulatory system. But it was usually a wrong number, something unimportant, a call for Candy or Timmy, which at least made him smile. Only at school could one know people with odd names such as Timmy's mates Spuffard, Fartibbit and Zgzdrynsk.

Worst of all was the lack of news from Stacey or Mara. Penn could contact her any time. She had indeed asked him to be in touch as often as possible rather than wait for her calls, which might be answered by Candy; but he was reluctant to approach her. For then he would tell her how much he missed her and that would be unfair to Candy, and Penn was not ready to introduce regular cheating into his marriage, however shaky it was. Or else he could ask her about the progress of her inquiries, but that would be begging and pushing. She had said she would ring if she had anything. So her silence was ominous. Perhaps she had found nothing. Perhaps what she had found was bad news. Perhaps she had given up. Perhaps even Stacey had given up.

Penn dialed Brown's London office.

"I didn't catch your name, sir," a pleasant woman's voice panted at the other end.

"Penn, Captain Penn."

"How do you spell it, sir? . . . Oh, Penn, I'm sorry, sir, I didn't recognize it at first. You see, I'm only helping out temporarily in this office, but I remember now. You crashed in Singapore, didn't you? What shall I say to the Chief Pilot, then?"

"Can't you put me through?"

"Not at the moment, sir. I'm sorry, but he's terribly busy and has people with him, you see, and he's already late from a conference and—"

"Just tell him," Penn interrupted her sharply, "tell him to call me *if* and *when* he has a moment to spare." He hung up. Terribly busy. Didn't recognize the name at first, but it must be the pilot who crashed.

He was still fuming when Candy arrived home. "Where have you been?"

"Guess. Just guess."

"Shopping?"

"Fantastic! Right first time. You win nothing."

"I could have helped you."

"It's quicker on my own. Besides, you'd worry all the time about the vast number of people who might have wanted you."

"I've just called Keith Brown."

"What did he say?"

"Er, couldn't talk to me just now. He's terribly, terribly busy."

"Most people are, you know."

"What are you trying to say?"

"Nothing."

"Well, I spoke to his secretary. She knew my name."

"And?"

"That's all. I said she knew my name."

"You're full of fascinating stories these days."

This was below the belt. And it hurt because it was true. In the absence of anything new happening, he was endlessly regurgitating his past and discussing non-events. People were too busy to talk to him. People were busy. He was grounded and redundant in every sense. He was losing his self-confidence and his grip on life. "I'll remember to invent more amusing stories specially for you next time."

"Do that. Alternatively, you could get a job."

"Alternatively." The word bugged him. He could hear every bit of her speech training. "How's your elocutionist these days?"

"Actually, it's an extraordinary coincidence"—she now really went for the caricature—"but I talked to him only a short while ago. However, I think we meant to talk about a job for you, not about him."

"I have a job."

"What? Sitting at home?"

"It's not my choice. And my contract—"

"Break it. AeroCorp offered you something better, much better."

"How do you know about that?"

"I don't know. Somebody mentioned it."

"Who?"

"Can't remember. Perhaps you. So why don't you accept it?"

"It's a desk job and I'm a pilot."

"Glorified bus driver in the sky, you mean." The phone started to ring. "When you work, that is."

Penn paused and breathed in and out. This could be it.

But it was only Brown. "Sorry I couldn't talk to you when you called."

"That's all right. I . . . I just wanted to find out if anything was happening at your end." At your end. Penn heard himself saying it and hated himself for the stupid and too transparent hypocrisy, as if things never stopped happening at his end and he only spared the time to complete the picture.

"Millions of things, of course, and we're still understaffed, as you know; but if you're asking about Singapore, the answer is nothing. Early days yet. You know how slowly bureaucracy moves."

"It's more than three months."

"Is it really? That's awful. I mean how time flies."

Penn suggested a drink. Brown thought it was an excellent idea and he would call as soon as he got through that paper mountain on his desk. But Penn tried to pin him down and invited him to dinner, offering a complete free choice of dates. Impossible to turn down.

Not that Brown wanted to. "Yes, next week, why not? . . . Er, wait a minute. Next week I'm doing the milk run to Istanbul, then a charter job down Acapulco way . . . er, yes . . . I'd better give you a buzz next month, old boy."

The way Penn put down the receiver told the whole story to Candy, but she was determined to play it out. "Is he coming to dinner then?"

"No, not just now."

"Pity. What a pity. And so unexpected, too."

It was soul-destroying enough to be in this limbo of non-retired non-employment without Candy's demoralizing remarks. "You never miss a trick, do you?" The doorbell rang. Candy was about to get up, but Penn was already halfway to the door. He had never realized how desperately he was grabbing at anything to do. Pity that the grass had already stopped growing. It was such a useful, regular duty to cut it—with the telephone in the open window.

As he opened the front door, Timmy rushed in and up the stairs. But Penn noticed the tears in his eyes and a few drops of blood on his shirt.

"Timmy! What happened?"

"Nothing." He locked the door of his room and refused to come out.

Candy watched the scene from the bottom of the stairs. Penn felt sorry for Timmy and did not want to shout at him or order him out. So he settled for talking through the door. "You had another fight?"

"Yes . . . the same boys."

"I hope you kicked their teeth in. Did you?"

"There were two of them." He was sobbing.

"I didn't ask how many there were. I asked what you did."

"I tried to run. You know, dodge them."

"And that's just why they always pick on you. You must stand and fight. Always."

The door opened so suddenly that Penn almost fell into the room. "Like you, Dad?"

"What?"

Timmy was crying freely. "Do you stand and fight, Dad?" He walked out and locked himself in the bathroom.

It was the second time ever that Penn felt ashamed to face the child. About the first occasion Timmy knew nothing. It was such a stupid thing, after all. Timmy was a toddler. Granny gave him some bells on wheels which he could push around at the end of a stick. It went clink-clank all the way and back and again. Penn had just come home from a long stretch of duty. He was tired, sleepy, short-tempered. When Timmy refused to stop the noise, he cut off the clapper while the child was having a bath. He never forgot Timmy's expression when, out of the bathroom, he ran to grab the stick and push the wheels again —only to find that the beautiful, beautiful noise had gone out of it.

At a loss, Penn stared at the bathroom door, then looked hopefully at Candy; but she turned away, marched down the stairs and into the living room, filled a tumbler with vodka over a token lump of ice, drank and left the house without a word.

Penn sat in the darkening room, willing in vain the phone to ring. He ought to call Mara. He ought to make a move. Scream and shout and make a nuisance of himself as Mara had first suggested. But the last time they spoke, she had begged him to wait a little longer. She had convinced him that, at the moment, she had the better chance to do something. Do what? If only she called him. But he had promised to give her until Christmas.

Timmy came in and without a word sat down next to him. Penn told him about the bells on wheels and the mutilation of the toy. They laughed about it. But Penn knew that the child was worried. Perhaps about the fight. Or his mother. "She'll be back soon," he lied hopefully. He expected him to ask where she was, but the question did not come. Perhaps he had guessed the answer from the lipstick on the edge of the empty tumbler.

Timmy sat up in bed when Penn went in to kiss him good-night. "Dad, may I ask you something?"

"Go ahead."

"Did you cause that accident?"

"No. You know very well I don't think I did. What makes you ask?"

"Nothing."

"Come on, tell me."

"I just thought . . . you know . . ."

"No, I don't know."

"Well, Spuffard heard two men talking about you."

"What two men?"

"I don't know. Somebody on the train. I think one of them works near the school."

"What did they say?"

"They said that you must have caused the crash and you must know it, because otherwise you wouldn't lie low. . . . Sorry, Dad, that's what they said, and Spuffard asked me if it was true.'

The Leopard proved himself a friend. And an invaluable planner, gag man and critic, too. The act was dreamed up to be funny, mesmerizing, even breathtaking as it reached its climax, and he insisted on a girl to share the stage with Barraclough throughout the act. Long legs, fishnet stockings, glamour if not outright sex appeal, preparing the boards, walls, bricks to be smashed and, above all, guiding the audience, showing them how to react.

"Fright is just as infectious as laughter," said the Leopard. "If *she* looks worried, they'll chew their nails off. So get yourself a girl and train her. It'll take time, but it's worth it."

Barraclough promised to think about it. That meant talking to Fraser. He hoped she would not even notice the delay in their plans, for it would take her quite a while to find the right shop anyway. He was wrong. She had been lucky. But she listened and accepted the new situation with a single nod. "Right. I'll play them along until we get the money." She then suggested that Sally, their own daughter, could be the girl in the act. Barraclough dismissed the idea out of hand. She did not argue. Which usually made him think again.

"What would be the advantage?"

"She could become part owner of the shop and the show; you two would get to know each other; and you could pick the moment to tell her about us."

"Would she do it?"

"Wouldn't you if the choice was between that and the typing pool?"

Barraclough did not answer for a while. He sank into one of his infrequent pensive moods, which ended with an apparently meaningless statement: "We must be coming up to infinity then."

But Fraser understood him. "Must be." He had a pet theory about parallel lives which run independently without any sign of physical or spiritual affinity but which, nevertheless, are bound to meet like the parallel halves of a railway line somewhere on the horizon, in infinity if not before. That's what destiny is, he would declare, and she had no reason to argue.

Barraclough wanted to make it a bit of an occasion when the proposition was made to "your daughter." At one minute to four on Monday afternoon, he stalked across the traffic in Piccadilly, noted the wind direction subconsciously, paused as usual to stare up at the clock and wait for the mute exchange of polite gestures between Messrs. F and M, checked his watch, reviewed the caviars on parade, delayed his order of tea, and was now ready to receive Fraser, Betty M., and "her daughter."

Sally, named after Barraclough's favorite aunt though the girl was not to know that, turned out to be a real treasure. On stage she looked no more than passable in fishnet, but she was enthusiastic, had some humor and a good sense of dramatic timing, and, above all, she was truly impressed and frightened by Barraclough's antics.

"She likes you," whispered Fraser into Barraclough's ear, and he quickly looked aside, cleared his throat, turned away, turned back, mumbled, "Right," and mumbled, "Well then," and for good measure smashed a few tiles with the edge of his stretched hand, hollering, "Huyyah!" The word was Sally's invention, better than his usual grunts for action, and the "Two Huyyahs" became the name of the act.

They had dress rehearsals every day now because the Leopard had at last won an audition for them.

"I don't very much like the venue," said Barraclough, because Pussy(cat), the name of the nightclub, irritated his sense of propriety, and it was obviously no place for Sally, but he accepted the argument that they must start somewhere.

The doorbell was an old-fashioned one that had to be wound up like a clock, and Candy knew that if she kept her finger on the button long enough it would bring the whole of East London to the edges of the lace-curtained windows. But she did not think about it.

"Coming! Coming!"

Candy smiled as she waited for her mother to open the door, smiled as Mother took a quick look around to check who had noticed Candy's presumably drunken arrival with the big Mercedes, and smiled as she stumbled in the dark hall, caught the hat stand and pulled it down with all the decrepit umbrellas which her mother never had the heart to dispose of.

"Sorry, Mum. Sorry." She went through to the kitchen and sat at the table. She looked perfectly sober, but her mother did not even look at her to check the state she was in.

"Are you drunk then?"

"What makes you ask?"

"You called me Mum instead of Mother or even Mather or whatever way you say it these days, that's what." She put on the kettle. "Want a cup?"

"Anything stronger, Mum?"

"Yes. Strong tea."

"I'll choose tea then, may I?"

"You may." She busied herself with the tea to give Candy a chance to collect her thoughts and say her piece. It used to work when Mr. Sharn came home in a state like that. But it did not seem to work with Candy. "All right. Out with it."

"With what?"

"Why you came here."

"That's a nice warm reception, I must say. Look at me, Mum. I'm Candy. Don't you recognize me?"

Mrs. Sharn turned around in regal slow motion. "Candy is a former air hostess. My daughter is a regular Maggie, if you must know, but that's up to you. If calling yourself Candy makes you feel more special, that's all right with me. So what brings you here?"

"I just popped in to see you. Satisfied?"

"Nobody just pops in to see nobody after ten. Not in West Ham, Maggie dear. But let's have it. Did Cornelius throw you out?"

"He didn't. And everybody calls him Corrie."

"And I call him Cornelius."

"Only because Dad always said that a man who has the time to go to the barber's in ordinary people's working hours deserves due respect?"

"Your dad knew what's what."
"You keep saying so."
"Because it's my opinion, young lady. I may be old, but I can still have my opinion, can't I? . . . Can't I?"
"Yes, yes, you can." Candy sighed.
"Thank you. And I could tell you a thing or two, but it's not for me to say. It's your life, your own making."
"Wish you could tell me how I could get out of it."
"You're out of your mind. You have a good life. With a good husband who cares about you. You're lucky."
"Am I?"
"Cornelius is a good provider, too. What else do you want?"
"I could have married a millionaire. Two, if you must know." Which was, in fact, true. Candy was the classic cool blonde who represented an instant challenge to certain male types who all hoped to really melt the iceberg for the first time. "One of them died recently, and I could be an heiress now."
"But you chose Cornelius because he had the glamour."
"He talked me into it."
"Every man does. Every good man, if you know my meaning. And he didn't make no false promises, now did he?"
"And I kept my side of the bargain, didn't I?"
"How? By taking everything that was on offer? Big house, big car, the cottage—sorry, you call it the villa, don't you? Not that you ever use it. No, you're too busy with four holidays a year in places most people get to only in wartime. Some bargain you had, hadn't you? Not to mention all the treats! You two spend more time in Soho and the theaters than a waiter and a tart put together."
"Because we have nothing else. Nothing to talk about."
"Oh that. I know what that's like. Your father was on the dole long enough. People were too poor to go to the barber's, so their women had to cut it for them. Oh, you should have seen some of them short backs and sides. Was that fun! But no laughs to your dad. He was bored and jumpy, and I had to keep

my mouth shut. For once we had too much time to talk and we didn't know how to. That must be it."

"It isn't. We know how to talk but not what to talk about. He always did most of his talking outside the house. With pilots and more pilots."

"Beats a whoring, drinking man every time."

"But now he wants to talk to me all day because nobody else has the time. He wants attention."

"Then give it to him."

"But I'm bored to tears with all that flying bullshit."

"Language, Maggie, language!"

"Sorry, Mother. I can assure you swearing's an acquired taste, not my lower-middle-class inheritance."

"But your tongue is just as sharp as ever."

"Sorry."

"You should put it to better use. To cheer up your hubby. If you don't like that pilot talk, talk to him about other things."

"But don't you understand? There's nothing. We have nothing in common."

"You have Timothy."

Candy stared at her for a moment, then turned away. "I wouldn't be so sure about that, Mum."

"And what is that supposed to mean?" She rounded Candy to face her. "Tell me."

"Let's leave it, shall we?"

"That's a good way out for you, isn't it? Because I put my finger on it. Because you do have something to share and love and cherish."

"Oh yes."

"If only you loved your family as much as Cornelius loves and worships his son!"

Candy's face flushed with anger. She backed away, bit her tongue, struggled to hold the words down, but up and out they came throatily just the same: "Whose son?"

Her mother watched her silently for a long few seconds, then turned to the cabinet under the sink, shifted a bucket, two old pots, some cleaning fluid and a watertight bag of salt in order to reach a half-empty flask of emergency brandy. She poured out a large measure for Candy, another for herself, carefully screwed the stopper back on the bottle and raised her glass to her lips. Only then did she ask, "What did you say, love?"

Candy's natural inclination was to say nothing and walk out on her. She stood up and started toward the door. She felt her mother's eyes on her back. The eyes that used to puncture her hubby's ego and reduce the chatty barber to the bearer of ulcerous, silent disapproval of everything. The eyes that bored holes now into her instinct of self-protection. Her energy to escape seeped out and away. "I only asked whose son Corrie worshiped," Candy said.

"And what's that supposed to mean?"

Candy shrugged her shoulders.

"All right, love, you don't have to say anything you don't want to. I'm your mum and only trying to be helpful."

Candy knew that her mother had stopped talking, but she was still listening to the other, unspoken sentences which hung in the air. You must know that I'm on your side. I devoted my life to you. You can throw away my goodwill, spit on my help, trample all over me, I'm still your mother/wife/sister, and you may turn to me any time as long as there is life left in my bones. The very sentences Maggie was determined to run away from. The Bible-hard pronouncements she was determined never to copy and utter. The menaces that could all be forgotten by Candy, the girl in the uniform that would protect her from the implied curse forever. If only she could answer with nothing but silent contempt. But no. Words gathered in her mouth. Perhaps because she wanted to hurt her. And herself. And Corrie. And to prove that she was not, would never be, the devoted, helpful, much-trampled-on mother and wife pouncing on every opportunity to cash in on her pains.

"I only indicated that Timmy might not be his son." Candy

drank up and held out her glass for more. "I can't be sure. He might have been born at about eight months, in which case he'd most probably be Corrie's. Or it might have been a full nine months, in which case . . . well, someone else would be the father. Do you want to hear all the sordid details?"

"Only what you want to tell me."

"I knew I might be pregnant when I first went with Corrie. It didn't matter because all the stews of four airlines were chasing him, and I thought I'd never see him a second time. But it went on."

"You mean you fell in love."

"All right. If it makes you happier, we'll call it love. Anyway, I always knew I'd have an abortion, but when it continued with Corrie, I told him about it. I offered to share the cost. But he wouldn't hear of it. He made an incredible fuss. He had some awful memories about his mother, who had one abortion after another and once called Corrie's birth an accident or something like that."

"What do you mean, something like that? Didn't you ask?"

"Of course I asked. And he told me, although I said he wouldn't have to tell me anything he didn't want to. I was there to listen and help and understand—" Candy suddenly stopped. The sentences. "Dad, I suppose, would have told you everything without even that much prodding."

"Your dad was an honest man. Let him rest in peace."

"Anyway, I wanted to go ahead with the abortion, and he really fought it. I told him how much I loathed the idea of motherhood. He refused to believe a word of it. He insisted that I'd love that child. That it would change our whole life-style for the better. He painted rosy pictures and he was fun. And of course he'd marry me right away."

"Very decent of him, too."

"Decent? It was a bloody trap. I fell for it because it was a laugh and sheer joy to see how envious the other stews were. But I was trapped all right like a bloody bird. Soon there was no way out, and then he made my cage so bloody comfortable that I didn't even want to escape any more. That's bloody corruption, isn't it, Mum?"

"Well, I only hope that Corrie won't ever find out."

Candy answered her with a slow smile. Her unblinking stare punctured the stain above the stove. "I wonder what it would do to him if he knew . . . if only he had an inkling . . . " It never quite surfaced in her consciousness, but she knew at that moment that her eyes were her mother's.

"Maggie, you can't!"

"Can't I?"

"He loves you."

"He loved my pregnancy."

"You can't do it to Timothy."

"No. Because it would be harder to walk out on the two of them. But I will one day, you'll see."

"You're a mother, no matter what."

"Unfortunately. Of course I could be like you and make motherhood a virtue or a shortcut to martyrdom or a trump card for emotional blackmail, but there must be something more to life than that."

"If there is, Maggie, you've failed to get its meaning, and if you want an honest opinion—"

"No, Mum, I don't." She walked toward the door, and her mother followed her. "Don't bother. I'll see myself out."

"Not in this house, you won't." She held the front door open for Candy, and for the benefit of any of the neighbors who might be listening, she shouted over the starting roar of the Mercedes, "Take care, love, and see you soon!"

Federal agencies, transport and safety authorities, research establishments, a full range of air-oriented Congressmen, reporters, specialists and a quorum of the rest of the informed kibitzers likely to populate air cocktail parties and junket flights—in other words, the aviation circles of Washington—

began to grow bored or irritated by Mara Boone. She consulted everybody everywhere and worked her way through all the available information concerning the Sarissa. She was now delving into the computerized records of all incidents. The basic data were rather sparse, but most cases, such as tire blowouts and inoperative storage rack doors, could be discarded without any further ado. None of the incidents seemed truly significant, but on the few which might be relevant to Penn's problem Mara sought further advice. Oddly enough, this was increasingly difficult. Some of her sources dried up. Friends failed to call her back. Old contacts sounded bureaucratically inclined just a touch more than before. AeroCorp employees were polite and cooperative but only up to a point. Where that point was could not be defined precisely. But she felt it all right, it was there, and if she could connect all such points, she could probably draw a map of the area out of bounds to her.

She pressed friends and so-called friends in the business for an answer: "Am I being stonewalled or something?" They assured her that she was not. But sometimes there was a slight pause, a resonance of uncertainty not louder than a pin dropping on stone, or a qualifying half-sentence of "No, nothing I've heard of to that effect or the contrary."

Her editor called her into his office for a heart-to-heart talk. He told his secretary to hold all his calls. So Mara knew it was serious. But he was impatient rather than unfriendly. Her usual steady flow of minor and major scoops had apparently dried up. Why? Had she any problems? Did she need help? Perhaps a holiday? Ah, oh yes, that preoccupation with the Singapore case. Was it not mere shadowboxing? What did she hope to find? Any reason to suspect some hanky-panky at AeroCorp? And, if not, would she not agree that it was becoming an obsession rather than a logical investigation? She ought to give it a rest. Perhaps chase some other stories and come back to this one eventually. He went on and on, and Mara knew that if her position on the reputable aviation weekly and her access to further information on the Sarissa were to remain tenable she would soon have to come up with something in other areas.

It was the paper's print night when, by sheer luck, she heard that Singer was in town. She called him, and he suggested dinner "to offset the loneliness of the long-distance executive." They chose an unassuming little French spot with red-checkered tablecloths in Georgetown, where the ladies'-man owner never blushed when charging vintage champagne prices for a carafe of *vin* (very) *ordinaire* to compensate him (more than amply) for the "dirt-cheap prix" of superb food. Singer drank a fair amount and, over his second Armagnac, mentioned the name of a rather unsavory aircraft salesman whose name had been tarnished if not completely discredited in the Lockheed scandals. After some gentle prodding by Mara, Singer revealed that apparently, under very peculiar but considerable pressure from high places on the Hill, the man was now in line for a seat on the Civil Aeronautics Board. It was an astonishing piece of information. Mara asked him if she could use it and Singer had no objections provided that the story was not attributed to him in any way. She promised to tell no one about her source. She spent an hour trying to verify the scoop from another angle but received nothing beyond no-comments, flat denials and some abuse for late calls. She telephoned her editor, who was very keen on using the story right away but wanted to know her source. She refused to name Singer.

"Tell me at least if you trust the source."

"Implicitly," she said. "Or, let me put it this way: he's never been wrong so far."

The editor decided to take a chance and run the story, complete with denials, mainly because he trusted Mara, who had an excellent track record. She had to call the night editor, who made some last-minute changes to let her be first with yet another sensation quoting a "usually reliable source." But right after it had appeared, a radio station had a counterscoop:

the man allegedly in line for the CAB seat had been dead for a week. The family had done everything in their power to keep the news out of the press because it had been a ghastly suicide and they did not want the children to find out about all the gory details. Singer could not have known, Mara kept telling herself.

Singer apologized to Mara, she apologized to her editor, everybody accepted that it was a genuine error of judgment, but it did nothing to improve her reputation or encourage her sources to be more forthcoming about the Sarissa.

She began to feel panicky. Christmas was near. Penn had not promised her he would sit tight beyond that.

A couple of "turbulence encountered" reports caught her eye in the computer printouts of the National Transportation Safety Board. Both were fairly recent cases. There were no injuries, no damage to aircraft, just two minor events, duly recorded by the pilots, nothing to add or investigate. One of them mentioned, not unnaturally, a considerable loss of altitude. In despair, she thought she would question Stacey, the investigator in charge. She knew he was on a long visit at AeroCorp to supervise some elevator bench tests, and called him there, only to be told that he had gone. Nobody sounded sorry about it. Was he back in London? They were not sure. So Mara asked for Drayton.

"Yes, he's left," Drayton confirmed, "and he ought to consider himself goddamn lucky, because I'd have throttled him with my two hands. A quite impossible character, Stacey."

Mara asked him about the two turbulence cases. Drayton promised to look into it, and only an hour later he called her back to report sadly that the company had nothing more than the NTSB computer. She was grateful but turned down his offer to meet and fly her to Chicago for dinner at Barney's, the scene of their first date.

The pickup was easy once the proper groundwork had been done, and Salah Termine did not believe in doing things by halves. He watched the girl for two days and nights, so now he knew who her friends were, north and south of Houston Street, how she spent her time, how badly she played the guitar, where in SoHo she bought her organic food (with a taste for oat flakes), and who supplied her downers and jelly babies (no hallucinogens) in NoHo. The girl he called the "New York Witness" seemed clean, most unlikely to have anything to do with Hannan's death apart from the accidental discovery of the body, but in Termine's book to leave it at that would have been doing it by halves.

He decided in advance that if success with the girl came his way too easily and the evasion of an insert might look odd or unnatural, she would have to be forced to do a blow job, for no matter how attractive she was, she was still hip, a freak, a dropout, the sort he had no time for. Because Termine was a man of principles and strict standards. He despised layabouts, refrained from making malicious remarks about the mutilated and the dead, and disapproved of adultery by women. He regarded himself as a serious man, though he was proud of his controlled sense of humor; jokes were not to make incursions into the kingdom of prudence. (It was amazing, really, how quickly it spread from Marseilles to Chevy Chase that he found jokes about his huge and agile Adam's apple distasteful. Besides, perhaps it was not so monstrous after all. Perhaps it was the fault of his schoolboy's neck, which was too thin to accommodate a perfectly normal Adam's apple. Until he could afford silk shirts made for him in London's Jermyn Street, he used to tighten the collar of his shirts at the back with paperclips.) He did not relish the prospect of his current self-imposed assignment, but he did not grumble; expediency must always take precedence over pleasure, principles and his own code of morality.

He had a passable command of hip culture and language. Sadly, his Guccis and other rewards of labor had to be exchanged for clothes to fit the job. His choice of residence, too, was to suffer. His observations completed, he moved out of the Waldorf and into a home for geriatric cockroaches in the Village. He spent his third evening in the vicinity of Washington Square Park, where he soon spotted a male creature, completely strung out, badly in need of a fix, performing his painful contortions among garbage and urine. Termine caught his leg, pulled him into the shadows around the corner, and undressed him without making any allowance for his moaning.

Back among the roaches on night duty, he put on the junkie's foul clothes, which almost made him puke but gave him the unmistakable touch of the genuine article. His dark pomade-smooth hair was sometimes a problem because he always refused to mess it up, but he had a successful technique. Rather than hiding his hair, he emphasized it as his very special feature, the hallmark of a true Valentino freak.

Half an hour later, he was in front of the house she shared with what appeared to be a whirlpool of a hundred people. He followed her to a loft studio party two blocks down the street, gatecrashed, offered her a joint, monopolized her most of the night and ended up with her in her half-attic, where she played the Gibson Heritage Custom for him, fed him with some Chinese whole rice, crabeye beans and sunflower kernels, and performed the blow job, too, just as he wanted it. Then she walked down three flights of stairs to pee, and in her absence he quickly searched the room. No papers, no real money, nothing to incriminate her; but Termine had to be sure.

When she returned, he stood at the loose-hanging sack that served as a door and greeted her with a Termine special. He could slap faces nine times every five seconds (faster with two-handed action), and the shock effect, especially on women, was tremendous. At first she just gasped, could not even scream, and by the time sound would have reached her lips, he had covered her mouth firmly with the junkie's jeans. He then picked up her guitar. "One loud word out of you and the guitar is finished. OK?"

She nodded, her frightened eyes blinking fast, ready for more slapping.

"How come you found that stiff by the fountain?"

"I went to Manny's to buy the guitar."

"Liar." He hit her from left and right in quick succession with a whiplash effect on her brain. "It's not open at that time."

She tried to explain it.

"Don't lie to me." He hooked the guitar by the first two strings on a nail in the wall. "Who dumped the stiff there?"

She began to cry. He snatched the instrument from the wall and strings A and E snapped with a pinnng that hurt. The interrogation did not take long. Termine knew what she had said at the police station, he knew that, eventually, the money had been returned to her, and felt sure now that she was no witness, just an innocent bystander. The killer might never be found. He dropped the guitar on the floor. "Forget you ever knew me, will you?" She did not need much encouragement to promise that. "And don't ever talk about it or I'll be back." He pulled on the jeans and longed to have a hot bath.

Halfway down the first flight of stairs, he stopped and returned to the attic. The girl was still standing there, stunned. He put his foot through the guitar and twisted his heel for good measure. She began to wail like an Italian mourner. "Now go and get yourself a decent job," he said without anger. He knew it was the right advice, and he liked to feel helpful.

Two hours later his brief report to Drayton via Singer was on its way. "Checked out witness in Hannan case. Propose no further action. No loose ends left." He knew that his boss appreciated initiative and thorough attention to every detail.

Now he felt free to relax, have a hot bath, and prepare himself for a job in London. Some investigator called Stacey was troubling the chief. According to Singer, there was a chance some competitors owned the man. Termine wanted to know more. Was he supposed to make an offer to buy this Stacey? But things like that could not be discussed with Singer, who seemed horrified and disgusted by a mere mention of direct action and refused to clarify his instructions: "All I'm saying is that the man is a born nuisance. Mr. Drayton said, "I wish somebody'd get him out of my hair," that's all. We've made certain discreet approaches to the British AIB to see if the man could be replaced by somebody else on the basis of total incompatibility, but they wouldn't budge. It's his case, and that's that. I think they may be only too pleased to have him out of the way, occupied with this relatively unimportant accident. But it would be useful to know more about him and his motives in case we need to cool his fervor. So I thought you might like to take a vacation over there and see what you could turn up." The man did not need to know that these were Drayton's ideas almost word for word, and Singer did not bother to anticipate Termine's interpretation.

Six hours after the hot bath, Termine caught a London flight to take a close look at the man in his chief's hair.

Candy made no secret of it, that she detested festive family occasions and that she could hardly wait to have Christmas over and done with. Timmy had a very poor end-of-term report, and it would have been a miracle if the tension in the house had left him unaffected. He had no appetite, and he only looked forward to his holiday in Wales.

Penn was subdued throughout Christmas. There was no news from Mara and he did not like the arrangement for Timmy to travel on his own to Swansea, where he would be met and taken to the cottage which was completely cut off from civilization in the Black Mountains. On Christmas Eve, there had been two intriguing developments. One was a call from Stacey, who wanted to "have a chat" in his office at AIB right after Christmas. The other was an announcement that the Sarissa international sales team was about to conclude the biggest contract in aviation history, and this started yet another avalanche of press interest in Penn. Would he care to comment on the news? He said no each time, but the temptation was tremendous.

He knew he had some hard thinking to do urgently. Although from the moment of hearing about Candy's pregnancy he had always given absolute priority to creating a happy childhood for Timmy and giving him the sort of home he himself had never had, he could now see the vague outline of abysmal failure grinning at him. He knew he had to reach some difficult decisions, but suddenly he was driven to realize that he had no useful experience in charting the course of his life. All the major turning points in his past were determined by outside forces, other people, circumstances. The divorce of his parents, the recession in aviation, rotten luck with the charter airline, Colombia, Africa, Candy, Singapore and Mara—these were the crucial factors rather than his own clear decisions. Now he would have to learn the hard way. But inertia, habits and conventional attitudes were a formidable opposition to break down. Even if his motto for easy going—"I make decisions for hundreds of lives in the air, must give others a chance to think on the ground" was not valid any more.

The morning after Boxing Day, Penn took Timmy to the station. Candy said she had some urgent shopping to do. Penn returned home and stared at the telephone for several hours until the prearranged call from Swansea came through: Yes, Timmy had safely arrived.

"You have too much time," Candy had said, and unfortunately it was true. For the same reason, Penn was more than an hour too early for his appointment with Stacey. He walked up and down in the Strand, stared at shopwindows without any interest, watched the entrance of a haughtily prewar office building, and envied the revolving door because it was busy.

Stacey's sparsely furnished, unlived-in office did not enjoy the magnificent panoramic view that the other rooms of the Accident Investigation Branch boasted, but then Stacey was not a man to indulge himself in gazing through windowpanes.

Had there been anybody in his life to inquire why he had no ambition to occupy a room with a view, he would have answered with a question, "What's the point?"

He greeted Penn with correctly executed cordiality and asked him if he would care to have some tea or coffee. The pilot asked for coffee. Then a creaky voice made him turn.

"With or without?"

The creature who stood by the hat stand behind Penn had cropped hair, a pair of precariously balanced glasses on the tip of a nose, a cigarette firmly planted in the corner of a mouth, and dusty-fluff clothes of which only the skirt was significant—it informed Penn that the wearer was a woman.

"Without sugar, please."

"But with or without?"

"Oh, sorry, with milk, please."

Stacey wanted to run through Penn's account of the accident yet again. What he did, why he did it, what his thoughts were at the time, what made him think those thoughts. The creature took notes. Stacey had still not warmed to tape recorders. Penn watched his quick weight/speed computations, and noticed he had aged a great deal since Singapore. The investigator looked haggard and harassed, and chewed his pencil vigorously. After a long pause he turned to look at some broken pieces of metal on top of a gray filing cabinet. Penn did not need to ask if they were parts of his Sarissa. Everything in that room was relevant to the case, which was now Stacey's life. The walls were covered with huge engineering drawings of the aircraft.

"They want us to say what we think the cause was, and if the answer is feasible everybody's happy," said Stacey, virtually to himself. "The important thing is to fit a case into a suitable slot. But do we ever understand what it really was that went wrong? We now call pilot errors the human factor, which is more charitable and sounds more scientific, doesn't it? But do we know what *made* you go wrong?"

"Are you suggesting—"

"No-no. I'm sorry. But something, perhaps something in your own mental makeup, perhaps something external, must have misled you. Or what if there really was a temporary breakdown in the elevator system as you believe?" He shook his head, anxious and bewildered. "There're gaps, inexplicable gaps. They may cost lives." He stood up and walked with Penn toward the door. Penn said goodbye to the creature in the corner. He had the distinct sensation of being hated.

Stacey opened the door. "Too many gaps." With his eyes half closed, he was still talking to himself. "And I have a hunch, no more, that some people are perhaps unwittingly but clearly withholding information." His eyes opened, and Penn was caught by the flash like a rabbit in a car's headlights. "Are you one of them?"

"Certainly not. What makes you ask?"

The beam went right through Penn, then Stacey shook his head and the lights went out. "No. He was wrong. I'm sure you told me everything you could. I'm sorry."

"Who was wrong?"

"White. Some relative of your dead flight engineer. He telephoned to warn me."

"It was the brother," the creature said.

"I didn't even know he had a brother." Penn was sure that White had never mentioned him. "Why did he phone? What do you mean he warned you?"

"It doesn't matter. Believe me. Probably it's just that we all need someone to blame, a target for imaginary vengeance. It makes tragedy more acceptable. Forget it, Captain."

Penn was tempted to suggest a long, long night's rest to the investigator, but decided to say nothing.

"Hello, Anthony. How goes it then?"

Barraclough almost swallowed his cup of tea in a single gulp as a rolled-up evening paper touched his shoulder.

"May I join you?"

Flushed by the hot liquid and the surprise, Barraclough half rose to gesture to the Brigadier. Yes, sir, please do. Fortnum and Mason's was supposed to be only a visual contact point.

"Long time no see, as they say these days, what?" Then in a more conspiratorial tone: "I thought it wouldn't do any harm if we had tea together just for once. Old colleagues, nothing suspicious." Nobody sat near enough to overhear them.

Only the old waitress paid any attention to the two men at the corner table. It was the second time that her lonely regular had had company. It disturbed her. Nobody's habits could be relied on any more.

Mott asked about Fraser and life in general, and Barraclough felt reluctant to tell him about the nightclub act and the nearness of his twice-postponed date of audition. He tried to convince himself that it was not shame that prevented him from mentioning it, but he was not sure.

"So you're still free then, I take it," said Mott.

"Well, yes, I suppose so."

"Good. Because the thing we discussed may be on again. Crazy, isn't it? So consider yourself back on the payroll as from now. Still only contingency planning, some basic requirements as before, but further emphasis on total untraceability of the real cause. The crate must sink, preferably over water. A confusing picture, isn't it?" The Brigadier laughed. "But you know what I mean. It's essential that the clues to the eventual discovery of a probable cause should be something natural. I mean technical, human error, whatever."

"Er . . ."

"Any questions?"

Barraclough was astonished by his own reaction to the job. If anything, he was disinclined to do it. But that was, of course, ridiculous. If he was called upon to do his duty, he would do his duty; no question about that. Except that . . . I must be going soft, he concluded. "It would have to mean a break-up in the air or something similarly sudden and disastrous to avoid the pilot sending any signals."

"Good thinking."

"But any sign of sabotage is out, you said."

"That's right."

"It's not easy."

"That's why we need you." There was just a whiffle of emphasis on the word *we*. Mott knew it would not be lost on Barraclough.

"You realize that the crew would not survive."

"Most unfortunate." And Mott raised his mental eyebrows: Getting squeamish in your old age, eh? "Any problems?"

"No, nothing, sir. It's just the timing of the job. It's so unexpected right now."

"Well, we can't control events, my boy, can we?" The Brigadier unfurled his evening paper so that the headline faced Barraclough: "Sarissas to Cloud the Sky . . . 300 Sales Confirmed."

"But that's a commercial aircraft."

"And?"

"I thought it was military."

"I never said that."

"That means a civilian crew and passengers."

"We'd pick a flight, if it ever came to that, which had no passengers on board. You seem shocked."

"To tell you the honest truth, sir, I'm surprised. As I understood it, we've always been involved with military operations. During the war and since the war—"

"But today this is the war. We fight on the economic front. For survival. With our back to the wall. And what we need is the spirit of Dunkirk. Or even the teeth-gritting determination of the Battle of Britain. Now we're fewer than the few, but survival still depends on victory in the air."

Barraclough was confused. This was too much from the Brigadier. It was not the real Mott somehow, though the sentences were right. "But the Sarissa is an American product."

"And?"

"It's a friendly country."

"That's what you think. And that's what we all would like to believe. But it seems that, in the commercial world, we have no allies; there're no friends, only enemies. Let me give you some examples. You remember the Tudor?"

"Vaguely."

"A fine aircraft, a world leader and British to the core. A couple of mysterious crashes, one of them in the Bermuda Triangle in the late 1940s, and potential British lead in four-engine passenger transport lost. To whom? Yes, the United States. Then the Comet disasters in the 1950s." With an impatient wave of two fingers he averted an interruption by Barraclough. "I know, I know. There were all those magnificently scientific findings about structural fatigue and all that, but I can tell you something—not all of us are convinced that there wasn't something much more sinister behind it. Why did those planes crash so conveniently into the sea where most of the wreckage would be lost? Oh yes, another crashed in India, but strangely enough the wreckage was buried or otherwise irretrievably disposed of straightaway. Right? The perfect crime. We know the technique, but was there a motive? Yes, the Comet was the first jet-powered passenger aircraft, a world-beater. Possible beneficiary of the crime? The United States aircraft industry. And more recently the Concorde. Do you really believe that ordinary citizens and environmentalists or whatever they call themselves caused all the holdups and trouble? Do you really believe that? Have you overlooked who the real beneficiaries of the whole Concorde fiasco will be?"

Barraclough found these strong, convincing arguments. And Mott had always been in the know. And the job was a challenge. It needed a planner of unique qualities. He was flattered. Except that mentally he had already retired. A short stage career would be a lovely flash to go out with, leading to a friendship with Sally and a life of contented, leisurely reminiscences. And how would all those people, including the Leopard, a true friend, react if he let them down at the last minute?

"Listen," said Mott warmly. "I know I sprang it on you out of the blue. You have to think it over. We're not soldiers any more. Well, I mean not in that sense. You know what I mean. Besides, all we're talking about is contingency planning for a possible emergency. You see, at the moment, the operation is still in the hands of active personnel on the payroll. The crash in Singapore had nothing to do with us of course. It was sheer luck. It raised serious doubts about the plane. Delayed new contracts and further development. At the moment it's perfectly satisfactory if those doubts can be stirred up once again by the pilot or somebody else making inquiries and accusations. Actually, we're about to activate one or two people in that direction. And this could be repeated in various ways again and again until . . . er . . . until the . . . You know what I mean. It's a competitive world."

"Where would I come in?"

"Ah. That's the point. If the investigation concludes with a complete exoneration of the aircraft, and if we still need more time, another accident would cause quite indefinite delays and so a fatal blow, particularly if there's no easy clue in the wreckage."

Barraclough felt like running away without a word. He mumbled lengthy apologies. Something about lack of time. Unexpected duties. Travel. Obligations accepted since the cancellation of the job. Mott understood. Or he said he understood. It deeply troubled Barraclough. He wanted to explain that to his old boss, but Mott had already gone. And as Barraclough looked up and saw people sipping tea and munching cakes, quite unexpectedly he began to feel free, inexplicably free. And it pleased him that from now on he could come in here just to enjoy himself like anybody else, on any day, without feeling duty-bound.

He stood up, pinched the cheek of the waitress, who almost fainted, paid his bill; and on his way out he gave Messrs. F and M something new to experience: the sound of whistling in this inner sanctum of alimentation.

With Timmy away, the house would have been depressingly empty and silent even without Candy's poignant mental absence. Her drinking made it only worse. The constant clinking of her glass, the cracking of fresh ice cubes choked by vodka, her smirk-and-stare each time he answered the telephone, her refusal to discuss the single Sarissa headline he had read again and again for two days ever since his meeting at the AIB . . . and now the phone. A girl.

"Captain Penn?"

"Yes."

She introduced herself as a researcher for BBC television. He was about to ring off. "Tonight we have a program about the aircraft industry with a lot of emphasis on the Sarissa, and we've been told that you might wish to talk to us."

"Who told you that?"

"I'm not sure if I can tell you, but hold on for a mo, will you?" A few seconds later she was back on the line. "Well, it was a Mr. White."

"White?"

"Yes, the brother of the flight engineer. You know, the one who was decapitated. I mean, you know . . ."

"I suggest you interview him."

"But he said, I mean the brother said—"

"Forgive me, but I'm not interested in what he said. I have nothing to contribute to your program."

Candy left without saying where she was going or how long she would be. Ten minutes later the phone rang again. A man this time. "What have you arranged with the BBC?"

"Who's that?"

"The program goes on the air in, say, seventy-six minutes, and if you want to make it—"

"Are you White?"

"Yes, how did you guess?"

"Now, listen—"

"No, Captain Penn, you listen to me. Because I'm calling you from Wales."

"From where?"

"You heard me. And I've got company."

"What do you mean?"

"You can guess what I mean. So listen carefully. On my travels in the Black Mountains I've picked up young Timothy."

"How much do you want?"

"Don't insult me, Captain. I don't want your money. And your son will come to no harm if you do as you're told."

"Which is?"

"My brother is dead. You or that bloody aircraft is responsible for his death. Nothing will bring him back, I know, but you owe him, we all owe his memory, at least the gesture to fight for air safety and prevent a repetition of the disaster. That plane must be grounded until the investigation is completed."

"I've no power to ground it."

"I know. But it would go a long way toward it if you made a really strong public statement on that program, beginning seventy-five minutes from now. The boy will be freed as soon as you've made your statement."

"Let me talk to him."

"Nope."

"Why not?"

"Because I don't want to. He's quite happy. Why excite him? He doesn't even realize what happened to him."

"And I say you're bluffing."

"Try me." There was a pause. A point of no return. If ever,

the bluff had to be called now. And they both knew it. "Well, Captain?"

"If I agree . . ."

"There's a good man. Just make it a strong statement."

"The case is *sub judice* and—"

"I know, I know. I don't want you to do anything illegal. Just say what your real opinion is, nothing more than what's already been said at the public hearing in Singapore."

"How will I know that you've released Timmy?"

"You'll have to find out. And until then you'll have to trust me. You have no choice."

"What if I withdraw my statement afterwards?"

"That's a risk I'll have to take. And the risk you'll have to take."

"I'll have to think about it."

"Naturally. You still have seventy-four minutes to think. And I'll know your decision from the program. Because if you think that I'll ring back to hear your decision, you're wrong. You might be tempted to set up some tracing operation with the police, and we don't want that, do we? We don't want to risk messing up young Timothy's red-blue-and-white-checked shirt, do we? So let's just say goodbye now as friends who share fond memories of a dead man."

The mountain cottage had no telephone. Perhaps the police could send someone there to find out what the situation was. But of course the police might just mess it up. Penn remembered the detective superintendent who had once asked him for advice concerning landing strips for small aircraft used for illegal immigration.

Penn dialed Scotland Yard and asked for Superintendent Bucken. He was lucky. The detective was there and understood the problem right away: "You certainly are in the shit, aren't you?" He suggested that Penn should go ahead, approach the BBC and make his statement. Bucken would contact the nearest police station. If it was more than seventy minutes' drive away, he would try to arrange a mountain-rescue helicopter to fly over the house and land nearby to investigate if possible. He would also try to locate or find out something about White through the engineer's widow.

"I never even knew that there was a brother," said Penn.

"I'll find him for you."

"Wasn't he stupid to give his name?"

"Why? It's your word against his. It won't be easy to prosecute him unless we catch him with some evidence on him. But don't worry. If we can't get him through the courts, I'll give you his address and promise to turn away while you settle your score. Now get on to the BBC."

What Bucken did not mention was the risk that, against White, there could be only one valuable witness: the boy. And the man would know that, too.

There was no time to apply makeup or hold some preliminary discussion as they rushed Penn into the studio to open the program with him. The lights were hot, the chair was low, his long legs in the way somehow all the time, people around a table in the background, but he had no idea who they were; and the interviewer introduced him to the audience with a touch of ill-disguised animosity. Penn half heard him talk about the Sarissa, and the clichés failed to stir him, but when he noticed that more and more people were gathering behind the window of the director's box, even he began to sense that tomorrow's headlines could be seen in the offing.

Penn stared at the camera and repeated his Singapore statement about the accident. He tried to look gloomy so as to make it sufficiently convincing for White.

"This is a very serious point, indeed," he heard someone saying. "So the question is What would you regard as the correct course of action?" But Penn's mind was elsewhere. How could he wink at the camera without looking foolish, what secret signal of encouragement could he give Timmy? "Captain? Captain Penn . . ."

"Yes."

"Are you all right, Captain?"

"Yes, yes of course. Sorry. What was your question?"

"Well, let me be blunt. Do you recommend the grounding of the aircraft, and I mean all Sarissas?"

"It's not for me to say."

"But you do believe that the precautions being taken are inadequate."

"I didn't say that."

"Your presence here and now certainly indicates something of that nature."

"Please yourself."

"Why else would you be here?"

Penn noticed some commotion in the director's box. It was hard to see the faces in there behind the glittering glass. The lights began to blind him as he kept looking up.

"Captain Penn?"

"Yes?"

"Would you care to say why you decided to speak out after all?"

Bucken was in there. Were they trying to kick him out? Was he gesticulating?

"Would it be unfair to assume," the interviewer pressed on, "that, in the light of your strong views on the matter, you were compelled to take this major step?"

"What do you mean, compelled?" Penn saw Bucken at the window. Two men tried to pull him away, but the detective shook them off and held up his thumb. Timmy was all right. It could have no other meaning. He might be watching the program right now. Bucken smiled and retreated into the darker part of the box. Penn turned to face the interviewer. This was the moment when he could retract the statement and explain his presence if necessary. Bucken would back him up. It was the right thing to do, he knew. But the expression on his face seemed to disagree. And the words that reached his lips attained a long-lost edge. "What the hell do you mean, compelled? Nobody tells me what to do. It was my decision to be here." It was not true. But he meant it. The blackmail situation gave him the impetus to do what he knew he wanted to anyway. And Timmy might see him as he stood up and fought.

"I mean that you might have been compelled by feeling guilty about your silence."

"Which was not the case. I had to raise my voice only because of the recent huge sales of the aircraft. Because this tremendously increases the risk. Until now, we could rightly suppose that the fault which caused my accident in Singapore was freakish to an extreme, almost unique and unlikely to recur in other aircraft already in service before the investigators have a chance to find it. But—and that's a big but—the new contract opens the floodgates. The number of Sarissas in the sky will multiply faster than the investigation can proceed. With that, the risk potential will increase not only proportionately but in some geometrical progression. And that may cause at least one major disaster. I believe that the victory march of this undoubtedly magnificent aircraft must be slowed down."

The rest of his words were lost in an uproar. Some people in the studio, including cameramen and technical staff, applauded. Others shouted abuse. The interviewer tried desperately to cool the scene to the level of ever-so-jolly public laceration of guests in routine television debates. He was not very successful.

Bucken waited for Penn at the door. In a loud whisper, to make himself heard over the noise, he told Penn, "The kid was out with his friend and the family all day in the mountains. They're back at the cottage now, everything okay. There was no"—he glanced around—"nothing unusual happened."

"Then White . . ."

"The engineer had no brother. Never had one. Somebody just invented him."

"But whoever that was must have known where Timmy

was and took advantage of the situation. It means . . ."

Bucken nodded. "I know what it means. We've taken some precautions."

Now it began to dawn on Penn how lucky he had been not to retract anything, not to use the kidnap as an explanation. He would have looked ridiculous with the excuse of a nonexistent person committing a kidnap that had never happened. He took a deep breath and smiled. The choice had been served to him on a plate, but the decision had been his own. Entirely.

Within the next hour, there were dramatic reactions to the news of Penn's statement everywhere. Wall Street reported some sporadic but immediate selling of AeroCorp shares before the Exchange closed. The stock fell almost two dollars a share. Airlines flying Sarissas began to receive cancellations. SupraNat, flag carrier of the Sarissa, suffered most, though their spokesman denied most adamantly that the situation could be described as anything like panicky. An influential French aviation correspondent was interviewed on radio. Subsequently he was widely quoted as saying that "SupraNat was not really an airline but a pilot project for a new minting process."

Mott received a single telephone call. It came from Corsica and he appreciated it. Not often did his current employers acknowledge his existence at all, let alone contact him directly.

"Congratulations."

Mott was inclined to say, It's easy if you know how, but restricted himself to a dignified "Thank you, sir."

"Perhaps you'd care to join us for a vacation on the island."

A tempting offer, and most gratifying, too, but he turned it down politely. Once his schemes had the necessary momentum, he liked to push even harder to keep at least one step ahead of the opposition. And he had yet to find a replacement to do the contingency planning. Most inconvenient and annoying. He wondered if he could find a way to make Barraclough change his mind.

"Will anybody get the goddamn thing out of my hair?" Drayton asked in a loud whisper as he opened his safe and took out Termine's file, bulging with information on Penn. "Use it," he said and scanned the faces around him. "And use your initiative. We have nothing to hide. It's in our own goddamn interest to get the goddamn airplane as safe as possible, but we're entitled to defend ourselves against malicious attacks. Aren't we? Aren't we?"

Confused nods and head shakes answered him. Singer, Ms. Etch and a select band of AeroCorp publicists and other executives found it difficult to choose; a nod could imply agreement as well as a denial of entitlement to self-defense. A shake could dispute the president's view.

"All we're asking for is that they should give us a fair chance to clear up the goddamn thing. Is that too much? We don't want anything illegal or illegitimate. We want to de-emphasize the problem, and make that goddamn pilot shut up. That's all."

Drayton was in a hurry; he was already late after a lunch with a Saudi delegation which appeared to be keen on picking up a fleet of standard Sarissas as well as a few dolled-up "specials" complete with a revolving mosque compartment which would be controlled by a direction-finder compass to focus it on Mecca at all times. Had there not been a stupid TV program in London, Drayton might have used the lunch as the opportunity to make a first announcement about Mark 2, the new Whispering Sarissa. Now it would have to wait. Drayton studied the faces once more, at a leisurely pace this time. Yes, there was hope for AeroCorp. Everybody in that room had a big personal stake in it.

As chief executive, Drayton always firmly subscribed to the idea of letting people be individuals who used their brains not their ears to decide what was best for AeroCorp, and it was now up to his executives to interpret his directives.

Vice-president Wheeler had no doubts about his job. He settled down to dial, lean on, stonewall or reward personally his endless series of press, PR and advertising contacts.

Ms. Etch selected a few unlisted numbers in Washington. People on and around the Hill owed a great deal of goodwill to AeroCorp. Drayton had always been generous with his favors —and nobody was better placed than Ms. Etch to remind them with her infallible memory which was a vast store of gossip and factual tidbits garnered from obscure sources such as Salah Termine.

Singer told his secretary to track down Senator Letson in Washington. "Good news, Alvin, good news," he enthused at once when the Senator was on the line. "Charles has authorized me to tell you that the junket you've planned for some of your people up there is on."

"Junket?"

"Well, I was joking of course. But you know which delegation I'm talking about."

"Sure."

"You give me the final details, Far East, Australia via Europe, you name the itinerary and the destination and leave the rest to us. We know how overworked the Eighty-ninth is. We're only too pleased to oblige."

"I appreciate that, Henry, I sure do."

Bastard, thought Singer. The junket budget for using the 89th Military Airlift Wing must already be pretty exhausted if Letson was pressing so very hard for a free flight somewhere. Not that Singer was against the principle. He only despised politicians and businessmen who had sung too readily when the recent international bribery scandals were revealed. What are we, he would frequently exclaim, a nation of masochists? A nation of flashers with a zeal for full-frontal politico-economic self-exposure? In his view, public self-flagellation on a national scale was not only suicidal but also naïve. He was a shameless champion of secrecy. Confidential deals depended on trust, and he found unilateral revelations as dishonest as pocketing perks without reciprocating as expected. Letson's hypocrisy was another of his pet hates. The Senator was a much-publicized scourge of corruption and a fearless condemner of bribes, while receiving—and often blatantly extorting—substantial favors from trusted "friends" such as Drayton. Had it been anybody else, Singer would have tried to be more subtle with his next suggestion—a direct demand for Letson to deliver—but now the pressure was on, and Singer had no time to playact or pussyfoot. "Incidentally, we'll have a specially converted luxury Sarissa up there next week. Would you like it to drop in for a little show at Andrews?"

"Would *I* like it?"

"Well, since the base is just across the road, so to speak . . . "

Letson answered with a long-drawn "yeeeah" and let it hang in the air.

"What I mean is that if you wanted to arrange something, a quick visit or anything like that, we'd gladly do it for the President."

"That's out of the question."

"No—no, you misunderstood me." Singer back-pedaled fast and cursed the Senator, who was either too slow or wanted to make him sweat. "I wasn't suggesting a flight. Oh no. All I had in mind was what you yourself mentioned to me in Washington the other day. I mean, with millions of American citizens living below the unofficial poverty line and with all the jobs dependent on the success of our Sarissa, I thought the President might want to *see* for himself the aircraft that would bring all those hard-earned millions and prestige, prestige above all, to our country."

"I see what you mean."

"Good, that's good. It could be just a routine visit, perhaps *en passant* to *Air Force One* if he's off to somewhere, especially if we had a chance to park the Sarissa in the right place." Letson was still not saying anything, and Singer knew why. Well, if he was paid to sweat, sweat he would. "No flying of course, just natural curiosity. He'd walk up the stairs and back, a few informal shots—there're bound to be cameramen." The pictures would then find their way to the press, prospective buyers would be given complimentary copies with Drayton's autograph, and if anybody misinterpreted the scene, well, who would bother to dispute or deny that the Sarissa was safe enough for the President to fly in?

"I'll see what I can do."

"I'm sure you will, Alvin, I'm sure you will. I'll tell Charles about it. He'll be delighted with *your* idea."

The emphasis conveyed the message. Letson sounded more cheerful now. "Well, it's our duty to prevent U.S. products from being forced into a position of disadvantage in the competitive international marketplace."

"Right. And, Alvin, I very much enjoyed our dinner the other night."

"You did? Good. I'm glad you didn't forget."

"Forget?" Damn you, Alvin, Singer thought, it's your turn to sweat. "Er . . ."

"What we discussed."

"Let me see . . . new French aircraft . . . the proliferation of massage parlors . . . European co-production projects . . ."

"People, Henry, people."

"But of course I remember." How could he forget when Letson had spent half the evening pushing for a break for some aviation-minded young man? Except that Singer could not yet figure out whether the young man was Letson's relative or somebody connected with the jet-black Southern belle who seemed to be Letson's third elbow these days and whom he desperately tried to impress throughout the dinner. "Yeah. I've already mentioned it to Charles," which was a lie, "and he thinks that everybody should be given a fair chance," which would be a likely answer from Drayton, who would want to retain the prospect of a job as a lever in the endless Byzantine mass of bargaining and swapping favors.

"Suits me, Henry, suits me. A fair chance is what we all want, no more."

"Bastard," hissed Singer as he hung up and made a mental note to talk to Drayton about Letson. The Senator seemed to have forgotten the crisis in Arizona when local politicians had fallen like ninepins, but those in the good books of AeroCorp seemed to have a charmed political life. Singer sent a longing glance toward the floor-to-ceiling bookshelf that doubled as the door of a wall-to-wall bar—and poured mineral water into an old crystal goblet which gave the liquid at least the color of whiskey. He felt a little sorry for himself; but, as his father used to say, *Ein Mann, ein Wort,* and Anna had made him promise. She was intent on making him lose weight, because she swore that thinner men were better in bed. Which remained to be seen. He shivered as he swallowed. He positively disliked water. It did not wash away the bitterness of the Letson conversation, and failed to warm him to his next task—calling London to track down Termine.

Mara had a thoroughly frustrating day. Most people she hoped to interview in connection with various Sarissa incidents seemed to have vanished. She chased a Captain Mellou, who allegedly had had a "problem situation" while working for AeroCorp on VIP flights. She was told that Mellou was in and out of the country and that it was up to him to return the calls if he wanted to. She never heard from him. She managed to speak to Captain Simms, who had been in one of the Clear Air Turbulence cases. She asked for a meeting.

"What do you want to talk about?"

"Nothing special. Just a chat."

"What about?"

"CAT."

"In general?"

"I believe you had some experience."

"Yeah . . . I had . . ."

"Well, how about tomorrow?"

"I'll . . . I'll call you back."

He did, too, within twenty minutes, but only to say that everything about his CAT experience was in his original report with nothing to add.

In the evening she saw an edited version of Penn's TV appearance. She knew it was past midnight in London, but she called him nevertheless. There was no answer. At dawn GMT there was still no answer. She then called a journalist friend in London, who told her that Penn had probably spent the night in a hotel because his house was besieged by the press.

Mara was ready for bed when her phone rang. It was Linda Greenway, a stewardess she once worked with.

"I hear you were looking for me."

"Was I?"

"Well, perhaps you didn't know it was me. Mrs. Waller. I got married last year."

"Congratulations."

"Make it a double. I divorced him two months later. But I don't think you wanted me to talk about that."

"No. I believe you've been in a CAT incident."

"Who hasn't?"

"Aboard a Sarissa. With a Captain Johnson, about six months ago."

"Oh."

"Oh what?"

"Listen, honey . . . No, tell me first, can you make it off the record?"

"If I have to."

"Okay. Not that I can tell you much about the case itself. A bit of turbulence at dinnertime. We dropped a few thousand feet, I guess. The big hoo-ha among the passengers, peas all over the place and salad with French dressing even in the john, then free Saricolas and Saribrandy for everyone, and boom day for the dry cleaners after landing, that's all. But there's something else."

"Go on."

"Don't ask me why, but your name is an expletive everywhere in the business."

"Anything official?"

"No. Just a dribble down the grapevine."

"Who told you about it?"

"Come on, honey, don't ask me that."

"Sorry."

"That's all right. As long as you understand that there's nothing personal."

"I do."

"Good. Then I'll tell you what. Let me know if I can help in any way. Just don't call me in the office. I'll give you my home number."

"Oh, it's like that, is it?"

"Don't be like that. You know that everybody likes and respects you in the industry, but they say there's something fishy going on which nobody quite understands and so they don't want to be involved."

"Can you tell me what the rumor is?"

"Yeah. They say you fell out with somebody high up at AeroCorp, and that's why you're stirring the shit on the Sarissa."

"Thanks for telling me. At least now I know."

Chief Pilot Brown felt like a deep sea diver who had lost his helmet. The pressure was unbearable. His sleepless eyes stared down on a misty morning over the Liffey, and he felt as if the twin towers of the SupraNat head office were swaying under his feet, ready to collapse into Dublin's river. Somehow, he had become the focus of all attention, press, superiors, colleagues and authorities, everybody who had anything to do with the

Sarissa seemed to want him and him alone on the telephone, all telex lines and in person; and it was an open secret that within the next hour he would have to disown Penn. That he hated the idea of kicking his friend in the teeth made it only worse. A lung-splitting shouting match over the telephone would have helped him to vent the pressure, but Penn remained so infuriatingly cool and unapologetic.

"You do understand, don't you, that there must be some disciplinary action and your pay will be stopped."

"I understand."

"No, you don't, Corrie, you don't understand a single bloody word. We'll have to dissociate ourselves completely from you, from every word you say, from everything you do—everything, everything, everything!"

"Naturally."

"What the fuck do you mean *naturally?*"

"Only that I had no choice."

"You're mad!"

"I must fight against what I believe to be a major hazard, and I must clear my name."

"Oh! Is that what you want? Clear your name, right? Well, I must say, you've made a head start. Great. Just look at any rag of the world press from the Wagga Wagga *Daily Advertiser* to the Wilmington *Evening Journal.* You're free game for every petty scribbler who cares to print that your name is a four-letter word."

Penn did not try to argue. He knew he could not, even if he wanted to. It seemed incredible what an overpowering amount of information and fact-related misinformation about him had suddenly become available to press, TV and radio stations throughout the world. There were so many details about his life in circulation, and there were so many well-prepared attempts at finding weak spots in his background, that Penn wondered who had dug it all up for them, and when.

They attacked his former employers, the Swiss charter airline. But they also questioned his conduct. Why had he not resigned sooner? Why had he let them push him beyond the legal threshold of fatigue? They spoke about his fights in South America. The dangerous missions. The series of Mickey Mouse jobs. The risks. The women. His heroism in saving children. His heroism in rescuing a man from captivity—a man who eventually became the head of an Equatorian republic and set up a national airline under Captain Brown, giving Penn his return ticket to regular commercial aviation. Most stories were not libelous, only credit-damaging by innuendo. If he answered them all, it would only fatten the headlines.

The self-destructive fury of impotence made Penn's stomach turn over and over. And yet that was not all. A vast amount of detail about the Paya Lebar accident was now being discussed. Passengers were quoted as saying that "the Captain seemed obviously embarrassed, even worried about the long delays because of all those ballet VIP's on board." The unasked question was in every reader's mind: Was he in too much of a hurry to take off? Was he pushing too hard? Some papers raised the old problems of "allowable deficiencies" with which aircraft were permitted to operate. Was too much left to the pilot's discretion? What was the cumulative effect of the difficulties at Singapore that night? Was the pilot's state of mind an allowable deficiency? Was the pilot the best man to judge his own state of mind? Was there too much pressure on the pilot to get away? Somehow, each of the implied accusations pointed ultimately at Penn. Yes, normally it was acceptable to take off with a long list of minor snags, with deficiencies ranging from the loss of a fuel gauge to having one of four generators inoperable, but was the combination of marginal visibility, bad weather, strike delay, search for a missing passenger, threat of sabotage, false engine fire warnings, messy communications and "personal problems" too much of a liability, one that should have been recognized by the Captain?

References to the personal problems hurt most. Somebody

must have tricked stewardess Tiny Malloy into a mention of "Captain Penn's night out with a lady journalist before the flight." Tiny telephoned the head office as soon as it appeared in print and offered to explain. She obviously did not mean that the outing had impaired Penn's ability to fly safely; but explanations would only have made it worse. The damage had already been done. And both Brown and Penn knew it.

"Well, in some cases, I'll have marvelous opportunities to sue for libel," said Penn.

"No doubt about that. And you'll win, too. With damages awarded and banner headlines," Brown enthused. "But how long will it take? How many years will the court cases keep you out of that left-hand seat? You should have thought about that and about that fucking Bloody Mary before you opened your big mouth!"

"You know it was toothless. No alcohol in it."

"Of course I know. And you know it, too. But who'll believe you?"

"Mara was there."

"A fine witness."

"The barman may remember."

"If he's still there. Stop kidding yourself, Corrie."

All Penn wanted at the moment was some sleep. He had driven to Wales and back with Timmy during the night, and because Candy had not yet returned home from wherever she was, he had left the child with her mother. Penn had breakfast with them, then read the first newspaper reports. When he opened the kitchen window to get rid of the thick smoke of burnt toast, he heard Timmy proudly telling the boy next door, "Here, that's my dad in every paper."

"Big deal. My dad shook hands with the man who knew Pele."

When Penn left the house he had the strange feeling of being followed by a motorcyclist. Ridiculous. Who on earth would want to follow him? Besides, all men in helmet and goggles and leather looked alike.

Stacey recognized Penn's voice on the telephone right away. "I thought you might call. You'd better come and see me."

"Thanks."

"You were very foolish. It was a damnable thing to do. And that's official."

"It sounds as if privately—"

"I don't care what it sounds like. I mean it's up to you, isn't it?"

Penn could hear encouragement in his voice and he was grateful. On his way to the Strand, absentmindedly he chose the wrong lane to leave Trafalgar Square. It would have been a struggle to cut across, so he rounded Nelson's Column once more. As he looked into the mirror, there was no motorcyclist behind him, but a silver hump on the road, a Porsche which seemed familiar. Hadn't it been in the lane on his right when he went around the first time? He dismissed the thought. He was disturbed, tired and strung up, probably a short step away from persecution mania.

"With or without?" asked the creature in Stacey's office, and this time Penn gave the correct answer. Stacey was on the phone and signaled to him to sit down. Penn was fascinated by a Red Admiral set in a block of clear plastic. There were several other butterflies on the desk in similar miniature showcases which made them look more alive than the live ones.

Stacey rang off and viewed Penn with all the severity of the indelible frown, but an unruly smile lurked in the corner of his eye and gave the game away. "As I said, you are a fool, aren't you?"

"What worries me is that—"

"Don't tell me. Anything you say may be taken down and used against you as evidence. Or something like that. Besides, I have enough, thank you, to worry about. But it's odd how everybody seems to have readily available information about you."

The creature brought them coffee.

"Thank you, Miss Beaver."

Penn guessed it must be a perfectly apt nickname and noted that probably the creature disliked it because she reacted with a most unfriendly grunt which released a cloud of smoke from her lungs. He wondered if the coffee was poisoned. She sank behind huge stacks of Sarissa documents on a twelve-foot desk, and from then on only the smoke signals rising at regular intervals revealed her continued presence. With a gesture toward her papers, Stacey said, "Just a few thousand details of weight reductions and other design modifications."

"What are you looking for?"

"Oh, nothing specific. Just routine, and it keeps us busy for quite a while. At least they can't make us redundant until we finish it, which is nothing to sneeze at these days. Still, if it ever came to that, I'd prefer to be made redundant, fired, kicked out, almost anything rather than be 'selected out' like this friend of mine."

"I like that." Penn smiled. "Where was he selected out of or is it out from?"

"The American State Department." The joke vanished from his voice and eyes. "He, like my other private informers, tried to help me unofficially in obtaining some information about Sarissa incidents, internal memos and other ideas for party games. His selection-out came at the most inconvenient moment. A coincidence, I'd say, wouldn't you?"

"Are you saying that Singapore wasn't my fault?"

"I don't know. And to be quite frank with you, I don't give a damn. I chase facts, that's all. Like I chase butterflies, set them in plastic, put them on show and get my kicks out of people saying how marvelous. But let's stick to your problem. Once you've started, you'll have to keep answering some questions, I expect. I thought it might help if you refreshed your memory about certain facts, such as statements by witnesses, things that passengers really said, not what they remember they said. And preferably not what somebody might have taken down and neatly summarized for what would be a brief strictly-to-the-point though meaningless model of a statement, like this one, here." Stacey was clearly working himself into a fury. "It's an American witness's account of a Sarissa incident. According to a stewardess, the 'passengers verbalized their discomfort.' Ver-ba-lized! Verbalized, if you please. Can you imagine a stewardess saying that? Can you imagine passengers verbalizing their discomfort while the aircraft is buffeting in a pocket of turbulence and drops out of the sky like it had something against the principle of heavier-than-air flying? How would you verbalize it, Captain?"

"Why don't you look at the originals?"

"These are the originals, I'm told. Or at least the ones which had been kept as originals."

The door opened. A man with a blond bushy mustache looked in and, without saying a word, left. He did not even bother to shut the door.

"It's not a bloody railway station," Stacey shouted after him.

Penn spent the day in the office reading documents. Yet the "witnesses" stack seemed almost intact by the evening. Stacey offered to let him borrow the photostats of passengers' statements for the night. The Beaver put them into a large buff "On Her Majesty's Service" envelope. As it was Friday night and nobody would be in the office on Saturday, he promised to return everything to Stacey's house, not very far from his own, in the morning.

Before he left, he called his home. There was no answer. He toyed with the idea of reporting to the police that his wife was missing, but first he called her mother, who told him that Candy had telephoned only to say that she was all right and enjoying herself.

The underground car park was almost empty by now, and

Penn's car stood on its own. In the semidarkness, something struck him as odd about it. Some seventy yards away, he could not figure out what it was. As he approached, it appeared that the car was leaning a little toward him. At about thirty yards, he saw that the front nearside tire had gone down. Bad luck. He did not relish the thought of changing wheels just now. Then he noticed that the rear nearside tire was also completely flat. A most unlikely coincidence. He wanted a moment to think. After a grossly overaccentuated glance at his shoes, he stooped and pretended to retie his laces. That he wore slip-on moccasins without laces would not be visible from even a few feet away, he was sure.

In the car opposite his own somebody moved. Somebody with a bushy mustache, Penn would have sworn. And that car was a silver Porsche. Penn stood up, looked at his watch, and tried to act like a man who had second thoughts about the car and changed his mind. Hoping that the pantomime was realistic enough to convince whoever was watching him, he turned to leave unhurriedly. But, a second later, he knew he had not fooled anyone. He heard the click as the door of a car opened, then feet, at least four feet, coming up fast behind him.

He could have tried to run for it but it was impossible to guess how fast those behind him were. If he turned to face them, escape would be more difficult. He chose to rely on his ears since he hoped to be level with a swing door to the stairs by the time they had caught up with him. They were almost there. The patter of running feet slowed to a shuffle. Penn knew they would now decide how to tackle him. If they chose to hit him over the head, he hoped to detect the ominous rustle of clothes, an arm cutting the air . . .

The door. Penn half turned and virtually dived through in a single move. But he stopped and held the metal fire door at the same time. And more by instinct than deliberate timing, he let the delayed door fly behind him as he ran up the stairs. A dull thud told him that at least some damage had been done. He did not stop to check it.

The Strand was dark and almost deserted. No taxis, no bus in sight. Penn could have turned into one of the side streets, but those were bound to be dead at this time, much more suitable for an attack. He looked back. At least nobody was following him. Apart from this reassurance, all he wanted at the moment was time to think. Who was after him? And why? He could not go to the police. What was there to say? That he thought someone might attack him? That two of his tires were down simultaneously? Well, sir, vandalism these days . . . Besides, did they hurt you, sir? No. Hit you? No. Say anything? No.

He kept vainly looking for taxis. He turned back yet again —and he was a few seconds late. The silver Porsche had caught up with him. The door flew open and the man with the mustache came at him swinging a spanner. Penn ducked to protect his head, but the man, rather than trying to hit him, went straight for the envelope, then turned to escape with it. Balanced on one arm, Penn kicked out, hooking his feet in full flight. By the time the attacker hit the pavement and blood spurted from his nose, Penn was up and snatching the envelope back. That was when the driver joined in the melee with a hammer blow aimed at Penn's temple. The pilot staggered back, off balance, but the driver was slow to exploit the advantage. Both men kicked out at the same time, but Penn's leg was longer, and although it missed its primary target, his heel hit bone in the driver's hip. The rewarding cry of anguish brought back the long-forgotten mean joy of fighting and drawing blood. Penn knew that the pain he had caused was sharp but short-lived, giving him just enough time to have a free go with his fists; and the temptation was great. Though not completely incapacitated, both his attackers were injured, and he knew he could finalize their defeat. Yet, if they were armed, there would be a risk of losing not only the battle but also the envelope. It was clear that they wanted him less than the papers. He owed it to Stacey to protect them.

Now Penn ran for it. But the momentary hesitation cost him most of the advantage. They were no more than twenty feet behind him. If only he could reach Charing Cross Station and disappear in the crowd . . .

Unfortunately, the station was well past its rush hour, and much of the main concourse had been evacuated for redecoration and roof repairs. Late commuters pretended to see nothing or swore and stared and got out of the way. Steeplejacks and painters enjoyed their grandstand view from mobile platforms and half-finished scaffolding. Nobody seemed inclined to interfere with the pursuit. Penn hurtled down the stairs of the lavatory, which, he remembered, had two exits. He burst through the door and turned at once to crouch behind the attendant's cubicle.

Within seconds, the two men arrived. They took a quick glance around, then one of them ran through to the exit at the far end while the driver kicked in every door to make sure that Penn was not inside.

"Very flattering, my dear," cooed one of the sitters. With his trousers down, he followed the driver out and pinched his chin. "Don't be shy, dear. Love comes in the most unexpected places."

That was a good enough cue for Penn. But he still could not gain more than thirty yards on his pursuers, who were now shouting, "Thief! He's got government papers."

Penn saw at once that this spelled trouble. Her Majesty's conspicuous brown envelope was too well known to anyone. He sprinted down platform 3. On both sides out-of-breath trains were puffing in slowly, and a bunch of hikers spread out in front of him, ready to have a go at the thief. It was too late to dodge them. Blows came from all angles. As he fell, a few of them kicked him, but he managed to roll free and grab a light scaffolding pole. He swung it around viciously to create some space, then charged through the gap, jumped into the pit of the track and scrambled up on the far side out of the path of the approaching train. He bruised his face and shoulder, but he reckoned he now had perhaps thirty seconds to stuff the documents into his pockets and pick up a newspaper to refill the envelope, which he then quickly sealed.

The train was still moving, but the two men were already on it. Penn struggled to get up, overemphasizing his injuries, and when the men jumped off the train, he ran, stumbled and dropped the envelope "accidentally." A few yards away he stopped and turned. The driver had already picked up the envelope. Penn now had to gamble on the assumption that they did not want to hurt him if they had the documents. So he leapt toward them yelling, "Give it to me," as menacingly as he could.

It worked. The men were not eager to fight him or explain to the policeman at the far end of the track why this time *they* had government papers in their possession. They escaped.

Penn called his home again. Still no answer. He did not want to go into the empty house, prepare food for himself and spend the night alone waiting for Candy, who would probably turn up drunk. He decided to book into the nearest hotel. Except that he never got beyond the reception desk. He was about to raise his voice when he caught a glimpse of himself in a mirror. And a frightful sight he was with his face bruised and bloodied, his clothes torn and dirty. He returned to the station for a quick wash and clean-up and only then did he realize that every bone in his body ached, his lips and left eye had begun to swell, at least one tooth was loose, and blood clots in his mouth and nose were filling him with revulsion. If it was hard to regain his taste for fighting, it turned out to be an almost insurmountable problem relearning the youthful art of coping with injuries.

A taxi driver took a good look at him and, with a keen judgment of character, suggested a hotel of suitably dubious clientele. It was a perfect choice. They took his money in advance, charged extra for a bath and a surcharge for hot water, but nobody was interested in his gibberish about some accident, and he was too tired to go elsewhere.

In a state of dejection, he lay on the edge of the bed so as to keep out of the crater in the middle, and for the first time since Singapore he was unable to fight off the lure of thinking about Mara. The warmth of her voice, the ripples her ribs gave the skin below her breast, the total abandon of her lovemaking and the ready tears of fulfillment. The memory was so vivid that if he closed his eyes he would have mistaken a pillow for her body. He missed her. He knew he had missed her all the time. But only now did he allow himself to admit that he had never missed anybody like that. He wished he knew whom she had been seeing since Singapore, what happened to the "close friend" at whose instigation she had come to interview him in the first place. But Penn was married; he felt he had no right to ask questions about her friends.

He got up and read the passengers' statements through the night. He found nothing useful. There could be nothing useful for his attackers either. But they did not know that. And perhaps it did not matter to them. Probably all they wanted to discover was what Stacey had given him and how much Stacey might know. The question was Who would need that information? Competitors had an interest in forcing Penn to stir up a scandal. AeroCorp would want to silence him. They both would need to know how the investigation was progressing. He would have to warn Stacey. And he would have to see the originals of the statements. Weren't there any tape recordings of the initial interviews?

The question gave him an irresistible excuse to telephone Mara, even though it would be midnight in Washington. Now the operator treated him with utter reverence, because she probably thought that he was Mafia—nobody had ever called America from that hotel—although she still insisted on the payment for the call in advance. When at last Penn heard

Mara's voice, he was on the verge of telling her how much he loved her. But the unquestionable presence of the operator on the line prevented him from saying everything he meant to say. So he only inquired about the progress she had made. She was more interested in talking about him and trying to find out why he sounded so tired.

"Couldn't sleep, that's all."

"I don't believe you."

"It's true. I had a lot to read. By the way, do you think you could find the originals of various witness records for me? I mean the notes or tapes or whatever, not the signed reports and formal statements."

She promised to try.

Drayton paused and cleared his throat purely for effect, then one by one he slowly looked at each member of his inner circle of executives seated now around the huge buhl-inlaid table in the private dining room adjoining his office. Then he smiled. "Gentlemen . . . it's Farnborough."

Nobody needed any explanation. The Whispering Sarissa would make its debut at the Farnborough air show, and the execution of Drayton's grand design would move into top gear.

Drayton listened to the standing ovation, joined in with the mutual handshakes, toasts and backslapping, then made his second announcement: "We'll have only a flying display on the first day with a special flight straight from here to Farnborough, which may be good publicity, especially if we break the West Coast-to-London maximum speed and minimum fuel consumption records. SupraNat will announce a large initial purchase there and then during the fly-past, and we'll open the goddamn order books on the second day of the show, when we bring back the airplane to join the static display."

He sat back to enjoy a second round of applause for his strategic genius. Pity that Mara was not there to share the fun and be impressed. He had some great ideas for a celebration of this occasion. Patience, he said to himself, patience. The prospect cheered him and, deciding to be magnanimous, he told Singer to let Mara have the scoop about Mark 2 and the timing.

Penn packed away the documents and ordered a cab to take him home. It was past seven in the morning, with sunshine and clear sky, but the lights were on in the bedroom, he noticed while paying the fare. So Candy was back. She liked to sleep with the lights on when she was drunk.

In the hall there was a dark spot on the floor. It was a pilot's cap. On the stairs he saw a junior pilot's jacket. On the landing, a chief steward's uniform in a heap. The bedroom door was wide open. Sandwiched between two men, both of them fast asleep, Penn saw Candy in their extra-large double bed. They shared a single sheet for cover.

She sat up with a defiant smile and let the sheet drop to her waist. As if she needed to emphasize her nudity.

"And where have you been, darling?" She giggled. Normally, sex sobered her up, so this time, Penn could tell, she was playacting to convey the memory of what jolly orgasms were had by all.

He walked to the bed and took the wrist of the man on the near side. He pulled him off the bed and let him drop.

"Now what the hell . . ."

Penn viewed him with indifference. He felt no anger toward him, no jealousy. "Out," he said quietly. The other man opened his eyes. "And you. Out." Both of them were young and drunk with sleep. Penn raised his voice only slightly. "Out."

It took the two only a minute to grab their clothes and leave the house. Candy was shouting abuse at all three men, telling her lovers to stand and fight and urging her husband to piss off, but nobody listened. She jumped out of bed and stood in front of Penn with her hips pushed out provocatively. "All right, go on, hit me. Go on. Will you kick me too? Or don't you love me any more?"

Penn turned to leave. She caught him from behind and rubbed herself against his back. He shook himself free and started down the stairs. She ran after him, caught up with him in the hall and began an alcoholic belly-dance routine. "Won't you beat me, luv?" She had lost her much-worked-on accent and style. "Don't you want me to bend over, then? That would be somethin' new, wouldn't it? And I wouldn't mind somethin' new, I'm sure. . . . Or would 'is lordship prefer to exercise 'is conjugal rights 'ere and now? Which will it be then?"

Penn watched himself from 30,000 feet up. An impassive, unruffled, disinterested man in the flat landscape of a mental void. The sight was barren and featureless, just as even the Pyrenees could lose their dramatic impact from up there. The aerial view also dwarfed the monstrous waves of turmoil inside him. And Candy? Her furious nude antics between the sumptuous flower arrangement and the umbrellas looked unimpressive, not even ridiculous.

He walked away without a word. In the living room, he collapsed in an armchair and gazed at the telephone, his silent companion for the past few months. It conjured up the vision of Mara for a second, but he dismissed it urgently. The dirt in the house must not contaminate it. He tried to introduce some order in his mind, and the most painful realization was that he did not feel hurt. Although he always dodged the issue and refused to put the truth into words, deep down he knew that Candy could never hurt him, whatever she did. Because she did not matter. She was merely a prop to the lie he had chosen to live, the dream that had to be acted out continuously to create the life and home he wanted to give Timmy. And the lies were well justified, for the love the child received was real, and the outward elements of the show made him feel happy and secure, Penn was convinced. Timmy obviously enjoyed their good life, their home and numerous friends, their travels and the opulence that was still within the grasp and appreciation of a not-too-spoiled child, and he took pride in having a beautiful mother and a pilot father.

Early on, Penn used to have plenty of doubts, but he silenced them all, fighting like a maniac to shatter the inherited vicious circle of unhappy children from cracked homes creating misery marriages with broken-hearted offspring. Now he dreaded the day when Timmy would ask more searching questions and he would have to try to explain that the lack of happiness was not the equivalent of unhappiness.

Shuffling feet—the chuckle of liquid leaving the bottle—Penn became aware of Candy trying to attract his attention. He looked up. Wrapped in his raincoat, she had just stepped out of a glossy men's magazine. She's really two-dimensional, thought Penn, yet not without the sex appeal of a World War II sailors' pin-up. He felt ashamed of the past decade spent with a magazine tearsheet and of mistaking their life together for a marriage.

He walked to the window and stared out. Nothing had changed, he tried to convince himself. He did not love Candy. He hadn't for many years. Therefore he could not love her less from now on. Penn knew that his thinking was irrational. That it went against his nature, his temperament. But he could not free himself from an old obsession at the adulterous drop of a skirt.

She stood quite close behind him. "All right, say it then. You want a divorce?"

He turned suddenly and his eyes made her back away. "You're still my son's mother. And he needs you."

"Oh no! I won't bring him up on my own. Make 'im a boarder if you like."

"He stays at home and we stay with him as long as he needs us." He almost choked on the words. How on earth would he find the strength to go on living with her under the same roof. But the same roof it had to be. To keep a lifelong dream out of the rain.

She viewed him with suspicion. Why did he not beat her? Would he kill her? Even if he did not love her, not even that much, she could not believe that he would fail to take revenge. "I know your game." She brightened up. "You want to pick the moment when you tell 'im about 'is whoring mother and all sorts of filth you didn't even see upstairs, don't you? Well, let me tell you somethin' for nothin'. I never wanted that child. And you can 'ave 'im if you want to. But he's my son, too, and if you ever tell 'im dirty stories about me, then perhaps I'll tell 'im how 'is great hero father really came to save those kids in Africa. All right?"

Penn's voice was unnaturally hollow like a knock on dead driftwood. "You do anything or say one word that hurts that boy, and I'll kill you. Because my son—"

"Your son! What makes you so sure that he's your son in the first place?"

She did not know what hit her. He did not know how or where or how hard he hit her. But now she was on the floor, her body following the line of the wall where the corner of the room had stopped her flying, slumping, sliding any farther. Her lips opened, and for a few breathless seconds sounds of pain and words of fury fought for priority; but nothing came through. There was murder in his eyes, and her voice failed her. And she hated him. Because it was through him that she could hate herself. For being weak, corrupt and mercenary throughout their married life. Mother was right saying that she had taken everything that was on offer. And her own silence was even more humiliating. For even now she lacked the strength to get up and walk out on him, his dreams and obsessions. She tried to will him to kick her out. To give her the license to make demands and go anywhere, do anything. He said nothing, and she stayed on the floor without the slightest effort to move, engulfed in amorphous and absurd notions of hate and hurt. Her left cheek was burning. Her left ear was throbbing. Maddening peals of bells filled her head. Her entire right side must have been bruised badly. Her right shoulder might be broken. She could not guess. She had never been hurt before. But she knew that her left eye was swelling and beginning to close. Must be a black eye. It pleased her. Timmy would ask questions. She hoped to find the will to answer them—to tell him about that single vicious punch.

He left the room because the temptation to kill her was great, and he was considering his options quite seriously. If she died in the house, some clues might be left. He would have to lure her to a suitable spot. Somewhere in a forest. Or near the river. At a building site with a deep excavation. It would simplify the future. Timmy would never know. And if anybody ever found out, I could tell them, he thought, that in fact I did my son and the whole world a favor. That stopped him. Those were the very words of his own father, a model he would never want to copy. He was grateful to the memory. It prevented him from going over the brink. But he still wondered if he could do it under provocation. Or in cold blood. As always, there was one question he refused to answer, contemplate or even acknowledge. It was whether he himself had ever suspected that pregnancy.

Saturday morning at last. Barraclough planned every move with his usual precision for military operations. His alarm clock stood on the checklist which was headed "Turn off alarm." Light exercise to loosen up, early breakfast, mental run-through of the act, check and handle items of clothes and equipment, loading of the car, pick up Sally, Fraser and the Leopard, drive to Pussy(cat), preparation of stage and props, rest and concentration—audition. Nothing was left to chance. Except that at noon, the manager who was going to audition him failed to turn up. At half past, the Leopard made some telephone calls and returned with the assurance that the manager would be there at one. At half past he was still on his way. At two, Sally was very hungry but agreed not to eat before the audition.

At ten past, the deputy manager and two friends arrived, promising that it would not be long now. At half past, three girls—an acrobatic stripping act—rushed in and demanded that they should be seen first and Barraclough's props should be removed at once from the small stage. The deputy manager offered drinks to everybody. The girls accepted, Barraclough's team refused. Then a flurry at the door: a chef, a waiter, four hostesses and, finally, the manager with two girl companions arrived. The acrobatic strippers agreed to warm up with a bottle and everybody settled in small groups around the tables where light refreshments were served.

The club was in complete darkness apart from a small lamp on the manager's table. Barraclough stood on the stage and reached behind a curtain to encourage Sally with a brief but firm grip of her shoulder. "The Two Huyyahs," he announced, and instantaneously a single spotlight hit him in the eye. A little nervously and blinking blindly, he began to talk about the martial arts and karate, its major styles, his preference for *Tae kwan-do,* the lethal Korean version, the distinction of *Kyu* grades for students, and then the famous Black Belts and the only 10th Dan title holder alive—and ignored the coughs and murmurs among the audience until the mere shadow of a man shouted, "Cut out the bullshit, will you?"

Invisible girls giggled. "Ladies, please," said the Leopard, "the act requires concentration."

Sally joined Barraclough on stage. A few appreciative noises. Then the man in the darkness: "Yeah, she's overdressed."

Barraclough picked up a knife, yelled, "Huyyah!" and lunged at Sally. She was prepared and tackled him but only when the point of the blade already seemed to touch her eye. Then Barraclough needed only a modest jump to help her throw him over her shoulder. There was some polite applause. Attacks. Counterattacks. Huyyah! Huyyah! She punched and kicked him endlessly.

"Very good, we'll let you know," the manager said.

"But that wasn't all, Jock, the best is yet to come," enthused the Leopard.

Barraclough was fuming. Which only made him shout "Huyyah!" even more fiercely than usual. That silenced them. Good. He turned. Fraser shot a spotlight at a large breeze block suspended in the background. "Huyyah!" He charged and smashed it with his palm heel. "Huyyah!" His fist broke bricks and roofing tiles. Stacks of them. His side kick made firewood of a three-inch plank.

A nod—and the whole stage was lit for the first time. Well done, Fraser. Mild applause. A six-foot-high and twelve-foot-long half-circle of houses was the set. Sally walked in with an outsize broom and began to clean up the mess. Chuckles. Barraclough pretended to be angry. Guffaws of laughter.

Barraclough turned his mock fury on the scenery, and began a thorough demolition job. His audience did not know, because at the beginning he had never had a chance to tell them, that the set included a small-scale replica of the three-bedroom Victorian house in Yorkshire which had once been demolished totally by fifteen unarmed karate fighters in six hours. So all they saw was the mad war dance by an old man with wildly flailing limbs. He went through bricks and more bricks, planks and boards and roofing tiles, using knuckles and palms and chops and kicks, and Sally screamed and looked truly frightened; but the fright infection never had a chance to spread once the laugh infection had firmly claimed control of the audience.

Drinks were poured and downed, girls' thighs were gently mauled under the tables, canapés were swallowed and regurgitated in renewed bursts of chortling. Barraclough's hand felt paralyzed with pain, but he bowed bravely to the ruins. This customary act of gallantry to the destroyed opposition passed virtually unnoticed—except that somebody in the audience shouted, "Huyyah!" It got the biggest laugh in the history of nightclub acts.

Sally and Barraclough bowed to each other. The manager

fought back his laughter but only just. "Very funny," he said. "Very funny and good. But nothing special, nothing. I'm sorry."

A stripper was running round and round in the background. "Heree!" she hollered. "Did you see him? Bang! Bang!" She pretended to hit the wall, the waiter, the tables. She bowed to chairs and bottles. Barraclough looked at Sally. She was in tears. Fraser appeared in the background, ready to punch anyone who laughed. The Leopard's face was melon-red with shame. He bit on his cigar hard and it broke in two. More fun for those who saw him almost swallow the half inside.

"Silence." Barraclough did not quite shout it. A loud voice, hardly more, was what he used. The effect was quite inexplicable. All sounds ceased. "Silence," he repeated in almost a whisper. He turned his back on them and started to build a waist-high stack of bricks. Then, a few inches away, another stack. Then the bridge: a single brick.

"Breaking bricks with foreheads is dangerous," he said impassively. "We'll be the first to employ this technique on stage." He stepped back.

This was not in the act. The Leopard rushed forward. Fraser shook her head. Sally was about to protest. But Barraclough's slightly raised broken finger cut them off.

"Silence," he breathed. There was no need to remind anyone. Nothing moved. Not a sound. He stood in deep concentration, with true showmanship. He had it in him.

"Huyyaaaaah!" The battlecry flooded and shook the room. He charged forward and down.

A dull thud. The brick shattered. The applause went up as soon as Barraclough's forehead hit the target—and it died in the same fraction of a second when, together with shrapnel-sharp brick fragments, blood showered everybody near the stage.

Women screamed. The club manager was covered in blood.

An acrobatic stripper threw up. Hysterical sickness was as infectious as laughter.

Barraclough towered above it all, chest out, head high, eyes ahead, hands firmly glued to the seams of his pants. His face was a mess.

Penn woke up at two in the afternoon. He could not remember when he had fallen asleep, seated in a chair at the window in Timmy's room. Exhaustion and the defense mechanism of the brain had given him a blackout of a sleep, and now, as the memories of the night and dawn began to drift back, he tried to convince himself that it was all a bad dream. Every bone in his body ached, the cuts and bruises made him reluctant to move, but he called Stacey as promised. There was no answer. Had he not said that he would be home all Saturday? Perhaps it was the wrong number. Penn dialed again and let it ring for a long time. No answer.

Penn had a quick shower and shave, then left the house quietly. He did not feel like even catching a glimpse of Candy.

It was only a twenty-minute drive to Stacey's house, a converted barn at the bottom of a quiet country lane. The doorbell did not work. The lion-head knocker was good solid brass. It sent minor explosions through the house, but nobody came to the door. Penn looked at the windows and noticed that all the curtains were drawn. That was odd. Unless Stacey, a bachelor, had been up late and was still asleep. But then he would have answered the telephone. Penn tried the door. It was locked. The nearest neighbors were about a hundred yards away. It was pointless asking them.

Penn walked around the house and shouted Stacey's name a few times but in vain. He tried the kitchen door. It was open.

"Anybody home?"

Neatness was written all over the place. And cleanliness. Stacey was a neat and cleanly man. His shoes stood to attention in the corner of the kitchen. His papers were stacked edge to edge on the desk in the large and friendly living room. His briefcase under the desk. On the wall and in numerous display cabinets, under glass and set in plastic blocks, his magnificent butterfly collection.

There were two bedrooms. None of the beds had been slept in. Or perhaps Stacey had made his bed. But the methodical man he was would have opened the curtains and the windows. More likely that he had come home, drawn the curtains, then gone out again . . . except that his shoes were in the kitchen. He might have worn, of course, another pair. But there were no slippers in the bedroom, and Penn felt sure that Stacey would certainly wear slippers at home.

Penn tried to tell himself that all this reasoning was quite pointless, but there was something odd about the place. Stacey had not slept there and had not returned in the morning, he was sure. He could not think of anybody to telephone. Perhaps the neighbors knew something after all. He left through the kitchen. Some fifteen yards from the house there was a massive old stable with an up-and-over garage door. It would not hurt to see if his car was there.

Penn was about five yards from the garage when he noticed a thin trickle of smoke seeping through the fine gaps around the edges of the door. He ran. He opened the door, and a black cloud of carbon monoxide enveloped him. The garage was so full of it that he could not even see Stacey's car. He backed away, choking, coughing, to take a few deep breaths. As the cloud grew thinner with the inrush of the light breeze, Penn held a handkerchief to his face and entered. A long gray tube attached to the exhaust pipe and leading to the front passenger window was the first thing he noticed. That told him the whole story, and he only sought confirmation as he pressed on despite the presence of the killer gas.

The passenger window was slightly open to allow the entry of the tube, around which cloths had been pressed into the gap to seal it. Penn tore the door open. Luckily, it was not locked.

Inside the car, the gas cloud was even thicker, and Penn knew he might soon pass out; but now he saw Stacey, slumped to the floor in a half-twist. Penn held his breath and tried to pull him out. He was aware of the sound of breaking glass under his feet, but had no time to pay any attention. His eyes were burning, the veins in his neck and temples swelled and pumped away furiously. His lungs demanded a fresh intake and it was no good telling them that only gas was available. Stacey's foot was stuck. And he was heavy. And there was no room to get a good grip on him. Penn knew he had to run out for fresh air, and it would only take seconds, but the thought that those few seconds might be Stacey's final ones made him keep trying. His lungs took control. They forced him to swallow the first gulp of gas. But the body moved at last. Penn was unable to lift it in the confined space. So he just dragged it along to the garage door, where he collapsed. He was dizzy and tried to suck in all the oxygen in the yard. He was certain that Stacey was dead, but he felt his pulse and banged his heart and gave him artificial respiration because there was nothing else to do and it was reassuring to know that at least he had tried.

Before going into the house to call the police, he shifted the body into a slightly more dignified position on the ground. Stacey had slippers on. He must have made himself comfortable before coming out here to die. A handful of cotton wool was stuck in his shirt front. Penn remembered vaguely that he had smelled something strange while applying artificial respiration. There was no blood, no injury.

While waiting for the police, Penn returned to the body and, without touching anything, looked into the garage from where most of the gas had already dispersed. A broken bottle was next to the open car door. The label was still intact. Chloroform. The peculiar smell. Of course. A good few seconds passed before he thought about murder. Although it was logical, his brain resisted the conclusion.

"It takes time to adjust to real death in real life," proclaimed the detective inspector, who was rather disappointed by the absence of blood and more dramatic clues. "But then, what could you expect on a Saturday afternoon? Everything, but everything, is dead around here."

The bare news of Stacey's death reached AeroCorp on Monday morning.

"Well, I can't say that I'm particularly displeased or distressed," said Drayton with a half-smile and, acknowledging Singer's worried expression, added unhurriedly, "What I mean is that I'm very sorry that he's dead, but let's face it, he was a goddamn nuisance and it's reasonable to hope that whoever takes over from him won't be worse. So if that's what bugs you—"

"No, it's Termine."

"What about him?"

"He hasn't been in touch at all since he checked out that witness in New York."

"Oh, well, I think you're a little overanxious, Henry. Termine can look after himself, I'm sure."

"I don't give a damn about him, for Chrissake! I'm worried about what he's up to. He is in London. Stacey is dead. It could be awkward if people started asking questions."

"What questions?"

"Well, you know, looking for possible links between us and this, er, tragedy."

"What the hell are you talking about? We don't even know if it was an accident, suicide or murder. Right?"

"Yes, but—"

"No buts, Henry." Drayton liked this conversation less and less, and made no secret of it. "We had nothing to do with this Stacey. We couldn't even wish him dead. It was always in our goddamn interest that he should succeed, and the sooner the better. His death is, in fact, a great inconvenience to us because it means delays."

"But did Termine know that?"

"I wouldn't know, Henry. How could I? He is on your staff. You tell him what to do; I hardly ever talk to him. Not only because he's such an objectionable creature but also because, as you very well know, it's one of my principles not to issue orders directly, over the heads of my executives. So, if he's in any doubt about his duties, it's because of imprecise instructions."

"I had to let him exercise his discretion."

"Good."

"So I just gave him your message."

"My message? I don't send messages through you. I don't regard you as a messenger boy. You must forgive me if by some stupid mistake I ever gave you that impression, because I can assure you that I'd never show that kind of disrespect to any of my trusted executives and least of all toward you."

It had the inevitable mellowing effect on Singer, whose tone grew now more apologetic. "You know what I mean, Charles. I conveyed the gist of our discussion."

"Which was?"

"That Stacey was a nuisance and it was for Termine to find the way to 'cool' him and get him out of your hair."

"Well, Henry, I trust your memory more than my own, but I'm quite positive that, if I said anything like that, the implication would be that there was no need for me to deal with this Stacey personally because other people had more time and, what's more, were better qualified to answer all his questions and give him all the support I'd wish to give him."

He buzzed Ms. Etch and asked for a computer printout of the minutes of the conference dealing with the Stacey problem. Within a few seconds, it came up on Drayton's data TV. Singer went pale. It seemed that Drayton had said a great deal more than he remembered. And what he had said was unemotional, not at all hostile, full of understanding for Stacey and ardent desire to help. The minutes would be based on Ms. Etch's notes, and her shorthand was legendary. Singer knew that, if necessary, even those notes could be dug up, and his memory would be no match against such evidence. And yet he felt sure that much of all this had never been said by Drayton. Which would make no difference. Not now. Copies of the minutes had been dated, distributed, filed and computerized at the time. If Ms. Etch had made a mistake or "revised" Drayton's words, her notes should have been queried right away. By Drayton.

"Have a drink, Henry." Drayton half filled a tumbler with Scotch—no ice, no water—while talking in a friendly, conciliatory tone. "Not that it matters, but obviously there was a slight misunderstanding. All I meant was that Stacey had no manners or tact, no goddamn tact, that's what I found so objectionable."

"How about his endless questions, Charles?"

"That was his job. We had nothing to hide."

"But you weren't keen to show him what you called 'those irrelevant details' in my personal safe, right?"

"I said we shouldn't flood him with unnecessary information. We must volunteer only what we think important and relevant, but give him everything he asks for. I'm certainly not in charge of the day-to-day running of our records, and if anything was withheld, it would be directly against my written orders to every goddamn employee of this company."

Which was perfectly true and Singer knew it. Once again the only problem was the interpretation of Drayton's initial verbal orders. An ear for emphasis, emotion, tone and implication in the president's voice was a prerequisite of success at AeroCorp, and the higher an executive rose in the hierarchy the greater precision of interpretation was expected of him. As for "those irrelevant details" . . . Singer did not want to think about them. Orders or not, he had not done anything wrong. Many of those confused details were not even required to be filed and preserved. But the interpretation of Drayton's orders for Termine was another matter. He knew how he understood them: make some inquiries, see what pressures could be brought to bear on various individuals and government agencies, and propose countermoves against unfair attacks on AeroCorp. But what would Termine make of it? He asked Drayton.

"You tell me, Henry."

"You know him better."

"Me? I've hardly ever met him."

"You recommended him to me."

"It was just a suggestion for you to accept or reject. But you took him on, and you've used him on your personal staff ever since."

"Well, if you put it that way . . ." Singer looked into the Venetian mirror, which he knew was Termine's gift, and thought he saw the rings around his eyes grow several shades darker.

"What else?"

"So, if he made any foolish mistakes or crooked moves, I'd have to resign, of course."

"Nonsense."

"There're certain things one cannot go along with."

"Naturally. But then you can't be expected to hold every goddamn guy's hand day and night. You must delegate. We all do."

Singer drank up. "You know what I'm talking about."

"I do and I'm sure you're drunk. I'll have to tell Anna to help you cut down on your liquid calorie intake."

"Do that, Charles. And let's hope that Termine got me right."

"I'm sure he did. You have a reputation throughout the entire industry for reliability and precision."

When Singer had left, Drayton buzzed Ms. Etch once more. "Thank you, sweetie, I really don't know what I'd do without you."

Ms. Etch nodded an it's-all-in-a-day's-work nod and turned away. There was no need to make an emotional exhibition of herself only to tell the man how much she appreciated, even after twenty-two years and seven months of service, that this big, big, beautiful man treated her as a member of the team, not just a goddamn secretary.

That evening, Singer took Anna to a restaurant which stocked a vast selection of Rhine and Moselle wines, and while she chewed her way through the menu, he settled down to some serious drinking. A few months earlier, when he had begun to suspect Termine's motives and designs on his own job, he decided to maneuver the man into a corner and let him make mistakes. It was not part of the plan that he himself should be associated in any way with those mistakes. Least of all the sort that were below the moral limit of Singer's stooping. The wine was supposed to wash his fears and suspicions away. And it would have done it, too, because it always did, if only Anna stopped asking questions and more questions. Weakened by wine and pressure, he buried his face in his hands and let Drayton's words swirl freely in his brain. *Make Penn shut up. Termine will know how. Find a way. Get him out of my hair. Like Stacey. Make him shut up.* And then his own words to Termine. *We'll have to get him out of his hair.*

Singer was not sure how much of all this he spoke out loud. He tried to remember Termine's questions. But the stream of Anna's questions confused him. And the most persistent thought throbbing in his mind was that Penn must be warned. Termine must be stopped.

"If it isn't too late already."

"What?"

"He must be warned."

"Warned? Who?"

"Never mind."

The blind landing systems symposium did not produce much of a story for Mara, and she was fed up with the speakers, with herself, her life, her work, her loneliness, and all the men who sensed that loneliness and tried to chat with her at the bar. She knew that a moon-faced pilot with a keen let's-be-jolly smile had eyed her all day, and so it was not a great surprise when during the afternoon coffee break he sidled up to her at last. He found her in a filthy mood.

"You must be Mara Boone."

"And you must be a speed reader," she snapped with a nod toward her conference name tag.

"Yeah, I've asked for it, haven't I? I'm sorry. And I only sought you out because I wanted to apologize."

"Okay. You're forgiven for whatever it was."

As she turned to go, her eye caught a glimpse of the man's badge: Captain Simms.

"You didn't even ask why I wanted to say sorry."

"No. But now I know. I once called you to ask about that CAT incident on a Sarissa, and you said 'Get lost' or words to that effect."

"Now I've changed my mind. Okay? I wanna talk."

Too much recent frustration had made her impatient and suspicious. "If you're looking for a story-for-a-screw swap, you're not on."

"No story, and that's a promise."

"No screw—and that's another."

Simms accepted it with a solemn bow and they sat down together, but it took him two cups of coffee to find his gambit. "Look, I really haven't much to say about that incident. Particularly not to a reporter. But if the guy who drove into the ditch in Singapore wants to ask me, I'll see him."

"I'll tell him." Simms had no idea why she was suddenly full of smiles. And even less did he know that he almost got a kiss for what he had said. "What made you change your mind?" Mara asked.

"I'm not sure. But there's something odd going on. . . . I don't know . . ."

"Odd? In what way?"

"Nothing I could put my finger on, you understand, but it's in the air and I don't like it. Nobody is saying anything. But they just make you feel that it's no good for your career to be a smartass and knock the airplane that pays your mortgage."

"I think I know what you mean."

"That's why I'd appreciate it if you didn't exactly advertise all this."

"Now I know precisely what you mean. And I'll tell Penn."

"Not that he'll gain much from a talk because I think that the Sarissa is great and he's a lousy flier, but I'll talk to him if that's what he wants."

"Good. I'm sure he'll soon be over here." All she had waited for was an excuse like this to call Penn and give him a good reason to come to America.

An hour later, she was on the phone to London. Although Penn said nothing of the sort, his tone told her how pleased he was. The conversation just ambled on and on, neither of them wanting to end it.

"I'll meet you in New York. Simms lives there," she said. "Can we make a date?"

"I'll have to call you back. But I promise to take the first available flight after the inquest." There was silence from the other end. "Mara? Are you there?"

"What inquest?"

"Haven't you heard?"

Stacey's death was news to her. And a considerable shock. She trusted the man. He was her best hope to clear Penn's name. She wanted to hear all the details. He told her everything except his own fight at the station. Why worry her when even the police refused to see any connection between the attack and Stacey's death?

"Do you know who takes over his work?"

"Some ex-pilot called Cleaff."

"You know him?"

"Not yet."

Barraclough refused to be taken by ambulance from the Pussy-(cat). He walked to hospital. The doctor asked him if he had run into the back of a bus. (He relied heavily on this question; it never failed to cheer up patients and relatives.) Barraclough answered, "No, I only tried to smash a brick with my head." Everybody laughed. "It's true," he insisted. Which made the nurses decide that he was a very funny man indeed.

They diagnosed two skull fractures and a broken nose, stitched up his face and forehead, found only a minor concussion and, on his insistence, allowed Fraser to take him home.

The two of them spent the weekend in virtual silence. To talk about the fiasco would have embarrassed them both, to talk about anything else would have been self-deception. Sally called them several times, and Fraser knew her job was to minimize Barraclough's pain. "How shall I put it? It's a discomfort, love, that's all. Looks worse than it is."

On Sunday evening, Fraser suggested that they should take Sally to their favorite Greek restaurant, give her a sherry or two, and tell her gently everything about their love and reasons for secrecy. Barraclough vetoed it: "Nod yed." Through the blob of bandages and with his broken nose, he sounded as if he were about to sneeze.

On Monday morning when he had finished his breakfast, she said, "I'm off."

"Where do?"

"Must cancel the shop and all."

"Nod yed." And because he knew that her stony face meant she was almost in tears, he added, "Waid a liddle. I've other blans."

He used a long-standing emergency procedure to contact Mott. He left a coded message with an answering service, and the following evening he waited in the cul-de-sac behind the Bull and Bush, the old pub near Hampstead Heath. The Brigadier arrived in due course, driving an ordinary cab, and picked him up.

Barraclough felt uncomfortable in the back seat, driven by his old chief. "Sorry I dragged you oud, sir."

"That's all right. I'm sure you had a reason. Anything to do with all those bandages?"

"No—no, can't say id does, sir."

"You run into the back of a bus or something?"

The same words which the doctor had used. Too much of a coincidence, thought Barraclough. He knew that Mott had his ways of knowing everything about people he was interested in. It was a little flattering and at least equally worrying that Mott would be that much interested in him. He would then also know about the audition. "Id's only thad I've been thinking."

"Never knew that thoughts could be so injurious," Mott laughed heartily. Yet he remained an alert driver at all times, checking the cars around them, merging into heavy traffic, cutting through deserted streets, only to double back again and again to make sure that nobody was following him. "So what have you been thinking about? No, let me guess. You've decided to do the job after all, right?"

"Sord of."

"Only sort of?"

"Whad I mean is id wouldn't be fair do led you down, sir, if you needed me, I mean if you still do."

"Yes, we do. You know it's not easy to find someone as good as you."

Barraclough appreciated the prompt compliment. For even if it was substantially true that a good replacement would be hard to come by, the Brigadier would have been justified in letting him sweat a little as a mild punishment for his hesitation and refusal when first asked. "Thank you, sir."

"All right. You're on the payroll as of now. We'll need an initial assessment of the problem within a week, preferably with your main proposal and alternatives." He paused and took a few sharp turns to see if a red car would follow them (it did not), then continued with a reassurance which showed that he read Barraclough's mind correctly. "I know it worries you that it's a commercial aircraft with a civilian crew, and I don't like it either, but it can't be helped, unfortunately. The decision has not been taken lightly."

Barraclough felt he had to reciprocate. "Your involvement is a good enough guarantee for me, sir." But he was not quite sure about it. He also knew he was crawling, and hated it.

Once again Mott sensed his mood. "Although we're in a bit of a hurry, this is still no more than contingency planning, you understand, and the actual job may never need to be done. After all, the aircraft is still suspect. If the investigation drags on and on as usual—and just now it's being delayed by a, how shall we say, fortuitous and indeed fortunate change of key personnel—the signing of the major sales contracts may never go through. In that case, we can afford to sit tight and do nothing. No point in wasting innocent lives, is there?"

Barraclough was ready to clutch at the faintest ray of hope. "And even if id came to the worst, you think we could pick oud a flight with no passengers."

"Absolutely. You have my personal guarantee of that." Mott paused for emphasis. "And, er, welcome back to the fold, old boy."

The effect on Barraclough was evident—just the sentence to make him feel warm. It was the comradeship he missed most, the sort he could never develop with people like the Leopard. And Fraser would be pleased, too. This one final assignment, and no more problems. No need to cancel any of their plans for the home run of their lives.

Impatient and restless though he was, Penn found tranquillity in the days of waiting for the inquest. Candy had gone to stay with a friend in Norfolk, and Penn spent all his time with his son. They went rowing in Regent's Park, played silly telephone jokes on some of Timmy's teachers, knocked on doors and ran away to watch the irate or puzzled reaction of housewives, and lived on hamburgers and chips, the ultimate in Timmy's dream menu. Penn knew that the child missed his mother, and several times he was on the verge of telling him everything. What held him back was the memory of his own father crying on his shoulder, a harrowing act which had wrecked his world because it came at a time when he was not ready to be treated as an equal and when he could not appreciate his graduation to confidant of a crumbling idol.

These days of close togetherness restored his balance and self-respect. The child trusted him implicitly, and it became impossible for him not to live up to that image. Only now did Penn fully understand the fate of colleagues who had survived crashes but almost invariably failed to survive for long the tension of major crash investigations. The unwritten code of conduct, the shackles of ethics, the traditions of dignified silence and passivity, the waiting, suspension, growing isolation, and the incessant self-examination of the guilty as well as the innocent shattered their nerves or made them prone to strokes or heart attacks. Only now did he understand the inertia that forced the condemned to kneel down readily and rest his head on the chopping block without a struggle. Penn thought about trying to explain it all to Timmy, but he never had a chance, because to the child it was perfectly simple and obvious; There had been an accident; much bigger disasters had to be prevented; who but his father was to do it? Even if Granny had to come over to stay and look after him.

The inquest was brief and mechanical. In the absence of evidence to the contrary, "foul play" was not suspected and Stacey's death was registered as suicide. A rather vague and inconclusive rider was added to the verdict, stating that there were no known reasons for him to end his life and therefore it had to be assumed that "under the stress of exceedingly conscientious devotion to his heavy workload" he had killed himself, probably in a spell of "diminished responsibility."

The police discovered no sign of a break-in (unfortunately, Stacey hardly ever locked his doors), nothing of value missing, nothing to indicate that Stacey had a visitor or that there was a fight in the house or outside. No surface had been wiped clean and, apart from Penn's, there were no strange fingerprints anywhere. The police report mentioned the possibility that an attacker might have worn gloves.

The most suspicious clue, the presence of chloroform, was eliminated. Stacey always kept some in the house to stun and kill butterflies without damaging them. It was recognized that a clever murderer who had a strong motive and was willing to study his habits might have taken advantage of this fact, but nobody was known to have a grudge against him. Miss Beaver, his assistant, mumbled something quite ridiculous about his being a nuisance and about his devotion which created many powerful enemies "in all sorts of quarters," but of course she had to be cut short with polite firmness, because records were not to be weighed down with intuitive dissertations and theories. The decisive factor against attaching much importance to the ominous presence of chloroform was that the post-mortem revealed no injuries to the body, and undoubtedly Stacey would have struggled—unless, of course, he was attacked in his sleep.

Death was due to the inhalation of carbon monoxide–rich fumes. The assumed sequence of events began with Stacey entering the garage of his own free will. He would shut the door, channel the exhaust through the window of the passenger seat, sit in the car, close the door, close all windows, seal the entry gap around the pipe with rags from the inside, turn on the engine and, in order to bypass suffering and the opportunity of changing his mind, knock himself out with the deliberate inhalation of chloroform. It was estimated that the gas tank must have been almost full when the ignition key was turned, and the engine ran until it stalled with some 40 per cent of the fuel burnt. Death would have occurred much earlier, at about six A.M. Saturday. The inquest commended Captain Cornelius Penn for his presence of mind, unselfish courage and efforts to revive the victim.

The funeral was a wet, bleak and rushed affair. There were no known relatives. The official AIB representative and three colleagues formed the only group at the graveside. A solitary neighbor stood well back. The London manager of AeroCorp's back-up services brought a small wreath, SupraNat sent another. Penn was a few minutes late and so almost missed the entire ceremony.

As soon as it was over, people began to talk airplanes, but the rain drove them away fast. On the way to the car park, Penn introduced himself to a Mr. Cleaff, Stacey's successor, and offered to cooperate in any way he could.

"Thank you." Cleaff looked him up and down. "I appreciate it even though there isn't much left to do. I've looked through —well, glanced through—the files, and it seems that everything necessary and more has been done, said or even repeated. So it won't be long now."

"You mean your report—"

"I'm sorry, I'm not supposed to discuss our possible findings at this stage, as you very well know. But I'm sure that you or your legal representative will be given a fair chance to comment on everything before it's taken any further, not by us, but by the Singapore authorities, of course."

Car doors were slammed and engines started. Penn watched them go. That was when he noticed the Beaver from Stacey's office leaving on foot, without bothering to open her umbrella. The rain worked freely on her cheap makeup and drew lines down her face. Penn stopped his car next to her and offered her a lift. She showed no interest and walked on. He stopped again and opened the passenger door.

"Get in. I'll buy you a coffee."

"Make it a beer," she said and cupped her hand to relight a rain-soaked brown cigarette before she would sit in the car.

The pub, too, was bleak, fitting the occasion. The woman's face was ageless and drained of all the juices of emotion. She drank slowly and thoughtfully, without once removing the glass from her lips until it was empty. Then she looked at him with bored and tired eyes. "All right, what do you want from me?" Only the natural ding-dong of her Irish brogue enlivened the flatness of her voice.

"You don't believe that he killed himself, do you?"

"I didn't say that." She looked alarmed.

"You didn't need to. You winced when they spoke about suicide."

"I didn't."

"I saw you. What was it?"

"Must have been the pain. I have rheumatism. It comes and goes and makes me wince, that's what."

"So you accept that he was a coward or a weakling who ran away from it all."

"Bullshit."

"Diminished responsibility, right?"

"No." She looked away. "Far from it."

He waited for her to say more, but she just stared out of the window. He offered to buy her another beer.

"Ta. Make it a pint this time."

Again she drank continuously, without any sign of enjoyment or the urgency of thirst, until she downed the last drop. Penn watched her in silence. He reckoned it was her wake for Stacey. "He liked you, you know," she said at last. Then her eyes were away once again. She nodded a few times, continuing the slow flow of some unspoken conversation. "He could have made himself very popular very quickly by accepting that Singapore was due to pilot error."

"Why didn't he?"

"He said that you miraculously landed some shot-up machine with kids in Africa. And that the same pilot wouldn't have made a mistake like that in Singapore. Not without a reason. That's what he said, bless his soul. Always looking for the reason, always asking all them questions."

"That's why he had enemies?"

"What enemies?"

"You said at the inquest that—"

"Oh, them. Yeah. He had enemies all right."

"Who?"

"Everybody who wanted quick results instead of letting him ground the Sarissa."

"I didn't know he wanted to."

"Nobody advertised it. And he only suggested it."

"But why?"

"Because he refused to accept half-baked explanations."

"Then why didn't he press harder for the grounding order?"

"He needed more evidence, that's why."

"What did he suspect?"

She shrugged her shoulders.

"Did he think there was a cover-up?"

"I don't know. And I don't want to know. I don't want to be involved. I don't want to inherit his enemies." She looked around nervously and lowered her voice. "He was watched all the time, wasn't he?"

"By whom?"

"He didn't say. But that's what he thought. And I don't want nobody to watch me. I do my job and that's that." She lit another cigarette. Her hands were shaking.

"But why? Why would anybody want to watch him?"

She looked away. Penn grabbed her wrist and with a vicious jerk made her face him. And he repeated the question, a menace, rather, the way it came out this time.

"He hinted everywhere that he had secret informers. That he received a lot of confidential information," she whispered.

"Was it true?"

"Don't know. But it worried them."

"Who?"

"AeroCorp? I don't know." Her voice was hardly audible.

"And that's why they watched him?"

"Stands to reason, doesn't it?"

He hated the thought that he had to agree with her. The aviation world he knew and wanted to know—the service, glamour and team spirit, the devotion, enterprise and fight for progress—excluded the shadows, wheeling-dealing, dirty tricks. But it stood to reason all right that if they felt threatened by his informers they would watch him—whoever they were. They would want to know how much Stacey had told Penn. They would attack him, too, to get the papers he was carrying.

"What did he hope to achieve?" he asked, without noticing that now he also was whispering conspiratorially.

"Only that they wouldn't risk withholding any information from him. Or somebody might panic and tell him all them secrets. In case he found out something in other ways and that would put them in a bad light. See what I mean? He was rocking the boat. He was an embarrassment."

"Did you mention this to the police?"

"How could I?"

"Did you or didn't you?"

"They wouldn't believe me. There's no proof, is there?"

No proof. He had no proof of the attack either, nothing apart from the meaningless scratches and bruises he was still nursing. But if AeroCorp or anybody else felt threatened enough to kill Stacey, somebody would have to keep up the menace. Penn decided he would hate to be that particular somebody.

She blinked several times and rubbed her eyes with her fist. "It's sad, very sad."

"What?"

"Times change. Your heroes perish as easily as only your villains used to in the books I read as a child." She cleared her throat. "He was a good man, you know, one of the few, bless his soul." There was a long pause. Her dull gaze went through the window and Penn felt grateful that it avoided him. He was ashamed of his near-violence a few minutes earlier. And it was even worse that she did not seem angry. She touched his hand gently, almost affectionately, for the merest fraction of a second. "Will you take over now and go on rocking the boat, Captain Penn?"

"Why don't you do it?" His voice was abrasive.

"Oh, I would, wouldn't I? But Mr. Stacey gave me too much to do, didn't he? Must go through all them weight reductions. I must do it because Mr. Cleaff won't have the time, not at first." Her eyes and voice cleared now and she managed to sound quite chatty. "Did you know that bit by bit they reduced the weight of every inch of the Sarissa? Just a little, mind you, but reduce it they did, and Mr. Stacey wants me to . . . Did I say wants? That's awful." Her eyelids began to flutter and her fists came up to rub them shut once more. "I meant he wanted me to list and grade all them changes from the original design."

"Did he think there was something wrong with those changes?"

"No, but when there's no explanation for a crash, he said, you must look at everything again before there's a really big accident. And now that the flight tests haven't turned up any snags . . . Oh well, I hope Mr. Cleaff will let me get on with it."

The message from Mott was brief: Barraclough must hurry up. Due to unforeseen factors, plans must be finalized well before the Farnborough air show. That gave Barraclough less than three weeks. And the initial week allowed for his basic study, report and recommendation was already running out. So just this once he decided not to have tea at F and M.

Drayton made no attempt to hide his fury from Singer. "What's this goddamn Captain up to?"

"I don't know."

Singer was embarrassed. He was still unable to contact Termine, and it was Drayton who had heard directly from his own private sources that in London Penn had been talking about some fresh and confidential information concerning the Sarissa and also about plans to arrange a test flight for himself to see if he could reproduce the snag that caused the crash.

"Well, perhaps it's a good idea to let him do it," said Singer. His speech was slightly slurred; he had had too many liquid lunches lately.

"Why?"

"It would be further proof of our goodwill and conscientious effort."

"Rubbish. We don't need any further proof. We've cooperated with the investigation in every way we could, and you know it. We've completed a costly research and test program and we drew an honest blank. I won't be pushed around by any goddamn whitewasher and troublemaker."

"Quite. I agree, Charles, I do. But what I mean is that, just as you always say, we should give the guy a fair chance."

"It's he who should give us the fair chance instead of going round with rumors about discovering our secrets. What secrets, for Chrissake? Do you know of any? Do you?"

Singer returned to his office and made yet another desperate attempt to find Termine. He had already left messages for him everywhere he could think of, and asked for help from several people, including a friendly private eye in London—to no avail. He had to admit it, Termine covered his tracks well. Which was all the more worrying. He had no clear idea what the man was up to—well, no idea he would want to admit or even take seriously—but the details of the Stacey inquest, reported by the manager of AeroCorp London, did nothing to allay his nightmarish visions. At last Singer decided he had to do something to prevent another potential accident or suicide. If nothing else, he could reduce his own actual or moral responsibility. He called Mara in Washington, only to be told that she was in the New York office.

"I need your help and it's very confidential," he blurted out breathlessly. Mara said nothing and he could visualize the suspicion spreading over her face. "Look, honey, I know how you feel. I mean, last time I gave you a scoop I was wrong and I might have got you into trouble. I know, and I'm sorry, and I apologize, but this is no scoop, it's nothing to publicize, and it's very urgent. Can you contact Penn and give him a message?"

"Can't you?"

"Let's not waste time on verbalizing our hard feelings or trying to score, honey, because this is serious. Dead serious. And I can't call him, because he wouldn't believe me. Or perhaps he'd overreact."

He sounded serious. "Okay. What's the message?" she asked.

"Tell him to hole up somewhere. Disappear. Go underground. You know what I mean?"

"Why?"

"I have a hunch . . . some madman might try to harm him."

"Tell the cops."

"I'll do everything that's necessary. But I need time. So warn him. Please." There was no answer. "Mara? Are you there?"

"He'll want an explanation."

"He'll get it. I promise."

"Okay, I'll tell him tonight as soon as I see him at Kennedy."

"Damn!" If Penn was coming to America, Termine might think it right to intercept him. "He must not come over here. Trust me, please. Phone him. Now!"

Mara found it hard to trust Singer since that off-the-record dinner in Washington, and it was difficult to decide if now he was being deceitful, hysterical or truly concerned. But the implication was too serious to be ignored. She dialed London right away.

"Captain Penn is out and I don't know when he'll be back, and from tonight he'll be in America or Siberia or somewhere.

I don't care," snapped Candy and slammed the phone down.

Mara called again. "It's a matter of life and death," she shouted over the line before Candy had a chance to say anything.

"Isn't that exciting."

"It is. And it's vital that he should call me before going to the airport."

"Split-second timing, isn't it? Essential for a busy, busy man like him."

"Mrs. Penn, please. This isn't a joke. His life may depend on it."

Candy took down Mara's name and all her office numbers in New York. "I underlined the word 'urgent' seven times. Will that do or shall I make it eight?" She rang off, screwed up the note, and burned it playfully in an ashtray. The flames lent a pretty glow to the red crystal.

Everything about Fraser was tidy and spotlessly clean. The bedroom was no exception. She sat on the bed—which she had covered with a plastic sheet because it would have been against her principles to bring even the bedspread into contact with outdoor clothes—and bent over a small adjustable table on which normally she served Barraclough's TV dinners. Neatly arranged stacks of filing cards surrounded her in a half-circle. A dozen reference books were piled up at her feet. She stretched, yawned and stood up a little shakily. She had not slept for more than thirty hours. But her urgently required brief essay on the comparative merits and demerits of a vast range of explosives was ready.

She looked into the mirror, put on some fresh lipstick (the same glowing signal-red she had begun to use some forty years ago), touched hard-lacquered hair to a renewed height of impeccability and went to the kitchen, where in disgusting chaos, Barraclough was burrowing under tons of books, aviation accident reports and other documents, wiring diagrams, chemical formulas, engineering drawings, notes and trajectories of falling pieces of wreckage from aircraft breaking up in the air at various heights.

"Bangers," she said and dropped her essay on a paper-free slot on the pine table. Barraclough looked at his watch. He said nothing, and the bandage disguised anything his face might have expressed. But no comment was necessary. She was three hours late and she knew it. He stuffed the product of her painstaking effort into an invisible filing system that might have been mistaken for the condensed contents of a dustbin.

"I must get some food in. You want anything?" she asked as she retrieved her feared-lost shopping bag.

"No. Just don't be long. I'll need more on the traceability of poisons on that short-list."

"I thought you'd dropped that line."

"Why?"

"Timing is very uncertain. At least one of the crew might react with violent sickness and so eliminate most of the effect; and if the chosen substance is administered in food, someone would have to be on board to poison everything the pilots chose to eat."

"Unless they all eat the same," said Barraclough, not because it was important, but because he did not like to be lectured, especially not by his own subordinates.

"They never eat the same meal. That's to reduce the risk of accidental food poisoning."

"You should have told me that before."

"It's in my report."

"I haven't had a chance to read it." And when she was already at the door, about to leave, he added, "But Betty M., er . . . thanks. I mean for the long hours you've put in."

She was astonished and did not know what to answer to the thanks, which was not a part of his operational vocabulary. She was inclined to draw the same conclusion as Mott: Barraclough must be getting soft. Or old. Or both. So she said nothing.

Barraclough's eyes were itching, burning and watering a great deal. The week had been too short to consider the possible alternatives, their advantages and disadvantages, and the numerous factors affecting feasibility. On the whole he would have preferred a neatly timed explosion above any deep part of an ocean. But he saw too many problems. There might be witnesses. Much of the wreckage might be recovered by special deep-sea equipment. The wreckage distribution would show quite clearly the break-up in the air. The pilots might have a chance to radio an explosion message unless the device killed them outright. But, above all, Barraclough distrusted the chance element. The flight could be delayed or postponed, the one Mott had in mind would not even be a scheduled service, the aircraft could be diverted en route, and any of these fortuitous events would jeopardize his plan. The explosion would then occur over land or even on the ground. Not good enough. Fraser's fine essay was doomed.

He found interference with the fuel an attractive idea because he liked to break new ground, but (a) he might not have enough time to work out the details of "optimum contamination," and (b) if eventually contamination was diagnosed, the aircraft would be exonerated automatically.

He saw, of course, numerous other possible options, and some of them were rather tempting. Structural weakness brought about in some clever way was his favorite but that again would need a great deal of work on the engineering problems, the use of an agent of high-degree technical know-how, sufficient access to the target at the right moment beyond which there would be no time or schedule to carry out any more preflight checks on the aircraft, and a touch of genius to tackle the most insurmountable obstacle of faking such a suitable fault. Metal fatigue could be distinguished easily from shearing or other deliberate interference, and the damage would have to look like the result of some faulty manufacturing process. On his list of pros and cons he noted as the chief appeal of this course that "a structural failure due to design error rather than operational overstressing—particularly if it impaired the elevator—would lend disastrous significance to the Singapore case, whatever had caused that one."

Barraclough examined the possible use of acids that could chew away their own container and cause damage to essential controls. Against it he listed "imperfect timing and traceability if affected parts were recovered. A leaking battery could be used as the explanation, but its presence in a crucial position would be indefensible."

Gallium was his pet idea. It would be something original, quite elegant, and deadly. The cons were similar to those which had already eliminated the use of acids, but he indulged in a little scheming for pleasure to see what parts of the aircraft would be most vulnerable to the corrosive effects of one of the world's rarest metals, widely used in minute quantities by industry. He found, in fact, one incident on record when liquid gallium had spilled on the aluminium alloy floor of a cargo charter aircraft. The case made him wonder what the effect would be on the plane's hydraulic system or even the fuel tanks themselves. Would the vital juices just drain away?

The most exotic thought occurred to him when he was toying again with the possibilities of knocking out the pilots. If an attack aircraft with the right transmitter was available (and, considering Mott's status, Barraclough was convinced, this would not even stretch the department's resources), a certain high-pitch sound could be transmitted on the frequency the target aircraft was using at the time, and in a few seconds the pilots could be incapacitated. There would be no evidence left to be discovered by the most meticulous post-mortem even if the bodies were found complete. It had to be discarded, however, because of insufficient reliability (perhaps only one of the pilots would be wearing his earphones or they might be tuned to different frequencies at the crucial moment) and because the transmission might be detected or picked up, with disastrous consequences, by another aircraft. The chance that an additional accident might happen upset him. While the unpleasant job in hand was at least inevitable because Mott regarded it as something vital in the nation's interest, Barraclough would certainly not want to cross the paths of other parallel lives inadvertently. And he hoped that he would never know who the pilots of the target aircraft were. For in his private code of fatalism, a clash between parallel lives was heavy with bad omens for everybody.

He made himself a cup of tea. He loved to drink it so hot that it required self-control and a high degree of pain resistance to swallow it at all. He then began to draft his main recommendation: "Knockout of entire flight-deck crew simultaneously by toxic gases." He paused to consider what would happen if he enlisted Mott's help in selecting and obtaining the most suitable gas. Would it lead to a reduction of his promised success bonus, the paltry sum of fifty thousand Swiss francs? The money reminded him of the unenjoyable prospect that at their next meeting, when submitting his proposals, he would have to ask Mott for an advance so that Fraser could put down the deposit on the sweet shop with the flat above.

The flight to New York was less than half full and Penn had three seats to himself. It was a good opportunity to catch up a little on long-lost sleep. Forty minutes before the estimated time of arrival he took down his flight bag from the overhead rack and had a sleepy shave with a battery razor. He then walked down the aisle for a quick wash. At ETA minus twenty-five minutes he returned to his seat, but his path was blocked by an attractive woman in high-heeled boots who was shutting the door of the rack above the seats. She half turned toward him, then bent down in haste.

"Lost something?" he asked.

"My balance," she replied lightly and straightened up.

"Pity you've found it so easily. I'd have volunteered to help you."

"Could have been fun." Her eyes wandered somewhere beyond Penn as if checking whether their ten-second encounter had been noticed, and she gave him the guilt-tainted pity-I'm-not-alone smile most men cannot help falling for. It flattered Penn and made him feel alive. Thawing out after the long freeze. Ready to meet Mara.

Inside the terminal, he grabbed a free cart and waited impatiently for his suitcase to appear on the fun-free carousel of the twentieth century. He saw the woman once again. She was talking to a man in uniform. She must have sensed his gaze on her back, because she turned, and again she smiled that particular smile.

At the customs, Penn opened his flight bag without waiting for instructions, to speed up the procedure. But the officer did not give it even a cursory inspection. He just waved Penn on and turned to the next passenger on whom, suddenly, another two officials were closing in. Pushing his luggage cart toward the exit, Penn noticed out of the corner of his eye that the passenger behind him was being directed toward a small cubicle. A smuggler caught or a nervous, and therefore suspicious, passenger inconvenienced, he concluded.

When Penn had not called by London departure time, Mara had telephoned his home again, but there was no answer. Later she found out from the airline that Penn was on the flight, so now she was waiting for him anxiously at the airport. A screen of craning necks hid her from his eyes, but he was easy to spot as he turned this way and that, fast, searching for her. She ran and half embraced him from behind but avoided his kiss to ask eagerly, "Why didn't you call?" And, seeing his startled expression: "Didn't you get my message?"

"What message?"

The flood of passengers forced them to move on. He led as they rounded a corner into a main thoroughfare of the terminal, and he glanced at her: "What message?" That was when he noticed the woman from the plane with the two officers who had converged on that suspicious passenger. They were well away from him, scanning the commotion systematically. Penn ducked. His memory emitted three quick flashes—the woman at the rack, the touch of guilt in her eyes not flattering any more but a telltale sign of being caught; the woman at the luggage carousel; the passenger being led toward the cubicle. Insignificant scenes, now so evidently ominous. Customs had had a tip-off. They had made a mistake. It was his flight bag that was supposed to be examined. It had been in the overhead rack. Had she planted something on him? Why?

The mental sequence went so fast that in the meantime Mara could say, "The message I left with Candy," no more.

Penn paid no attention to it. "Take my suitcase, put it in your car, be at the Arrivals gate in ten minutes and try to wait for me," he rattled off and he was away. He had to examine that flight bag if he was not to be caught "in possession" of whatever it was. If anything.

Mara looked around to see what was going on, but then controlled herself. This was not the time for her to understand. Whatever was happening only confirmed her worst fears that Singer must have been right after all.

Penn zigzagged among the crowd, keeping his head down. He needed a hiding place for a few moments but he had to avoid the obvious ones which would be the first to be checked. The corridor opened into a large hall, with a deserted circular information desk in the middle. As he jumped over the counter, he noticed a woman's consternation. He gave her a smile of reassurance but she would not be satisfied.

"You have no right . . ."

He could not wait for the rest. His pursuers had appeared at the far end, and the woman's fussing would soon attract their attention. He ran down more corridors, soaking up the curses that trailed him, and went through a door. He was behind the building. A slow-moving train of luggage trolleys approached him. He dropped his flight bag in its path and gave a sound something like "oy!" to the driver, who stopped his machine and leaned out to see the bag better. Penn hit him right on the chin. It was a perfect punch. He caught the falling man in time, pushed him back among the luggage, piled a couple of hold-alls on top of him, put on the driver's cap and took his seat. A door opened and he saw the woman and one of the officers in the stronger light. Penn drove on, slowly. Another officer joined the people at the door. The woman stayed there and the two men ran out to the left and right. Penn heard their footsteps, one of them would soon catch up with him. He began to whistle a tune softly. The man ran past him. Penn kept whistling. The man turned, looked around and, reassured by the red cap of the driver, the only obvious feature in the semidarkness, ran back toward the building. To show his lack of concern, Penn whistled on and on until, quite involuntarily, he slapped his palm on his own mouth to silence it. He had been whistling, "Which is the way to London Town? To see the King in his golden crown. One foot up and one foot down. That's the way to London t—" He was lucky. His performance was less than perfect, or the man did not realize that the luggage handler's tune was an old English nursery rhyme.

Penn stopped the machine and looked at the unconscious porter behind him. He hoped that the man would not recover and require a second dose before he had a chance to check the flight bag. His luck held. He removed a couple of bulky items from the bag and saw at once the little white plastic sack that had slipped to the bottom. Some sort of drug, he decided. Must be. He was about to take it out when it occurred to him that if it was ever found with his fingerprints, he would have no defense against jail or deportation or both. So he used a paper tissue to hold it until he could drop it in a drain hole.

Mara stopped her car at the Arrivals gate—and found herself surrounded by police and customs officials. Questions rained from all sides, and she decided to tell the truth. She did not know where Penn had gone.

"Didn't he say anything?"

"Only that he'd meet me here."

Penn walked straight up to them and tried to look sufficiently surprised when they escorted him back into the building. He was interrogated for almost two hours. They lent him a coat so that he would not stand naked while his clothes and flight bag were subjected to a thorough search. They found nothing, and the only answer they could press him for was an explanation of why he had run down those corridors.

"It may sound ridiculous to you, but I forgot to bring a present for my girl and hoped to find something while she was collecting her car."

They did not believe him but they had no justification to disbelieve him. Particularly not when it was discovered that the woman who had given them the tip-off was gone. They apologized to him: a mistake must have been made. Penn hoped that the redcap, having recovered, would first get his load checked for theft, and by then there would be nothing to connect his flight and the attack even if some policeman noticed a coincidence in timing.

The woman was in the restaurant of the next building. She did not smile any more and she looked shiverish as she held the phone close to her lips. She did not think of old hopes, promises of bright lights and fast living any longer. Only fear governed her words: "Please don't be angry with me, it wasn't my fault. . . . No, they made a mess of it, I guess. . . . I'm sorry, what else can I say? . . . Yes, yes, I'll do that, I swear." She hung up. There were shiny sweat marks all over the receiver. Her hand was shaking a little. She hurried out. The last thing she wanted was to stay permanently in the bad books of Salah Termine. Particularly not now that he had promised this would be her final mission for him.

Later that evening, over brick-size steaks at Gallagher's, Penn's meeting with Captain Simms was very disappointing. Simms had virtually nothing to add to what was in every report about his CAT incident. "Yes, it was a little tricky to handle it, but what do you expect? . . . No, nothing special, considering the intensity of turbulence that day. Sorry if you had the impression that it's worth your coming over just to see me."

Mara felt that the man was uneasy. She wondered why. Was he embarrassed because he had nothing more helpful to say? Had he changed his mind since their meeting at the symposium? If yes, why? Or would he just prefer to talk to Penn without a witness? She excused herself.

As soon as she left them, Simms leaned closer to Penn. "Listen. I've told you everything that could be useful to you. But, if you want some advice, go home, shut up and wait. I don't know what's going on, but you're bad news. In fact I may be doing myself a lot of damage by simply talking to you. None of us is invulnerable, you know what I mean?" By the time Mara returned, he was gone.

"Who are the other pilots I could talk to?" asked Penn. Mara's list did not seem very promising.

"I'm sorry. Perhaps it was a mistake," she apologized. "I shouldn't have called you."

"Why?"

"Because I should have known that Simms was not a good enough reason. It's only that I wanted to see you."

"That's a good enough reason. Because I wanted to be with you." He kissed her. But his mind was elsewhere.

He proposed to call Singer right away and ask him about the warning. "It's pointless," she said. "He'd only deny everything. I can't prove that he did call me at all."

"Then why do you think he tried to warn me?"

"I don't know. It's one of the things we'll have to find out."

"Not we, Mara. It's for me."

"Why?"

"It's . . . it's a one-man job." He could not tell her that he intended to take over Stacey's role, to let the shadows snipe at him in the hope that he could spot where the fire was coming from.

"I want to help."

"I'm really grateful."

"And I still have a lot of contacts."

"I know. Even at AeroCorp." The second bit slipped out even though he had never wanted to refer to that morning phone call in Singapore when she was reluctant to talk in front of him.

She knew exactly what he was thinking of. "Don't you trust me?"

"I do."

"But my special relationship with AeroCorp still worries you."

"Just one of the manufacturers, I suppose."

"Stop it, Corrie."

"All right. Would you like to tell me what your relationship is?"

"Drayton used to be my lover."

"Oh. Is that how he persuaded you to muzzle me in Singapore?"

"He didn't. But I understood that you'd soon be in even more serious trouble if you didn't shut up at that stage. And by then I was on your side."

It sounded so simple and sincere that there could be no argument. "Thanks."

"It was Charles Drayton's idea that I should interview you. And when I returned home from Singapore, I told him right away that his scheme had failed. My two-dimensional infatuation became three-dimensional love. He put it that way. But he offered to remain a friend in the hope that one day you'd return to the original status of being a paper lover."

"So now it's 'just good friends' time."

"Don't you believe me?"

"I want to—so I do."

"Pity I'm not the only one you want to trust."

"What do you mean?"

"Maybe you trust people too readily."

"Maybe. But I'd rather be fed *to* the worms than be fed on them."

"And live with them rather than leave them? . . . I'm sorry. I take that back."

"Don't."

"That's one thing I never meant to say. It's only that she risked your life by not giving you my message."

"I know. And I know I must be mad. But you cannot wipe out a lifelong obsession overnight. And you don't throw away a magnificent jigsaw only because one of a thousand pieces is a misfit."

"Perhaps you don't. But it ruins the picture."

Dawn began to light up her apartment near the park by the time he had finished telling her about his obsession and Candy.

"Everybody is entitled to live with his self-made misery. You didn't owe me an explanation," she said.

"I owed it to us."

"You don't seem to understand. I love you. So you owe me nothing. Or do you always have to balance the books?"

"Yes."

The honest brevity of the word stunned her. He apologized. She refused to accept it. "You don't owe me apologies either."

It was hard to explain it. Because he had practically no experience in talking about himself. About his self-imposed self-control that had encased him in cement with very few peepholes for the outside world. About all his relationships that had to be worked out and worked on. So instead of talking to her, he now merely permitted himself to think aloud.

"We love each other, and it's as simple as that," she said.

"To you, maybe. But I must try to understand it. And see it

in shadowless surgical lights. Because I grew up without a model and I had nothing against which I could measure my own relationships. So I had to create emotional yardsticks for myself."

"Your son must have changed all that."

"I wouldn't be so sure."

Her silence offered help. His new silence did not make it easy for her. They fell asleep in a shiverish embrace, fully dressed, on top of her bed.

Over breakfast, they went through Mara's research notes once more.

"Who's this Captain L. W. Con Mellou?"

"Used to fly VIP trips for AeroCorp. That's about all I know," said Mara. "Right at the beginning somebody mentioned to me that he had some sort of problem situation with a Sarissa."

"That's odd."

"What?"

"I'm sure I haven't seen his name or this problem situation in Stacey's files. I ought to meet him."

"He seems a little elusive but we can try."

"Let's. And the sooner the better."

Mara rechecked the lists of incidents she had from NTSB and AeroCorp. Mellou was not mentioned by either source. She called her best contact at NTSB, only to be told that there was no Mellou/Sarissa incident or accident on record.

"It may be a lie," said Penn.

Mara disagreed. "They know that under the Freedom of Information Act they could be forced to show me whatever they have on file. So I'm sure that if it's ever been there it's now been removed."

Singer was not available, but Penn's call was put through without any fuss to Drayton. "Your message once offered to help me any way you can."

"I remember," said Drayton. "What can I do for you?"

"I'd like to do a few take-offs under test conditions."

"Test flights are strictly for professionals. That's one of the few things I cannot allow you to do, Captain. There could also be some legal problems."

"I'm the only one who really knows what the controls felt like at Paya Lebar."

"You've told us everything, I believe, and we ran a full series of tests."

"Then I'll have to arrange it some other way."

"I can't stop you, unfortunately, but I strongly advise you against it. Anything else I can do for you?" He made it sound as if he had already done a great deal for the pilot.

"Yes, please. Could you put me in touch with Captain Mellou?"

"No." The answer came too quickly. As if Drayton had expected the request. Had anybody warned him? Someone from NTSB? Unlikely, but not impossible. Drayton explained hurriedly: "I mean, I don't keep track of every goddamn pilot who ever worked for us, so how could I put you in touch with him? Try the usual channels, Captain, that's all I said."

"And you wouldn't remember if Mellou had a Sarissa incident or minor accident while in your service, would you?"

"No . . . nothing that springs to mind readily. . . . So, *if* there was anything, it couldn't have been important. But, if it's any help to you, I can run a check through records."

"Please."

The result was negative. Mara telephoned a designer who used to work for AeroCorp. "Yes, there was once a rumor about some incident involving Mellou and one of those VIP flights," he said, "but I thought it had more to do with drinking and sex at thirty thousand feet than flying troubles."

Mellou's current employers told Mara that he was on extended sick leave and off flying but refused to give her his address. She could only trace it through a policeman friend. Penn accompanied her to the fairly luxurious house with a Mediterranean portico, on the edge of a Westchester country club. An old housekeeper with a creaking Greek accent told Mara, posing as a friend of Mellou's, that the Captain was at home.

"You mean in the house? Can we see him?"

"Don't you know nothin'? What friend are you? Home is where mother lives. Near Jackson, Mississippi."

"So that's where he's hiding out." Mara tried to make it sound casual and lighthearted.

"Greeks don't like hidin'."

"What then?"

"He's spittin'. That's what."

Penn had a distinct sensation of being watched. He turned quickly enough to see a shadow move behind a clump of trees. But he could not be sure. The area was too dark and the wind forced the branches to gesticulate.

Messrs. Fortnum and Mason were either fifteen seconds late or Barraclough's watch was fast. He stared up at the clock impatiently because he disliked departures from the routine. The doors opened and the figures emerged at last. They were about to exchange courtesies when a taxi stopped behind him.

"Your cab, sir."

Barraclough turned quickly. He recognized the voice. Mott wore a felt cap pulled right down on his nose so that he had to tilt his head back a little to see the road at all. Barraclough sat in behind him.

For ten minutes the Brigadier drove in silence as he went through his lose-the-tail-if-any routine. "I'm greatly impressed with your proposals," he said at last.

"Thank you, sir."

"You've come down strongly on the side of some gas, and I can see why. But I'm worried."

"So am I, sir. It'll need a great deal of thinking and experimenting."

"We may not have much time. And I remember the disastrous results we had with those knockout sprays."

"There wasn't much wrong with the sprays, sir, but the gas tended to disperse too fast in the open air to cause the required effect. But, in this case, much of the problem would be eliminated by the fact that the flight deck is a strictly confined space, the volume of air and the speed with which the air is changed could be measured and safely predicted, and if the substance is released fast in sufficient quantity . . . Well, I wouldn't quite say, Hey presto, but something like that, I suppose."

"I see what you mean."

"Besides, the sprays we used were children's toys compared with what's available right now."

"What do you have in mind?"

"Well, a little bird tells me that the MoD chemical research plant at Nancekuke did a lot of useful work on improving Sarin GB, the stuff developed by the Germans during the war, and on other new nerve gases."

"Naturally." Mott hoped he sounded sufficiently knowledgeable, well-informed and therefore bored. "And you've also considered the Americans' Big Eye, I suppose."

"That, in fact, may be just the stuff we need. I mean a version of that, because, as you know, President Nixon stopped further development of that particular nerve gas, but our chaps at Porton Down did a little homework off their own bat, and the results are not bad, not bad at all."

"Not bad may not be good enough. How good is it? I mean, I can't recall any details offhand . . ."

"Well, at least in confined spaces, it produces almost instantaneous incapacitation."

"It's the word *almost* that worries me. A few seconds may be enough for the pilot to radio a Mayday message."

"Most unlikely, sir, with the NQ version, I'm told. The gas is quite colorless and odorless, you see, and although a knockout jus'-like-that is biologically impossible, the presence of NQ is first detected only by its effects, which are violent convulsions and a certain degree of stupor accompanied by a lack of muscle coordination. It attacks both through the lungs and the skin, and affects the nervous system while the blood carries it directly to the brain. The first couple of breaths of NQ would produce sufficient incapacity to prevent a pilot from recognizing the threat, noticing that the rest of the crew is also affected, putting on his oxygen mask and sending out the Mayday." Barraclough's voice reached a crescendo; this time he was unable to hide his pride.

"Sounds good."

"It is good, sir."

But Mott was not yet convinced. "Then why don't we use it against skyjackers?"

Barraclough smiled. "That's the point, sir. We're not sure about the long-term effects. Or the precise short-term effects, for that matter. I mean it may kill indiscriminately by respiratory failure or suffocation due to vomiting. Which wouldn't matter in our case, because our crew would be bound to die and there would be no passengers anyway, but nobody would take that sort of responsibility in an ordinary skyjack situation. And of course the skyjackers would probably be in various positions instead of just the sealed and confined area of the flight deck."

"What if the crew happens to be wearing oxygen masks for some reason at the time?"

"The attack through the skin alone would be slower but just as effective. You see, an old chum of mine at Porton Down says that—"

"Wait. Can't the stuff be pumped through the oxygen supply?"

"It's possible, but it's unlikely that they'd be on oxygen."

"Mm. Yes. Sounds quite ingenious, I must say."

"Thank you, sir. So if you approve of this line of further practical investigation, perhaps you could arrange first a small sample and then a sufficient quantity of NQ for my use."

"That's out of the question. Quite impossible." Did Mott sound alarmed? "I cannot be associated with the project in any way. It's you who'd have to get on with it."

"Oh." Barraclough was very disappointed. Even his most peculiar requirements used to be no problem for Mott in the old days. Supply of anything, information no matter how secret, cooperation of all defense and intelligence personnel, used to be the Brigadier's province. If now he himself would have to approach friends at Porton Down, go to see them at Salisbury, convince them with some cock-and-bull story, and accept the risk of being implicated afterwards . . .

As always, Mott gauged his mood correctly and back-pedaled a little to soothe him. "I know it may mean delays and additional difficulties, but there isn't much I can do. . . . I mean, I'll see if I can help, but this is a special case and it's well recognized by all of us"—and with a finger thrusting toward the sky—"and all the way above. By the way, I've been authorized to offer you a sizable increased advance on your expenses without affecting your final remuneration. . . . You'll find something for you under the foldaway seat."

"Thank you, sir." Barraclough shook his head slightly with undisguised and respectful amazement. Mott was something quite unique. He always looked after his men better than anybody else. Barraclough was bothered by his almost categorical rejection of giving any help. It broke the usual pattern and so upset him. But it was not for him to question Mott. And he was grateful that his request for a fat unmarked envelope had been anticipated.

Captain L. W. Con Mellou's taste buds were almost virginal. Unspoiled by his non-smoking, non-drinking, and not too gluttonous ways, they reacted with an abundance of protective salivation to the lump of tobacco which he had by now rolled and sucked diligently for almost fifty minutes. The juices began to thicken and grow sleek and slippery like mucus on water, as his master, old Henry, used to demand it. And old Henry had standards. Nobody would ever dispute that. Mellou's strong jaw continued the rhythmic vertical motion, now varied with just a hint of gyration. His stance loosened a little from the hips up, his eyes focused on the tin spittoon fifteen feet away, and his cheeks monitored the stillness of the air, ready for the faintest of breezes that might need to be allowed for in his aiming. Silent onlookers, a few of them with folding chairs, moved in closer; they knew the signs. Mellou noticed a pair who did not belong. Dark-haired girl with a tall man. That must be Penn. He had been warned. But right now his job was to concentrate on the target. In the last couple of days his accuracy had left a lot to be desired. The juice felt right. The quid well rolled. Still no wind, came the latest weather report from his earlobe sensors. He raised two fingers to the corners of his mouth and spewed out the projectile with a blast of air and the supporting forward jerk of the body from the hip up. The trajectory was near-perfection. The clink of the spit hitting the rim of the cuspidor was his reward. A truly great shot. Old men nodded, children clapped. Mellou's tongue continued to roll, flatten and roll the carefully measured lump of golden tobacco. The national championship was little more than a night away.

Mellou did not particularly like or dislike tobacco-spitting. He was "kind of born into it," as he sometimes explained. His father had left the island of Poros in search of employment and emigrated to America in the early thirties. In New York he had heard that there was a town called Athens in Georgia, and he found the lure irresistible. Lack of work made him drift from Athens across Alabama, then into Mississippi, where a kindly farmer set him up in business to cement the friendship of his two homelands with good kebabs for good Americans. He named his first American-born son Lincoln Washington Constantine and, because Raleigh, Mississippi, the scene of championships was nearby, he concluded that tobacco-spitting was more American than apple pie, therefore a must for all Mellous wishing to Americanize themselves. On his deathbed he made all his sons promise to keep up the tradition, but by now only L. W. Con spat competitively. And even he was rather ashamed of it when away from Raleigh and among non-spitters. It was a relief to him that soon these double standards of his life would end. His flying days were over. He would run the kebab house, even expand it, perhaps, and marry someone, preferably Greek and acceptable to Mother, someone who could appreciate an honest-to-god twenty-boot spit.

The light had begun to fade and Mellou decided to try a few distance shots before calling it a day. He rocked well back and snapped his neck forward hard for increased firepower, but even his best effort appeared too puny. He measured the flight of the spit with his special twelve-inch boots, walking heel-to-toe down the range. The landing site was nowhere near Snyder's famous, record-breaking 31½-booter. Still, the sweet clink of the spittoons kept ringing in his ear. Accuracy contests had been won by much worse shots than his last. He kept his eyes on Penn and the girl, and he knew he could give them the slip easily enough in the crowd of spectators, but all the time he prayed that they would go away, leave him alone, spare him from making decisions. For, since his nervous breakdown, the world was full of menace, and he found it almost completely impossible to sleep in the dark or to say no to anyone.

An hour later when he saw Penn approaching the restaurant, he shut himself away in his room. But Mother would have no such behavior in her house. If he had visitors, he was to see them.

He quickly drew the curtains when they entered. "Please go away," he whispered.

"Why?"

"I had enough trouble. I don't want any more."

"What trouble?"

"Go away. We shouldn't be seen together."

"Why not?" Penn noticed that Mellou's hand had begun to shake. "Who shouldn't see us?"

The approaching throb of some heavy vehicle came through the curtains. Mellou froze and listened. The sound passed the house and stopped farther up the road. Mellou turned off the light and peeped out. A large pickup truck with a tarpaulin-covered back stood about fifty feet away from Penn's hired car. Mellou rearranged the curtain to cover the window and switched on a small bedside lamp. "Please go away. I can't tell you anything." He appealed to Mara.

"All I ask is that you should listen to me for five minutes," said Penn. "Then, if you want me to, I'll go away without asking questions. Isn't that reasonable?"

Mellou's whole body was trembling now. He nodded, though he would have liked to say no. Penn told him about Paya Lebar. About the pressures to make him shut up and counterpressures to make him move. About Stacey's death. About his suspicions. About the tremendous risk of Sarissa disasters.

Mellou shut his eyes. "My case was different."

"What case? You have no case on record."

"Then why are you here?"

"That's just it. You had a case but nobody wants to know about it."

"Neither do I."

"But you're a pilot. Like me. And you know there's a cover-up. My friends and your friends will die because of your silence."

"It was my fault. But it was nothing. Just nothing. The wing tip hardly touched the ground. Nobody was hurt."

"Then why isn't there anything on record?"

"Because of those fucking, drunken VIP's, that's why! Not because of me. Because it wasn't my fault." He stopped. There was a faint creaking noise in the ceiling. Then silence. Then more creaks. As if someone moved on the flat roof of the sprawling one-story building. "I told you. I told you there would be trouble. Go away." The shake was now uncontrollable.

"Only if you tell me more," said Penn, and he hated himself for it. "When did it happen?"

"Just eight months ago."

"Where?"

"I'll talk to you tomorrow," Mellou whispered. "After the championship. In Jackson." He scribbled an address on a card. "I'll meet you there. Now go." He saw them to the door and shouted, "Go away and never come back, because I'll never talk to you!" for the whole empty street to hear.

As Mara and Penn opened the doors of the car, somebody jumped off the restaurant roof and ran toward the pickup. A hand lifted the tarpaulin for him, and as he jumped on the back the engine fired. Penn would have sworn the driver was the coquettish woman from the New York flight, the one who had planted the drugs on him. He had to find out.

The pickup went slowly, and Penn followed it from a safe distance. They did not notice him or just did not care. Using a cross-country shortcut, they headed east, northeast. Penn could keep well away from them because the open fields offered unrestricted views, but soon clusters of trees appeared, first sporadically, then forming a young forest, and he had to close in if he did not want to lose the truck. The road became more winding and undulating, but speed was increased. The tarpaulin moved and someone looked out. They accelerated. Then another look. And more speed. Penn swore at the hired car. It could hardly keep up with the truck, particularly on the bad road.

"Let me drop you off before I try to cut in front of them," he said.

Mara refused it. "You'd lose them. There're too many side roads they could take."

It was true. And it was no good trying to pretend anything any more. Penn forced the out-of-breath engine to the limit and kept some ten feet behind the truck. The road became even bumpier. Cut into a hillside, it now banked steeply to the right.

Something glittered. Water. The road formed the shore of a huge reservoir. The wall on the left was rocky and some protruding boulders reduced the width to a single lane.

The tarpaulin was lifted slightly once again. The road was now wrapped around a bay, some ten feet above the water level.

"I wish you had a gun," said Mara in a matter-of-fact tone.

"What for?"

The truck accelerated. Penn tried to push his foot through the floor. The tarpaulin was swept aside and two men appeared holding some large conical objects in the shadow. With that, Penn's vision was suddenly blanked out. He never had a chance to notice, let alone recognize, the powerful jets erupting from the large industrial fire extinguishers and covering the windshield with sticky foam. Nothing but the fast-fading memory of the curving road guided him. And only his subconscious knew that he had been trapped deliberately. The offside fender hit a boulder. But he was still in control, steering, slowing down. He tried to smash the windshield but only damaged his knuckles. Gently he touched the brake. The fender hit rocks again and the car spun around. He thought he heard Mara swear. Their necks suffered a tremendous jolt as the whiplash effect tried to remove their heads from their shoulders. Then the splash of water as the front wheels left the road.

Balanced precariously, the car stood on its nose for a long second, then overturned with slow dignity and began to sink. The foam was washed away; only now did Penn catch a glimpse of what it was. He realized that there would be nothing left to show the cause of the crash. Their deaths might be as much an accident as Stacey's was suicide. Water began to seep through around the edges of the windows. His mind worked, but thoughts had to rise through fog; shock still deprived him of clear logic.

"Don't move. Not yet," he whispered as if afraid of being overheard. There was no answer. For the first time he tried to pierce the darkness and look at Mara. She was held by the safety belt, hanging in her seat. The car was upside down. He smelled blood. "Mara . . ." He could not see her eyes. She must be unconscious. He longed to touch her and find out what her injuries were, but it would have been foolhardy to make any except vital moves.

He felt their sink rate begin to slow down. If the car was about to settle on mud, any rocking would help to bury it. "Mara . . ." She did not respond. He rested his head on the roof, positioned his left shoulder to support it, and unbuckled his seat belt. Then, as gently as he could, he lowered Mara, too, to the roof. Once the windows were open, he would have to get her out fast. If only she could help. He pulled her across, moved her head toward the window, and pressed the tab to operate the electric winder. There was a buzz, but nothing happened. He tried it again. The buzz was fainter this time. The electrical system must have been soaked or breached. Another buzz—hardly audible. Now he wished he had a gun. Or any tool to break the glass. With Mara squeezed to him, he could not reach up to his own feet fast, so he tore off her shoe. She moaned. He shook her and shouted at her.

"What happened?"

"We're under water. We must get out." He hammered the windshield with the heel of her shoe, but he could hardly swing his arm and it took several blows to make any impact, let alone smash a hole in the glass. And each blow rocked the car, giving them the distinct sensation of sinking deeper in mud or weeds. Now she began to realize what had happened. Shock paralyzed her and made her sob. Water burst in. The hole now seemed big enough. He tried to wriggle through, planning to pull her out, but she blacked out again and the pressure of inrushing water prevented him from shifting her out of his way. Which left him with no choice. Water filled the car and he was running short of breath. He had to risk pushing her out first. Something stopped her halfway through. Whatever it was had to give. Fast. Treading on the back of his seat he freed her with a jerk.

Something tore through her dress and flesh. The pain made her come to. She opened her eyes and panicked. She tried to hang on to the car, and he had to fight his way through the gap no matter what. Flashing lights began to blind him, the throbs in his ears grew into the deafening cacophony of drums.

Candy was quite determined to take the child. Her mother tried to argue, then cried and begged her not to. "I promised Cornelius to look after him while he's away."

"But I'm his mother."

"Some mother."

Timmy wanted to know where she had been. "Later. I'll tell you later. I'll tell you all sorts of things a little later. Now get your things."

Her mother stood in the door. "Won't you have a cup of tea, love?"

"Not now."

"How about a little something else. I've got it somewhere." She began to rummage in the cupboard for any leftover alcohol in old bottles.

"Not now." Candy took the child's hand. Her mother tried to hold on to him. "Do you want me to get the police? He's my child, you know. Shall I get them?"

Her mother shook her head. How would she ever face the neighbors if the police turned up here with flashing lights and sirens, yelling "Freeze! Freeze!" Or whatever they would shout off the TV screen?

Now Timmy, too, began to cry. But Candy was deaf and blind to everything except the memory of what the overage American hippie in the expensive kid-glove leather gear had told her. The man who sought her out, took her to expensive discos, adored her, pampered her and explained that her future could be bright. Yes, it could be if only she persuaded Penn to return to Britain at once and stop stirring things. And yes, there would be money and help to get her the best sort of separation from

Penn, and above all there would be prospects, anything to please her, a life of her old dreams—"Real electric, baby," a life of her own with no strings. Besides, Timmy would be all right with his father, wouldn't he?

The front page of the local paper was shared out between two headlines. One welcomed the day of the championship, the other announced, "Crash Pilot Crashes Car into Reservoir." Penn did not understand how the local scribe knew about Singapore—nobody had asked him or Mara about it—but there was no time to investigate such petty details. His memory of the last phase of leaving the car was almost completely blank. The only sensation he remembered vividly was the first lungful of air, a fraction of a second before he pulled Mara to the surface by her hair. Then the kiss of life that brought her back, followed by the long hours of looking for help, dragging her along, afraid of leaving her alone anywhere. Now she was in the hospital for a check-up, while step by step he managed to convince the police that he had not been drunk and had not tried to kill her. It was pointless mentioning the truck and the foam, which had disappeared from the scene. He called Mellou's number, but there was no answer. By now, everybody would be at the range. At last the police began to show some sympathy toward his plight and offered to take him to Raleigh, because, he explained, it was vital for him to see Mellou most urgently.

The Keeper of the Cuspidor checked and rechecked the distance. The competitors had been chewing diligently almost since daybreak in full sight of the judges, who monotonously repeated their warnings—"No licorice, no foreign substance, no artificial salivators"—more to emphasize their own importance than to doubt the spitters' integrity.

Mellou was unhappy with his own preparations. The quid in his mouth tasted a little sharper than usual, even bilious. He tried a few practice shots, then popped another lump of his own brand of tobacco mixture in his mouth. It tasted no better. Some odd rigidity spread in his muscles, but he chewed away, thought about his standard mouth-watering breakfast and saw no reason for the strange aroma. He felt dizzy and numb. His salivation began to reach the right level. Swallowing the liquid was the best way to test its viscosity. His throat greeted the juice with slight revulsion. A little pain in his stomach never had a chance to grow up into a big pain. Mellou swayed, heard the approaching siren of a police patrol car, collapsed and died by the time his body hit the ground.

Poisoning was thought to be the cause of death even before a toxicological investigation could be undertaken, and it was recognized that any number of people might have had access to his tobacco. Penn was interrogated for several hours about his relationship with Mellou, but the locals, and that included the police, were inclined to suspect the scores of visiting spitters in the first place. After all, what better motive could anyone think of? Who would benefit from "our boy's untimely departure" more than an aspirant to the accuracy title? Mellou had achieved at last his father's ambition: he died as a local good ole boy.

Apart from gashed flesh and a cut near the hairline above a peach-size bump on her forehead, Mara's injuries were very minor, and sedation had taken care of the direct shock effect. She had fought hard against the gushing tears of fright but succumbed to them at last when she realized that the police still treated Penn as a potential suspect rather than the potential victim of a renewed attempt on his life. He had to promise to keep reporting his whereabouts to the police and remain available for further questioning, but they would let him go and take her back to New York.

The old amorphous fear grabbed him by the throat as they left the police station. Whoever killed Stacey and Mellou must have been an expert at making deaths look like accidents or suicides. In Singapore and London, the violent attacks must have been warnings. The planted drug was a last non-lethal attempt to keep him out of the States and the investigation. Perhaps his death was then considered to be too conspicuous, something that might cast an outsize shadow over the Sarissa case. But now somebody must have decided that he was a greater menace alive than dead. So he had succeeded, at least partly. He had called the shots on himself, and here they came. Except that he could not run away. Not without betraying Stacey's memory and his own image in Timmy's eyes. And not without his father and the dead bomber crew yelling, "Poltroon!" at him. But whatever could be done had to be done in a hurry. Time was running out, he knew.

Mara gave him Singer's private number and he called it from Jackson while waiting for the New York flight.

The news about Mellou shook Singer. "Can't believe it, just can't . . ." he kept repeating.

"Lucky it didn't happen a day earlier," said Penn. "Then he couldn't have told me about his accident."

"What accident?"

"Don't you know?"

"I don't know what you're talking about."

"It's his famous flight with the VIP's on board. You know, a junket."

"There was no accident!"

"If you mean that there's nothing on record—"

"I mean there's nothing to be on record. It was all among VIP's, an entirely private affair, nothing to report to us or any aviation authorities."

"How about the damaged wing tip?" The pause that followed the question, the only factual reference available to Penn, demonstrated that he had touched a live nerve.

"Oh that . . . Yes, I remember now. That had nothing to do with the flight. It happened on the ground while the aircraft was being towed, and the damage was quite insignificant. We can discuss it any time you wish. Any time. But I can't discuss what some Congressmen get up to, if you know what I mean. That's private, you understand, I'm sure."

"Yes, but the way I understand it, it can be useful to me and an embarrassment to you."

"To me?"

"You're the company troubleshooter, aren't you? Well, sometimes, the troubles shoot back. This may be just the occasion." Penn was not quite sure why he said that. Perhaps he felt that it was time that others should grow as worried as he was.

And if that was his aim, he achieved something. Singer tried in vain to contact Termine, then Drayton, and when both failed to call him back, he got rather drunk and asked Anna to drive him to his office, where he wanted to check all the confidential Sarissa papers in his personal safe.

Penn's call to London was not very productive. The Beaver was alone in Stacey's old office, but she sounded harassed and, although not unsympathetic, reluctant to talk to him. She had strict instructions not to discuss the case with anyone. "Gone are the days with Mr. Stacey, bless his soul. Only my rheumatism is the same." She confirmed, nevertheless, that there was no record of Mellou's accident or incident, whatever it might have been. "When do you think it happened?" she asked.

"Just eight months ago."

"That figures."

"What?"

"The date. It would place it in the batch of minor incidents Mr. Stacey used to ask all them questions about."

Penn heard the click of her lighter as she lit another cigarette halfway round the world. "Is the new man asking the same questions then?"

"No. I mean, can't say he does." There was a pause, and then she whispered urgently as if that would protect her from anybody overhearing their conversation. "Don't ask such things. Things are different now. Mr. Cleaff is much quicker. He's about to wind up the case, if you know what I mean."

Cleaff, in fact, processed the available data most efficiently. He had no special respect for Penn's flying skill, and no intention to allow himself bias one way or the other through personal contacts. Yes, pilot error seemed rather obvious to him, but he was not prepared to jump to conclusions and apportion blame on the basis of superficial evidence, particularly not when he could outline—if not pinpoint—the underlying problem, the cause behind the cause, the circumstances that brought about the pilot's error, the invisible hazard that might endanger other pilots and other aircraft—human fatigue under excessive stress. In the draft of his report for the Singapore government he planned to indicate a borderline case and argue that, due to annoying delays, technical difficulties and weather problems, the pilot's reactions might not have been at their sharpest at the crucial moment when the aircraft reached the point of no return. With that he tried to explain Penn's action, not vindicate it. He found it "unfortunate" that international regulations and the airlines did not make allowances for such factors, and that Penn himself had failed to anticipate the potential effect of adverse conditions.

Cleaff discussed the case with SupraNat, whose Chief Pilot Brown promised to take another "long, hard look" at the problem of human fatigue induced by special conditions. At the same time, Brown tried to defend Penn, although he conceded that his friend could not be fully exonerated from blame. All he hoped to achieve was that Penn's reputation should not be tarnished to the extent of rendering him unemployable. That Penn's lifelong career hopes were at an end was a foregone conclusion to Brown. With all the bad publicity Penn had received, Brown could give him only a reasonable desk job or suitable references if he chose to emigrate to some underdeveloped country where he might fly cargo and the like.

The first part of the report Cleaff drafted was the appendix. It contained the summarized results of Stacey's arduous technical investigation. Privately, over a friendly jar in the Coal Hole, he admitted to colleagues that Stacey's findings were as petty as the man himself, but on paper he was fair enough to pay lip service to the dead man's effort and communicate every bit of it to the manufacturers as well as all Sarissa users. A typical example of Stacey's discoveries was that, when among hundreds of parts the thickness of the pilots' instrument panel had been weight-reduced, the corresponding reduction in the length of the panel fixing screws was not affected. When he informed AeroCorp, such "technical blemishes" were noted. In due course they would be rectified on all new aircraft coming off the production line. It did not add up to much of a eulogy *in memoriam* of an accident investigator "who could not take the pressures and the recognition of his own failure like a man."

The haunting memory of that calamitous audition at the Pussy(cat) formed a strong bond between Sally and Barraclough. She visited him frequently, laughed at his little jokes, accompanied him on long walks, listened with admiration to his wartime exploits, and bossed him about as he had never been made to jump since his earliest days in uniform—and he loved it all. Fraser, Betty M., was pleased, fulfillment in this life was, could be, in sight after all. "When shall we tell her about us?" she kept asking him, but did not mind when he answered, "Not yet, not just yet," every time.

Barraclough wanted to complete the job in hand first, and he had nothing to complain about; progress was quite satisfactory. Old friends at the various chemical warfare research establishments still trusted him implicitly and supplied him with minute gas samples for his experiments. He worked in a rented lock-up garage, with Fraser sitting in the car just outside the door, partly to keep out visitors, and partly to check from time to time if he was still alive. The latter duty she imposed upon herself despite Barraclough's angry protestations, because he used himself as a guinea pig, knocked himself out several times, and injured his head when he collapsed once with violent convulsions. Another time, he would have probably choked on his own vomit as he put his head into a plastic crate, the scaled-down model of a flight deck with its limited volume of air, where just a whiff more than the intended sample of gas had been released accidentally.

Having finalized his choice of gas (and Mott promised him at last to help him obtain a sufficient working quantity of the NQ), Barraclough now concentrated on the method of delivering his blow. He studied virtually every word that had ever been published about the Sarissa and its special worldwide operation, and noticed—in view of the heavy promotion, it would have been impossible not to—the tremendously profitable spinoffs of the Sarissa marketing operation. Among all the Sarissa bags, caps and badges, Sarissa chocolate and tinned Sarissa snacks, Sarishirts, Saricigars and Sarifreshments, the Saricola and the Sarinade caught his eye. The presence of such bottle splinters and splashed soft drinks would always remain quite inconspicuous even if some unforeseeable factor caused the crash to happen at a spot where the wreckage could be recovered and examined. In flight, the bottles would have to be concealed from the pilots, but that as well as installation were Mott's province. Having surveyed the layout of the flight deck, Barraclough decided to recommend that the containers should be hidden in the small cavity behind the map rack.

The experiments reached a crucial stage. He made some tentative decisions, but Mott's early approval was essential. At his usual table in the tea shop he read the *Financial Times* and watched the patisserie counter over the edge of the page. The Brigadier appeared, bought a few cakes and noted, with a slight nod, the unmistakable pinkness of the paper signaling that Barraclough wanted a meeting. An hour later in the security of Mott's cab they discussed the projected fate of an unknown Sarissa crew.

"How good is your fitter, sir?"

"Pretty good. On the staff of AeroCorp."

"Will he have sufficient time and opportunity to fix and conceal the containers?"

"I should hope so. But he'll need precise orders. What's your plan?"

"It's like this, sir. We could fit a barometric switch to the containers to trigger off the spray when the aircraft reaches a certain height, but if, fortuitously, the crash occurs overland, the presence of surplus altimeter parts would immediately indicate the possibility of sabotage. The same would apply to any timing device—with which there might be an additional problem if, for instance, the flight is delayed for any reason. But if our man could connect the trigger mechanism to one of the standard altimeters of the aircraft . . ."

"Wouldn't the connection be traceable?" Mott interrupted him impatiently.

"Not if we used a specially molded thin and brittle strip with a printed circuit. It would be shattered to powder by the impact."

"Would the same thing work if the flight happened to be on autopilot at the time?"

"No difference at all. In fact, if possible—I mean if it's a long transAtlantic or Pacific flight—I'd set the trigger to work in two stages. It would be armed when the plane went through, say, 34,000 feet on its way up, and it would fire when the flight descended crossing the same altitude once again."

"Why 34,000?"

"Just a convenient height. The Sarissa cruises above 35,000 feet."

For the first time, Mott smiled. Barraclough was a gem. Pity he was growing too old, finicky and jittery. "Good show, jolly good."

"Thank you, sir." Barraclough touched his nose with embarrassment. He was afraid he might blush. "What I'm working on is a quick fixing system. I want to make it easy for our man at the plant. Is he a mechanic, sir?" Mott glanced at him, and Barraclough apologized hurriedly for the question he was not supposed to ask.

"Let's say he has access to the aircraft."

"Could he declare an altimeter faulty?"

"Perhaps."

"I could then supply the device complete with an altimeter and he could just swap one set for another."

"Mm. Yes. Work on it." Mott pulled up at a red traffic light and closed his eyes to envisage the installation of the device. The light changed to green, but Barraclough would not disturb the chief. If he wanted to move on, he would. It was not for subordinates to urge and advise. Drivers held up by the cab began to honk. Mott gave them a leisurely two-finger salute and drove off, in true cabby style, so slowly that they were all caught by the lights already turning red again behind him. He winked at Barraclough in the mirror. "You must work on your cover, right?" He then had a few questions about the expected behavior of the gassed pilots and the aircraft. "What happens if they're on autopilot when they pass out?"

"The chances are, I'm told, that if they're set on level flight, the plane would carry on straight for quite a while. In principle, it could fly on and on until it ran out of fuel, but more probably the nose would tend to tuck under slowly and gradually. If the descent had already begun when they were knocked out, the aircraft would just continue on its course, at a steeper and steeper angle, straight into the sea."

"I must have some more details about that, but you need not be concerned. I'll get it." And after another pause. "Yes, if you were looking for an OK, you have it. Go ahead. Any other problems?"

"A few technical ones, but I'm working on them."

In Mara's New York apartment the phone rang.

"Can I talk to Captain Penn?"

"Sure. Who's calling?"

"I want to do him a favor, so never mind the name."

"Hang on." Mara held out the phone to Penn, but covered the mouthpiece. "I've no idea who she is, but the voice sounds a bit familiar. She wants to do you a favor."

Penn took the phone. The woman spoke to him rapidly but with pauses in odd places as if her speech were sprinkled with irrational punctuation. Or perhaps she was reading from illegible handwriting. "You must stop going around suspecting secrets everywhere. That's why you'll get a chance to read all the confidential documents that exist. There's nothing else. You understand?"

"Go on."

"Go to the public library. . . . You know where the big library is?"

"I'll find it."

"In the main card index there'll be an entry under your name. That'll tell you what to do next but only if you go there alone, you understand?"

"Doesn't sound very complicated."

"You must be alone. If you're not alone all the way from where you are, there'll be no card for you. Be there at noon precisely." She rang off.

Mara tried to persuade him not to go. "We can't prove it, but we've just survived an ingenious murder attempt devised to look like an accident. You're dealing with determined professionals."

"They've bungled it, haven't they?"

"That's no guarantee that they'll go on bungling it. If your interpretation is right, they've already succeeded with Stacey and Mellou. You want to be the next?"

It was pouring non-stop for the third day in London, and Candy felt caged in, staring at the silent phone as Penn used to not all that long ago. Timmy kept asking questions about where his father was, why he could not stay with Granny as arranged, what important news was Candy waiting for. At last the call came. That his language was a little passé did not bother her. His hip talk was quaint and excited her. She gave him the nickname "My Ugly American."

"Sorry, baby, couldn't suss out where your man was until now. But now you can ring him in New York."

"Where?"

"At his chick's place. You got the number, right?"

"Yes. And where are you?"

"Still in the States. You remember what you have to say?"

"Er . . . yes, I suppose so."

"You sound wired. You're not sure."

"I'm worried. Wired if you like. You can push a man only so far. And I've pushed him way beyond that already."

"You can't flip out now, baby. This is no time to be uptight or develop new hang-ups. Remember what a groovy time we had? You really buzzed, baby, and we'll have lots more of the same, with plenty of bread and anything you dig. And I do mean anything, if you do the right things now."

"He'll kill me."

"Trust me, baby, trust your ugly American, just as I trust you. And I'm getting good vibes, so don't blow your cool. Nothing will happen to you."

"I hope so." She tried to understand what attracted her to him. It was not just his money, and certainly not his huge Adam's apple.

He hung up, and she dialed Mara's number in New York. There was no answer.

The headlines were full of Sarissa Mark 2, the secret project: Drayton's achievement in keeping the new version from the press throughout its development, plans for a Farnborough spectacular for the world trade, and above all the magnificent prospects for new deals which would make aviation marketing history and cloud the skies with Sarissas. AeroCorp executives, aviation commentators, airline officials, managers of SupraNat and government representatives were interviewed in seventeen countries. They spoke in glowing terms of what they already knew about the aircraft. All those who had been photographed, too, were now seen toasting Mark 2 in Sarichampagne, a special reserve, bearing the date of the first Sarissa's first appearance on the drawing board. But no picture of the aircraft as yet. That was to appear only on the opening day of the international air show. The papers were bursting with true, half-fictitious and completely fabricated stories about ruthless security measures, armed guards and helicopter patrols of the AeroCorp base to prevent any unauthorized and premature sighting of the plane.

Penn pretended to read it all avidly as he sat on a bench in Bryant Park that was already teeming with unsavory characters. He felt uncomfortable among them, and would have hated to stay on there after nightfall, but this seemed to be the best place to check if anyone had been following him. He was sure that only a drunken, tottering, ageless and sexless bundle of rags had come into the park after him, and it remained there in a glassy-eyed stupor when he left. He walked down 42nd Street, along the public library block adjoining the park, stopped on the corner of Fifth Avenue to buy a pretzel, and munched lazily away at the tasteless reheated crumbs so as to give himself a final chance to take a look around. He glanced at his watch: 11:58—time to go in. It annoyed him that he could not spot his tail although he had been warned that he would be watched all the way. Perhaps the woman was bluffing. Perhaps there would be no note for him in the catalogue.

Anna Singer shed the outer layer of rags, dropped it behind a bush and hurried out of Bryant Park. She stared up at the university building opposite the library and raised her hand. She could not see anyone behind the fourteenth-floor windowpane, but she knew that Singer's friend, a private eye, was there and would see her just as he would have seen Penn. By now he would have spoken to Singer, who was running the operation from a public phone booth in the library.

The unexpected flight to New York and Singer's vague explanations had puzzled Anna. The peculiar telephone call she had to make and the masquerade of tailing Penn with the detective had upset her; now she felt tired and uneasy climbing the stairs to join her husband as arranged.

P-a . . . P-e . . . Pembroke . . . Pepys . . . he had gone too far. Then a few cards back a William Penn, and then a similar card with a typed note under his name: "Use microfilm reader No. 2. When you've finished, leave film where you found it, then leave building."

Penn looked up. Nobody seemed to be watching him. He found the room with the bank of microfilm machines. No. 2 was the second from the left in the last row. A note on it showed that it had been reserved for him. A film was already in the machine. A librarian asked him if he needed any assistance. No, it was simple enough.

The first picture came up: a pilot's statement about a Sarissa incident. Strictly confidential. If Penn was caught reading or just being in possession of such material, he could be charged with theft and industrial espionage. Even if there was no conviction, the muck of court reports would stick. He decided it was pointless to worry about it. If somebody wanted to trap him, it was too late to run for it. If the caller was trying to help him, it would be worth taking a chance.

A few handwritten notes. More signed statements by crews, passengers, airport staff. A jerky, disjointed two-page report by Mellou. It read as if a third page in the middle had been removed. The Simms case. Transcripts of the first taped accounts. Passengers about the in-flight turbulence. Nothing startling, but at least it was the stuff Stacey wanted to see. The originals instead of edited summaries. An avalanche of harsh words immortalized in the report writer's vernacular: "Passengers verbalized their discomfort." It appeared that they had plenty to verbalize. Simms's account itself testified to that. But Penn had to admit that there was nothing anybody would deliberately want to keep secret. Perhaps Stacey should have been grateful for being spared from reading all this waste and by-product. On the other hand, someone might have given all this to Penn to mislead him and to prove that there was nothing else to look for.

Another two "CAT encountered" incidents. A Captain Johnson described the aircraft response to the control input as "sluggish, at times . . ." Sluggish. Quite understandable in the circumstances, but the word stuck in Penn's mind. A statement (from Tape 723/B5) by Linda Waller. That must be Linda Greenway, Mara's friend. In flowery language she briefly described the flight and her irksome confrontations with a couple of peripatetic drunken ass slappers who constantly tried, with all sorts of tricks, to get extra service of free Saribrandies, and who "found themselves covered in piss and peas and French dressing when at dinnertime we must have dropped a few thousand feet." After it had hit the unexpected pocket of clear air turbulence, the flight became quite bumpy. The weather deteriorated fast. Johnson switched the Fasten Seat Belts on, ordered the girls to stop cleaning up and serving dinner, then went off autopilot to fly manually and, guided by the weather radar, maneuver around the eye of the storm. That was when the controls felt sluggish. Hadn't Mellou used the same expression in the description of his landing? Penn checked back. Yes, Mellou did use the very words. Penn thought about Paya Lebar. "Sluggish response" could have been an apt definition of his initial impression about the developing emergency in Singapore.

His progress was slow. The film might take all afternoon to read. He looked up and around. One of the many keen readers was probably there only to watch him. Which one? Would anyone stop him if he tried to walk away with the film?

The private eye grew impatient. Anna had promised to take over from him after an hour or so to give him a chance for a pee and coffee. Yet no sign of her—and he was not supposed to lose sight of the microfilm.

At the time when Penn settled down with the machine, the Singers had coffee. Anna wanted to know more about the whole mysterious operation, but Singer was not in a talkative mood. "I think I'm entitled to some explanation."

"Later, honey. Another time. But don't think I'm ungrateful for your help. It was your greatest performance ever."

"Thank you. But omit the curtain calls, because I still stink from those rags."

She urgently needed a wash and facial restoration. He knew a small bar nearby, just the place for it. Once there, it would have been foolish to miss the opportunity for a quick liquid lunch. By the time she returned to join him, refreshed and thirsty, he was on his second refill. He was now more relaxed, she noticed right away. Her years as a Washington aviation lobbyist had taught her to see the signs. And she was a good listener. Words began to pour out of him. Disillusionment with Drayton. Suspicions about Termine. The limits of stretching his own business ethics in the service of AeroCorp. Of any company. The fears of being set up as the whipping boy. "If Penn suspects me of being in charge of a cover-up, others might get the same idea. And I won't have it. Not that. Not me."

"Has there been a cover-up?" she asked lightly.

"No. Well, not in that sense."

"Not in what sense?"

"Nothing that would affect the safety of our operations. Or anybody's operations. Or the design of the Sarissa. Nothing like that. But it's my job to protect the good name of AeroCorp and not to help our competitors conduct a smear campaign."

"Against the Sarissa?"

He nodded. "And against Congressmen and others on whose

goodwill we must depend. Nobody on the Hill would talk to us any more if we publicized their junkets."

"Then why are you giving information to Penn?"

"Because I want him to know that we have no secrets. At least I have no secrets. No dirty linen, no skeletons in my personal safe. And I want him to know that."

"But are you going the right way about it? I mean, I'm worried, honey, worried about you."

"And I love you, too."

"Listen," she said and squeezed his hand, "why don't you discuss the whole thing with Charles?"

"He wouldn't understand. He's just against releasing any information that's not absolutely necessary. He thinks it helps to de-emphasize things. It's part of his covering his own tracks."

"What do you mean?"

"It's a long story. But take it from me, he's covering himself in all sorts of devious ways. So now it's my turn to look after Number One." Singer drank fast. It helped him to convince himself.

"Charles won't take things like that lying down."

"How would you know?"

"You always tell me. And I know his reputation."

"There's no way for him to find out about this. Even Penn doesn't know who's giving him the stuff, because it was you who called him."

She touched his face. "Do me a favor, honey. Let me go back and grab the film before the damage is done. Then talk to Charles. Don't fight him. He's too powerful."

"Not for me, he isn't. For I'm the only one he cannot touch. I know too much, you see? Far too much. And I can dish out a little of his own medicine, you see, because he's a good master to learn from. So don't worry." He looked at his wafer-thin gold Omega. "Anyway . . . one more for the road and time to go back."

While he ordered, she wanted to go and make a phone call to her mother. "Do you think we can visit her in the evening? She'd be hurt if she knew that we were in town and didn't even call."

"We'll see. Just don't be long, honey."

Penn's eyes began to burn as he stared into the sharp light of the reading machine through the microfilm. And yet more documents to scan, others to recheck more attentively. "Sluggish response." The words kept echoing in his mind. He ran the film back to Simms. This time he read the reticent pilot's statement more carefully. There was no reference to any sluggishness. But, at some stage Simms "had to fight the controls." And that would have described Penn's take-off emergency even more precisely. Certainly worth asking the man about it.

The library was about to close when Penn stood up from the machine and, leaving the film behind as instructed, walked away without trying to spot the tail any more. Now that the street was dark, it would have been an impossible task for him anyway.

The private detective recovered the film, handed it to Singer, collected his honorarium in cash, and wished the couple safe journey back to California.

Anna made another phone call and returned with good news to her husband: "You're off duty, honey. I'll see Mother alone and meet you for dinner. You've been spared."

"I didn't mind going."

"No—no, it would have been a chore. Besides, she wants to talk to me alone for some reason."

It meant they would need two cabs at this busy hour, because Singer had been against using one of the company limousines. They walked toward the Avenue of the Americas, where the direction of traffic would suit both of them and where, Anna suggested, they would have the best chance. After only some twenty yards down 42nd Street, a cab stopped and disgorged its fare right in front of them. Anna took the cab, which pulled away fast. Singer walked on.

The bunch of muggers pounced as he reached Bryant Park. There were four of them. One hit his head from behind, the others caught his arms, held his limp body upright, shielding it from passers-by, frog-marched him into the park, dumped him behind the bushes, and were all over him like piranha devouring all his possessions within seconds. They left him unconscious, bleeding from several deep skull wounds.

A soft sun shone on Angmering-on-Sea and spotted the few glittery corners on the tiny shopfront among the spreading patina patches of neglect. "Nothing a good coat of paint couldn't put right, sir, nothing at all," Collins, the old tobacconist insisted. "You seem to be just the man to do it, if you don't mind me saying so. Just the man. A few new glass display shelves and it'll come up beautifully, bright as a button. Because only what you do for yourself is well done. Nobody puts his heart into paid work these days, sir. Not any more."

"Yes, my *husband* is quite good at these things," said Fraser, Betty M., with as naughty a smile as she would ever manage.

"I'm sure he is, Mrs. Barraclough. It shows when a man is good with his hands. As the late Mrs. Collins used to tell me . . ." and the tobacconist was away, repeating the only thoughts that occupied his mind, how he and the wife used to hope to grow very old and die together serving at the counter, how cancer had cheated them, and how he knew, just knew, that the shop and its loyal customers would be in good hands with the Barracloughs.

Since he had accepted the assignment, this was the first day Barraclough was willing to take off from work and spend away from his experiments. It was the first time that he met, over lunch, Betty M.'s sister who lived by the sea, and that he saw the shop. And he was pleasantly surprised. Talking family was less disconcerting than he had feared, and yes, Betty M. was right, he would discover a new, completely different life to be lived out in the sleepy retirement belt of the holiday resort. Sally might be a little bored by it all, but nobody expected her to spend all her time with her newly found father. Not that he would mind, far from it, but it was best not to expect too much.

On their way back, they had a small compartment to themselves on the train. It was a good opportunity to think aloud together, go through the plan step by step, and let her kitchen logic spot and wipe out any snags he might have overlooked. One aspect that worried him was the proportion of gas to the volume of air in the flight-deck enclosure. He aimed to achieve oversaturation, but the speed of releasing the gas was limited because he was against the use of special pressurized containers or fans, which would leave numerous telltale pieces of wreckage.

"Would it ruin the operation if the door happened to be open at the time of release?" asked Fraser.

"No, but it would slightly increase the chances of somebody sending out an emergency message."

"Then you'll have to reduce the chances of the door being kept open. I mean permanently. Perhaps I could think of something."

Psychological warfare was Fraser's speciality. She had often achieved more with a bit of clever scaremongering than he would with his loud bangs and flashes. The plan she now devised was simple. A gradual threat campaign must be aimed at AeroCorp and one or two Sarissa operators. It must be serious enough to gain attention, but a bit amateurish to avoid calling for new, extreme defense measures. There could be vaguely political messages from some obscure organization or impassioned protests from religious or anti-pollution fanatics, and threats that a Sarissa would be skyjacked in flight. If it was not overdone, it would be in nobody's interest to publicize it, and the reaction would probably be no more than stricter boarding checks and additional in-flight security measures, such as instructions to keep the flight-deck door closed whenever possible.

"We're a good team, Betty M.," Barraclough said. In his terms, praise like that was worth a Nobel prize. And Fraser knew it.

In a hectic three-hour stretch, Mara and Penn left fourteen messages in nine towns for Captain Simms, who was on leave. In the New York head office, the airline for which Simms flew refused to say more than that as soon as he returned to duty the word to contact Miss Boone would certainly be passed to him. When would that be? As the irate duty officer looked up the rota, Mara read the names of Simms's crew over his shoulder. The list contained Linda Waller. Mara called her from a phone booth in the lobby.

"You once promised to help me, strictly off the record, if you could. I need that help now, Linda."

"Oh yes."

"I'm looking for Captain Simms."

"Oh."

"Can you put me in touch with him?"

"Well . . ." Linda hesitated. "Why me?"

"Because I'm running out of other possibilities. And you could at least tell me the route you're due to fly with him."

"How did you know about the schedule?"

"A friend told me. Does it matter?"

"No. Not really. It's an L.A.–Miami–Caracas flight, but we'll take it only on the first leg, because first we have to pick up the plane at the AeroCorp plant where some work's being done on it, and ferry it to L.A."

"That's the day after tomorrow."

"That's right. You know everything."

"Except where Simms is. Can you help?"

"I can try. But don't expect much from him. He's a bastard."

"Has he gone to ground or something?"

Linda laughed nervously. "It's a good question, honey."

"Will you answer it?"

"His wife is rich and a bitch."

"Better than being poor and a bitch."

"Yeah, because she can afford to have him tailed. So he must be careful. But he's always on the lookout for light relief, if you know what I mean."

"Do you know where he's holed up now?"

"Only because I promised to pick him up tomorrow and drive him to Kennedy."

It was one of those studio apartments in a small old house near the eastern end of 35th Street. All the windows were dark and nobody answered the doorbell. Penn had no choice but to wait there all night if necessary while Mara returned home so that someone should be available if Simms had received one of the messages and decided to call.

At two o'clock in the morning a taxi arrived. A sparrow of a woman stepped out and opened the door of the house while Simms paid the fare.

"What a lucky coincidence to see you, Captain," exclaimed Penn. "I meant to get in touch with you all day." Simms made a dash for the door, but Penn caught him by the arm. "Are you inviting me in or would you prefer a loud discussion in the street?" He knew it was below the belt but he was past caring.

Simms glanced furtively up and down the street, then pulled Penn toward the door. "Yeah, come and have some coffee."

The girl friend was not much to look at, middle-aged and somewhat dumb, and if that was Simms's refuge from his wife, well . . . But Penn tried not to feel sorry for him. Or at least not to show it. Particularly not when Simms refused to discuss any aviation matter. "I told you everything I could when we met the first time. I even tried to help you with . . . er . . . some advice, right?"

"You mean you warned me off."

"If you like."

"I'm grateful."

"Then go now."

"I don't like it, but I must ask you for a favor. My future, your life and the safety of the Sarissa may depend on it."

Simms turned away. "You never give up, do you?"

"I can't. Not until I've flown the Sarissa once more. I don't want to take risks. I don't want to experiment. Just an ordinary take-off to see if it's my memory that's playing tricks on me."

"Talk to your Chief Pilot. Or AeroCorp."

"They won't let me do a test flight."

"Then how can I help you?"

"You're ferrying an aircraft from AeroCorp to L.A. Let me join you."

"You're out of your mind."

"It only shows how important it is." Penn could not admit the growing self-doubts to Simms. Perhaps he was mad at Paya Lebar. Perhaps the controls always felt like that. He could not be sure any more. He had to feel and try it once again.

"Get out of here or I'll call the police."

"It's the perfect opportunity, Simms. The perfect setup with the two of us on board."

"The two of us and the rest of the crew. You're crazy."

"It's only the two of us who matter. Me because I had the accident, so I know what the elevator felt like at Paya Lebar, and you because you described exactly the same thing when you said you had to *fight* the controls."

"Did I say that?"

"Yes. In your initial statement, which was later, well, sort of edited before you signed it."

"And how do you know?"

"Does it matter?"

"I'm interested."

"Somebody showed me some bits and pieces of microfilm which never made the official dockets. Now if I went on that ferry flight with you . . ."

"I'll have to think about it."

"Why? Don't you see what we could perhaps achieve?"

"Only because I *know* what we could achieve. We could break up the damn thing and kill ourselves and the crew in the process. It's crazy. It's a crime!"

"Then why think about it?"

Simms shrugged his shoulders. "Because I see your point. And I want to be fair."

Simms promised to call Penn at Mara's before the night was out. Penn did not believe him, but it did not matter. He already knew what he wanted in the first place: Simms had agreed to doctor his initial statement because the expression "fight the controls" must have seemed truly unimportant while it would have been a free catch phrase for headlines and so bad publicity for the Sarissa.

When Penn opened Mara's door, the first sentence he heard was "No, hang on. I think he's here." And then she shouted, "Corrie?" He walked into the living room. Mara looked pale and worried as she held out the phone to him. "Captain Simms for you."

Simms sounded agitated and a little incoherent. But his decision was clear. He had thought it over and now he was ready to break all the rules in the book and let Penn come on board. Yes, he would sort it out with the rest of the crew, and if they all agreed he would let him do the take-off. Because aviation safety was more important than their careers. And their lives. He sounded a little drunk. But Penn did not care. Linda was wrong. Simms was not a bastard after all. Or not a big enough bastard to let information with potential relevance for safety be kept out of the official records. Because there was no doubt about it. The mention of that microfilm had been the turning point in his attitude.

"Do you read me loud and clear? I can't promise you anything. I don't even know about it at this stage. Is that clear?"

"Yes, yes, I understand."

But Simms repeated it yet again: "Don't expect any help from me. How you get on board, that's your business. But if you're there at oh-six hundred, we'll see what we can do. I can't wait for you one minute."

"Tell me one thing. Where will the plane be parked overnight?"

"I have no idea. In a hangar, I suppose, or on the apron. Your guess is as good as mine."

Mara received his news gloomily. She tried to interrupt him several times, but Penn was so full of it that he had to speak first. "You're not going there, of course," she said at last.

"Of course I am."

"You're out of your mind."

"That's what Simms thought at first, but he came round, didn't he?"

"You can't get to that aircraft. Not in the AeroCorp grounds. It's not on."

"I'll see."

"You'll see nothing. The place is full of alarm systems, armed men and guard dogs. It has a treble security perimeter. You know Drayton's got this thing about secrecy. It's partly a genuine paranoia and partly his gimmick for obtaining government contracts."

"I'll put it to the test."

"Not if I can help it."

"You can't. But you could book me on the earliest available flight while I pack a few things."

"You must ring Candy first. She called twice while you were out."

"Why didn't you tell me?"

"You wouldn't let me. But she said it was urgent. Something to do with your son."

Candy answered the phone right away. Penn asked if the child was all right. "He is . . . At the moment."

"What the hell!"

"Listen, Corrie, and listen to me carefully for once. I want you to be back here within twenty-four hours. By, say, eight tomorrow morning. And in everybody's interest you must stop doing whatever you're doing. I mean it's not your job to play the investigator."

"And it's not your job to tell me that."

"As you wish. But if you're not here in time, I'm going to talk to Timmy. Talk. T-a-l-k. I mean really talk to him. You know what I mean?"

"I think I do. And if I'm right, I'll wring your neck, slowly and for a long time." His voice was so cold and surgical that Mara, though without a clue of what it was all about, began to shiver. She poured herself a large measure from the nearest bottle. It happened to be gin, and she downed it in a seemingly endless gulp.

"I'll have to take that chance," said Candy. Her voice grew a little weaker. "But if it ever comes to that, you'll also have to kill your son if you ever want to erase the memory of what I'm going to tell him." She hung up and waited for the phone to ring again. Yes, she guessed correctly. It was Penn.

"Let me talk to Timmy."

"He's not here," she said. "And don't try to call again, because I'm going out right now and we won't be back until eight tomorrow."

Penn knew that Candy was not bluffing. For some—to him obscure—reason she must have decided to play her one and only trump. And there was nothing he could do to prevent it. Nothing apart from returning to London in time. His life was built on the obsession that he must be loved and admired by his son at any price. Now it was time to pay up. "I must get a seat on the first flight to London," he said quietly without looking at Mara. He heard her pouring herself another drink, which again she killed in one gulp.

"You can't run away, Corrie, not forever, whatever you're running from."

"I'm not running."

She did not argue. And she did not ask what Candy wanted from him, but the question hung heavily in the air. He longed to tell her, but did not know how. He never discussed his problems with anyone, not even with himself, not since he had talked to Candy about them. And, if he now told Mara what Candy's threats were, he would have to tell her that Timmy might not really be his son, and then there would be no way to stop and avoid destroying the image Mara loved in him.

There was a sad little smile in the corners of her mouth. The gin had misted her eyes. Her voice was warm but lacking softness, a quality he found peculiarly American and irresistible. "You've been under a lot of conflicting pressures. People wanted you to fight and do nothing. I tried to make you fight and sit back. Your conscience and pride, your doubts and professionalism, your sense of duty and loyalty, and probably many other things urged you once to fight and then to be patient and wait. But now you must lump the lot together and make your decision." She lit a long thin cheroot which gave her the excuse for not looking at Penn and trying to sound cool and practical. "I just wanted you to know that, whatever you decide, I'll be around. If that's what you want."

It was the second time since Paya Lebar that they found themselves lying on the bed fully dressed, side by side, touching from shoulder to ankle, motionless, silent, but very much awake. Then, halfway through an unspoken sentence, he blurted out a few words. Then more words and disjointed sentences. Facts without any hint of self-pity. About Timmy. How he had talked Candy out of having an abortion. "She'll tell that child the most gruesome details. She's quite capable of it."

"He may not believe her."

"Perhaps not. But she'll want to destroy the man Timmy loves in me. And so ruin me. Life is all a matter of images. That's what my life has always been. Like being an airline pilot. A nicely wrapped up ready-made image, something to admire, something to trust, something to live up to. But Candy will talk about my flights as a mercenary, flying anybody and anything anywhere if the money was right, my mistakes and dirty fights, the lies I lived to create the make-believe world of happiness for him, yes, yes, I know, it's out of loving him, but will he understand it? And that won't be all. Candy will try to be more specific. She'll talk about the false image I built for myself. It's impossible to know how it all began. Perhaps with the odd omission of some fact, the convenient oversight of some uncomfortable circumstance, then the half-truths, then the lies."

He struggled to admit that his image for his son had been created to help him see himself through the child's eyes. "After the long wait after Paya Lebar, when I began to fight to clear my name and became Timmy's hero once again, he thought I was out to win. And I conned myself into believing him when I knew that in this battle there're no heroes, nobody wins, and I can only reduce the number of losers, if I'm lucky. So how can I let Candy tell that child that his strong, brave father, who's supposedly in cold control of magnificent airplanes and hundreds of lives, is no more infallible than a newcomer to skateboard riding—and just as panic-prone. Yes, panic-prone, and I mean it. It's only that I've learned to live with it. And swallow hard when it grips my throat.

"My father was a war hero. Most people said so. He was, he was not, that's how I saw him. And he despised cowards. Poltroons, he called them, bloody poltroons. And anybody afraid of anything was a sissy. Damned perverted sissy. And he convinced me that one should never be afraid of anything. When the fright comes, he'd argue, it won't make any difference that you've spent half your life being afraid of it. So I feared nothing.

I grew up totally fearless. Except that it left me with a low panic threshold. Something that Candy knows about. I always felt I owed her the truth. So she knows that my famous African mercy flights left me bathed in my sweat of fear."

"That's what makes a hero, that you did continue them just the same."

"Hero? Do you know how my greatest moment of heroism came about? It was only because on the way out, when that Dakota was first shot at, I panicked and diverted to a seemingly safer landing strip. She'll tell Timmy about that, too."

Neither of them remembered when they had fallen asleep during the night. It was Mara's clock-radio that woke them up with the early news bulletin. And sleep was still in their eyes when the voice mentioned a mugging case. At dusk. In Bryant Park. The victim was a high-ranking executive of AeroCorp. He had died of his injuries in the hospital during the night. His name was not disclosed because the next of kin had not yet been notified. The attack must have been needlessly brutal. The victim's pockets were completely emptied by the muggers who, oddly enough, overlooked an exceptionally valuable wafer-thin gold Omega.

Mara knew that watch. "Singer," she mumbled as she switched off the radio. "Another of your losers."

"You're wrong. He's a winner. His death has just made the decision for me."

Mott turned up at Barraclough's workshop unannounced. He wanted to examine the device and see a test run right away. Barraclough warned him about the risks, but he held out two sealed packets of pink pills. "P Twenty-three," he said and, seeing that it meant nothing to Barraclough, added, "Antidotes. Based on pralidoxime mesylate." He did not elaborate any further. Barraclough did not need to know that the chemical had been developed by the defense research establishment at Porton Down to enable soldiers and airmen to survive about four times the lethal dose of most nerve gases. He tossed one packet to Barraclough. "Swallow them."

"All four?"

Mott nodded. "One is absorbed in the blood right away, the others act as boosters for six hours." Then he rolled up his trousers to above the right knee and produced a flat box containing two peculiar contraptions with hypodermics. He gave one to Barraclough and strapped the other to his own leg. "That's just for insurance. At the very first sign of feeling any effect of the gas, sickness, dizziness, convulsions, just anything, you press that button. It's spring-loaded and it will fire a needle into your skin. It will hurt a little, but considering that it's a derivative of the killer nightshade, it's not too bad, I'm told."

Barraclough attached the autoject to his leg, swallowed the pills and asked no questions. It was a matter of trusting a superior. He then removed a few bricks from the wall to clear the way to a hidden safe. He spun the combination lock and took out a large Saricola bottle with an unusual billiard-ball-size stopper which was connected to an altimeter.

Mott took a good look at the device, handling it with respect. "How will it be positioned?"

Barraclough led him to the back of the garage, where pieces of hardboard, some canvas and empty beer crates shaped a mock-up of the Sarissa flight deck. He fitted the bottle behind a small box and positioned the altimeter in front of the crates that served as seats. "Would you like all bottles in position, sir?" Mott shook his head. "Then take a pew, sir."

The Brigadier hesitated. He looked toward the closed doors and windows.

Barraclough understood: "Shall we increase the volume of air just as an additional precaution?"

"Yes, good idea."

Timmy sat in a corner and refused to say hello to Granny. His eyes were red, he looked bewildered. "One day you'll be grateful to me," said Candy and turned toward the door. She was carrying a small suitcase.

"What am I supposed to do?" asked her mother.

"Whatever Corrie told you to do."

"He was ever so rushed on the telephone."

"Not my fault, is it. Is it, Mum?" She opened the door. "I'll be in touch, Timmy, don't worry."

The child said nothing. He stared at the door long after Candy had gone. The old woman had no idea what to do or say, so she sought security in routine activities and began dusting, polishing all the knick-knacks with the hem of her skirt. Her eyes fell on the old brass clock. "Dear me, have you had any breakfast?" Timmy did not answer. "What would you like? I mean you must eat. We all must. And take care of each other. That's what your dad said."

"*My* dad?"

"Who else?"

Until ten past noon, Pacific Time, everything went according to plan. At ten-thirty, Mara interviewed the head of the design team that had worked on the new Whispering Sarissa, and at eleven-thirty she met the Chief Test Pilot, who spoke about his work and showed her around the AeroCorp airfield. She saw a Sarissa going through the final checks after a major overhaul in a hangar next to the main runway. The plane was now prepared for a ferry flight to Los Angeles. At ten past noon the pilot's bleeper came to life. The message was for Mara. Mr. Drayton had finished a conference almost an hour earlier than expected, and his driver would pick her up in a few minutes. This upset the timing, but Mara hoped that Penn would be ready. But the message was encouraging at least in one respect. Drayton retained his old habits; he would take her to his favorite haunt, the Scandinavian restaurant in the Sacramento suburb, only half an hour's drive away. If all went well, Penn would not have to fall back on their standby plan, which would be even more of a risk.

The driver dropped them off at the main restaurant, then drove into the crowded parking lot. He was lucky. A man in white overalls had just finished some work in a convenient corner and removed the *keep out* sign in deference to the gold Corniche convertible. The driver locked up and hurried toward the cheaper "Quixervice Smorgashboard" end of the restaurant. Penn, in the white overalls, watched him. The driver's lunch would give him a minimum of thirty minutes. It was reassuring that, so far, Mara had been right about the routine. But it was a stinging thought that Mara had ever had "routine outings" with anyone else.

In the restaurant, nothing seemed to have changed. Many faces were familiar to Mara, most of the menu reflected the same old unpronounceable luxury she once found so flattering, and the *maitre d'* greeted her by name without any sign that would question or even acknowledge her long absence. He led them to the table by the window still permanently reserved for AeroCorp top brass.

"You look tired," said Mara, omitting to mention that Drayton looked worried and subdued, too.

"There's been a lot of goddamn pressure on me."

"You? You're the boss."

"Nobody is boss, and I mean really and completely boss any more. The pressures come from above and below, and I fight both ways like anybody else."

"Still, you tend to win."

"Don't try to butter up the old man, sweetie."

"I meant it."

"Nobody wins any more. Everybody loses a little. Those who lose least are the winners."

"That's odd." Mara looked out of the window. It gave her a chance to check her watch surreptitiously. Ten minutes of Penn's time had gone.

"What?"

"Oh, just that somebody said almost the same thing to me only the other day."

"Who?"

"Can't remember. . . . Does it matter?"

"Was it Penn?"

"What makes you ask that?"

"Come on, Mara, you know better than that. You know that I must always hear things about people who interest me. Was it Penn?"

"Yes."

"I thought he was more of a romantic."

"He has some ideals and principles. That doesn't make a man a romantic."

"Is it because of him that you're here?"

"It's most peculiar that, different as you are, you resemble each other in many ways. It's . . ." She twiddled the winder wheel of her watch nervously. Mentioning Penn was no part of the agreed plan. He would be furious. . . . "It's as if you two could have been friends in different circumstances."

"Are you complimenting me or insulting him?" Drayton's self-induced laughter grew out of the rumble of a restless volcano, shattered the cutlery tinkle music of the room, and died away just as suddenly. "So what is it you want, sweetie?"

"Live up to your old principles. Give him a chance."

"Which one in particular?"

"Every man deserves a fair chance. Give it to him."

"What sort of chance?"

"A test flight."

"Why?"

"He wants to be sure about his recollection of the aborted take-off."

"There's nothing he could prove, and I think he only wants to embarrass AeroCorp. That's what he really wants."

"No. It's important to him."

"How important is it to you, sweetie?"

"Very."

"Let's be more specific. Would you do me a favor in return?"

"Yes."

"Would you sleep with me?"

She looked straight into his eyes. "It's not your style to ask for sexual favors."

"I'm asking you now."

"No, you're not." She hesitated. "But if you were, well . . ."

"Well?"

"I'd *try* to talk you out of it."

He turned away and buried his head in the wine list. "You know something," he said without looking up, "I envy the bastard no matter what happens to him."

Penn had worked systematically through a set of skeleton keys. An engineer friend had warned him that the trunk lock of a Rolls-Royce might be mighty tricky, but after twenty minutes of patient trial and error there was a faint click and the lid was free to rise open. Penn detached the successful key from the bunch and taped it carefully under the bumper. He then put his tool box and a small oxygen bottle into the trunk, and climbed in, pulling the lid shut.

Usually, lunch with Drayton was as relaxed and leisurely haphazard as a commando raid, but today he seemed to be in a mood of luxurious time wasting, and there were no reminder calls from Ms. Etch. Mara knew that, with any luck, Penn must already be inside the Corniche. The longer the driver had to wait for Drayton the greater the likelihood that he would want something from the trunk. She said she was not very hungry but Drayton insisted that she must try some smoked reindeer in wine à la Prince Bertil. "You're nervous," he said casually. "Did I upset you?"

"No."

"Then you're quite willing to congratulate me?"

"On what?"

"On my divorce, for instance."

"Oh. I didn't know."

"Nobody does. It's quite sudden, really."

She knew he was hoping for some questions from her. He never had anyone to discuss his life with. Not unlike Penn. But she was not interested. And she did not want to be more of a hypocrite than absolutely necessary. "Congratulations. I hope you'll be a happier man. What else?"

"The Sarissa, of course."

"Oh yes. Farnborough will be a great moment of triumph."

"Don't say that. It's eight days away and you know I'm superstitious."

"I'm sorry. I should have said we *hope* it'll be a triumph."

"Yes. For me, for the aircraft, for AeroCorp, even for the United States."

"In that order?"

"Why not?"

The ride back to the plant was mercifully fast and unexciting. At the gate the Corniche was waved through without even slowing down. Mara knew that the trunk was large and Penn had the oxygen for emergencies, but she would have preferred to be sure about the survival chances inside. Except that there had been no time to find out more in advance.

Having said goodbye to Drayton, she took advantage of her Class A visitor's name tag that gave her the freedom of the plant. In the press room of the main administrative building, she sat by a window pretending to look through her notes while watching the Corniche in the parking lot. She cursed the driver, who was busy polishing some spotless chromium bits to a new pinnacle in the history of shine. She was running out of patience and considered putting through some fake junk call to lure the driver away when at last he left the car and entered the building. It took her only forty seconds to reach the car, locate the key at the agreed spot, open the trunk and let Penn out. She was ready with some cock-and-bull story should anybody ask her, but their luck held and nobody saw them walk away.

She had a list of several hiding places for Penn until dawn but he thought that doing some work would be safer. "So you'd better leave now. I'll call you after the flight."

"You don't even know where the flight-crew lounge is."

"I'll find it. Thanks for everything. I don't want you to take any more risks."

"Don't argue with the guards if they spot you," she said as lightly as she could. "They're armed in this country."

He walked away swinging the metal box, stopped at the corner of the building, studied a manhole cover knowingly at length, and took his time to produce a twenty-yard tape measure from among his tools. He banked on the universal respect for the measuring man. And he was off to a perfect start. People rounded his chalk marks on the ground cautiously and tiptoed over the metal strip or waited patiently for him to make notes, nod and raise his index finger in appreciation, and wind the tape back into its case at the pace which implied anticipation of a great deal of overtime on the job. Mara watched him anxiously and tried to cheer herself up by recalling Penn's solemn conviction that history would have taken a different turn if Caesar had had to cross a tape measure rather than the Rubicon.

By nightfall, he had measured his way everywhere and gained unquestioned entry to hangars, workshops and the flight-crew lounge. According to his plan, he had another hour to waste. He had a couple of sandwiches for that purpose. Squatting on the tool box in full view of anybody who cared to look, he munched away, on the assumption that thieves, spies and other intruders are supposed to be always in a hurry, therefore eating men must be innocent. He watched the Sarissa being towed out on the apron.

"And what are you doing here?"

Penn turned slowly. A keen young guard with his Alsatian had crept up on him. Penn held up the remains of his sandwich in answer.

"This is a restricted area, didn't you know?"

Penn nodded and took a big bite. Saying sorry with his mouth full, he hoped to avoid questions about his English accent.

"Where's your badge anyway?"

Penn looked down at his overall as if surprised to see that it was missing. He began to search for it.

"ID card."

Penn went through his pockets one by one in vain. In the open space around the runway he would have no chance to escape from the dog even if the guard turned out to be a poor shot. "Must have left it in my locker."

"Okay. Let's go."

As they walked toward the hangar, Penn remembered the bolt on the inside of the heavy sliding door. From there a metal staircase—only seventeen feet away—led to a gallery of small glass-cage offices for dispatchers and supervisors. One of those had a window—yes, that's right, Penn hoped he was right—opening onto a roof where he could run in the direction of the crew lounge . . . Pity he had never measured that distance.

Penn pretended to look for his ID card all the way. He seemed annoyed, but the guard was too fresh in the job to allow himself the luxury of sympathy. Penn opened the sliding door enough to get through almost sideways. The guard was right behind him. Penn had no choice. He dropped the tool box, turned and pushed the guard back, trying, at the same time, to yank the heavy door shut. It caught the guard's foot and the man yelled with pain. Penn had to ease back the door to free the foot and kick it out before he could secure his escape. But as soon as the door moved the dog leapt at him, snatching his left arm. With his right he picked up the tool box and brought it down on the dog's head. He heard a crack and felt sick. But the dog was no more than dazed, unhurt enough to hang on. Penn tore his arm away, leaving some of the overall between the dog's teeth. As he shut the door, he saw the guard pulling his gun. But the bolt was on before the first shot rang out, and the heavy metal gave him protection.

He took the stairs in threes, shedding the overall on the way. He wore a pilot's uniform underneath. He jumped through the window on the adjoining roof and raced across. There he saw a trapdoor but had no idea where the stairs underneath it would lead him. So he chose to climb down the chain of a crane, and he ran into the next building. Then up the stairs and along the corridors that looked familiar enough to keep him in hope that he was moving in the right direction. He dumped the overall and the tool box in the open well of a freight elevator. That would create quite a task for the dogs. He sneaked past the open door of the airfield controller's office, and three minutes later he was in the crew lounge. Through the window he saw guards running in all directions. He took off his tunic and crushed cap, and lay down on a couch. He had his own ID card and pilot license as well as a faked letter (by courtesy of Linda Waller) assigning him to the ferry flight at dawn. There was a fair chance that his name would mean nothing to any of the security guards who would find him eventually. He had not planned to be in there so early, because it increased the risk. But that could not be helped now.

It was after midnight when he heard the ferocious barking of a dog outside the door. Somebody knocked and entered.

"Anybody here?"

Penn sat up, switched on the light and pretended to be just waking up.

The guard noticed his uniform. "Sorry, sir, security. Your papers please." As he was about to examine the documents, the boom of a beer-swilling voice was approaching. "Well, I s'pose you can't complain. You had the luck of seeing all the theories put into action, right? You should have plenty and more to write about." The chief of AeroCorp security and Mara came into view.

"Oh, hello. I didn't know that you were already here," said Mara cheerfully.

"Hello," Penn grunted. Because of the surprise, even that was an effort.

"You two know each other then," the chief concluded brightly.

"Of course. The Captain is one of the pilots assigned to our flight."

Penn noticed that Mara had carefully avoided using his name. She could not be sure what he had said to the guard, who now returned his papers without having looked at them and whispered to his chief, "Sorry, sir, I just thought I'd check the crew lounge, too, in case—"

"Don't you apologize, my boy, don't you apologize. I'd have you by the balls—excuse the language, Miss Boone—if you failed to search every nook and corner. Just get on with it."

Mara chose to stay in the crew lounge for the rest of the night. "I decided to write something about security, so I spent the evening with the chief," she explained after the men had left. She hoped it sounded casual enough. "It was just an idea."

Penn understood and thanked her for it. "But you're not coming on that flight."

"But I must. The chief knows I'm going. It would look odd if I changed my mind in the middle of the night."

At 0435 the telephone rang in the crew lounge. It was the first officer for the flight calling from the main gate where he had been stopped with a telex message. He wanted to check with the rest of the crew on what was going on and, even more, to vent his frustration. "I mean it's ridiculous, isn't it? Couldn't they have told me earlier that they've rescheduled the crew? What am I supposed to do now, for Chrissake? I've let my cab go and—"

"Isn't there something about transport arrangements for

you?" Penn interrupted him. "They said something to me on the phone if I remember rightly."

"Oh, hang on . . . yeah . . . another cab's supposed to be here . . . What? Oh yeah, thanks. Hello, are you there?"

"Yes."

"The guard is just telling me that it's here. And I see it now in the telex, too. Sorry."

Penn hung up and swore at the fool who had not read the message before calling the crew lounge. "For a second I thought that you'd forgotten to mention and order the cab or that Linda had given you the wrong sample text."

The flight engineer arrived ten minutes later. He was too sleepy to question Penn's vague explanation about the change of crew. At five o'clock, Linda and Simms entered the crew lounge. The Captain went pale when he saw Mara and Penn, but in the presence of the engineer he chose to say nothing. It was time to go and check the weather and get their briefing for the flight, but Simms appeared to be delaying it until the last possible minute.

Drayton was dozing on a sofa in his private lounge behind his office. The buzzer woke him up. "The surprise for you has arrived, sir," said Termine on the phone. "Would you mind coming right up?"

Crammed between the executives' rooftop swimming pool and the screen wall, Termine had posted three civilians with rifles and night telescopes. He led Drayton to a pair of powerful binoculars with light intensifier on a tripod. "You wanted him in a fix where we can tell him to shut up and toe the line, sir. So here you are." He gestured, a little too theatrically for Drayton's liking, toward the infrared viewer. The night was dark, but Drayton could easily pick out the small group walking toward the Sarissa. Mara, another woman, Penn, a stranger and Simms, who kept looking around and back as if waiting for something or somebody.

"I thought you'd keep him out of the States."

"I tried, sir. I've tried everything to give him a chance, as you said. Even his wife begged him to go home, stay with the kid he adores and shut up. But when he wouldn't . . ."

Drayton noticed that the three gunmen kept circling slowly, inch by inch, keeping the target group in sight. "How did you get him here?"

Termine suppressed a small smile of vanity. "He wanted to be on that flight. So Captain Simms helped me a little. He feels kind of indebted to me, owes me a favor or two if you know what I mean, sir."

"It seems he may not be the only one. But don't let that go to your head. Having too many debtors may be just as big a liability as having too many debts."

"Yes, sir. Now what would you like to do? We can arrest the two intruders and discredit Penn or we could have them shot and then there're no questions and arguments afterwards. In my family it was always thought to be best not to turn your back and walk away from the man who has a pitchfork and the will to stick it in you."

Drayton winced but refrained from commenting too hastily on what he regarded as gutter-crook philosophy. He eyed Mara's long legs in close-up. "You have a lot to learn, Salah," he said at last, noting with satisfaction that he had managed, after all, to call the man by his first name.

"I'm willing."

"Yes, that's very much in your favor. But hyperactivity can be a risk. It may start an avalanche. You know what I mean? Like when you're careless on a ski slope."

"I don't ski, sir."

"No, of course not." And communication with you is not quite as subtle as between a kid and his hedgehog. But that he did not say. "And don't think that I fail to appreciate your effort and your devotion. You did a good job getting Penn here. But now you must let him put his head in the noose. Let him fly.

Let him try what he wants. He's virtually skyjacking that airplane. So let him. If they complete the flight, he'll be found out at the other end. Nothing to do with us. If he gets into trouble in the air . . ." Drayton swallowed hard as he watched Mara, who would also be in trouble up there. "Well, we'll have an even stronger case. Even alive he'll be as good as dead. And if, by any old chance, he turns up trumps and finds something useful, he'll be our boy, a winner for us, because *we* always back everybody who fights for AeroCorp."

Termine was not too keen on this strategy. In his experience, a one-sided shootout was always a better way of settling a conflict than a lengthy talk-out. But he was willing to learn. And he hoped that Simms would not take it too badly.

On that particular score he was wrong. Simms was furious. Termine had promised him that Penn would be prevented from boarding that Sarissa. What was he to do now? Chicken out? Pretend to be sick? Try to expose Penn, who could always claim that initially Simms had been a party to the plan? Linda poured coffee for everyone from a thermos, and Simms made up his mind. This could be a good opportunity to get Termine off his own back. He had already taped a couple of telephone conversations with the AeroCorp hatchet man, and in one of them there was a veiled reference to this flight. From now on, perhaps, he could swap threats with the bastard. He would only have to cover himself a little more. When the flight-deck voice recorder was already switched on, he turned to Penn. "Well, considering the circumstances, I have no choice but to assist you flying the aircraft and so ensure the safety of the flight and everybody on board."

The engineer stared at him; the Captain's remark did not make sense. But Penn understood him only too well. Simms would let him do the take-off and wash his hands of all the consequences. Penn had no objection to that. Knowing nothing about the secret deal with Termine, he even found some admiration in his heart for the man's courage. About the flight itself he had no doubts. When his hands were on the controls once again, he would recognize if he had misinterpreted a perfectly natural feel at Paya Lebar.

He took Mitchell's seat (he had heard just the other day that his co-pilot in Singapore was now out of the hospital) and began to run through the checklist, chanting it a little ceremoniously as if it were a canticle for the occasion. Mitchell always hummed his sums as he checked his take-off data chart, Penn remembered. Simms worked silently. V1 would be 125 knots. Rotate at 140. The engineer began to read out the pink checklist from flaps to transponder.

To the two women, the empty silent cabin gave an eerie sensation. They sat side by side in first class, with the thermos between them. They did not need to look at the warning signs: they strapped in automatically and would not smoke during take-off anyway. Initially, Linda held down her questions bravely, but now she asked, a little meekly, what Mara thought Penn would be up to. Experiments?

"Don't worry. He may be crazy, but he's no fool."

Up front, the checklist reached "transponder."

"As required," answered Penn. Without thinking, the old routine led his eyes to recheck a few items—cabin signs on, autopilot off, and then a quick scan all around. He gently moved the column forward and back, and the half-wheel ailerons control left and right. No resistance at all. No problem. He was about to ask his customary "all set?" when a cold grip on his throat and chest tightened quite suddenly. He knew that no sound would come out. He reached behind his seat, where he had seen a bottle of Saricola. Two good gulps helped. "All set?" He released the brakes and told the tower that he was ready to go.

Simms started his stopwatch, then focused in on his speed indicator. Penn eased the throttles open. Acceleration was normal. The green lights of the threshold. Penn played the pedals of the rudder to support nose-wheel steering. The speed was seventy knots. Penn glanced at Simms. The Captain seemed to apply just slight, normal pressure on the stick to keep the nose down. Approaching eighty knots.

Termine had sent his henchmen away. He stood half a step behind Drayton. Both of them watched the take-off run through binoculars.

"Well, at least we should wish them luck," grunted Drayton. On the apron, behind the roaring aircraft, he could still visualize Mara's walking legs as if they belonged to a ghost.

"Wishing them luck just reminds me, sir. May I be the first to congratulate you on the two coming events?"

"What events?"

"Your divorce and wedding, of course."

Drayton spun around. "How do you know about that?"

"I thought it was my duty to know things and prevent crises."

Drayton did not like the faint smirk on Termine's face. It seemed to suggest that everybody must be indebted to someone.

Penn let go of the steering wheel, placed both his hands on the control column and took a firm grip. "I have it." The speed indicator kept moving up. His concentration was absolute. It left no room for thoughts about the clamps on his throat: "110 knots . . . 120 . . . V one . . ."

Penn's eyes were focused on the far end of the remaining length of runway, his ears were tuned to Simms and his monotonous speed calls, but his ultimate awareness was congealed in the second digits of his fingers, ready to pull the half-wheel.

"130 . . . 135 . . . Rotate . . ."

Penn pulled softly. The wheel gave. More back pressure, and more again in a continuous movement. The nose was lifting off, almost imperceptibly. No trace of resistance. Nothing wrong with the Sarissa. Nothing misleading. Had it been his fault after all? Penn felt it was pointless to continue. He might as well abandon the flight, return to London, apologize to everybody, get out of aviation, and change his name to spare Timmy from the shame. Except that he would not be able to stop the aircraft now. It was well beyond the point of no return.

The Sarissa lifted off with smooth elegance. Simms nodded an eighth of an inch, no more. Some pilot, this Captain Penn. He felt sorry for him. It was no fun that awaited him at the end of their 400-mile hop.

The altimeter moved steadily. They were climbing to their assigned altitude. Penn took another gulp of Saricola before asking Simms at what altitude his problems had occurred.

"It's impossible to recreate that scene. The descent was plain routine, but there were pockets of CAT that day. How do you want to stage that?"

It was clear air turbulence that Mara and Linda were also discussing.

"Once or twice it frightened the hell out of me," said Mara. "Was yours with that Captain Johnson very bad?"

"Well, you know, the whole thing was less memorable than the mess afterward. And the godawful bunch we had on that flight. They were returning from some football game, all plastered, and trouble all the way. Two damn ass slappers were the worst. When I got the first whack, I shouted, 'Cut that out,' but the guy just laughed, and the passengers thought it was funny. So I told them that it was a felony under the Federal Air Piracy Act to assault, intimidate or threaten crew members and interfere with their duties, and that they could be fined and jailed for up to twenty years for it, but that got the biggest laugh of all, and they began to slap the girls real hard. They followed them around and kept calling them. What made it even worse was that it was one of those free Saribrandy flights to publicize the new goddamn brand. And they wanted it, but how!" Infuriated by the memory, Linda unbuckled her seat belt and jumped up to demonstrate the tumult the ass slappers had caused.

The flight engineer had sensed from the start that his two pilots had some private conversation going. Now, as the aircraft shuddered once and the ride became a little bumpy, he thought they had gone bananas. Penn had been flying manually, on a normal descending course, but when the bump came he snorted, "Christ. That must be it."

Simms grabbed the controls. "I have it. . . . Oh! You're right!"

It was not impossible to fly the aircraft. Just difficult. Requiring a great deal more force than usually. It behaved like a horse that had different ideas from the rider's about the desirable direction. As if it had a will of its own. That was exactly what Penn had noticed at Paya Lebar. Except that then there was no time to experiment.

"As soon as I reduce the pressure on the wheel, she wants to rear up," said Simms. He looked baffled. "Try it."

"I have control," mumbled Penn. Yes, he had to struggle to retain full control. He glanced at the autopilot. It was off. "Warn the girls to stay put and strapped in."

The warning came a little late. Linda had been on her feet for a minute or two. "I don't like shouting for help, but I was about to call the Captain," she recalled, standing in the aisle. "One guy out here, making a nuisance of himself, the other up and down like a yoyo, hitting the call button every time, shouting for service, pressing the button like this—oops!" As the aircraft shuddered, she lost her balance and laughed. "I'm getting drunk from the memory. But, as I was saying, one guy just stood there beating out some mad rhythm on the button, and I couldn't even pull him away because his finger seemed to be glued to it. Hey! Looks like another bumpy ride."

Mara could only stare at her antics and the call button. "Chuck Denning is the name," she heard distinctly. The man in turpentine. A simple man of simple tastes for waltz and schmaltz, a man who wanted only some coffee and a smoke and attention and reassurance.

Linda let go of the button and sat down. By the time Simms warned them on the PA system, she had her seat belt on.

The resistance of the elevator control ceased as suddenly as it had started. There was nothing to fight any more. Penn pulled the column up to level flight, up again to ascend on a fine slope, back to level and descend again—no problems. It might have been many things, but turbulence it was not. "We'd better tell AeroCorp right away," said Penn.

"We might as well land it and make a full report in L.A., unless . . ." Simms bit off the rest.

Unless they had a crash. The fault might recur during the landing phase. Penn remembered Mellou. That was a landing incident.

"What the hell's going on?"

Nobody answered the engineer's question. Mara appeared in the door. She looked sickly. Linda stood behind her.

"Get back and strap yourselves in," Simms snapped.

"There's something you must know *now.*" Mara told them about Chuck Benning. How he kept calling for service, how he would not sit down or remove his finger from the button, and how he was catapulted to his death when the crash came. Then Linda began to look sickly, too. She spoke about the ass slappers who had also played rhythms on the call button.

"It's impossible," said Simms. "There can't be any connection."

"There's no other explanation," argued Penn.

"It's impossible. The call signal cannot interfere with the controls. There's never been a problem like this."

"Had there been one, they'd have sorted it out long ago." The engineer asked a few impassioned questions, then shrugged his shoulders. "There's only one way to find out."

It had to be Simms's decision. He was in charge. He could have reported their suspicion on the radio to his head office and AeroCorp at the same time, but he felt he had enough trouble as it was, and the last thing he wanted was to look foolish, too. But he could extricate himself from the situation if they produced some explanation for Penn's crash and all the incidents. "Okay. Strap yourselves in and wait for instructions." He took over the controls. "We'll try it on level flight." He turned to Penn. "Tell the girls to press the buttons . . . now."

Penn took the PA microphone. "All set. Go ahead." He kept the system open. Ten seconds passed. Nothing happened. Thirty seconds. Fifty. "Feel anything?"

Simms shook his head. It required no effort to hold a straight and level course.

Penn wriggled out of his seat and went into the cabin. The women had their fingers on call buttons on both sides of the aisle. "Leave it," he said and returned to the flight deck.

"It's no explanation then." Simms sighed with hesitant relief.

But Penn was still puzzled. "Listen. We both felt during descent as if she wanted to go up. Right? What if she only tried to fly level. Once you complied with her, she didn't resist us."

"Makes sense," said the engineer.

"Okay, you win." Simms set the aircraft on a three-degree descent course.

"Feels okay?"

"Yeah. Tell 'em to press it."

"Go ahead, girls."

They counted the seconds. At one: nothing. At two: nothing. At three: Simms cried, "Sheet!" It was as eloquent a diagnosis as anybody could wish for. He was clearly struggling with the column.

"Let go of the bloody button," Penn yelled into the microphone. The next second the controls felt normal again. There could be no doubt about the connection. The question was why, at Paya Lebar, during the take-off run, the Sarissa had tried to stay down or even go into the ground instead. Had she then also been trying to maintain a level course?

Simms declared an emergency and asked for immediate clearance to return to AeroCorp rather than enter the overcrowded Los Angeles airspace.

Formal politeness took the assistant deputy manager of the George V Hotel of Paris to the brink of reverence, but that did not make his resolution waver. Far from it. He could leave the choice of weapons to the opposition, because he was well equipped to parry contempt, provocation, tears, threats, hysterics, seductive smiles or any other secret device in the client's armory in lieu of cash. Candy, in fact, had no secret weapons. She was just lost for words. He explained that her two-room suite had been booked by a transatlantic telephone call and duly confirmed on the arrival of actual cash by special delivery. But that covered only her first three days. Now that another three days had gone, the manager felt it would not be unreasonable to present her with the bill or ask her by what means she intended to cover the accumulating debt.

Candy had no money. She had left London with a grand "I don't want your money" gesture, taking only a hundred pounds from their joint account. Most of that had already gone. If she used her credit card that would be charged to Corrie's account, and she would, in effect, throw in the towel yet again. But she had no choice, even if she felt sure that, of her many mistakes, this last one, involving the child, was irremediable. She asked for the bill, paid with the credit card, and promised to move out at once.

The assistant deputy manager apologized. He was absolutely positive that the inconvenience must have been due to some unfortunate misunderstanding. He encouraged her to take her time vacating the suite. "Shall we say three o'clock this afternoon?"

She agreed. It gave her fifty-five minutes.

What she could not understand was that her ugly American had not even telephoned her. Some men had maltreated her in the past. But she had never been ignored. He had promised to meet her in Paris. He must have had an accident. He would soon call and apologize.

Candy checked the bulk of her luggage at the hotel. She made arrangements for them to take messages for her. Then she took the bus to Orly. Airports, she knew, gave the cheapest night shelter for well-dressed vagrants. Only there would nobody question a lonely woman sleeping in a corner. And there would be washrooms and breakfast and telephones and transport back to town until the next night and the next. She made no decision about how long she would rough it, waiting for the call, in Paris.

At about the time that Candy left the George V, the Sarissa landed without any difficulty on the AeroCorp runway. Two cars and two trucks ran alongside the aircraft as it slowed to a halt. It was immediately surrounded by armed guards, the doors were locked, and the entire crew was driven to the executive building. To Penn and the others who had never seen Drayton's collection the Venetian mirrors were a surprise and a little disconcerting. Ms. Etch served hot drinks with as much noise and presence as a curtain fluttering in hot air above a heating duct. Drayton introduced Termine as acting crisis manager, "a likely replacement for our late Mr. Singer, a great accidental loss to us all, a great accidental loss indeed."

Penn was under the impression that he had met Mr. Termine somewhere before.

"What of it?" His tone was as crude and provocative as flashing a switchblade. There was a momentary silence and Termine recognized that he would soon have to master yet another language, just as he had once added Long Island smooth to his Brooklyn tough and then West Coast hip, too, because it was useful down in the Village and impressive to some chicks overseas. "I mean it's possible. Right?"

Drayton led the group into an adjoining conference room, which bore proof that idle he had not been in the forty minutes since he had heard about the emergency. In one corner, a mobile switchboard had been set up. There were several loudspeakers, each marked according to who was already on the conference line. The NTSB had two participants: one in Washington, one via his car radio, on his way from San Francisco. There were airline representatives, an FAA official, a congressman and several aviation correspondents on the open lines. Just when Drayton entered, a free speaker was labeled "AIB, London." Cleaff, the man in charge of Penn's case, had been traced and connected. At the far end of the room a door was opened for the first arrivals among the AeroCorp specialists who had been summoned and collected, by helicopters where necessary.

Drayton made a brief and impressive opening statement. He vowed that the good names of the Sarissa, AeroCorp and American craftsmanship would be most vigorously defended. "You all know about our tremendous struggle to clear up the Singapore mystery. You all have, in fact, participated in it. Even the press helped, because we helped them and never tried to de-emphasize the importance of even the most insignificant incident, operational occurrence or routine technical snag report. But now at last it seems we have a serious lead to a solution. And if there's anything, and I mean anything, to it, I promise you all that we'll get to the end of it and cure the snag before the great international air show in Britain." His executives applauded and he added that "Mark Two, the Whispering Sarissa, will make a flying debut at Farnborough as planned, no matter what!"

Drayton's performance was not to everybody's taste, but they all had to admit that his stage management was first class. The press lines were now cut off and work commenced. Once Drayton had declared that all credentials have been checked, nobody questioned why Mara and Penn were present. Other potential complications had also been sorted out before the conference began. The alert security guard with the foot injury had already received an award for his bravery, and everybody who might have heard about the night breach of security had been given the sad news that, according to three witnesses, produced by Salah Termine, the unknown intruder was never caught.

Simms and the rest of the crew made their brief factual reports. Penn understood that his role in the flight would be subject to disciplinary procedures but he was anxious to contribute to the investigation and answer any questions. The Chief Test Pilot listened to it all with contemptuous skepticism. He felt some compassion toward the crew, which must have erred, but they were knocking the Sarissa, and that he found intolerable. "Are you sure, gentlemen," he asked with cutting irony, "that you were not trying to fly on autopilot and manually at the same time?"

Simms blushed. "Checking that the autopilot is off is part of the take-off checklist. So I hope you're not putting this as a serious question."

"But I do, sir. You may recall that man and machine may be in conflict if flying in such circumstances. And I was thinking about your 'tests'—after flying on autopilot for a while."

Penn sat up. The chief's remark had started a different train of thought. "I'm quite positive that the autopilot was off," he cut in before Simms could retort. "It's my personal habit to recheck cabin signs after take-off checklists, before going manual and in many other phases of operation. And on the Sarissa the autopilot tabs and the cabin sign warning lights happen to be on the same panel . . . as *you* may recall."

"Gentlemen, gentlemen." Drayton tried to suppress an outburst of indignation and acrimony which approached a crescendo around the table and through the speakers.

"But that's not the point." Penn raised his voice and dropped his fist on the table at the same time. "The questions about the autopilot, whichever way they're put, may be more relevant than anything else. Because it seems to me that, unwittingly, the chief could be right. Perhaps we *were* flying in conflict after all. Perhaps the autopilot was on even though we'd switched it off! It would explain everything."

There came another wave of technical interventions and solemn declarations of why his suggestion was quite impossible. But, after a few minutes, it became obvious to everyone that Penn was not listening. He kept nodding to himself until the objectors ran out of steam, and then he spoke slowly and quietly. He just thought aloud, and the idea began to seem more and more feasible.

The take-off was normal. At the end of the climb they had gone over to automatic control and it was set for level flight. Then they had tried to recreate the situation in which Simms had once experienced difficulties. Therefore they started a manual descent. That was when the service call button was pressed. If that, unknown to them, reactivated the autopilot, there could be a phantom force opposing the pilot. It would want to achieve level flight. Could the pilot win? Yes. Every time. It was a standard safety feature that pilots should be able to overpower the autopilot. But it was a matter of time. One would have to allow for the pilot's reaction, recognition of the problem, and experiments to decide how to cope with the unexpected. After this delay, he would have to fight to retain full control, and the flight might become a little bumpy as a result.

When Penn stopped, there was total silence. Mara stared at him and raised her eyebrows slowly as if afraid of making a noise or voicing the question everybody else was reluctant to ask: Would this explain Singapore? Penn nodded and carried on with more half-sentences. "Yes . . . all SupraNat pilots would normally descend on autopilot and then land manually . . . nobody would then reset the autopilot. What for? No need. When I took over I'd make sure it was off. I'd want to use it only after the initial climb-out. . . . Poor Chuck Benning. He was on his feet during the take-off, wasn't he? And pressed and pressed the button. . . . If that activated the autopilot, it would want my crate to go down when I wanted to rotate and up . . . Wouldn't that make the column resist me? Wouldn't that feel like an inoperative elevator? . . . Wouldn't it? With no time to spare?"

Everyone around the table suddenly discovered a vast range of directions all of which enabled them to avoid looking at Penn. Nobody wanted to commit himself.

"Pretty fancy thought, Captain," the Chief Pilot said at last. He paused, shook his head as if rejecting the idea, then shrugged his shoulders and smiled. "Yeah. Fancy concept like flying itself. Wanna give it a try?"

The entire conference adjourned to the Sarissa on the runway. It was to be a ground test. The engines were started, the autopilot was set for descent, but its switch was put in the Off position. Then all the people in the cabin pressed the service call buttons and Penn, watched by the test pilot, pulled the column as if rotating. There was no resistance. The test pilot took over and tried it.

"Piece of cake. And yet I'd bet my bottom dollar that you're right only because it's such an outrageous idea." He suggested they should try it with a level flight setting. Elevator up—down. No resistance.

Penn returned to the cabin. "I'm sorry. I was wrong." He was ready to leave. Drayton watched Mara's face, and envied Penn. Termine volunteered with a grin to escort Penn to the gate so as to avoid complications with security. The PA system came to life: "Captain Penn, could you return with Captain Simms to the flight deck, please?"

The test pilot wanted them to start all over again, as if preparing for a take-off. They went through the first checklist. He then suggested that Drayton and the others in the cabin should disembark because he proposed a short flight but no tests during take-off. They all insisted on staying on board. "Go ahead," he said to Simms.

The take-off was smooth. They prepared to repeat the maneuvers carried out during the previous flight. The test pilot monitored all their moves. They were ready to start a slow descent. Penn looked up.

"Is that what you did during the flight?"

"Yes," said Penn. "I was checking that the autopilot was off and the cabin signs were on, just in case."

"The cabin signs were not on when we did the test on the ground."

"Does it make any difference?" asked Simms.

"We don't know, do we?"

The descent began. As soon as Penn asked for the service buttons to be pressed in the cabin, the stick gave Simms a fight.

When they had landed, the test was repeated on the ground —but this time, with the seat belt and no-smoking warnings on. And the technical impossibility happened again and again. The autopilot worked against manual efforts.

Baffled technicians gathered in the cockpit. But Drayton was already on his way to organize a worldwide alert. Top priority telex messages flashed warnings to all Sarissa users even before the FAA could issue mandatory Airworthiness Directives. Pilots in the air all around the globe were instructed to forbid the use of the service call buttons. Upon landing, the service call circuit was to be disconnected immediately. All aircraft were to be tested before any flight could be undertaken. This would amount to a virtual temporary grounding order—at least until the necessity of formal grounding was decided. Drayton's argument was that the disconnection of the system would restore complete safety even before a satisfactory explanation of the fault and the modification to cure it were found. It made sense.

Press inquiries were to be handled by AeroCorp lawyers. They would give standard answers to everybody: "A minor fault has been discovered. Remedial action has been initiated. AeroCorp is quite open to any scrutiny and,"—borrowing a phrase from a recent Hollywood legal dispute—"we'll gladly discuss the full implications with anyone, but we'll not respond to anything relating to the facts."

Mara was bored listening to the mumbo-jumbo. She went into Drayton's private office and told him that she intended to file her report for her magazine.

"Why are you telling me?" he asked.

"I thought it might help you to know. I wouldn't like to add to your troubles."

"Thanks."

"So you have no objections."

"What if I do? Can I stop you? Can I control the freedom of the goddamn press?"

"No, but I wouldn't want to be ungrateful."

"Then just listen to the press conference," Termine butted in, "and report what you hear there like the rest of them, no more."

She turned back to Drayton. "Is that what you're asking me to do?"

"Surely not. I mean you can go easy on us and kind of de-emphasize certain aspects of the case, but it's never been my policy to interfere with the press, and you may report that, too. For it's one thing to restrict the flow of premature information, and quite another to muzzle a reporter. No, that's not me at all."

As soon as Mara had left, Termine rushed to the door. "I'll do it, sir." The thin neck could not hide the ridiculously bouncing ball in his throat.

"You do nothing without being told to do it."

"I mean I could delay her or something."

"I know you could. But is that what we want?"

"She knows almost as much as we do. If you let her publish it, you might as well make a full statement to all the pressmen out there."

Drayton watched him with a sad little smile. Singer would have needed no prompting. And Singer's decadent eyes would have given more fitting reflections in the Venetian mirrors. But Drayton was a realist. He knew he could not have everything in one man. Perhaps Termine would learn his ways one day. So he explained patiently. "If I made a full statement and gave them all the facts straight from the hip, the whole world would suspect that we were covering up something far more sinister. But if we play it cool, appear to be cagey or even evasive, and let the truth be discovered by some wily reporter, people will just lap it up. They believe anything these days if it seems to be the result of some clever detective work. If Mara wasn't here, we'd have to invent a "deep throat" and engineer a leak. Learn to think, Salah. Think before you start the engine of a car in a garage. Because it can backfire, you know. So think, and above all, ask me. Ask if I like muggings and undue violence."

"It was an accident, I swear on my . . ."

Ms. Etch came in with a report that some ozone-protectionist crank had telephoned stupid threats to skyjack a Sarissa. Airlines using the aircraft in four countries had already received similar threats. "They don't sound very serious, but security thinks that we ought to take some additional precautions for a while."

"Agreed, sweetie. But no publicity."

Penn felt more drained than jubilant. Nobody had had time to praise him very much so far. It was early afternoon when he had his first chance to call his home. He hoped that Timmy would not yet be in bed. Granny answered the phone and told him that no, it was not too late. She shouted for the child, who, he could overhear, flatly refused to come to the telephone. "What do you mean *no?* It's your daddy calling and it costs a pretty penny, too!" Then into the phone: "Wait, Cornelius, I'll get the rascal. It's not for me to say, but he's impossible since his mother's left. And I really can't cope with this house. It's too big for me. I mean at my age, and I'm neglecting my own house, and I never know what mess I'm going back to if you see my point."

Penn stopped her forcing Timmy to talk to him, and listened for a while to her complaints. No, there was no news about Candy, but Cornelius really must make some other arrangements soon, because an old woman could not be expected to cope with a big house and a growing child and the prospect of not knowing what mess she would be going back to in her own home.

Barraclough scanned the headlines in the evening paper on the top deck of the bus. His work was finished, he had the time to travel slowly, and as a pensioner he was entitled to free bus rides—an irresistible temptation to get something for nothing. He read the report about the Sarissa and paused when he came to the cocksure statement by Charles Drayton that the Whispering version would make its flying debut at Farnborough as planned, no matter what. There was also a quote from an organizer of the air show, explaining that the appearance of Mark 2 was being treated as an exception to the rules partly because the aircraft had such tremendous international significance and partly because the ability of its crew, headed by the Chief Test Pilot of AeroCorp, was well known to the Flying Control Committee. Normally, the FCC would insist on a full demonstration of each pilot's proposed program, but the Sarissa would not land at Farnborough at all, it would not perform any aerobatics or special maneuvers, and its possibly record-breaking flight from California would be timed to the second so that its arrival fitted precisely into a reserved slot in the tight flying display schedule.

Barraclough reread the names of the crew. Parallel lives, he thought. They would never know that their lives were tragically intertwined with the old man's on the bus. He nodded. He had no doubt that this was the sort of spectacular and much-publicized ferry flight Mott must have in mind.

The report about the investigation mentioned the involvement of an English pilot. Captain Penn. Yes, he knew that name, too. It was Penn's accident that had caused the cancellation of his original assignment and forced Barraclough to seek the alternative employment which led to his ignominious fiasco. He touched the sore scars on his nose and forehead. He felt no animosity toward Penn. It was just another parallel life.

He walked down Piccadilly, crossed the road with no regard for the steady stream of cars, stopped as usual on the traffic island facing the clock, noted that he would have to wait seventeen seconds for the doors to open for Messrs. F and M—and he was not surprised when a car stopped behind him and the familiar voice announced, "Your cab, sir."

Mott was in a hurry. He drove Barraclough to the workshop and picked up two sets of the neatly prepacked knockout device.

"We'll be in touch," he said.

Barraclough asked no questions. There was only a week until Farnborough.

Nobody thought about going to bed that night at AeroCorp. The entire routing of the autopilot and service-call circuits were checked, tested, exposed, stripped and rechecked, but there was no sign of design mistakes, no pointer to the cause of the fault. A special enigma they discovered was that, although several more test flights confirmed Penn's theory, not all the ground tests could reproduce the malfunction even on the same aircraft.

It came about naturally that Penn started to work with the AeroCorp task force, helping and helped by everybody. Early on, he felt like somebody cooperating with the enemy camp on compassionate, humanitarian grounds; but soon he began to feel part of the team to which nothing seemed to matter except the success of the aircraft.

They knew that all users were checking their machines. The results were to be telexed immediately to AeroCorp. The first trickle of information began to arrive within a few hours. Most airlines reported by nightfall. But in some countries there were delays. The team treated contemptuously flimsy excuses such as "During the night—local time—we have no personnel available to do the job; tests will have to wait until daybreak." At first the degree of their fury puzzled Penn. By midnight he could have kicked anyone for less than full support. Over breakfast at four in the morning, his own potential violence frightened him; he could have killed for the Sarissa.

At noon, people began to doze off. Penn held out as long as he could, but then his previous two nights took their toll. He slept for five whole hours in an armchair with one foot on the desk, without ever moving an inch. He woke up with a groan. His entire body felt paralyzed as if set in plaster of Paris. Mara put her hand on his face. "Take it easy."

"What's the time?"

"Seven past eight."

"How long have you been here?"

"Couple of hours."

"Why didn't you wake me up?" He shifted his foot with his hands. "Any developments?"

"Don't know."

"Why not?"

"I'm a reporter, not a member of the team."

"Since when?"

"This morning. My editor released my story to the entire world press."

"Oh."

"Drayton was frantic."

"I'm surprised they let you come in at all."

"Only to say goodbye to you. Or are you coming with me?"

"No. I mean, where to?"

"New York, then London, then Farnborough. I booked this assignment for myself quite a while ago. I was hoping to be with you over there."

"I can't go. I'm needed here, I think."

"Is that the real reason?"

"What else?"

"Sooner or later you'll have to face Timmy."

"I know. But I have a lot to sort out here."

"You're playing for time."

"Partly, perhaps. I must think out how I go about it. It won't be easy to rebuild that relationship."

"Rebuild?" She shook her head. "You'd better start fresh. This time without protective lies out of love."

Penn tried to stare at her through Timmy's eyes. He wondered if the child would ever put up with a strange woman in the house. He forced himself to turn away from her, struggled to his feet and stretched. The stiff joints began to thaw out but still hurt him. "Will you do something for me?"

"Of course I'll go to see him. What shall I say?"

"Give him my love. Tell him I won't be long here."

"That's all?"

"No. If you feel up to it, tell him I'll have to face some disciplinary procedure. They may take away my license. It would be better if he heard it from you than the telly or his schoolfriends."

There was no time to kiss her goodbye. Cleaff from the AIB had arrived and wanted to be briefed by Penn.

The renovation of the abbey, one and a half nautical miles northeast of Farnborough, necessitated a correction in the published list of Aerodrome Obstructions. The scaffolding had added temporarily a couple of feet to the overall height of the spire, and all users of the Farnborough airspace in its busiest fortnight had to be notified.

This was the week of the rehearsals for the flying display programs. The derelict showground area sprang to life at the magic touch of some four hundred exhibitors from all over the world. Chalets and giant hospitality marquees were erected. The two great yawning permanent halls swallowed people and equipment at an incredible speed until everyone had to fight for more elbow room, as if they were in the bazaars of Karachi. Chaos and rubbish turned into thick carpets, soft music, subtle lighting, electronic showcases, gleaming marvels of engineering and sophisticated demonstration stands. Dozens of aircraft, some complete with bombs and rockets, were positioned for the open-air static display. Public facilities—from one-way systems and car parks, to food stalls, first-aid tents, mobile lavatories, bars, pressrooms and lost children's collection points—had to be set up to receive 150,000 people on the three open days, in addition to some 30,000 trade visitors and 2,000 reporters and photographers from virtually every corner of the globe.

The organization and timing of the flying displays had grown into an art in its own right over the years. SATCO (the Senior Air Traffic Control Officer) argued vigorously against the inevitable special arrangement to accommodate the fly-past of the Sarissa Mark 2, because the split-second timing of the show could easily be upset if the aircraft was delayed by weather or other adverse conditions anywhere on the long trek from California. At last a compromise was found: the flight must arrive at 1503 on Thursday, the mixed last trade and first public day, when there would be only an afternoon program, and the appearance of the Sarissa could be squeezed in between the flying start of an IS28 powered glider and a short-take-off Jaguar demonstration. If then the Sarissa failed to turn up or reported some delay, the Grumman Tomcat, already holding at 4000 feet to the south, could be brought in fast to fill the gap with its planned touch-down-and-go or low overshoot (at pilot's discretion) on runway 07. SATCO still failed to warm to the idea, but public interest in the aircraft had been whipped up sufficiently to demand some concession

The Flying Control Committee sent its rules and recommendations to AeroCorp concerning the approach route, communication and emergency frequencies, radio-failure procedures, and diversion aerodromes in the vicinity of Farnborough.

The FCC session was concluded with a review of the ejection area reserved for military aircraft in distress, and the finalization of the revised aerodrome obstructions list including the scaffolding on the spire, a chimney only ninety feet above runway level, a TV mast, control towers, temporarily positioned cranes and rigs, and a massive white building which housed the Concorde test bed and was now to be surrounded by a no-go area of a thousand feet in every direction.

What puzzled everybody at AeroCorp was that the malfunction seemed so very elusive. Each time they failed to reproduce it on an aircraft already known to be faulty, they checked and rechecked all the factors, but the common characteristic was still missing. A junior mechanic made a mealy-mouthed observation that whenever the relevant circuits were fully exposed for examination, the interference with the autopilot could not be achieved, no matter what rhythm they beat out on the service call and cabin sign switches.

This was, of course, an absurd suggestion, because it pointed an accusing finger at the final assembly and outfitting of the aircraft, even though it was proved clearly every time that there had not been any departure from the thousands of precisely prescribed procedures. "Building an aircraft is not a hit or miss affair," he was lectured by an engineer, "or else all of us in the hot seats would fall like ninepins."

And, of course, the engineer was right. The birth of each aircraft was governed by several hundred thousand engineering drawings, and every one of these had to be strictly adhered to. So in the rest of the lecture the word "even" was featured prominently. For *even* the most junior of employees should have known that duplications and triplications of systems and fail-safe designs ensured perfection, that the fitters' tasks were devised to obliterate Murphy's Law (anything that *can* go wrong *will* go wrong sooner or later), and that, for example, not even the least significant nut and bolt could be assembled merely to "feel tight," because the degree of tightness was predetermined meticulously and achieved by the use of wrenches and screwdrivers with calibrated torque gauges.

It was most unfortunate that the absurd observation of the junior mechanical ignoramus happened to be correct, which only added yet another one to the investigators' headaches.

By now, most of the airlines had reported their findings. The malfunction did not affect every aircraft. A quick comparative examination of the available data revealed that those airlines that had taken the earliest deliveries had never experienced what was now known as the "Paya Lebar syndrome." So the date of manufacture of each aircraft might be a potential clue to the problem.

The earliest minor snag report in connection with turbulence encountered, which seemed a probable example of the malfunction, was nine months old. Captain Mellou's VIP incident had happened just eight months ago, Penn recalled. Simms knew that his report came within the nine-month limit, and so did all the other similarly suspect cases.

On Sunday it became obvious that the snag would have to be found among the numerous modifications and improvements introduced between the first and second generations of Sarissas. A matter of time, a mere matter of time it is to find the culprit, members of the various design, technical and operational investigation groups kept encouraging one another, but they all knew that the pressure of urgency was tremendous. Time was running out on Drayton's grand designs. Most of his team were already at Farnborough. He and Termine were due to leave for England that afternoon. And it was no secret that Drayton had had several thousand redundancy notices printed and prepared. If the public doubts and suspicions about the aircraft could not be wiped out fast, the Whispering Sarissa campaign might never get off the ground, competitors might have a chance to catch up with AeroCorp, the future of the company and dozens of its subcontractors would be in jeopardy, and those dismissal letters would hit the mail as fast as the franking machines could churn them out.

Four hours before his departure, Drayton gave a pep talk to

a mass meeting of everybody who had anything to do with the investigation. He quoted various Senators, aviation authorities and newspaper columnists who had recently expressed their unassailable faith in the safety and bright future of the Sarissa. He only failed to mention that most of these statements had come about at his personal instigation. But he sounded as optimistic as ever: "It's a wild race against goddamn time, I know, and it may appear that the odds are against you. Thousands of components may need testing, and you must work through tons of documents. But! And in my book, there's always a but!"

There was a round of applause and Drayton waited patiently. Penn stared at him, through him, without hearing or seeing him. Tons of documents. Paperwork. A woman behind a paper mountain. As the noise subsided, Penn looked around trying to find Cleaff. They were separated by some fifty people, so he had to shout: "Stacey!" He was hushed angrily, but he did not seem to hear. "The Beaver may have it at her fingertip. Come on!" The two men fought their way through the crowd toward the exit. Drayton ignored the disruption. "And the *but* in this case is the spirit of AeroCorp," he enthused. "I know you. All you want is a fair chance to get on with it. Well, I'm giving you that chance. And I know that you won't let me down. We have four days until we show Mark Two to the rest of the world. I'll be there, waiting for you to prove me right!"

Then Termine stood up to address the meeting. It was Drayton's final master stroke. Although there was no information about any threats from competitors, Termine's job was to create a siege atmosphere. "I cannot reveal much of what we already know. It's all very confidential and there isn't enough evidence to fight off some legal action against libel and things like that. But I can tell you this much: we're up against it. They want to stop us, and I mean that. I mean I really mean that. They want to stop us, no matter what it takes. We'll take certain security measures, but the risk is there, and, as Mr. Drayton says, that's a risk that must never be de-emphasized, because we're on our own!"

Drayton nodded, but winced mentally. I must stop myself wishing I could swap him back for Singer, he thought. But then he had to admit, at least to himself, that the wish did not stem entirely from Termine's objectionable style. Singer's return to this life would also spare him the now inevitable change of course in his private life.

Barraclough seemed chuffed, yes, positively chuffed, Fraser observed as they drank the first glass of Demestica over their traditional end-of-assignment Greek meal.

"He said he was grateful to me. They all were, he said, because I really got them out of a tight spot," Barraclough told her.

"That's odd."

"What?"

"The chief used to be more of a praise miser."

"Perhaps he's going old and soft." Barraclough laughed.

"Who did he mean, 'they all'?"

"The department, I suppose."

Which sounded even more peculiar to her. Mott used to regard himself as a one-man department. But Fraser knew her place in this world. Who was she to question Barraclough, let alone Mott? Particularly now that Barraclough had agreed to tell everything to Sally—and seemed chuffed about that, too.

The shoebox of a shop at Angmering-on-Sea was almost theirs by now—only a few lawyers'-delight technicalities had to be sorted out—and Barraclough planned to make his will immediately so as to ensure that Fraser and Sally would inherit everything he had.

On their usual after-dinner walk through Hampstead toward their whisky in The Flask, both of them were preoccupied with the same thoughts but did not know how to discuss them. What would be the best way to tell Sally? How would she react to it? Would she be shocked? Would she understand? Would she mind going to their wedding? Would she start calling him Dad? How would he feel about it? He could certainly not start suddenly calling his bride love, dear, Betty, the missus, Mrs. Barraclough and names like that when she was just Fraser or Fraser, Betty M., if the mood was right.

"When?" she asked at last.

"When what?"

"When do you want to tell her?"

"Oh, that." He hesitated. "How about Fortnum and Mason?"

"Tomorrow?"

"Er . . ."

"Thursday, then."

"All right."

His visits there would soon have to stop if they moved to the seaside. Pity. He would miss those quiet afternoons of vanilla-fragrant atmosphere, heavy though with expectations of the Brigadier's unannounced appearance at the patisserie counter. He did not like to change his routines. It made him feel gloomy. The longer they walked up Hampstead Hill the gloomier his mood grew. And it was their longest ever after-dinner stroll. The end of the last assignment. The irrevocability of retirement. The inevitable death of a Sarissa crew. Chief Test Pilot. What sort of a man would that be? Barraclough never liked to know unnecessary details about his target. Now he felt curious. They passed a deserted newsstand and a school. Would the pilot have children? They turned into an elegant tree-lined road. Where would the man live? And was this gloom due to the fact that, he knew, the parallel lives were now converging? He shook himself like a wet dog, hoping that instant drying was feasible.

A fine Georgian house in front of them was the end of the road. It was a cul-de-sac. They had to turn back.

Mara sat with her back to the window and half listened to Granny's non-stop moaning. She felt Timmy's steady, unblinking stare on her. It was the open gaze of a man-child's desire and curiosity, the embarrassing mixture against which so few women have any except rude defense.

"Maybe it's not for me to say, but it's really the parents' duty to be here with their offspring if you don't mind me saying so."

Mara kept her eyes away from the child by studying the room methodically from left to right and back. It was well, though somewhat ostentatiously, furnished, with good pieces, all in style, but a home it was not. And there was certainly no trace of Penn's personality anywhere. She wondered what the room could tell her about Candy. It was not much. She wished the old woman would stop yapping. Then perhaps she could hear the words of the mute conversation going on between herself and the child. For she had no doubt that such a conversation was well in progress, deciding whether there could ever be a friend ship between them. And the longer she failed to hear those words the bleaker that prospect grew.

"So what's keeping Cornelius over there? I mean if you don't mind telling me."

"His presence may be the key to the success of the investigation. It's a hell of a fight for the safety of that aircraft."

Timmy walked over to Mara and, staring from only an arm's length away, captured her eyes. "Is my father a fighter?"

"Yes."

"A good fighter?"

"Yes."

"Stop asking silly questions, Timothy. . . . Timothy, can't you hear me? You see, he's always asking silly questions," Granny droned in the background.

The child remained unperturbed. "The sort of fighter who'd stand up and fight no matter what?"

"If he thinks it's right, yes."

"Even if two men are against him?"

"Yes."

"Even if three?"

"I think so."

"Even a million?"

"Yes."

"Do you love him?"

A trained interrogator could not have made the switch in the line of questioning so swiftly. It was more a flash in her mind than clear-cut recall of what she had said to Penn about relationships without lies. And she answered quietly, "Yes. I do love him."

"And I love him more," the child counterpunched, ready for an argument.

"Stop being so silly and go to your room at once." Granny closed in on them. "Your father has a wife and the young lady knows it."

Timmy paid no attention to her. "I love him more," he repeated defiantly.

Mara smiled. Contact had been made. "May I tell him that?"

"Why?"

"It would make him happy."

Miss Beaver spent the weekend with her sister in Ipswich and went to her office straight from the station on Monday morning. That was why Penn could not find her until then. But the stacks of documents she had worked on for Stacey were still on her huge desk. In a single drawer she kept a plastic file of summaries under various headings in her childish handwriting: a touch of homeliness and fallibility that used to convey more than a computer printout to Stacey.

"What modifications do you need?" she asked Penn.

"Everything that was introduced on aircraft that began to leave AeroCorp, say, ten months ago."

"That's a lot."

"I'm ready to tape it, so just give us the list of the relevant document numbers."

"They'll be under different headings—things concerning the undercarriage, fuel tanks, passenger seats, pilot's windscreen heating, minor structural changes, electrical improvements, weight reductions, galley equipment, hat-rack locks, and so on. Are you sure you want the lot?"

"Hang on for a sec."

Penn conferred briefly with Cleaff. Faulty aircraft in the suspect batch must have come off the production line nine or ten months before. From the date of orders received it would take about four months to prepare additional drawings according to customers' special requirements and designers' modifications. Then it would take about fourteen months to build the various parts at AeroCorp and the numerous subcontractors' plants hundreds of miles apart, deliver everything to the AeroCorp production line, put it all together like a giant jigsaw, fit everything from wings to the last Exit sign, paint it all according to individual airline specifications, do the preflight tests, test-fly it and deliver.

Cleaff took the receiver from Penn: "Would it speed up and simplify matters if you first gave me all modifications that were introduced between nine and twenty-eight months ago?"

"No, because that would include almost everything I've got."

"Oh. Then would you have a heading under which you classified all structural and electrical changes which might affect the autopilot and cabin sign circuits?"

"No . . ." She thought for a few seconds. "But there might be a way. . . . You see, Mr. Stacey used to have a blowup of the Sarissa layout on the wall and he had a code to mark the spots where all them modifications were made, because he had this idea, you see—"

"Never mind that now," Cleaff interrupted impatiently. "Do you still have the blowup?"

"Yes, I think I could lay my hands on it; but you see, it

wouldn't mean much to me because I wouldn't know, would I, whether a change in the lavatory layout had anything to do with your circuits, sir, or not." She stopped and there was some rustling of fine paper. "Here, sir, I've got it."

"We'll arrange for one of the inspectors to help you right away."

"Yes, that would be good, sir. Pity Mr. Stacey isn't no longer with us. I mean he would know, wouldn't he? And he would know how them detail drawings fit together."

"What details?"

"You know, sir, things that were too small to be shown on the big picture. Now you mentioned the autopilot. That, for instance, would be on a separate sheet with markings to show that the weight of the instrument panel had been reduced and the depth of the cavity or what you call it behind the panel was better utilized . . ."

Cleaff went white. Miss Beaver was still talking on the line, he still held the receiver to his ear, but he did not hear her any more. He felt sure that a simple answer had been there staring him in the face all the time. When he had written that appendix to his draft report, he regarded it as a gesture to the pettiness of his dead colleague. Now he would have sworn that the "technical blemish," the unnecessarily long panel-locking screws, might be the culprit they were looking for.

Followed by Penn, he ran along corridors, across workshops, toward the faulty Sarissa, summoning help on the way so that they arrived eventually at the head of a small army of mechanics, designers, and electricians. Cleaff pointed at the 20x5-inch plastic panel on which the autopilot, navigation light, landing lamp, No Smoking and Fasten Seat Belts switches were located. The autopilot controls were only an octave away from the cabin signs.

The panel was removed. Behind it was a multipin plug, rather like a brush with three dozen wire hairs fitting smoothly into a miniature honeycomb. The honeycomb was in a fixed position, forming the end of a bundle of wires which was clipped to the back of the panel. The brush could be moved freely for quick disconnection and reconnection during maintenance. Its pins continued in individual wires, held together in an outer sleeve, leading to the various switches.

A small puncture on the sleeve of the fixed bundle of insulated wires was hardly noticeable. But it was there—right at the tip of a locking screw which protruded from the panel a good quarter of an inch. Under a magnifying glass it became clear that the screw had penetrated the outer sleeve and touched two neighboring wires—one to the main autopilot On switch, the other to the cabin signs.

If the screw did not damage the inner insulation outright when the panel was fitted originally, it would surely cause chafing through the constant vibration, particularly when the aircraft was on the ground with the engines running. Once the wires were bared at some point, the presence of the screw would create contact between them at least intermittently, and the power used for the cabin signs could stray into and activate the autopilot.

This would explain the mysterious stick resistance. It would also answer the question of why the fault could never be reproduced with the circuits exposed. When, in order to check the entire system, the instrument panel was removed, the locking screws had to be taken out first, and with that the contact had gone. The trips and contact breakers guarding the circuits against shorting and malfunction could not differentiate between the stray electricity and ordinary application of power, and so allowed free passage to the accidental input.

Old, skeptical boffins and technicians stood around the magnifying glass in a funeral circle burying, yet again, the notion of perfect safety.

At first sight it was assumed that the untimely pressing of the service call button must have intensified the stray power input. At what point this would occur was one of the questions to investigate without delay.

The other questions were more historical, concerning the origin of the fault. It seemed obvious that the series of improvements were the main cause. All the instrument panels, like thousands of other parts of the Sarissa, had been subject to weight reductions in the course of a determined program to achieve even greater fuel economy. Lighter alloys and plastics had been introduced where possible, grooves and holes were cut in the metal to eliminate dead weight. Instrument casings and their fixing flanges had also grown thinner in the overall slimming process.

Who was the designer who had overlooked the length of the locking screw? Why had not anybody reduced the specification to fit the thinner panels? Somebody might of course defend himself by saying that the jutting out screw tip would have been an inconsequential technical wart if there was no reduction in the depth of the cavity behind the panel. And this was perfectly true. For maximum space utilization, instruments and wiring in there were compressed a little, with fixed location for everything. The result was a gain of a few extra inches for the crammed flight deck—and unexpected proximity between the wires and the forgotten screw.

At a quarter to four in the morning, Drayton's deputy chief executive declared that some heads would surely have to roll. He wanted to know right away why only the hair-splitting Stacey of the AIB had ever questioned the unwanted length of that screw. But the investigators were more concerned about the full extent of the problem. Their team, backed by all resources of AeroCorp, began yet another day-and-night fight for a solution in time for Farnborough.

That Monday, the first of the trade days at the air show, it was vintage champagne for everyone who happened to come anywhere near the AeroCorp chalet. Not that aircraft manufacturers were particularly stingy with their PR and sales hospitality at other times, but today everybody was to celebrate with the Sarissa makers. On the huge terrace behind the chalet, overlooking the static display of aircraft, 250 people were expected to lunch. They would enjoy the flying display in comfort over their coffee and brandy.

Mara watched a glowing rejuvenated Drayton as he faced the relentless question barrage from the international press. She wished him well despite her recent suspicions about some underhanded company techniques and outright crimes for which she was inclined to blame Drayton's minions. She felt sure, and kept telling herself she felt sure, that he would have nothing to do with such things. If only she could understand how or why Drayton put up with the constant company of that creep Termine, lately never far from his chief's elbow.

One of the reporters turned to Termine. "You told us last night that Sarissa users had nothing to worry about, all was clear. Was that true?"

"Yes, sir, that was the truth."

"Then how is it that now you tell us that this morning the fault has been found? Does it mean that yesterday the aircraft was unsafe?"

"Well"—Termine struggled for words—"to tell you the truth, it was the truth I told you yesterday, but now, how shall I say, that truth is inoperative."

Drayton winced and butted in fast. "What we mean is that our previous safety instructions are now inoperative because, instead of preventive measures, we can now offer a complete cure. Our team is working on the details and I've been assured that we'll have everything ready within the next forty-eight hours." Drayton turned to face an American television camera. "That's why I now have a message to our men conducting the investigation at the plant. As a reward for the team's tireless devotion and ingenuity, we'll fill up the Whispering Sarissa and I invite all of them to England for a free holiday—and they can bring their families, too!"

"That was a clever ploy," Mara told Drayton after the press conference. She was about to say more, but Anna Singer's unexpected appearance silenced her.

"Hi, Mara."

"What are *you* doing here?" Mara could not hide her astonishment.

"What a question." Anna slipped her arm under Drayton's. "Helping my fiancé, of course, with his social duties."

"Oh. Congratulations," Mara forced herself to say, studying Drayton's face all the time, trying to discover what on earth could have compelled him to take this step he could have taken long before Singer's marriage but certainly never wanted to. Drayton knew exactly what she was thinking about, and it was one of the rare occasions in his life when he felt embarrassed. He wondered if the success of an aircraft was really worth all the personal compromise and private indebtedness he had run up in the past few weeks. But there was no answer to that. Anna knew too much, and knew how to protect herself even from Termine.

Penn was among the lucky few who managed to grab a few hours of sleep that morning. He was up again well before lunchtime and helped Cleaff, then joined the Chief Pilot for another test flight. While they were in the air, shortly before 1400, Pacific Time, one line of investigation was concluded.

It was already known that a change-of-specification notice about the length of the panel screw had, in fact, been prepared. But it was not docketed on the assembly line and, apparently, no copy had ever been issued to the shop-floor stores or CeMaS, which stood for Central Material Supplies. It was now discovered that, instead of distribution, all the copies of the change-spec notice had been clipped together and filed with the original in the designers' Drawings Depository. Responsibility for the admin error was traced to a junior clerk who had long ago left AeroCorp.

A message from Drayton about the holiday bonus was received by the deputy chief executive. He immediately arranged to set up three television sets at strategic points so that the whole investigation team could watch the boss in the special feature about Farnborough.

Barraclough spent the evening weeding out his possessions. He threw away all the nonessentials of his future in Angmering-on-Sea. The flat above the shop was too small to store the lifelong by-products of two households.

More than ready for bed, he propped up his eyelids to watch the late-night news. The interview with Charles Drayton gave him as sickening a jolt as his first-ever reveille in the barracks at Aldershot. That target Sarissa would be full of people. And children, too. Mott might know nothing about it. Mott must be warned.

Barraclough followed the standard "urgent contact requested" procedure, but the Brigadier failed to respond. By Tuesday afternoon, Barraclough was very nervous and impatient. Mott might be away, out of touch completely. Or he might plan to make contact on the regular Thursday at F and M. Which might be too late. Unless he had already heard about the unexpected passengers on the flight and canceled the operation by now. Usually he knew what was going on. He would not take kindly to warnings and interference. Except that this case was different. Or so it appeared to Barraclough.

Termine lied convincingly. He said he found it outrageous what the hotel had done to Candy. She wanted to believe him because it was flattering and a boost to her deflated self-confidence. The days of sleeping at the airport, calling in vain for messages at the hotel, and not knowing which way to turn made her highly susceptible to a good meal and kind words. So now her path was clear again. She would stay with her ugly American for ever and ever. Which was not Termine's idea about the future. Far from it. He had slipped over to Paris only for a couple hours. She must now be persuaded to apply for a job with a Brazilian charter airline that supplied executive jets to people Termine was interested in.

"The future is real electric, baby," he crooned.

"I'm talking about the present, not the future. If I wanted to be away from you and lead that sort of life, I . . . I . . . Oh, I don't know."

"That's right, baby, you don't know. You're just wired again, and you need help to shape the future and make you buzz."

Oh yes. She felt good again. That man had the answers. She kissed him. There was something in him that made her forget his ugliness. "Did you say Brazil?"

"That's my baby. A little help, that's all I need from you, because I'm in trouble right now. So will you save me, baby?"

No man had ever asked her to save or even help him. They all wanted to help her. Or so they said. This was a new experience. "How about my child? Can I take him to Brazil?"

"I thought you wanted to leave him with his father."

"I've changed my mind."

"Oh."

"Does it matter?"

"No," he drawled, "I suppose not. Sure you can take him once you got this job going in Brazil. If that's what you want."

"The longer I leave him the more difficult it will be to take him from Corrie. He'll see him again as God in that left-hand seat."

"I wouldn't say that, baby. He's finished you know. He'll never fly again. He'll be pleased if someone gives him a desk job."

"Then he might as well be dead."

Termine shrugged his shoulders. He was more concerned

about Candy's future. Would she cooperate and become a useful agent or would she have to be disposed of? He liked women agents; promises were cheaper and in better supply than blackmail data.

The house in Wimbledon looked more luxurious than Barraclough imagined it. Through a piece of accidental intelligence he had known for several years where Mott lived, but he never mentioned it to his chief and always resisted the urge of curiosity to go and have a peep. On this Wednesday morning, in sheer desperation, the temptation became irresistible when he telephoned Farnborough and discovered that the Sarissa flight was still as planned, except rescheduled to arrive two hours later.

He watched the house from the corner, a good fifty yards away, and decided to wait until noon. If Mott did not appear, he would knock on the door.

At ten to twelve a chauffeur-driven near vintage Rover passed Barraclough and stopped in front of the house. A few seconds later Mott appeared in a black pin-stripe suit. The driver opened the door for him. Barraclough associated the scene with government. He was impressed. But Mott was not when Barraclough raised his hand halfheartedly to call attention.

Through the open window of the car, the Brigadier spoke a little abruptly, clipping his sentences to a military short-back-and-sides. Barraclough understood. He had never broken regulations and procedures before.

"Yes, I know about the unexpected cargo. And I'm concerned. Naturally. Just like you. And I've taken the necessary steps, of course."

"Of course." Barraclough felt rather foolish with all the fuss he was making.

"And I'd have contacted you in due course."

"I just thought . . . just that it might be . . ."

"Too late?"

"Yes, sir."

"What if it was? What would you have done?"

"I don't know, sir."

Mott watched his face. Barraclough was a sad sight. An old man growing jittery. Even squeamish. Pity. "Now that the op is off, we'll have to make alternative arrangements. Will you be available to help?"

"Yes, sir. Of course." The keen emphasis on the last two words contrasted with the hesitancy of the voice.

"Good. I'll join you for tea tomorrow." And just before the car pulled away from the curb, he added, "Look after yourself."

Mara was almost in tears. Chief Pilot Brown of SupraNat had just told her that Corrie's flying career was over, of course.

"I thought you were his friend."

"I am. But that has nothing to do with it. I'll try to help him in every possible way."

"He'll be grateful, I'm sure." The edge of her voice hurt him, she knew. Just what she wanted.

"He's been fully exonerated, of course, but other circumstances must also be considered. You must understand."

"I'm beginning to."

"I mean, how would you feel as a member of the flying public if Corrie's voice came up on the intercom announcing at thirty thousand feet that this was your Captain, that much-maligned Captain Penn, speaking. Would you feel safe?"

"Yes."

"But you're not the flying public."

"And neither are you, Captain Brown."

Drayton agreed with Brown when Mara told him about the conversation. "Penn had too much bad publicity."

"Then it's time to give him some good publicity," Mara argued.

"As a goddamn journalist you should know that mud sticks.

And no big revelation of the truth will ever whitewash it completely."

When shortly before midnight Penn telephoned her at her hotel, she tried to sound more cheerful than she felt. She was tempted to tell him about Brown and Drayton, but decided against it. He would lose nothing by the delay in facing the problem. There was plenty of time.

He asked about Timmy. She blurted out what she had planned to be a surprise. "I'll take him to see the air show tomorrow. Drayton promised to give us a lift in his chopper to meet you wherever your flight landed. Would that be Heathrow?"

"I'm not sure. I'm just a passenger."

At five in the morning, Piccadilly was dead. An old drunk was angry. He began to shiver as he was sobering up and the police were late. By now they should have picked him up, run him in, and given him a decent cell for a few hours' rest.

An office cleaners' van stopped in front of Fortnum and Mason. An elderly man gave the door the merest perfunctory wipeover, then took the ladder from the top of the van, climbed onto the canopy above the entrance, and began a more thorough cleaning of the clock face and the doors on both sides.

At the AeroCorp plant it was still Wednesday evening. The flight was supposed to leave at nine o'clock (0500 GMT) but there would be a two-hour delay due to a change of schedule at Farnborough.

The Sarissa stood on the tarmac ready to go. Mechanics had just finished their last-minute checks. One of the altimeters had to be replaced because of some suspected malfunction. It was a trusted, experienced fitter who changed the complete unit.

The hangar nearby was packed with the passengers. The

members of the investigation team, who had not seen a bed for four days, sought corners for a nap while waiting, but their families were in a holidaymakers' noisy mood. Penn could have withdrawn to some quiet office, but did not want to ask for special arrangements. It was, after all, a favor that they were giving him a free ride home. He settled down, uncomfortably, on a bench, and he knew that as soon as he closed his eyes no noise, no amount of willpower could slow down his sinking into the dreamless, featureless marshland where the worn-out slept. But there was one sound Penn failed to reckon with. A tinkle. It was high-pitched and continuous. Penn did not need to open his eyes to recognize the source. But it would not go away.

Penn looked up. A little girl, perhaps three years old, was pushing a stick attached to a red telephone on wheels. It twirled as it tinkled as it twirled, up and down and again.

Somebody hushed. "Stop it, dear," a young woman said softly. The voice lacked conviction. And the little dear knew it.

Penn wished he had the energy to get up and run away. But his body refused to move. His head stubbornly tried to sleep, ready to dream about a belly dancer whose trinkets tinkled as she twirled as they tinkled.

Mara picked up Timmy at half past ten in the morning to drive him to Farnborough.

"Where is my dad now?"

"Let me see . . . They left the West Coast at seven o'clock our time."

"Our time" was a careless reference. For then she had the hopeless task of explaining what time zones and Greenwich Mean Time meant, why it was night in San Francisco when morning in London, and how one could gain or lose a day of one's life by flying across the international date line in the Pacific Ocean. The awesome turmoil of the crowds saved her from further interrogation—only to expose her to even more probing questions about radars, missiles and the hypnotic flickering of electronic equipment.

At two in the afternoon the flying program began. Mara borrowed a pair of powerful binoculars for Timmy and impressed him with snippets of inside information about the two electronic clocks that ruled the rhythm of an air show. She showed him the two glass cages on top of the tower—one for the group captain in charge of the Flying Control Committee, and one for the official commentator—and gave him a map of the airfield.

"And how did you get *that?*"

"Shh."

The child's eyes opened wide. "You scrounged it!" he shouted in a whisper. "You really did."

She smiled with open vanity. It was sheer joy to be appreciated like that. And that was not all. She arranged with an AeroCorp communications engineer that Timmy could sit with him and listen in on the laconic exchanges between tower and aircraft.

"Are we breaking the law?" Timmy whispered.

"No. Lots of people come with radios."

The child was clearly disappointed.

A Northrop fighter zoomed in low, giving a pleasant thrill to some sixty thousand spectators.

"Two minutes," said the cold voice on the radio. Timmy turned to the engineer with alarm.

"It has two minutes to go. The next in the show, a new twin-engine Piaggio P-166 is already at the holding point, ready to go. Over there . . . look."

"One minute."

Silence. The fighter turned. It was coming in: *"Northrop F5 downwind."*

The Piaggio began to roll slowly toward the runway. The

show was in full swing, but Timmy was more fascinated by the radio. Pity they were all so taciturn, even if the virtual radio silence helped the show pilots' vital power of concentration.

Aboard the Whispering Sarissa, the passengers had lunch at 1300 GMT, when their stomachs were about to develop a daybreak craving for fruit juices and cereals; their body clocks showed only five A.M. So when the Saricola, Sarinade, Saribrandy and other containers as well as the rest of the plastic garbage of a meal in flight were cleared away, almost everybody pulled down the window blinds and tried to catch up on missed sleep.

At 1400 GMT, the Chief Test Pilot, who occupied the left-hand seat, decided to inform Farnborough that, helped by a 150-knot tail wind, flight Aero 616 would probably break the route record and arrive early at the holding area. His call would be picked up by one of the powerful aerials on the Welsh coast and piped to the heart of the network, the London Air Traffic Control Center, which, in turn, would relay the message to the Farnborough controllers, whose receivers covered only a fifty-mile radius.

At 1523, the pilots reviewed their position. Coming in on Upper Green One, the transatlantic route of all heights above 25,000 feet, landfall should be at Strumble Head in about thirty-one minutes. ATC would drop the flight to 30,000 feet at about Fishguard and set it on a straight line over the southern slopes of the Cambrian Mountains, the Rhondda Valley, across the Severn Estuary, over the Cotswold Hills and the Hampshire Downs to Farnborough. They would leave 30,000 at Brecon, join Lower Green One, leave the airway under radar control and descend, as directed, step by step, to about 6,000 feet at Lyneham, from where they would contact the show controllers at Farnborough. The Estimated Time of Arrival: 1625. It meant they would have to hold at somewhere 3000 feet on

Farnborough radar, waiting for the reserved slot in the flying program.

The Chief Test Pilot was pleased with the speed. Approaching the end of a distinguished career, he would leave yet another micro-entry or at least footnote in the history books of aviation.

The tea counter was exceptionally busy, but Brigadier Mott did not mind. He was just browsing. Between the Chinese and Indians he could keep an eye on the entrance and the street beyond. From time to time a bus, using the reserved lane, obscured his view of the slim tongue of a traffic island opposite where now a cab was stopping. Mott checked his watch: 1554 and thirty seconds. A slight nod of satisfaction was quite irresistible. He felt the eyes of a morning-coated assistant on him. It was his turn to be served. Mott looked around and found what he wanted: an impatient old woman. His mute gesture of the turn of the century told her "After you, ma'am." It was appreciated. The world was not yet wholly void of chivalry.

The uniformed doorman and a security man of authoritative courtesy stopped customers at the door and begged permission to glance into large handbags and briefcases. There had been a bomb threat, they explained. No, nobody took it seriously, but the house owed its patrons a certain degree of vigilance.

At 1555 the driver got out of the cab and walked away. That was all Mott had been waiting to see. Now he asked the assistant to pack some dark oolong and green Ceylon tea for him. "I'll be in there," he said, and walked unhurriedly into the tearoom, where he took Barraclough's table. The waitress was about to protest, but Mott was quicker: "I'm expecting the gentleman who usually sits here, thank you."

At 1555, the Sarissa was cleared to descend to 30,000 feet. The Chief Test Pilot knocked off the altitude hold and dialed 500 feet a minute to be the descent speed, but then he changed his mind. After the boring hours of transatlantic inactivity, he would treat himself to some decent hand-flying. He switched off the autopilot, then cut short the irritating woof-woof and flashing red lights that would have warned him if the disconnection was accidental. He throttled back a little and put the nose down. Like every pilot, he had his personal habit of instrument-scanning pattern. Frequent circuit of eye movement was his preference, pausing mostly on the largest instrument face, the artificial horizon, right in front to monitor the attitude of the aircraft. The other main staging post for his eyes was the barber pole, the red-and-white-striped needle in the airspeed indicator which would alert him with the piercing sound of a klaxon if he ever reached the "never exceed speed."

Leaving 35,000, approaching 34,000 . . . He was in no hurry and kept well below the barber pole.

Barraclough stopped at a pillar box in Piccadilly and posted a handful of lilac envelopes. He wondered if the income from the small shop at Angmering-on-Sea would enable him to continue playing the anonymous benefactor and well-wisher. He was sure that Fraser would have no objection to that. Which reminded him of Sally. Pity that the moment of truth had to be postponed, but the discussion with the Brigadier could not wait. He offered Betty M. the chance to talk to the girl alone, but of course she preferred to make this happy turning point the first true family occasion. They would nominate the date as Sally's second birthday—she would have two celebrated each year, like the Queen.

The Chief Test Pilot wanted to see the map of the Farnborough area. The co-pilot leaned forward to reach the map rack. That was how he became aware of the strange hissing sound.

"Can you hear it, sir?"

The chief shook his head. The engineer leaned toward the

co-pilot's seat. He heard it, too. "It's like oxygen escaping from a pressure bottle."

The co-pilot shook violently. The engineer felt faint, tried to reach out toward the pilot, but his hand would not quite obey.

"What's going on?" the chief wanted to ask but never quite finished the sentence.

By the time the convulsions came, none of them felt anything. The colorless and virtually odorless gas quickly filled the flight deck, but the efficient ventilation system began to disperse, dilute and clear it away by the time the Sarissa left 34,000 and continued its gradual descent.

At two minutes to four, Barraclough approached the Royal Academy. He looked up and noted that the sky was mostly clear, the chilly wind from the north had dropped, but low clouds were racing westward over Green Park. That was when he suddenly recognized his mistake. He had recommended setting the barometric trigger of the gas device at something like thirty-odd thousand feet. It would achieve the maximum drop, dive and destruction. But that sort of height would be crossed during descent toward the end of a long flight, which meant the aircraft might crash on land, not into the sea. Lucky that the operation had been called off this time. He would warn the Brigadier at once, though he was ashamed. He would never have made such a miscalculation in his younger days.

Barraclough stopped in front of the Academy, executed a stiff left turn, and crossed the road as if there was no traffic. His customary beeline for the F and M clock had to be broken. A parked taxi at the narrow traffic island forced a slight detour.

He glanced into the cab; it was empty. Mott must already be in the tearoom. Barraclough raised his wrist to check the time. According to his watch, the doors had two seconds to open for the red and turquoise grocers up there. Now. And there they were, gliding out to meet and bow to each other.

What he did not see was the metal pin protruding from Mr.

Fortnum's feet. It touched a short piece of raw wire and activated a single-tone miniature radio transmitter. The code was picked up by the cab radio. The explosion was deafening.

Three passers-by were slightly injured. Their cries for help demanded attention. It took time before somebody noticed Barraclough, because he did not ask for help. His body had disintegrated.

At 1603 the Captain of an Aer Lingus flight for Barcelona reported a near miss over Wales. He expressed his displeasure with Air Traffic Control in his least melodious Irish brogue. Cardiff ATC swore there should be no aircraft at 28,000 in the area. The pilot just swore. He certainly had not dreamed up the near disaster. Even though the ghost aircraft was an odd one. It looked like a Sarissa but it was not quite like a Sarissa. None of the crew had ever seen anything like it. "It was in a steep descent cutting right through our path, I'm telling you! Wait!" The pilot broke off for a few seconds. A pale stewardess had rushed into the flight deck. She had witnessed the near miss. "Both pilots were asleep, so help me. Their heads were tilted at an odd angle, even bobbing, like two drunks on a mule."

By then ATC had clarified the position with London. The only aircraft that could be there was the new Sarissa. It would explain why it looked familiar and yet unfamiliar. But it should certainly not be at 28,000.

"We saw it, I'm telling you. Until it disappeared into thick clouds."

Efforts to contact the Sarissa were fruitless. "Aero 616, come in . . . Aero 616, do you read me?"

All aircraft and radar stations in the area were alerted to look out for the flight that would not answer any radio calls.

The shock waves of the explosion had hardly dissipated when a well-drilled evacuation of the shop and tearoom began. In all the hubbub of excitement, Brigadier Mott alone remained perfectly unruffled. He raised his teacup and drank a few sips to the memory of an old comrade.

His calmness would be in character. At the moment he was not supposed to know if anybody had been killed or hurt. His alibi was perfect. The cab driver was as trustworthy as Barraclough used to be. A little later, on being told about the tragedy outside the shop, he would have the correct opportunity to seem frightened. Had he not been early at their rendezvous, by Jove, the explosion might have killed him, too.

He would then add his thoughts to the post-slaughter speculation and support the mindless-random-violence viewpoint. After all, there had been warnings, no bombers were seen, the cab radio must have been the trigger, and the transmission could have come from anywhere, most probably a passing car. Had there been any remains of clockwork or electronic timing device in the wreckage, police might suspect that Barraclough was intended to be the victim. But, without such discoveries everybody would fall in with the irrefutable random-violence explanation. Barraclough himself would have been proud of the planning of the operation.

In three or four days, Mott would borrow the cleaners' van just once more and remove the transmitter from Messrs. Fortnum & Mason's feet.

Penn was dreaming about a belly dancer. He sensed it must be Mara, but he wanted to be sure. As she danced nearer and nearer, he tried to touch her, stop that crazy whirl and check her identity with a kiss, but he could not reach her. He stirred and grabbed at those trinkets around her hips, but the metal slipped through his fingers as if it was melting snow. The sound began to fade away.

He opened his eyes. The telephone toy had passed him, dragging the stick behind it. That damn kid . . . except that the child was nowhere to be seen. The tinkler rolled on of its own free will. Penn's brain was still fogbound with sleep, but it registered that something was odd. Steeper than normal descent had made the toy roll. There was a clanking noise behind him. He turned. The bewildered face of Joan, the head hostess, as she tried to restrain an unruly drinks trolley.

Penn unbuckled his seat belt and felt drawn toward the seat in front. He had to push himself back and away from it to get out. Something whizzed past his ear. Joan struggled with the trolley. Bottles flew off and landed with minor explosions. People began to wake up.

Penn stepped forward and was at once driven to hurry and slide like a hiker on an icy ski slope. He burst into the flight deck with sharp questions at the ready, but the sight of the crew blunted words and intentions. The engineer was hanging sideways, held by his seat belt. Penn had to shove him out of his way. The co-pilot, doubled up, seemed to be trying to squeeze his head into the map rack. The Captain's lifeless body rested gently, as if just taking a breather, on the control column, pressing the nose further down and the aircraft into a dive.

The air was heavy but Penn had no time to ponder over that. From a loose-swinging headset (the wire, by now, almost parallel to the floor), through noise and incessant, excited patter, came a yelling voice: "Aero 616, do you read me? . . . Aero 616 . . ."

Penn grabbed the Captain, released his seat belt, and tried to shift him. The stiffness of the body resisted any movement and, in the confined space, Penn had to support his own weight on one hand to avoid falling onto the control column.

New voices were added to the cacophony. Some radar operator thought he had spotted the bleep that might be the missing Sarissa: "There . . . the one leaving 26,000 now . . . 20 due north of Swansea?"

Penn found a firm foothold. He heaved, but the Captain's shoulder slipped from his grip. Penn caught his collar and gave it a desperate jerk to the right. The Captain's flailing heavy left arm fell on the stick. It might have been that extra push or an unexpected gust outside or people moving in the cabin that shifted the attitude of the aircraft and forced it into a much steeper dive. For, quite suddenly, everything went unnaturally light. Penn had to hang on to the back of the seat so as not to float away.

The Mach warning horn came on. Then the klaxon of the VNE, the never-to-exceed velocity. Lights began to flash. Warning flags lit up. Violent shivers and shudders shook the Sarissa. Mach buffeting, Penn's brain registered without looking at the mad dance of the airspeed indicator. But the virtual weightlessness, caused by the aircraft settling firmly in this catastrophic dive, helped Penn to slide and float the Captain out of the way. He could then pull himself into the seat.

In the cabin a child cried out. It only emphasized the stifled silence. When the dive reduced the force of gravity to zero, a stewardess sailed gently to the ceiling and there she stayed in a state of blind shock. Blankets, and then some heavier loose objects, soared to fly freely around. The tinkling toy tried to creep up an old woman's leg. She sat there, watching it, hypnotized. The drinks trolley struggled to become airborne. Oxygen masks fell out. Some people grabbed them and pressed them to their mouths as taught: at least something to hang on to.

Nobody knew how long this took. Might have been five minutes or more. It was, in fact, ten seconds. The sense of time was the first to be lost. The sense of direction was the next.

To Penn it seemed as if he was watching the high-speed replay of some documentary film. His lifelong scan pattern—eyes slipping along spokes of an imaginary wheel from artificial horizon in the hub to instruments and back—asserted itself automatically. His first moves were equally instinctive. Must reduce speed. Pull out speed brakes. God bless the Sarissa designer who made them effective up to maximum speed. But they stopped moving. The tab assisting them must have jammed. He pulled harder. Somewhere between two hand movements he buckled his seat belt and flipped the Fasten Seat Belts switch. But what if . . . no . . . it couldn't . . . it was checked . . .

The old panic rose from his stomach. It pressed his chest out as if trying to make room for an extra lungful of air, and grabbed his throat in the same move. But, strangely, the pressure began to ease as fast as it had begun. Perhaps in this situation there was no fear left to the imagination, no scare to be ashamed of. Even Father would not call him a poltroon now, despite his sweaty palms. The thought gave him a heady sense of new freedom. His hands were on the control column. He was not sure whether the unsteady stick made his arms tremble or his shaky hands caused the jitters. In training, he had done dive practice at the hair-raising fifteen-degree angle—now he was diving at forty-two degrees, still a little steeper every second, at a speed which guaranteed he would punch a big hole in some green pasture within three or four minutes.

Must reduce speed. No point in aiding and abetting the dive, he heard his old instructor's words. They still made him smile. He throttled right back. Engines idling. He would need them later. If they were still there. The aero-elastic structure of the aircraft would endure a lot of battering. But then flutter would be caused by the excessive speed. It might affect just a tab or a wing or everything. It could be cumulative. If only there was a crew to help, just help him think clearly and fast. Another shudder ran from the stick through his arms. Slow down, bastard!

The speed was still 10 per cent above VNE, just about the design limit for dive proving by test pilots. Beyond that, only another 10 per cent as a safety margin. Then the aircraft could come apart like an Airfix model assembled to perfection—but without glue.

He did not realize that in the few seconds in the driving seat he had begun to speak aloud to himself. "Easy," he kept saying, "easy," as he pulled gently on the yoke. A single hard move would snap the fragile structure or make the wings fold up and clap. Easy. But was the stick moving at all? He remembered the Pacific Airlines crash in California. It was a Fairchild. The pilot had been shot. The plane went into a dive. Two men could not pull the stick back even with the aid of the trim tab. It had tipped over at 25,000 and begun to come out of the dive at 11,000. By then it was too late to recover.

The tip of Penn's thumb sought out the small wheel on the column and rolled the elevator trim just a fraction. Easy . . . slowly . . . His arms, chest and diaphragm tightened. He backed them with the weight of his torso. But they did not seem to achieve anything.

Normally, only about forty pounds of power-assisted pressure would be needed to pull the aircraft out of a steep descent. Designers never made it feel too light because of the danger of pilots overcontrolling and cracking an aircraft by hardly more than a flick of the wrist. So, as the speed increased, sensitizing the controls more and more, the built-in artificial feel made it gradually harder for Penn to nurse the stick back. By now, using both hands, he had to exert about a hundred pounds pressure, yet the conflicting forces must remain very delicately balanced, as if he were testing the sturdiness of an eggshell.

Penn could not be sure about anything any more. In the last few seconds he had had the distinct impression that there was no response by any of the control surfaces. Was there an aircraft behind him at all? Was he just hurtling toward the ground in command of half an aircraft? What damage had the excessive speed inflicted? Was it the tremendous force of the slipstream at high speed that had paralyzed the elevators?

There was a hint of yawing and rolling to the left. The risk of spin and an unstoppable spiral occurred to him. An irresistible temptation welled up in his fingers to actively control it and wrench at the column violently.

At 22,000 feet, the Sarissa entered thick cotton-wool clouds with bright glare at the edges. He would now have to rely on instruments he could not trust fully any longer. There was no time for troubleshooting or conducting comparative diagnostic experiments with the help of the crew—he had no crew.

He would have to revert blindly to old-time flying by the seat of his pants like legendary pioneers of the transatlantic run—and pray.

Height was the only safety factor left to the Sarissa. And that he was losing fast. He must pull out. But slowly . . .

In the next three minutes, he would drop some four miles. Not more, he hoped.

Sweat was running freely down his spine. Pull hard, pull slow, pull hard, he kept telling himself, pull slowly, slowly! The movement of the column had to be almost invisible. Not more than a quarter of an inch every seven seconds. With five and a half inches to go.

A hole in the clouds gave him a glimpse of the ground. It was coming up fast. Too fast.

"Two minutes."

Timmy loved the cool voice. It conjured up blurred and indefinable yet chilling sequences of drama in his mind. He looked up at the Harriers hovering only about a hundred feet above the runway. He saw their swivelling nozzles. The eight aircraft turned, like carbon copies of their leader, then suddenly, the whole flock slipped away.

"One minute."

Mara stared at the sky toward the west. She hoped to catch an early glimpse of the Sarissa. It must be near now, she knew. She also felt it in her bones. Drayton glanced at his watch, then nodded toward Mara. He also knew.

London's Air Traffic Center desperately urged Aero 616 to "ident." They could not know that only a single pilot was fighting for the survival of the aircraft, and he would have no time or opportunity to press the identification button on his transponder that would enable radar operators to recognize him and note his location.

"Aero 616, please ident . . . Aero 616, what frequency are you on?"

An unidentified blip was spotted in the ten o'clock position. Judging from the flight plan, it could be the Sarissa.

The horrified pilot of a private aircraft reported a fast-descending jet in a near dive. His position report coincided with the intruder blip on the radar.

Air Traffic Control received a top priority D and D call. The distress and diversion organization had picked up a May Day call on 121.5 VHF, the emergency frequency for civil aircraft.

The Sarissa was now positively identified, just leaving 15,000 about seventy miles out of Farnborough. Still no contact could be made. The pilot must have hit the May Day button. But why did he not answer any calls?

"Aero 616, please confirm that May Day is intentional . . . Aero 616 . . ."

The controller called Farnborough and told them about the emergency. "She's coming in toward you in a straight line. She seems to be in a dive."

"Just keep her away for Chrissake." The emotional words contrasted with the slow and deliberate voice, but the message was panicky. "Take her to Boscombe or anywhere. Just anywhere."

"We don't know if she can maintain height and where she's going. We'd better keep everything out of the way."

The first consideration had to go to the pilot and the aircraft in an emergency. How long can it stay up? Where will it come down? And how? As soon as contact was made with the Sarissa, they would beg the pilots to go away, anywhere, if possible. For if the aircraft missed the runway, it might plow into buildings —or the crowd. The temptation was great to try to evacuate the public enclosure. But there would be no time. A sudden announcement might cause a stampede, killing as many as or more than a crippled aircraft for which the airspace had to be cleared.

Timmy sat up and stared at the radio. He was not sure that he had heard what he thought he had heard:

"We've an aircraft in probable emergency. Break off display, turn south flying to 2000, contact Farnborough radar on 1244 and hold until further instruction."

The Sarissa broke out of clouds just below 15,000. Its speed was still much too high at 400 knots, the angle of descent, twenty-four degrees, still catastrophic for the remaining height. It was about to enter denser air, where increased resistance would be likely to cause most of the potential pull-out damage.

Penn had no choice. He now had to pull with every muscle and every ounce of his weight, still hoping that the change in the attitude would be reasonably gradual. And he needed the power of the engines to help him break the dive. The aircraft shook and shivered. In his mind's eye he could see torn and distorted tabs, elevators, rudder package, entire wings and engines.

Some warning lights went out. Others came on. Yellows flickered. He was losing hydraulic pressure.

350 knots, twenty degrees.

Several options ran through his mind. How he could counter the various possible damages. Spoilers, split-flap configuration, engines to answer problems. If the Sarissa could still fly and would be at all controllable.

A bang distracted his attention to the right for a second. A shadow flew off. Then a tremendous jolt from behind. Fire warning! The aircraft yawing to starboard.

The outer starboard engine had vanished. It might have hit the tail plane. The damage was totally incalculable. But the dive was broken and he could risk using one hand away from the stick.

He shut down the fuel to that engine at once. And shut the flow of hydraulic fluids that way. He could lose it all. He fired the extinguishers. As he adjusted the power on the other engines, he had grave doubts about the efficiency of the remaining hydraulic pressure. He trimmed the aircraft for rudder. But there was no response. "Reduce power!" he shouted at himself.

Fly the aircraft, fly the aircraft, he kept repeating. But there was no elevator response. Not only that, but he was suddenly quite certain that the elevator must have jammed in a position that was forcing the Sarissa down, farther down, and faster. At that speed, nose down, he could not even attempt to land with half a chance of success.

In the cabin, the pull-out of the dive slammed a pressure lid on everybody. Two stewardesses, who were helping mothers with children, fell to their knees without a hope of getting up. Everybody else was riveted into their seats, hands and feet held down firmly, fear and G force combining to keep them there. More oxygen masks fell out.

Joan, the chief stewardess, was the first to overcome the disabling pressure. She knew the sensation from training. She was determined to grab something and pull herself if not up at least forward. She must get to the flight deck. There was no logic behind it. She just had to know.

Then that frightful bang. Then the jolt from behind. Anticipated horrors in bulging eyes—unborn cries of anguish ready to greet the disintegration of the walls.

Freedom hit them unexpectedly. It seemed incredible that they were able to move and that the aircraft was still in one piece. At least as far as they could see it. But freedom released not only the hands and bodies but the throats, too. Several men, women and children howled uncontrollably. Others could not even scream. They were afraid to breathe.

Penn's doubts had gone. He knew he had not enough aircraft to fly, experiment with, turn and aim in the right direction at the right moment. He would just have to land, and land as fast as possible, on a runway, an open field or in a tree.

He could exercise directional control only intermittently. It meant the rudder was still there but probably displaced. And it might soon go altogether.

Longitudinal control was his most immediate problem. Whatever fields, roads or runways lay ahead, he could not approach them nose down. He tried a little more engine power. It began to arrest the angle of descent but his speed increased dangerously just when the survival of the empennage might be in the balance.

The instruments went haywire. Many of them had their take-off points in the damaged tail, and some of the crucial gyros were there also.

"Never mind the instruments, fly the aircraft," he said aloud. It was answered by a half-suppressed gasp. Joan had entered the cockpit and hit herself hard on the mouth so as not to let the sight make her shriek out.

"Strap in." Penn was surprised to hear his own voice from somewhere far away, weak, tired, as if beyond caring. He wasted a precious two seconds thinking about the best use he could make of the unexpected helper. The girl went white as she handled the stiff body of the co-pilot. Penn hoped she would not vomit. She did not. Good girl. Keep her occupied and she would be all right. All right? Shouldn't he send her back into the cabin? No, it would make no difference.

"Headset. Take the headset."

"It's the Sarissa!" The controller's uncharacteristic outburst reverberated in the semidarkness of the London ATC center. Contact had been made at last. Help could be offered, questions could be asked even if no ready answers were forthcoming. But all joy vanished with the realization that it was a woman's voice which had made the call. What had happened up there? There was no time to think. The same voice declared that the aircraft was hardly controllable, the starboard wing was burning, and the Sarissa would land wherever it could.

So there was no chance to keep her flying, make her try turns, divert to an airport which would offer the best emergency facilities.

Farnborough and all airfields in the area were notified. Emergency units had their engines running. It might be a long, bumpy, cross-country dash to reach the wreckage and salvage whatever might be left of structure and flesh.

On the ground and in the air at Farnborough all activities ceased. For no apparent reason, crowds backed a few steps away and compressed like sheep before a storm.

"If she comes here, I hope she won't mess up the runway," said SATCO in the tower. Time-honored tradition was to keep the air show going if at all possible, the way the program had continued in the wake of past disasters even before the wail of ambulances and fire engines could die away.

The well-rehearsed emergency drill went into first gear. No more could be done. No more could be said. In the strained, ear-splitting silence, all eyes scanned the sky.

"We'll have to get the nose up," Penn said. It was an incredible relief to have someone to hear his words. He was still alive and fighting.

A white powder puff of cloud floated past the windshield. From it, he would have sworn, his father smiled at him. No son of mine would ever be a poltroon, eh? Poltroon. Father's famous escape with the crippled bomber.

"Speed brake! . . . That one . . . Pull. Pull."

Eight thousand feet, 320 knots. Descending at fourteen degrees. He must reduce the angle without increasing speed. He had tried everything. Can't be done. Not unless . . .

"PA mike . . . Give me the mike and hold it."

Joan leaned across to reach his mouth with the microphone of the public address system.

"Attention please." He knew that everyone would now freeze in the cabin. Yet there was no time to pull punches. "We have a stinker up here. We'll need your help to get rid of it." He gave them a second to let it sink in. "All adults must unbuckle their seat belts . . . Now! . . . Be ready to walk, slowly walk . . . er . . . twelve seats aft, toward the tail that is, when I count three . . . twelve seats . . . It'll be crowded but stay there until further instructions. . . . Ready?" He grabbed the column with such force that his fingers went white, and pulled hard, hoping that it would contribute to the effort. "One . . . two . . . three!"

The aircraft became as unsteady as a skateboard on mud. But the attitude of the aircraft was changing. As the center of gravity moved aft, the nose began to rise!

5500 feet, 300 knots, nine degrees.

"Good show! Thank you everybody." At least he would be remembered as a polite man. He watched the horizon director. The aircraft was sinking in a nose-up attitude. But the presumably jammed elevator had already begun to force the nose down again. It's quite an aircraft if it's still flying, he thought.

Timmy retreated from the radio and held Mara's hand. "It's . . . it's . . . I must tell Dad about it. And Mum," he whispered. Mara squeezed his hand. It hurt. He wanted to protest but then noticed her other clenched fist. Her nails dug into her palm and began to draw blood. So he kept quiet.

In the AeroCorp chalet everybody knew about the emergency. But nobody had bothered yet to tell them that it concerned their aircraft. It would have been pointless.

A receptionist brought in a telegram for Salah Termine. He read it at a glance, then showed it to Drayton. It was about Brigadier Mott. Termine had had him under surveillance for several months, but the investigation revealed nothing. Not even whom he worked for.

"Quite an operator," said Drayton.

Termine nodded in agreement.

"Could be useful to have him in our team."

"He might not be willing."

"See if you could persuade him."

A foam truck was moving on the far side of the runway. Drayton turned away from Termine and walked out on the terrace to take a look. It also helped him to dodge the worried faces and unasked questions inside the chalet. They all knew that the emergency might concern the Sarissa. An accident would ruin Drayton, the project and them all. Sabotage could be propaganda capital but the evidence would have to be irrefutable. Drayton could not afford even to contemplate the possibilities.

Two and a half minutes had passed since moving the passengers, and Penn was a little amazed to see that his crate was still in the air. All his starboard extinguishers had been used up, but the fire was not out. The sink rate was more acceptable now. Speed down to 220 knots. Considerable achievements but still hopelessly fast for a survivable emergency landing. And the jammed elevator was demanding a steeper descent. When it came to lowering the flaps, Joan could help him. The speed would be reduced but it would also push the nose farther down. Normally, he would balance it with extra engine thrust. But that would cause acceleration—something he still could not afford. Could he risk moving the passengers just once more?

Penn looked up. The outline of various structures on the ground looked familiar. Twenty seconds later he was sure. Some fourteen miles ahead and 2400 feet below—Farnborough.

His instinct urged him to move his passengers, climb away, and crash into the first open field just to avoid the crowds.

The card pinned above the radio told him the various call frequencies en route. Farnborough, on 126.4 VHF, was the last but one on the list. He tuned in. And told Joan what to say.

The tower was ready for the emergency call.

"We have the field in sight," she whispered in such a hoarse voice that they could not understand it.

"Please repeat, Aero 616."

"We have the field in sight."

"Can you maintain height?" the controller asked, clutching at the last hope to get rid of the menace.

"Can we maintain height?" she asked.

"Negative. Tell them negative."

"Negative!" she shouted. For now she knew that it was an approach with no chance of correction or going around again for a repeat performance.

"Runway is clear. You're cleared for a straight-in approach on runway zero seven, repeat, zero seven. Surface wind one eight zero, repeat one eight zero, five knots, QFE one zero one zero millibars."

The last three minutes were a blur in Penn's mind. When he wanted to drop the undercarriage, he was not sure that the hydraulic pressure was enough to do it for him. If he had to crank it down with Joan manually . . . but it was pointless to try guessing it . . .

Two minutes and seven miles out, he lowered the flaps twenty degrees, the take-off position. Speed and the nose dropped. Then flaps to thirty degrees. He could not risk more flaps. He increased thrust fractionally. Even so it would be a hard landing and much too fast.

He had the runway in sight clearly. If the rudder worked just once more . . . yes . . . yes, they were in line for touch-down. But the angle was still too steep. There was no choice. The nose had to come up without increasing the speed.

One minute from probable touch-down he asked for the PA mike.

"We're doing fine. But one more correction must be made. This time it's only the men. When I give the word, all men hurry farther aft. Stop when I say and hang on for dear life. Everybody else straps in. Share seats and belts. Good luck."

The Sarissa began to yaw to starboard. The flames shot up at the wing tip. He had no idea how he would keep the aircraft on the runway and how he would stop it or where. Wasn't there a swamp beyond the far end? Or was it the other way around?

"Now!"

The aircraft shook under the feet of running men.

"Stop!"

They piled up near the tail end, grabbing seat belts and overhead racks, ducking behind seats, the galley and lavatory doors.

Seventy tons thumped the concrete. Tires blew out. Sparks flew.

Penn was aware of the fire engines racing alongside.

"I don't think we'll taxi back to the terminal this time," he mumbled. Joan began to laugh hysterically.

Mott sat in the back of his car and listened to the news on the radio. The bomb in Piccadilly was the first headline. It was followed by a brief account of some miraculous landing at Farnborough. According to the news desk duty wit, the Whispering Sarissa had arrived with a bang. There was fire and there were lots of broken bones. Inexcusably, it had held up the air show for almost eleven minutes.

Mott turned it off. The news was the past. He was more concerned about the future. He could not imagine what had gone wrong. But he could well envisage what a frenzied investigation would now begin. It would never lead to him, about that he was certain. The altimeter swap and the Saricola bottles would throw the suspicion on the AeroCorp fitter. Of course the man was perfectly expendable. Information about him might become, in fact, a valuable property, suitable for auction. International auction, Mott corrected himself.

He told the driver to slow down a little so that he could pour himself a small brandy in comfort. He tasted the drink on the edge of his lips, and began to list the potentially interested parties. AeroCorp would need strong proof of sabotage—or else they might have a fully vindicated but unsellable new type on their hands after all.

Mott smiled. The thought was intriguing. It was gratifying to hold the aces even when one was apparently a loser. Yes, a good auction. With that scoundrel what's-his-name, that not only crooked but unforgivably ill-mannered Termine as a keen bidder. Probably the keenest, all told. Pity, Mott thought, that these days one was not entirely free to choose one's vis-à-vis in business.